PHANTOM'S LAMENT

MW00509392

PHANTOM'S LAMENT

The Shadow's Creed Saga

Volume Two

Noelle Nichols

Published by Phantom Ink Press

Text copyright © Noelle Nichols
Cover illustration and map artwork © Noelle Nichols

All Right Reserved.
No part of this book may be reproduced in any form or by any electronic
or mechanical means including information storage and retrieval systems,
without permission in writing from the author except by a reviewer to quote
a small passage.

Names, characters, places, and moral issues were created from the
imagination of the author and are not to be mistaken for real life.

ISBN-13: 978-1-949051-05-6

Noelle Nichols
www.noellenichols.com

Printed in the United States of America

The Shadow's Creed

A Shadow seeks peace within himself
and the world around him.

A Shadow stays true to his beliefs, letting
compassion guide his actions.

A Shadow does not condemn, searching
for the truth with unclouded eyes.

A Shadow does not take life, killing only
when no other option can be found.

A Shadow protects the innocent, using
his strength to aid those in need.

A Shadow does what he is capable of; no
more can be asked of him.

A Shadow serves until he is no longer able,
his life freely given to the people.

The Seven Virtues
of the Shadows

Justice, Courage, Compassion, Honor,
Loyalty, Truth, and Strength.

Kiriku
Land of Hope

moshe desert

kiren forest

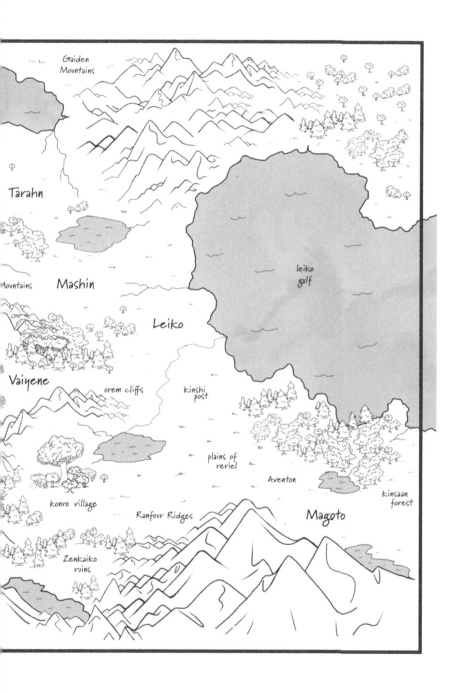

part five
HITORI

chapter thirty-nine
The Council

B lood still stained the floor of the council room.

It was all that remained of my father.

The seven council members responsible for my father's murder sat on an elevated platform in the middle of the large stone chamber. They were older, most in their fifties or sixties, with aging and sagging skin. As they stared down at me, their smiles twisted with arrogance. They thought themselves clever for exerting their power over me and calling me here for a futile meeting.

I smiled.

Soon, the council's time would come to an end.

"Did you receive word about my request for support?" I asked, trying to keep my voice as pleasant as one could in the situation. Summoning all of the council members to bear witness to a simple request was nothing short of mockery, unnecessary given I already knew what they would say.

Tenzo, the oldest council member, steepled his fingers in front of his long white beard. He gazed down at me from his high position, no doubt believing his superior position made him more intimidating.

"Your request has been denied," Tenzo said.

His arrogance echoed off the chamber walls.

"And the reason?" I asked.

"They said they only dealt with the old lord."

My father.

Whom they had killed.

"And what have you done to rectify the situation?" I asked. "Surely the ones who killed the old lord should have some sort of plan to save the town they are sworn to protect."

There was a momentary pause before Reina, a woman at the far end of the table, cleared her throat. Her bulbous cheeks waggled as she turned her head.

"The lord has to provide for the people."

Walking around the platform and ascending the stairs, I spread my arms out and approached the group from behind. Their heads turned as they kept keen eyes on me.

"And yet you won't allow me to do what needs to be done," I said. "You continue to undermine me in whatever ways you can, keeping Magoto locked in this pitiful state."

I stopped a foot away from Tenzo and glared at him, but he didn't flinch away. Instead, he sneered, his lips curling back to reveal yellowed teeth.

"Your father wouldn't have had any problems getting the supplies he needed."

I slammed my fist against the wooden table in front of him.

"Do not talk about my father! You miscalculated, thinking you would be able to get rid of me by framing me for my father's death. But all you did was deepen the people's hatred and thus secured my place as ruler."

I withdrew my hand and walked down the line of council members.

"Once my powers with the Skills grow, you will no longer be able to control me."

If I didn't need their presence to subdue the townspeople and to use their names to secure supplies, I would have already slit their throats. Magoto's people believed them to be the pillars of this town, the ones who would save them from my tyrannical rule. But the truth was, the council members were the ones strangling the town from within. They stank of corruption. Shoddy deals and lack of accountability fattened their purses while the people suffered for it. Patiently, they waited for the people to rise up against me before they assumed complete rule of Magoto.

My father had foolishly believed the lies they fed him, considering their intentions to be genuine. When the opportunity presented itself to be rid of an outsider like my father, the council took the opportunity to eliminate him. Now they waited to do the same to me.

But I was not weak like my father.

I saw through their filth and lies. While I had no great love for Magoto, my father had bequeathed it to me. It was mine, and *no one* took what was mine.

"You are free to do as you like to attempt to save this town," Tenzo said, drawing my anger back to him. "We will be here to rebuild when you have finished destroying it."

Smiling sweetly, I turned to leave.

"In time…" I whispered under my breath. Let them think they had won this time, that I had been placated into not acting. It would make their demise that much more satisfying.

As I slid open the door, I burned their smug faces into my memory. Saitou, my personal bodyguard, fell into place behind me. He waited until we were on the other side of the castle before speaking.

"You did well to keep your temper."

"As if any of it matters," I replied, my voice bitter. "Neither the council nor the people will ever see me as anything other than the enemy."

A child tainted from war.

That was all they saw me as.

My father had promised that "in time" they would come to accept me as their ruler. But he never heard the cruelty of their words when he was not around. Despite my attempts at pointing out the people's hatred to my father, he had insisted I learn patience to win them over.

I scoffed.

What had patience earned him but death?

Now that he was gone, and the council had failed to make up for his lack of charisma and charm, the last remaining towns in the area had begun pulling their support from Magoto. I needed to act, and quickly. We could not continue to appear weak, or others would take advantage of that weakness.

The Skills were the answer.

With their power, I would be able to bend those who were unwilling to listen to my will and take back control.

As Saitou and I continued through the castle, toward the entrance, our footsteps echoed against the stone floor of the great hall. The space was inadequately lit by torches on the wall, casting elongated shadows across the floor from the guards who stood at the entrance.

"We'll head to Tenraishi first to collect what is owed," I said to Saitou, striding out into the courtyard and looking to the north.

A man dressed in leather armor stood ahead. At my approach, he came toward me. He was one of the guards from the lower quarter. Suspicion crept over me, and I glanced over at Saitou.

"Lady Hitori," Haru said, bowing at the waist.

Saitou cleared his throat. "I have asked Haru to escort you around the lower quarter so you may see for yourself what the state of the town is."

I held back a groan.

The council had recently begun to lie about even the most trivial things. They disregarded the true state of provisions, inflating the facts out of proportion to keep me from taking adequate action.

Saitou gave a calculated smile. "It's been a while since you've been there."

I nodded stiffly. "Very well."

It was a necessary task.

Haru stepped back to allow me to lead. I descended the steps, following the edge of the castle to the gate leading out of the courtyard. The sun was out, warming the stone walls and casting shadows as we headed deeper into Magoto. Overhead, a ladder creaked, and I lifted my gaze to see a small child carrying a vase on his head. An older woman with a pole balanced two large buckets on her back and followed after the child. The rickety wood groaned under their weight, but it held. The two scurried between white buildings carved from stone, slipping into an alleyway. I followed after them, keeping my distance as I turned sideways to move between the buildings, shuffling my hands against the wall in front of me. It was a lesser-known route, one of the quickest from the castle to the lower tiers.

Once through the tight space, I brushed off the dirt from my hands and robe, looking around the courtyard. The buildings lining the perimeter seemed to have deteriorated more since my last visit. The stone tiles were worn and dirty and the weeds that had begun growing between them had withered and died.

Even the people seemed dirtier and more skittish than usual.

Shouts came from around the corner, and I headed toward the commotion, Haru following me. A long line of people stood between the rows of stone buildings, waiting as a man was positioned behind a storefront guarded by what looked to be bags of rice.

Rations.

Behind the line, men and women continued to shout, forming a circle around two people exchanging blows.

I exhaled heavily.

At least a dozen of the same hot-headed people were locked in the cells beneath the castle. One of the men observing the fight noticed our approach. The patch over his right eye and the deep grizzled scar indicated his experience as a fighter. His one good eye was bright blue, and a chunk of skin was missing from the bridge of his nose.

His head raised, as if he recognized me, then he shouted.

"You! This is your fault!"

Haru swore at my side and drew his sword. He stepped forward, placing himself between the crowd and me. The man with the eyepatch, emboldened by the crowd at his back, rushed us, directing the crowd's displeasure at me.

"If it weren't for you," the man shouted, "our lord would still be alive, and we wouldn't be fighting for scraps like beasts!"

More shouts came from the crowd, indicating a consensus.

The crowd moved to surround us.

Haru held his sword steady. "You need to leave, Lady Hitori."

I didn't move.

Something struck the side of my face, and I flinched. A flash of white appeared before my eyes, and blood trickled down my cheek. I fisted my hands at my side. The pain from the impact didn't faze me, nor did the blood. What angered me was their audacity, their privilege, and their misguided hatred.

Haru glanced back at me. "Get out of here!"

His words were muffled as I reached out to the Skills in the air.

Striding past Haru, I ignored his shouts, focusing on the man with the scars and eyepatch. When he saw me coming, he ran to meet me, his fist drawn back. Haru dashed in front of me, slashing at the offender's shin with his sword. My vision narrowed as the crowd of people surged forward. More rocks were thrown, but they bounced off a thin barrier of the Skills set against my skin. The Skills burned inside me as the air grew thin. Unwillingly, the people dropped the stones in their hands as I forced the Skills down onto them. A few grasped at their necks, unable to breathe. With the remainder of the Skills in the air, I unleashed a wave of force against the lead man. He tried to fight against it, bending over as he dug his fingers into the ground, but he slid back uselessly, his fingers trailing blood across the broken cobblestone. I stepped over him, drawing the short sword secured to my lower back. Twisting and conducting in the air, the Skills lapped around the blade.

The man's eye grew wide, and I allowed the illusion of fire to swirl around the blade, inching it closer to his neck.

He curled back his lips. "You filthy little—"

Before he could finish, I slashed the blade across his throat.

He fell to the ground, blood pooling across the cobblestones. I glanced down at my forearm, noticing a slight tinge of black over my skin. Releasing the remaining power of the Skills in a burst of energy, I purged myself of their toxic effects.

The people fled.

And the eyepatch man twitched on the ground. Blood bubbled from his gaping mouth, and I watched him with no remorse. Haru drove his sword through the man's chest, twisting it to end his suffering.

Haru's gaze locked onto the sword in my hand.

Did he feel it?

The Skills obeyed me, unlike the people in this town, who despised me for my existence. I could let the people starve, keep all the stores of food for the guardsmen, and forsake the people's pitiful lives. I could toss them out into the cold, force them to endure the harsh winter without the supplies I provided for them.

It would not take long for them to die.

Haru flicked his blade to rid the blood from his sword, refusing to meet my eye.

Did he despise me?

"I see the people still hate me," I said.

"Of course they do. There's nothing for us to live for." His voice was quiet, but he met my gaze defiantly. "The people would hate even the old lord if the circumstances were the same."

"It's not my fault if the weather does not cooperate and the harvest is poor." My words were icy. I had seen the reports on the production of our own fields. Was I to be blamed for natural occurrences in the people's day-to-day lives?

"Ever since you closed the border, food and coin have been becoming scarce," Haru said. "We used to be able to bargain for things on our own and leave these walls to provide for our own families. Now, living here is a death sentence. We are powerless to do anything, and most of us are just trying to find some small reason to live."

Closing the borders had been to protect the people from the threats outside our walls, but as always, the people interpreted my actions the way they wanted to, focusing on the negative outcomes over the good I had done for them.

Haru sheathed his sword, his hand fisting at his side. "Why are you even still here? Everyone knows you care more about the Skills and the people you experiment upon in Leiko." His voice dropped lower as the treasonous slander escaped his lips. "Maybe the council would be able to do something in your absence."

I stiffened at his words.

"If you think the council cares for Magoto, you've fallen for their lies. It is because of the council this whole situation has arisen." I stopped myself from going further. What was the point? He wouldn't believe me even if I explained how the council continued to blacken my name among the towns, making the chance of outside aid even slimmer than it already was, or how the council cared more about getting rid of me than feeding their own citizens...

"If you wish to be relieved of your duty because you are dissatisfied with my rule, you are free to find another lord to serve."

Haru's eyes narrowed. "I swore to protect Magoto. I have no desire to go back on my word."

"Then remember who it is you speak to!"

Haru gave a small bow, biting off any further retorts. Earlier he had used the term "us" to describe the lower quarter. If he counted himself among them, his loyalty would always be to them first.

I gestured to the body at my feet. "Clean this up, and take care of the tension in the lower quarter. I no longer need you to escort me."

Haru straightened, and I left him to deal with the crowd and the aftermath of my altercation. My thoughts burned as I walked back to the castle. The people here didn't respect me. They hated me. Even in Haru's eyes, I had done wrong. The guardsmen, the very people who were supposed to be loyal to me, didn't even believe in me. Like most, they thought the council would save them, and that I had killed my father.

Clenching my fingers into a fist, I hardened my resolve.

What I needed was an army, more people so I would be able to acquire resources and power before I eliminated the council. None of the council members were skilled with a sword, like the guards were, so killing them would not be difficult. What would require a certain amount of tact was putting measures into place to keep the people complacent. To keep them from revolting against me.

The most immediate of our needs were food and supplies.

Our attempts at cultivating our own fields had failed, and while the nearby ocean provided a small measure of fish for the town, even that source had dwindled due to circumstances I could not surmise. And so, Magoto relied on other towns to provide for the people. My father had been able to nurture those alliances, but after the council had killed him, we'd been left to take what was needed, as the neighboring towns didn't care to work with me.

This was where my army would come into play.

Already, I had recruited a number of people, dubbed the "False Shadows" by their counterparts, the Shadows. The Shadow group was a small idealistic force from a village deep in the Miyota Mountains. They were known as peacemakers across the lands, spreading goodwill and maintaining order between towns. Originally, I had copied the Shadows' bond and used it for my own group as a means to an end: vengeance against the Shadow leader, Phantom Kural, who had tried to control my knowledge of the Skills. But as I had studied more about the Skills from the book I had found, I learned there was a link between the silver casing around a person's arm and the ability to withstand the side effects of the Skills. I had begun experiments around the revelation, focusing a majority of time on learning more about the connection and the power of the Skills.

Using the False Shadows thus far had allowed Magoto to survive. The people feared me, giving power and pull to my campaigns. Most villages conceded to my requests, not wanting to fight. However, my group's numbers had dwindled of late.

My footsteps slowed at the gate leading into the castle, my mind churning to the cells deep within Magoto's castle. Saitou stood inside the gate, and when I passed him, he aligned himself slightly to the right of me, avoiding the long robes I wore.

"I see Haru is no longer with you," Saitou commented lightly.

"Haru is cleaning up the mess in the lower quarter."

"You seem in rather high spirits about it."

Glancing up at Saitou, a wry smile spread across my face. "I'm going to release the prisoners. Most of the False Shadows have not come back from their missions, and if I'm going to eliminate the council and secure what we need to survive as a town, we will need a larger force."

"I see," Saitou said.

At the doors to the castle, I paused next to one of the guards on duty. She thrust her arms to her side as she approached, bowing hastily at the waist.

"Lady Hitori," she said, keeping her eyes downcast.

"Raise your head," I said, not caring to delay with courtesy. "I have a message for General Gai. Tell him to bring a group of his men and meet me in the main hall. They are to begin training the former prisoners into warriors."

"Yes, Lady Hitori."

Entering the castle, we walked along the side of the main hallway before heading down a passageway that led to a narrow stairway. The hall was cramped and hidden in shadow, smelling of stagnant air. Held below were those who had either committed crimes or directly defied me.

"Are you sure about this?" Saitou asked.

It was a rare interjection on his part. Ever since my father had placed me on this path, I had not been able to turn away from using measures more drastic than the previous lord. Everything I did required force. He knew this.

"If you know of a better way, speak of it now," I said.

Saitou opened his mouth as if to say something, then shook his head, letting out a long breath. "I suppose it does not matter about the prisoners' crimes or their hatred of you. Those surrounding you would betray you just as easily as the people in the cells. Lord Shingen's desire for you was always a vain one."

I fisted my hands at my side.

Lord Shingen had adopted me as his daughter and made me his successor. He had found Saitou and me, survivors of the war across the sea. Whatever had possessed him to look after us, I didn't know, but there were days I hated him for his kindness. He should have left me on the battlefield and gone on with Saitou, who would have made the better lord. Under his influence, this town might have had a chance. But my adoptive father had chosen me, and this rotting town was the only piece Saitou and I had left of Lord Shingen. And so, we continued on like this. Saitou at my side, and I with the burden of the town's future.

Drawing back my shoulders, I raised my head, recalling the council members and their disrespect as I fixed their smiles and their arrogance at the forefront of my mind.

It was the motivation I needed to continue.

"I will not allow the council to take what is mine," I said, feeling my temper flare as I regained my sense of duty. "I have never hesitated to do what was necessary; I will not start now." Whatever I had to do to survive and protect my father's legacy, I would do it—even if it meant dealing with those who had tried to kill me.

Taking the first step into the dungeon, I wrinkled my nose as we descended. The air was humid and stale, and a hint of human feces reached my nose. Puddles of water pooled at the bottom of the steps, leaking down from a crack in the ceiling. It sickened me to be here, for more reasons than the smell. The prisoners were scum, not even worth my time, but I here I was forced to deal with traitors.

Holding my breath, I started forward.

The woman in the first cell stared blankly ahead. Her eyes were glazed over, and she didn't seem to register who I was.

Or perhaps she simply cared little about me.

In the next cell, a man stirred. He was livelier than the woman and seemed anxious. Pacing around his confines like a rat, he muttered to himself, his eyes flicking from left to right. When my shadow passed over him, he stopped. He came to the bars of his cell and sneered at me.

I recognized him as one of the people from the lower quarter. The people must have continued fighting in my absence for Haru to have thrown him in here.

"This is all your fault!" he shouted, his lips curling back in disgust. "Senshou is dead because of you!"

In the cell adjacent, a woman grabbed the bars and spat in my path.

"Die, scum! Return to the land you came from!"

As I turned toward her, a chorus of jeers and insults echoed throughout the prison. The people were becoming aware of my presence. I smiled. I didn't recall who this spirited person was, but she certainly seemed to remember me. Saitou adjusted his grip on his sword behind me and leaned down.

"She tried to assassinate you a few years ago," he said, whispering into my ear. "The council hired her. If I remember correctly, she killed a handful of your guards before reaching you."

Ah, yes.

It had been an admirable attempt on my life. One of the many failed endeavors by the council to eliminate me when my father was still alive. Given her history and hatred of me, she could not be trusted to join my ranks.

But that didn't mean she could not be useful.

I stepped closer to the assassin. The woman had a pale complexion, with a smile as cunning as a fox. Her deep-set eyes were rimmed with black circles.

"What was your crime?" I asked, toying with her.

The woman's lips peeled back. "You don't remember?"

"I have far more important things to do than remember insignificant details."

"Murder."

She seemed pleased to admit it, almost boisterous in her proclamation. I needed people like her. Those who were not afraid to do whatever I commanded them to. Perhaps others in this prison would have the same drive.

Turning my back to the woman, I cast my eyes over those in the cells. "I have a proposition for all of you," I said, adding a touch of sweetness to my voice. At the mention of a deal, the woman and a few others perked up.

"Join my army, and I'll set you free."

A few more of the prisoners' eyes settled on me. They were interested. If I could get one to join my cause, the rest would likely follow.

"If you let me out, this time, I *will* kill you," the woman jeered.

I kept my face emotionless. I hadn't expected any of the prisoners to give in—not right away. Resting my hands on the bars to her cell, I allowed the Skills to pour into the cell like water. Once inside the cell, the Skill particles split in two, their energy igniting into flames around the woman.

She jumped back, the edge of her shirt burned at the fire's touch.

"What is this?" she hissed.

Exclamations from other prisoners erupted around her cell. Smoke wavered before me, blurring the woman's outline. She tried to keep a collected demeanor, but I saw the tremor of fear in her eyes.

"Work for me, and you'll gain your freedom," I said, now turning to the other prisoners in their cells. I wandered down the line, meeting each of their hardened gazes.

They hated me.

Loathed me even.

I returned to the assassin woman. The fire continued to rise, the plume of smoke caressing the top of her cell as it spread across the prison. A bead of sweat formed on my brow. The temperature in the dungeon climbed. It would not take long for the smoke to begin choking the prisoners' lungs.

Leaning closer to the cell, I whispered, "Pledge your loyalty to me, or the fire will consume you."

The woman scoffed. "Kill me."

"As you wish."

Rearranging the particles in the air, I stripped any moisture away to create a torrent of flames. The woman's flesh singed, and she swore, backing herself into a corner. She patted at the fire with a dirty blanket and stomped on it, unaware the Skill fire could not be extinguished traditionally.

"I'll do it!" she shouted, but it was too late.

The flames crawled on top of her, burning her skin and clothing. Gripping the bars of the cell, she jostled the metal in a desperate attempt to get me to stop. Her skin began to blacken. And she clenched her teeth together, tears forming at the edges of her eyes as she struggled not to scream.

"I'll join you!"

I pulled my short sword from my back, diverting the flames into my hand and sliding them over my blade. Without hesitation, I slashed forward, cutting through the metal bars and into the woman's chest. The fire lapped against the wound, searing her and turning everything within the cell into a blackened pile.

I scowled at the other prisoners, the flame still curling around my blade.

"Now, who wishes to swear their loyalty?"

The woman's ashes smoldered behind me, the flames still slapping against the cell and erupting into the hall. They began to trail across the ground until finally, one person stepped up to the bars of their cell.

"I'll pledge my loyalty," he said.

"I will as well."

"And I."

The rest of the prisoners voiced their agreement. Spying the guardsman cowering at the end of the hall, I waved at the cells.

"Release them."

The guard hesitated, but after eyeing me, he untied the loop of keys at his belt. With shaking hands, he unlocked the cells, and the prisoners stumbled into the hallway. I met each person's eyes, daring them to try something. Most individuals placed a high value on their life, and because they did, they would do whatever was necessary to prolong it. Even if that meant committing acts they had never thought themselves capable of.

Like joining someone they had sworn to kill.

"Today is the start of your new lives," I said, heading back to the main floor of the castle. "Because of me, you will be given the chance to die for something worthwhile."

I hoped they appreciated the gesture.

The prisoners said nothing as they followed me. Even though the air had been depleted from the Skill fire, making it hard to breathe, the prisoners didn't voice a single complaint. I smiled to myself. Typical. Despite their earlier bravado, they had become complacent because of their fear.

The light from the main level of the castle poured across the steps. I shielded my eyes with my arm as I made my way up the steps, standing to the side as the prisoners lined up in the main hall. Opposite them, the guardsmen stood dressed in full leather armor, awaiting my orders.

Haru and his father, Gai, stood in front of the rest.

"You are to obey Commander Gai," I said to the prisoners. "He is in charge of your training. If you disobey, try to escape, or do anything foolish, I've authorized him to use whatever force is necessary to regain control."

I walked down the line of prisoners.

"Do not forget that, as you are, your lives mean nothing to me. Eliminating you would lessen the burden on our resources, so there would be no great loss if you were to die. But if you put in the effort to learn how to fight and help me restore power to Magoto, perhaps your lives can be worth something and you can ascend to something more than fodder."

Whether or not Gai could use the Skills I left as a mystery. The uncertainty would ensure they obeyed him. Though as a commander and a strong warrior, he had other options for those who disobeyed him.

"In three weeks," I said, looking over at the general, "we will leave Magoto and head to the Tenraishi. There we will secure the resources we were promised."

"Yes, Lady Hitori," General Gai said. "I will see they are trained as best as they can be in such a limited time."

I nodded slightly, acknowledging the point. We did not have the luxury of spending time training those who would immediately die in battle, but three weeks would at least allow them to last a short while.

Next to the commander, Haru stared ahead.

For a moment, I saw a flicker of something within his eyes, but I dismissed it.

He and the others would prove their loyalty in Tenraishi.

chapter forty
Where Loyalties Lie

We camped in the Plains of ReRiel.

The prisoners turned warriors were with us, as well as a dozen of my False Shadows who had returned from their missions across Kiriku. Of the guardsmen, only Haru had come; the others had remained in Magoto. The exact number of men and women under my control fluctuated. Many died on missions, while others tried to escape. Those who did attempt to escape were executed. Considering the False Shadows from the latest mission had failed to return, I suspected I would need to intervene soon—before the system of control crumbled and the people began to believe I would not go through with my threats.

A roar of laughter came from the opposite side of the camp. It was in stark contrast to Saitou's silence as he added logs to the dying flames of the campfire between us. Usually, he spoke little, but since we had left Magoto, his silence had become more noticeable.

I sipped on some warm rice wine. "Are you upset with me, Saitou?"

Adding a branch to the fire, he sat back on his heels.

"Why would you think that?"

"Because my father would never attack a town to ensure they upheld a trade deal."

Saitou carefully placed a large log on the fire, his eyes keen on the growing flame. When the wood didn't take, he prodded the hot coals with a crooked branch until the bottom log collapsed and embers burst into the sky.

"You are not your father."

He said it so mildly I couldn't decide if it was an observation or an insult. He seemed more guarded today, which proved he was indeed upset with me. Saitou picked up the whetstone he had placed at his side and drew his sword. With care, he held up his sword against the flames, inspecting the edge.

I let my eyes unfocus on the flames.

When the logs burned, they became black and fragmented.

Lifeless.

Many of my experiments with the Skills involved rocks and plants. All of them had some measure of the Skills within them, but the amount was not distributed evenly in each as some objects carried more energy than others. It was one of the aspects of the Skills I didn't understand yet.

"Will you at least talk to the town's lord before you attack?" Saitou asked.

I blinked, letting the image of the fire and my thoughts of the Skills disappear.

Saitou poured water from his flask onto the stone and scraped the blade over the whetstone in a steady rhythm.

So that was what had been bothering him. He thought I would raze the town without offering them a second chance to fulfill our trade agreement. While I doubted it would make a difference, if it made Saitou happy, I would make the attempt.

"I'll talk to them first," I said.

Saitou dried his sword with a rag and unstoppered a vial, dabbing a little of the oil onto the rag before he began greasing the sword.

He glanced up at me briefly. "Keep your back straight and your eyes sharp when dealing with others. Trust no one who cannot meet your eye.'"

It was something my father had said often to Saitou and me. They were words of advice on how to gauge the worthiness of others.

Saitou ran his finger near the edge of his sword.

"Do you find that's true?"

"I do," he said. "Although there's always an exception. If the lord can meet your eye, you will know if their will is strong and if they are willing to defy you. That can be trusted. If they are sheepish in their regard, be cautious. They might try and feign weakness to lower your guard. Your father used to be grateful for those who lived by truth, even if it was in opposition to what he believed."

"He was a fool," I said.

Saitou smiled. He finished applying the oil to the sword and sheathed the blade, standing up. "I will bring something to eat."

I nodded and watched him leave, letting my thoughts drift back to the Skills, the fire, and the defiance of those who stood against me.

––––––––

The wind blew across the gulf, sending a chill through my body. Saitou rode next to me, as did Haru. We went as envoys, leaving the rest of our forces over the hill next to the town, hidden from view.

Only a few hundred people lived in Tenraishi. They occupied a small sliver of Leiko gulf but had claimed a large portion of the fertile soil inland. Despite its size, it was a wealthy town, selling much of its excess rice to neighboring towns.

As we approached, the townspeople stopped their work to stare.

Saitou dismounted and approached a young woman.

"Can you tell us where Lord Igai is?" Saitou asked. He kept his voice more pleasant than he did when he spoke with the guards or even with me.

The woman glanced over at Haru and me, then pointed to the edge of town.

"The lady is supervising some of the fishing operations today."

"Thank you," Saitou said, taking his horse's reins in hand.

Haru and I stayed mounted, following Saitou toward the docks.

A woman wearing a sky-blue robe and an elaborate pin made with white pearls was bent over at the waist, digging up oysters with a shovel. She placed her shovel on the ground, straightening at our approach.

"Is there something I can help you with?" she asked. She brushed off the dirt from her oversized pants. The sleeves of her robe were tied back with a white strip of cloth.

"We're looking for Lord Igai," Saitou said.

"He died some months ago from an illness," she said, drawing her shoulders back and raising her head. "As his daughter, I've taken over the responsibility of this town and have inherited his name and title. You can call me Lady Igai."

Saitou looked up at me, and I dismounted.

"Tenraishi made an agreement to help Magoto in times of hardship," I said, getting straight to the purpose of our arrival. "I've come to collect on that debt now."

Lady Igai's lips pressed thin. "That agreement is no longer valid. It was drafted by the old lord. Even if it wasn't, we don't approve of what you're doing and will never offer aid to Magoto."

Anger burned inside me.

"It is not for an ally to judge what another does."

Lady Igai took a step forward, throwing her arm out to wave the others away. When she lowered her arm, and the others began to leave, her tone became icy. "I will not bend like the others, Lady Hitori. I've heard about your experiments in Leiko, as I heard about the eradication of Mashin and the attack on Tarahn. Those in your group parade themselves as Shadows, yet you are nothing like them. We will not tolerate your behavior."

She drew a fan from the sash around her waist and flicked it open. The sharp edges glinted in the sunlight.

An open threat.

I turned my back on her. "So be it."

From his mounted position, Haru lit the arrow in his hand, before setting it against the bow. When I nodded, he released it over the gulf. The shaft shrieked and whistled over the waves, creating a trail of smoke in its path.

I watched it briefly before returning my attention to Lady Igai.

"If you do not offer your aid, we will take it," I said.

Undeterred, Lady Igai shifted into an offensive position as the ground began to rumble. Haru shouted a warning behind me, but his voice was drowned out by a trampling stampede of horses from the north.

My group should have been coming from the south.

"Mercenaries," Saitou said under his breath.

Green banners jostled in the air as riders came into view. They whooped and hollered as they drew near. From the south, my own army appeared. The townspeople still on the shore ran toward the town, clearing the beach for the two opposing forces. Horse hooves pounded into the sand, crashing against the waves. The mercenary army and my own collided, and sword met sword in a flurry of movement.

Saitou drew in a shallow breath beside me, his hand resting on the hilt of his sword. "They won't win," he said.

The prisoners' training had barely covered how to defend against an attack. They were nothing more than fodder—they always had been—but the mercenaries were not in my calculations, and therefore my plan was miscalculated. The capabilities of the mercenaries hired by Lady Igai surpassed our own. If I didn't do something to change the course of this battle, it would be meaningless for us to continue. It didn't matter how many people I sacrificed to slow them down.

With a low growl, I pressed my lips thin.

I disliked battle.

The chaos and repetition made it tiresome.

But there was something I hated more than becoming personally involved: wasted time. If we lost here, the time spent preparing and traveling would have been for nothing. We would be forced to attack another town, thereby losing more time and resources.

And we would have to begin anew somewhere else.

"I'll take care of it," I said, walking toward the beach.

I needed to be quick and fast.

Deadly in my force.

These were trained mercenaries, and they would adjust quickly to my tactics.

Drawing a dagger from the pouch at my thigh, the metal hummed a melodic tone. *Death,* it seemed to sing. It was what the blade wanted and what I needed to end this town's stubbornness and take what belonged to me.

I walked over the sand stained with the former prisoners' blood. The Skills continued to drone inside me. Raising my hand, the dagger was now heated to an almost unbearable temperature as waves of the Skills wafted over me. The mercenaries had but a moment to turn their heads before I threw the blade. The ground cracked, shifting with the force of the Skills, sending out a burst of energy across the area. The mercenaries on horseback struggled to stay seated, unsteady as the earth moved. Staring at the dagger, I felt the churning of the Skills around me until they raced inside the blade.

I released my hold, and another wave of energy burst forth.

The blast seared the mercenaries' flesh and riders and horses fell.

When the ground stabilized, the remaining mercenaries rose from the ground. Not by choice, but because I had exerted my desire into the Skills that touched them. I had overwritten their desire to move—to strike me—by holding them in place with my own will.

The mercenaries' eyes trailed me as I approached them.

Hatred lay within their eyes.

A green banner shuddered in the wind a few paces away from me, the cloth flapping wildly against the pole, trying to break free in the wind.

I had seen the colors before, in Leiko.

These were the mercenaries who had aided the Phantom.

Anger flashed within me, and I slashed out with my short sword, decapitating the man nearest me. As I released my hold on him, his body crumpled to the ground. I stepped back to avoid the blood spurting out from his severed neck. Making quick work of the remaining men, I paused before two quivering figures. My control over them was not absolute. Their grip on their weapons trembled—one even managed to move slightly at my approach.

They were strong of will.

It was a pity they wouldn't pledge their loyalty to me. But I knew better than to try and sway these men to my side. They were loyal to their general, and they would die before even thinking of betraying him.

The taller of the men sneered. He was bald, with a neatly trimmed beard. Without a second thought, I removed his head with my sword. An intense rage collided against my mind, and I reeled back. My control of the second mercenary broke as he screamed. He snarled at me, the scars on his face wrinkling as he lunged. His sword cut deep into my thigh, and I cried out in pain. Before I was able to retaliate against the man, Saitou was in front of me, his sword slashing at the man who had cut me.

I shifted my weight to my left leg, tears stinging my eyes as I pressed down onto the wound on my right thigh. Blood gushed and seeped through my fingers.

I pressed down harder against the wound.

It was too deep.

"Saitou!" I yelled.

When he did not respond, I searched for him, but he was no longer within sight. Panic overwhelmed me as the edges of my vision darkened. I could feel my strength draining. Frantically, I glanced down at the ground. Somewhere, hidden underneath the bodies and blood, was the blade I'd thrown.

If I could reach it with the Skills…

Closing my eyes, I searched for the dagger. Its presence was faint, cold against the battlefield—against the death around me. The earth shook, cracking open and slithering with momentum, a black trail of the Skills following in its wake. When the sinister trail was almost upon Saitou and the man who had tried to kill me, Saitou leaped back. The Skills consumed the other man, rotting his skin, and blackening it as his life was sapped away.

He fell to the ground in a heap of ash.

I shifted my fingers; the blood was still oozing out from my leg.

Panic returned to me.

"Saitou!"

He ran to me, kneeling on the ground as he looked at the wound. Noticing the green banner near us, Saitou retrieved it, cutting the fabric from the pole into strips.

"Keep your hands steady until I'm ready."

I nodded, tears still at the edges of my eyes as he tied the fabric above the wound as tightly as he could. He grabbed another strip.

"Move your hands."

I did, and the green fabric immediately turned brown.

The blood wasn't stopping.

My breathing became ragged and stunted as panic overtook me.

"Stay calm," Saitou said as he wrapped the fabric tighter.

Pressing down on the binding, he looked straight into my eyes. His jaw was set, fierce and determined. His green eyes were narrowed, still battle-ready. I wiped away the tears on my cheek with the back of my hand, suddenly self-conscious under his regard.

"We need to finish it," I said through my tears. "Erase them all so no one will question me again."

Saitou nodded stiffly, his attention focused once again on the wound.

Wings beat overhead as the caw of a bird echoed. A large black crow landed on the shore, blinking its vacant eyes at me, waiting.

I clenched my chattering teeth.

"How much longer will it take for the bleeding to stop?"

I was tired of sitting in this cold, smelly place.

Saitou pressed down harder on the wound, his hands stained with my blood. "You're lucky it was not deeper," he said.

I took his words to mean "be patient," and I let my agitation and pent-up rage seep out in a deep, disgruntled growl. I needed better men who were already battle-trained to keep Magoto from the grasp of the council members. Saitou stayed by my side because of his loyalty to my father. Others stayed because I had ensnared them into doing so. The prisoners I had freed stayed because they wanted their freedom. But mercenaries, they worked for money, and they were powerful. It would be easy to pay people to join me, and it would be less complicated than my previous ventures of twisting and manipulating people's connections to force them into servitude.

Magoto had some amount of wealth, but it wasn't in excess.

"Saitou, have you any experience working with mercenaries?"

"Only in battle," he said, mildly. "Money cannot buy loyalty."

"Some people do though."

"Some buy others' loyalty, yes."

If I could grow my army with trained mercenaries, situations like these would not happen. I could take what I needed without exhausting myself. Gathering people from the lower quarter of Magoto would no longer work; most had not even held a sword before, and none grasped the nuances of swordplay. Training worthless men exhausted our time, and with villages and towns gathering their own forces against me, I needed another tactic.

Saitou removed one of his hands from my wound and replaced it with one of mine. "Keep putting pressure on it. I will have to sew it closed."

After he stood and left me, I glanced down at the blood soaked into the sand beneath my leg. I had seen people injured before—I had caused a lot of injuries myself—but I had never been on the receiving end of a wound like this.

At the edge of the shore, I noticed Haru. He was with a group of False Shadows and the prisoner-soldiers. He and Saitou exchanged words before Haru grabbed one of the saddlebags from the horses. As they both came to my side, Saitou pulled something from inside the leather bag. A needle. At the sight of it, I averted my gaze. Saitou knelt beside me and held out a thin piece of what looked to be a tree root.

"Chew on this. It will help with the pain and give you something to focus on."

I kept the pressure on my wound and opened my mouth, biting down into the bitter root. It was unpleasant, but the action of chewing was, as Saitou had said, something to think about besides the needle.

With deft hands, Haru lit a small fire and held the needle to the flames. It turned red, and once he had rotated it all the way around, he threaded it. Saitou leaned forward, blocking Haru from my view while he moved the fabric from my robes up, leaving them at the edge of the wound above my knee.

"Try not to move," Saitou said gently, taking the needle from Haru. Before putting the needle through my skin, he addressed Haru. "How are the townspeople?"

Haru sighed and shook his head. "They're keeping their distance. At least, for now. We weren't able to track down Lady Igai among the dead either. We believe she and a few of the townspeople fled."

I clamped down on the root when the needle pierced my skin. Wincing, I tried to think of something to keep my mind off the pain, but all I could think of was the sting of the needle as it closed me up.

Blood still wept from the wound.

"I sewed Lord Shingen up on the battlefield quite often," Saitou said.

Before going back to his stitching, he glanced up at me briefly. Whenever he spoke about my father, his expression reflected how much he had loved the man.

"Lord Shingen always found himself outnumbered," Saitou said, continuing. "He always insisted on putting himself in danger's way. It made protecting him a rather difficult endeavor." Saitou chuckled. "I learned how to sew a wound closed and how to take care of the sickness that haunts the battlefield. All because your father had no restraint. I figure if he was charging into battle, risking his life, I might as well learn how to put him back together again. That way, we wouldn't have to wait for the doctor. He was the last to be treated too. Always wanting his men to be taken care of before he was. He was a good man."

A tear fell from my eyes, emotion welling up inside me. This time I didn't try to hide the tears. My father had been a great lord, a great master, and a leader of men. His mistake had been adopting me into his family, an outcast who should never have been allowed to follow in his footsteps.

"Thank you," I said, my throat too choked up to say anything more.

I appreciated Saitou's loyalty and compassion. He had saved my father's life countless times, and he had stood up against people's lies about me. Through it all, he had stayed by my side. I was nothing like my father, but his loyalty had never swayed, even when I doubted his intentions and grew short with him for fear that one day he would find someone else he would rather serve.

Someone better than me.

Saitou pulled the thread in my leg tight, and I scowled. The skin puckered. Turning away from the sight of the wound, I closed my eyes against a sudden rush of dizziness.

"I can watch over Lady Hitori if you'd like," Haru said.

"I would appreciate that," Saitou replied as he began winding the cloth strips around my leg. "I will see to the townspeople and ensure there is order."

I opened my eyes, regretting it instantly.

I vomited to the side.

Haru reached out a hesitant hand toward me, but I swiped him away.

My eyes were heavy, exhaustion taking its toll. I wanted nothing more than be rid of this place. Instead of helping me, Haru went over to the horses and brought one over.

He and Saitou stared at one another for a moment.

"It would be best to move you to Leiko, where we have the medical resources to tend to your wound better," Saitou said, frowning. "It will not be an easy ride though."

Grunting, I held out my arms. Saitou slipped one arm under my shoulders and the other under my knees, scooping me up. Pain shot up my leg and spiked through my spine. I sucked in a deep breath. Saitou raised me over the horse's girth, seating me in a sidesaddle position.

"Can you manage by yourself?" Haru asked, looking up at me.

The pain in my leg was almost unbearable. Nausea and dizziness still plagued me, and as much as it annoyed me to accept his help, I didn't relish the idea of falling from the horse.

Gritting my teeth, I pressed my hand over the wound.

"Ride with me," I said to Haru.

With a slight nod, he threw his leg over the horse and situated himself behind me. I cursed as he bumped my leg.

"Sorry," he said.

I felt sick and didn't care to respond to him, only wishing for it to be over.

"I'll meet you both at the main camp," Saitou said. "Seiji should be there to offer medicine. I'll follow shortly after I deal with the affairs here."

chapter forty-one
Moshe Desert

My leg ached intensely. Pressing down on the wound in my thigh, I stood up, wincing as the stitching in my skin pulled. I shifted my weight from my good leg onto a stick Haru had found for me to lean on. If I kept moving, it wasn't as bad, but when I remained seated or immobile, it took a while before it would loosen enough to walk.

"You shouldn't be up," Haru said, following behind me. "We've only been in Leiko for five days. Your wound hasn't even begun to heal."

"I need to see how things are progressing with the experiments," I replied, stubbornly continuing to walk. With my injury, it was slow getting anywhere, excruciatingly so, but I was bored of sitting around the main camp doing nothing.

Saitou still hadn't returned, leaving me under Haru's prolonged care.

One of the keepers of the Skill experiments walked by. When she noticed me, she stiffened and began fidgeting with the papers in her hands.

I searched my memory for her name.

"Reka?"

She jumped and almost dropped the papers. "Y-yes?"

"Show me the notes from the last few weeks."

She handed me the papers, shrinking back away from me. It seemed not much had changed since I'd last been here. The people were surviving the Skills training, though it never was as intense unless I came to administer the tests myself.

"Take me to see number thirteen," I said.

"Yes!" Reka's voice squeaked when she answered, reminding me of a mouse.

I limped after her, passing the row of wooden buildings. Inside each was a single person. Currently, the experiment was based around improving a person's endurance with the Skills. The keepers took note of any adverse side effects, and we tried different ways to manage them and to improve a subject's capacity. Each subject was numbered according to the order in which I began testing them, and so far, most of the first twenty subjects had already died. I flipped to the last page of paper before turning back to number thirteen's notes. He was an arrogant test subject with a fiery temperament, but so far, his capacity for the Skills was the highest out of all the test subjects. Whether it was because of natural talent or his desire to gain power to escape, he was stronger each time I came to see him. If any of the participants were going to progress to become one of my False Shadows, he would be the first candidate of my choosing.

"How is he doing today?" I asked as we approached number thirteen's building.

The wooden planking had become weathered during the winter. We hadn't had the proper time to seal the wood, having rushed through the preparations to accommodate as many of the people as we could before the weather changed.

"Fine in terms of the Skills," Reka said.

I raised an eyebrow. "And in other terms?"

"He seems bored."

"Bored?" I had expected some other type of complaint.

"I think he finds doing the same experiment over and over to be tiring."

Did he now?

Well, I had some time to fix his complaints.

"You're free to go," I said, sliding the door open to the building and leaving my wooden crutch outside. It was dim and musty inside the building. Number thirteen stood immediately, his white eyes glowing in the darkness.

He seemed eager to see me.

"Would you like to try something new today?" I asked, moving toward him.

The ropes tied to his legs and hands slid across the ground as he came forward.

"I'm ready whenever you are," he said.

There was an eagerness to his voice I didn't like, but I ignored it, considering this the perfect opportunity to assess his true talent.

Number thirteen extended his hand for the silver pendant around my neck.

"Not this time," I said, holding out my hand. He raised his eyes to me, and a momentary flicker of something passed across his face.

Keeping my hand outstretched, I explained: "Since you've become adept at using the Skills, it would be good to judge how far you've come in terms of being able to channel them without the use of the pendant and with something living. You should be able to feel the Skills upon contact where the metal threads are wrapped around my arm. The Skills are drawn to metal, so even though your point of contact will not be against metal, it will be near enough for you to sense. We'll see how long you can last with the Skills when it is from someone of power."

Number thirteen grinned, his pointed teeth jagged against his lips. Grabbing onto my forearm tightly, he dug his fingers into my skin.

It was a challenge.

Posturing to see if he could scare me.

I looked at him mildly, unafraid of what he thought he could do to me. With the Skills, I could crush him in an instant—especially with direct contact. By moving the particles in the air or altering the natural flow of the Skills from a person, one could drain the life of the target or overwhelm them within minutes. Seconds even.

I had tested it more than once on a group of rats.

"Ready?" I asked.

He nodded.

Feeling his fingers on my skin, I began to focus on the metal around my arm, willing it to burn brighter as the Skills grew within me. Without allowing the Skills to gradually flow in a controlled manner, they poured from me into number thirteen without pause. The test subject winced as the warmth became uncomfortable. He tried to pull away from me, but I turned my hand and grasped his forearm.

The skin around his arm became black.

His eyes widened. "Let go of me!"

"Why, what's the matter?" I asked sweetly, digging my own fingers into his skin. "I thought you were bored? Were my trials not challenging enough for you?"

He jerked back his arm, and I released him, watching the skin blacken on his forearm further. Without warning, he lunged at me. The ropes around his wrists and ankles jerked as I stepped back from him.

He snarled. "You little—"

The door to the building slid open, and Saitou ducked under the doorframe.

Briefly, his attention rested on the man straining against his bonds before he focused on me. "Lady Hitori, there's something I need to tell you, but if now's not a good time..."

"I was just leaving," I said, turning my back on the experiment.

Saitou slid the door closed as number thirteen yelled after me. Taking the wooden crutch from against the building, I began to limp away, drawing the attention of Reka and the other keepers.

"Keep an eye out for signs of the Skill poisoning," I said, raising my voice for all of them to hear. "Let me know how long he survives."

Normally, a test subject with severe Skill poisoning lasted only a few days. It would be interesting to see how the poison progressed in someone whose desire to overcome it was high.

"Was that necessary?" Saitou asked. "Out of all of the people in your experiments, he was the one who showed the most promise."

"And if he survives, he will be even stronger of a prospect," I said. My irritation had returned in full. "What did you want to speak to me about?"

"We took a portion of the rice in Tenraishi, as well as dried meat, fish, and venison. I sent three of the False Shadows to Magoto to deliver it with carts. They should arrive within a couple of weeks."

"And Lady Igai?" I asked.

The issue of supplies didn't seem enough to warrant him interrupting me.

"It took us some time to find her, but eventually we managed to get the information out of one of the townspeople. They are hiding her in one of the storehouse buildings close to Leiko. What would you like us to do?"

If they were hiding her, it likely meant she was injured and could not immediately retaliate. There would be townspeople with her willing to give their lives to defend her, which would mean losing more False Shadows if we attempted to recover her. We had already obtained our objective, albeit not under the best of circumstances.

"Leave her."

Saitou turned a questioning gaze toward me. "She will likely rise up against you in the future."

"We lost nearly half our forces. If we lose any more, the appearance we are trying to keep will crumble. We need more people who will fight for us before we begin waging a war."

My leg was beginning to bother me, but I didn't want to go back to the main camp and deal with anyone there. Leaning against the stick, I began lowering myself down to rest against a tree. Saitou held onto my arm and helped me sit down.

With stilted breath, I pressed my hand against the wound and leaned my head back against the tree.

"Do you know where we could hire mercenaries?"

"There is a place," Saitou said, seeming reluctant to answer.

"Where?"

"If you ride a few days north, you will reach the Gaiden Desert. Nestled against the mountains, there is a town that acts as the go-between for many of the extreme northern regions." Saitou leaned against the tree opposite me, crossing his arms as he gazed back toward the camp. "You should be able to hire mercenaries there."

"Good," I said, closing my eyes. "We can head out tomorrow." Rubbing my sore leg, I amended, "A week, no longer."

"As you wish."

———

I squinted my eyes against the reflection of the sun's rays in the sand. Despite it still being winter here, the sun didn't relent in the desert, burning my skin and chafing my lips. Why people lived here, I would never understand.

Licking my lips, I tried to moisten them before speaking.

"What do you know about the people here?"

Saitou's face was shrouded in a headscarf. "Your father once struck a deal with them—their oil for Magoto's swords." He paused, raising his arm to shield his face as a gust of wind blew sand and bits of ice against us. "The people here respect strength above all else. It is their language. Do not show them any kind of weakness."

I nodded. I had no intention of bargaining with anyone. Instead, I was intent on demanding service by whatever means were necessary.

After two weeks, the wound in my thigh still ached. It had healed enough so I could hobble around without a crutch, but I would have to be mindful—others might see it as a weakness.

I smiled to myself.

Not that I would have any problems making a point if I was pressed.

Gusts of wind sculpted an ever-changing landscape with sand. The dunes and hills shifted, constantly recreating the terrain. Through a blurry shield of grit, a town came into focus on the horizon. Tall rocks formed a circular wall, the edges chiseled and positioned to block out the wind. Towers lined the entrance, with tall poles sticking out of the sand to define a path into the town. Within the rocks, deep gorges created a dimpled texture. The guardsmen in the towers didn't bother to call out to us as we passed through the entrance, but we didn't move unnoticed. Through their coverings and wrappings, we were being watched.

What interested me more than their attention was the smell of stagnant water permeating the town. It seemed to come from a trickle of water flowing down from the surrounding rock formations.

Intrigued, I wandered toward the stone pillars at the edge of town. The stone was not smooth, as I had initially thought, but textured. Large grooves on the surface funneled a spiral of slow-moving water into tiny micro-grooves. Compared to outside the walls of the town, the air here had a slight humidity to it. The residents had created a funnel that collected the water in the air—likely the sole source of water in all of the desert.

No wonder this was such a prominent town.

I returned to the main cobblestone street with Saitou at my side, continuing through the town. Out of the corner of my eye, I began observing the people as closely as they watched me. They carried themselves with confidence, their shoulders pushed back and their heads held high. Near the eastern side of town, a crowd gathered, and it seemed to be a source of excitement in the town.

It seemed as good a place to begin as any.

As we drew closer, the crowd seemed to have formed a makeshift arena. Standing in the center of it, a short man with thick muscles shouted a battle cry. Throwing his fists toward the sky, he goaded and encouraged the people in the area to do the same. The people cheered as another man stepped from the crowd into the center of the circle. The two men paced around one another, the newcomer cracking his knuckles before he struck a pose.

The crowd roared with approval.

The first man was bare-chested, with more scars than smooth flesh. He had a dark beard with golden beads braided into it, which contrasted against his almost black skin. His challenger, on the other hand, was tall and lean with no apparent battle scars. The champion pounded his fists together, drawing my eyes to the gleam of metal on his scarred knuckles. At his side, a sword was tied. He remained still as his young opponent bounced around him from foot to foot.

"They say he never has to draw his sword!"

"He's undefeated!"

"No one's even been able to lay a hand on him!"

Judging by the whispers from the crowd, they thought highly of the first man.

I inched closer to get a better view, keen on the outcome.

The young challenger sprang forward, jabbing at the older man, who dodged his feeble attempt at an attack. The champion seemed uninterested, avoiding the first attack and catching the next blow with ease. He twisted the challenger's arm, snapping the young man's wrist. Screaming, the challenger fell back, clutching his wrist close to his chest. Hastily, the crowd parted around the injured man, allowing him to shuffle away.

Without hesitation, I grinned and limped into the circle, taking the challenger's place. What easier way to find someone worthy enough to join me than to challenge him myself?

I caught Saitou's pointed stare. He was displeased at my decision.

He didn't, however, move to interfere.

Which meant he knew I was stronger.

"Get out of here before you get yourself hurt!" the champion said, his smile widening across his face. He waved me away with both hands.

The crowd joined in with laughter.

I drew a dagger from my hip and slipped my fingers into the circle at the end. Allowing the Skills to transfer from my body into the metal, I cocked my head and smiled at the man. A surge of energy coursed beneath my bones; the Skills were as eager as I was to put him in his place.

I threw the dagger at the champion, not surprised when he side-stepped the attack. The crowd roared even harder, then quieted when the ground cracked open under the dagger.

Beneath my blade, the land pulsed with energy.

Moving as one, the people took a collective step back.

I directed the Skills to spread out from the blade, feeling every movement of the crowd as I narrowed my focus and found the champion's feet. I willed him to stay and drew the short sword from my back. I ambled forward, the blade held horizontally in front of my chest. The champion's eyes widened as he tried to move, finding himself unable to do so. When I sliced into his shoulder, he pulled free from the Skills and his arm shot out. He caught my wrist, keeping me from cutting through his muscle to the bone.

His will was strong if he could defy the Skills.

With a quick glance at the crowd, I decided my next move, releasing the man and stepping back. I needed something showier. Something that would spread my name across the northern regions. It would need to spook the crowd, without killing this man.

Kneeling on one leg, I dragged my fingers across the sand, revealing the stone tiles underneath. I began withdrawing the Skills from the area. The sand and stone lost their color, blackening at my touch. The crowd collectively inhaled as I released my hold on the Skills. A circle formed, the sand whipping into the air to create a whirling tempest. Turning toward the crowd I jabbed the dagger into the nearest man's arm. His will to move was momentarily frozen by the Skills. Like the earth beneath him, his skin blackened. The crowd screamed and scattered, and I released the bystander, who fled, the drops of blood from his arm the only color in the area.

I turned back to the champion.

He had yet to move.

"Who are you?" the man demanded of me. He was no longer smiling. Instead, he finally seemed to be taking me seriously.

"Hitori, Lady of Magoto."

He pointed his thumb at his chest. "The name's Gaiden."

I cared little about his name or any pleasantries we might exchange, wanting to get straight to the point. "I am in search of mercenaries to hire. If you work for me, you'll be well paid, and if it interests you, I can promise you will face skilled opponents."

Gaiden considered, looking at the blackened ground. When he returned his gaze to me, his upper lip curled back into a sneer.

"There is something else I want, in addition to money."

Anger coiled inside me. I knew immediately what his demand would be

To give away the knowledge of the Skills for such a cheap price! It was belittling, but I reconsidered my initial reaction, mulling it over. Controlling others who could use the Skills would give us an edge against the Phantom—if they were obedient. But something about the eagerness in his voice irritated me and made me want to hesitant to trust him. However, I needed someone with brutality and strength to buy me time against the council. If he believed he would eventually learn the Skills by serving me, what was the harm in agreeing?

"When you prove your worth, I will teach you."

Gaiden smirked and held out his hand to me. I extended my hand, feeling the strength in his hand as he squeezed mine. "It's a deal."

I met Gaiden's eyes, not flinching as he squeezed my hand harder.

"Who else do you know who can join me?" I asked.

Gaiden released his grip and pointed north, farther into the town. "There's a group of scoundrels who hang out at the local tavern. If you ask there, I'm sure you will have more than enough who are willing to join you."

"Lead on."

After giving me a mocking bow, Gaiden started down the sandy cobblestone road. Buildings of mud lined the streets, with large open entrances instead of doors. A man stepped out of one of the structures, a large broom made of dried brush in his hands. He began sweeping the sand outside, which seemed a pointless gesture as the wind immediately started to blow the sand back across where he had swept.

Gaiden gestured toward a crooked stone building where a wooden sign hung from metal chains. The Crow's Wing. A crowd lingered outside the tavern, and the people turned their heads as we approached, their conversations dying as they noticed Gaiden and me.

Their eyes followed my progress into the tavern.

I glanced over at Saitou, who seemed unperturbed by the whole endeavor.

I was beginning to like this town.

Already they were cautious of me.

Inside, the tavern was dark. It stank of booze and dust, a fitting place to gather a nefarious army. There were at least three dozen patrons inside, and it was still early in the afternoon. Each person's appearance seemed as dingy and dirty as their manners. Chairs were strewn about and glasses were spilled over, with liquid pouring onto the ground. Someone lay on the ground before me nursing a black eye.

I stepped over the man.

Gaiden looked down at me, his sneer a permanent fixture on his face. Something in his eyes made me believe he was testing my character by bringing me here.

As if seeing someone unconscious or dead would deter me.

I strode into the middle of the tavern, where a musician was playing a flute. The notes and melodies were mediocre, and the tone of his music was bland. It was nothing compared to Saitou's soulful playing. It did not elicit any sort of desire to listen to it further and it was the perfect position to address the entire tavern at once.

Gaiden sank into an empty chair, slouching against the table behind him, waiting.

Saitou stopped next to the stage, helping me up onto it.

The musician glared at me as I climbed onto the platform. I shifted the Skills in the air, drawing them in, calling them to gather in this dark place.

The musician lowered his instrument. "You can't be here."

"Oh?" I replied, glancing around at the patrons who continued to talk. "No one seems to care."

The musician's hand tightened around his flute, and he stood up and stormed out of the tavern, the bartender yelling after him.

Loudly clearing my throat, I drew one of my metal daggers. I rested my hand over the blade, feeling the Skills from my skin merge into the metal. The Skill particles broke apart, igniting with energy. I moved my hand over the dagger until it succumbed to my will of fire.

A few of the people in the tavern noticed it.

Throwing the dagger, smoke streaked across the tavern. As the dagger hit one of the tables in the center, a giant plume of fire shot up toward the ceiling.

"I'm Lady Hitori of Magoto," I said, raising my voice to be heard over the exclamations. "If any of you are looking for employment and are willing to do as I command, I'll be waiting for you outside this hellhole."

"Ooh-ho!" Gaiden shouted, slapping his knees. He downed a glass of what looked to be liquor, then wiped the foam from his mouth. "You heard the woman! Move!"

I stepped down from the platform, heading toward the door and eyeing the flames from my dagger as they cascaded down onto the ground. A few patrons tried to extinguish the flames, but upon sticking their hands into the fire, they turned their attention to me.

It was not real fire this time.

Outside, I watched as, one by one, people exited the tavern and gathered.

"It seems you no longer will have a problem with numbers," Saitou said mildly.

I smiled.

Everything was going according to plan.

chapter forty-two
New Information

We left the Moshe desert a week later with four dozen mercenaries. Gaiden was put in charge of the mercenaries since I found myself content with not having to constantly contend with the newcomers. They seemed to respect Gaiden, so for now, it was a good enough chain of command to keep order.

Our course was through the Gaiden Mountains, at the recommendation of the mercenary bearing the same name. He had boasted, comparing himself to the steep cliffs and the difficult terrain, saying the climb would prove how strong our force was. While it was an unfounded boast, the mountain was indeed a challenging climb. Gaiden had assured us it would be more pleasant than traveling through the desert again, which was all I needed to hear to convince me to take that path.

At the edge of the forest, near the base of the mountains, exhaustion slowed me. My throat was parched and sore, and the wound on my leg ached. I licked away the blood from my lips and inhaled the moisture in the air, feeling immediate relief from the harsh desert.

Off in the distance, the roar of water echoed across the mountains.

"Split up and search for the source of water!" Gaiden yelled at the mercenaries.

Often, his orders were met with some sort of a challenge, but given the past few days of limited rations, all seemed keen on replenishing our dwindling supply of water. While they obeyed him, it didn't seem to be for any other reason than Gaiden was the strongest and the loudest. It was their dynamic, their language, and should anyone else challenge that, the mercenaries would surely gravitate to that person. They were no different than a pack of wild animals.

Only the strongest survived.

Saitou brought his horse up next to mine, allowing Gaiden's men to search for water. He held the reins against his horse loosely, but his eyes were narrowed as he tracked the number of mercenaries who left us.

He had yet to relax around them.

"The mercenaries seem competent," I said offhandedly. "They know the basics of survival at least."

When Saitou didn't answer, I cleared my throat.

He glanced over at me and seemed to refocus on the conversation. "Something about them bothers me."

I raised an eyebrow. "And that is?"

"I'm not sure yet."

I nodded dismissively. When Saitou could put evidence to his suspicions, then I would consider if it was worth my time or worry. Feelings and gut instincts had no place in any decision; they were too misleading to trust.

A series of shouts came from within the forest, and Gaiden turned and began to head north. I set my horse after him, keeping the animal's pace relaxed. Through the trees, the mercenaries gathered in single file, heading upstream to follow the river higher into the mountains.

"Are we still headed toward the plains?" I asked Saitou.

"We are," Saitou responded. "There is a mountain pass that spans the remainder of the peaks and drops down on the southern side of the Orem Cliffs. Although, if we head down the mountains before the pass, we can reach the plains without having to traverse the worst terrain. Traveling across the plains would be easier on the horses."

In matters of direction and the best route, I trusted Saitou's judgement. As with people's names, the specific geographical locations of mountains and rivers escaped my memory. My preference was to take the quickest route, but following a path Saitou knew would ensure we didn't walk into a trap Gaiden had set. While I had promised to pay the mercenaries well, and the lure of the Skills remained, I didn't trust any of them. People were biologically wired to look after themselves. If they found another person who could pay more, or if they tired of me, they would do what benefited them the most. This arrangement would undoubtedly be short-lived. That much I knew. And I smiled to myself, daydreaming about how I would end Gaiden with the very thing he desired the most.

The sun was low in the sky when the mountain became steeper and the air grew cold and damp. A cloud of moisture hung in the air, making me shiver. Water roared in the distance, and the conversations between Gaiden and his men became garbled. A sizable lake spread out before us, fed by a small waterfall coming from the higher peaks.

Gaiden's men spread out and began filling their canteens with water.

I dismounted, leading my horse to a vacant place near the water. When the animal's head lowered, I untied the canteens hanging from the saddle packs.

"We should reach the plains by nightfall," one of Gaiden's men said, coming over to where Saitou and I stood.

I nodded to dismiss him, but he hesitated to leave. Putting the stopper into the canteen, I stood up, looking the man over.

His skin was fairer in color and less damaged than the others. Almost all of Gaiden's men were scarred, their skin twisted from battle. This man's hair was a shade of red with shadows of black near the base of his neck, and his skin was heavily freckled with brown specks.

His fingers curled in on themselves while he stood in front of me.

"Is there something you wanted?" Saitou asked.

The man flinched at the words, glancing nervously at Saitou, who stood almost a foot taller than him.

"Gaiden mentioned there's some sort of power you have. I was wondering if..." His voice faded as his eyes rose to meet mine.

So Gaiden was already talking about the Skills to the others in his group. With as much lust and desire as Gaiden had for them, the others would surely be as eager to learn of them.

"What do you know of it?" I asked.

The man flinched.

If he wanted to learn how to use the Skills, he was going to have to prove himself capable of standing his ground. As he was now, he would not be able to withstand even the endurance trials.

"Don't ask me again until you can look me in the eye," I said, causing him to shrink further away from me. "This is not something you ask for on a whim. It destroys those who are weak of mind. Already, I can tell you could not handle such a power."

His mouth hung slightly open, as if he were taken aback by my words.

I thrust the reins of my horse at him. "See that the horse gets a chance to cool down while we rest."

The man nodded; his eyes still wide from shock.

I passed by the other mercenaries, searching for their arrogant leader. Gaiden sat on a rock near the far side of the lake. He took a swig of water from his canteen, downing a large mouthful before he exhaled slowly and wiped his mouth with the back of his forearm.

"I don't appreciate you telling others about the Skills," I said, keeping my tone as level as I could. Gaiden clearly thought me someone he could toy with. He needed to understand he was here because I allowed him to be. Everything hinged on whether or not he was useful in accomplishing what I tasked him to do.

He was a means to an end, nothing more.

I could replace him as easily as I had found him.

"Until you've proven you're useful to me, you will learn nothing about the Skills," I continued, allowing my voice to carry for the benefit of those he had told about the Skills. "No one will learn anything unless you bring us to Leiko Gulf and secure the towns in the surrounding areas under my command."

I reached out to the Skills, shifting them in the air to create a weight to press down on Gaiden and his men.

"Do you understand?" I asked.

Gaiden sneered and stood, acting as if the added weight upon his back was not crushing him. He stared down at me, nearly two heads taller than I was. His eyebrows were low on his brow, creating a scowl that shadowed his boxy face.

"You'll get your villages and supplies," he said, his words sharp and to the point.

"Good," I said, matching the iciness in his tone.

Keeping my commanding posture, I turned my back on him and returned to my horse. Gaiden's men were undoubtedly watching me, analyzing me and sizing me up against their commander. Any signs of weakness would be seen as proof I was someone they could take advantage of.

"We head down into the plains," I said, changing our course to descend the mountain's southern slope as Saitou had advised. A leader always made bold decisions, and Saitou's advice seemed sound.

The mercenaries looked toward their leader.

Gaiden shrugged. "As you command."

After the group refilled their remaining canteens and the horses had time to graze and drink, we set off. This time, Saitou led the way. He seemed confident in his choice of path, and no one complained. For a time, the mercenaries were quiet, but as the miles stretched out, they began joking and talking with one another again. Eventually, the mountain leveled out, allowing us to see an unbroken view of the plains below. They were expansive, and the wind whipped the tall grasses in a rhythmic display.

"Hitori, look," Saitou said under his breath, nodding toward something below.

Approaching the mountain were three riders. From this distance, I could tell nothing other than how many were in their group, but the urgency in Saitou's voice hinted at something more I should have noticed.

"One of them has a bond," he said quietly.

I squinted and made out the glint of metal. Shadows. What luck! If we had continued along the mountainside, we would have missed the opportunity to cross paths with our enemy.

"Gaiden," I said, looking to my left. "Have one of your men follow them. I want details of who they are and where they are going."

If they led us to their camp, we might have the opportunity to take out a larger group, and if the Phantom was with them, we could eliminate our biggest threat.

"Braigon," Gaiden called. A short man with burly shoulders and a square jawline approached us from the back of the group. He had burn scars along his jaw and creeping alongside the muscles in his thick neck.

"Track the group and report back to us," Gaiden said.

The Shadow group turned at the foot of the mountain, keeping close to the foothills. There was not much time left before sundown, which meant they would need to seek shelter soon, and when they did…

I smiled.

Braigon left the company, his stocky horse making little noise as he slipped into the forest. Allowing Gaiden to retake charge of the group, we began moving higher up the mountain to stay out of sight of the Shadows. While we waited for Braigon to return, we continued moving at a slow pace.

When Braigon returned, he reported directly to Gaiden.

"They're camping at the base of the mountain, along the White Dragon River. If we wait until they're asleep to move in, the sound of the river will cover our advance."

Gaiden nodded. "Anything else?"

"One carries a long staff... "

I held my breath. Could it really be the Phantom?

"...some woman..."

My heart sank at the news.

"...and two others. One of the men carries a long polearm. The other seems not to carry any weapon. After listening to their conversation, it seems they're traveling across the plains to the north somewhere."

Their destination would most likely be Vaiyene, in the Miyota Mountains, but why were there Shadows outside of Vaiyene? Were they doing their own scouting missions to determine my weaknesses?

"What would you like to do, Hitori?" Saitou asked.

The attention of Gaiden and all his men fell on me.

If the Phantom was not among them, it was not a pressing matter. But if we had the opportunity to capture some of the Shadows, perhaps we could extract information about the Phantom's whereabouts and his plans. While I was impatient to head to the gulf and return to Magoto, a quick diversion to apprehend these Shadows could prove beneficial to my plans.

"Capture them," I ordered.

It would be the first test for the mercenaries.

Gaiden dismounted from his stallion and looked over the mercenaries. "I will only need three additional men. Even if we were up against more, a handful of my men would be able to secure them without trouble."

"However you see fit," I said, losing interest. I could have captured them by myself, without anyone's help.

We descended the mountains on foot with a force of seven. Saitou and I followed to keep tabs on the main group, partially because I wanted to witness the mercenaries in action, but also because of my continued distrust in them.

Through the forest, the glow from the enemy's fire became our destination. We fanned out, encircling the Shadows. I ducked under a low branch, shifting my feet as quietly as I could over the ice-crusted snow. Saitou reached out his arm, and I held onto it, using him for support. When I placed my foot on solid ground, he leaned over me and pointed at one of the Shadows—a tall, lean man with red hair tied back at the nape of his neck. His clothing was different from the normal Shadow attire; he wore a bright blue tunic decorated in silver accents instead of the more natural brown and green tones. A large stave lay balanced against his chest.

Slowly, he swiveled his head, as if listening.

"He senses us," Saitou whispered.

A moment later, Gaiden and his men burst into the camp. The man with the stave immediately moved toward the threat, thrusting his spear into one of the mercenary's legs. Judging from his lack of a bond and quick action, he was no Shadow. The woman who was beside him wielded a staff. She also didn't have a bond. The only one whose arm was wrapped in silver was a man standing on the opposite side of camp. The silver threads wrapped around his arm were the same pattern as my own.

So, he was one of mine.

They were not Shadows at all.

I clicked my tongue in disappointment.

The woman and man fought together, back to back, defending against the three mercenaries. Gaiden had cornered the False Shadow, who had his back to me. Compared to the other two, he seemed hesitant to fight. I left my place in the forest, and the woman noticed me. She ducked under an attack from one of the mercenaries and placed herself in between me and my target.

Gaiden drew his sword, taking a step toward the False Shadow.

"Leave him to me," I said. "He's one of mine."

Narrowing my eyes, I tilted my head to inspect the woman who opposed me. She had the same posture and defiance as the Phantom I loathed. Her brown hair was tied up in a loose bun, and her brown, nearly orange eyes flickered between me and the False Shadow. Glancing over at the False Shadow, I drew my short sword. How arrogant and cocky he was to go up against me knowing full well who I was. His fingers curled into fists as he turned around. Pausing, I momentarily lowered my weapon. The man's hair had grown longer, more unruly since the last time I had seen him.

When Ikaru had not returned from his last mission, I thought he had died. He had the same emerald eyes as his sister, Rin. How I hated them both.

"I never expected you would so openly defy me by joining a group that is working against me," I said enjoying the terror in his eyes. "Did you really think you could escape me?"

Ikaru clamped his jaw tight. He had a sword tied to his waist, but he had yet to draw it. From what I remembered, he was no warrior. He wouldn't dare draw his blade against me.

The woman took a step forward to block him from my line of sight.

"Ikaru is free of you now," she said.

"Shenrae, don't," Ikaru said, his presence growing meeker. "Forget about me. I told you it was only a matter of time before she would find me."

"You're not afraid of me, are you?" I asked the woman called Shenrae.

"Why would I be afraid of someone who lacks common decency? Anyone who treats those who follow them like a dog is not someone I will cower before!"

Gaiden's men wrestled to hold onto Ikaru's other friend. The mercenaries had possession of his stave now, and he wriggled and twisted in an attempt to escape from the hold he was in. Blood dripped from a wound at his side.

"Just stop, Shenrae," Ikaru pleaded. He glanced over at his friend. "Akio needs your help more than I do."

"No!" Shenrae said, glancing over at Akio. She seemed torn between standing her ground and intervening in this fight. "We know Rin isn't with her anymore. You don't have to obey her."

I smiled, finding her bravery amusing. "You say you're not afraid of me, yet you're clutching your staff so tightly your knuckles have turned white."

Shenrae drew in a deep breath and crouched down, ready to attack.

Saitou moved to intercede, but I held out my hand to stop him.

I would face her.

From across the campsite, one of the mercenaries yelled, "You filth!"

The mercenary held onto his wrist, blood dripping from it. Akio had managed to escape from the men. A dagger flashed in Akio's hand, and he jammed the blade into the man's neck before he could recover, snatching back his stave. With his weapon back in his hands, he lunged at me, swinging the sharp end at my side.

"Get out of here!" Akio yelled to his friends.

As I sidestepped the point of his spear, Saitou drew his sword to engage. I turned my attention back to Shenrae. Using her staff, she thrust at me and hit me in the chest. I braced myself against the impact, sputtering as my breath was cut off. Rage built inside me.

With all of Gaiden's men, how were we losing?

I summoned the Skills to me, feeling them float across the ground as they created a deadly mist. As if Shenrae sensed what I was doing, she began to spin her staff. Using the wind of her pole, she pushed the Skills away from her and Ikaru's feet.

I narrowed my eyes.

She knew about the Skills.

Shenrae jabbed her staff toward my side, but I dodged her attack, reaching my hand across my blade to summon fire. She eyed the red at the edge of my sword and hesitated in her next attack. While she was distracted by the fire, I ensnared her with the Skills, immobilizing her.

She tried to move her foot but couldn't.

With my blade, I slashed at her chest. Ikaru threw his arm out to block me. Instead of cutting into Shenrae, the blade cut into

Ikaru's bond. He gritted his teeth as the fire on the blade seared his arm.

"Ikaru!" Shenrae yelled.

The hold on her legs loosened, her anger and will tearing through my control of the Skills. I stepped back, and she came at me with her staff. With the momentary break in my command of the Skills, I was left vulnerable. Recoiling from the impact against my side and fighting against the pain, I pulled a dagger from the pouch at my side. Before slashing at Shenrae, I infused it with the Skills. It cut into her, and she winced as the flames sizzled across her skin.

Saitou moved in front of me as he slashed forward with a one-handed grip. Shenrae twisted her staff up to block it. Planting her feet and bending her knees, she braced herself against Saitou's strength.

Gaiden had engaged with Akio.

The Skills in the air became cold, and I glanced around to find the source of the disturbance. Ikaru had drawn his blade. He held it with both hands, the blade held steady in his palms as it vibrated and pulsed. The air became even colder. Ikaru's brow creased, and he lunged, thrusting his blade between Saitou and Shenrae. A white flash burst from his sword, and I threw my arm up to shield my eyes, cursing under my breath.

When my eyes had finally adjusted, Shenrae, Akio, and Ikaru were gone.

A patch of ice was in their place.

In the wake of the white light, a sort of mist hung in the air. I reached out my hand to touch the moisture. The cold in the air had mixed with the heat of my blade. Had Ikaru planned that, or was it a lucky occurrence?

Seeing Saitou's silhouette in the mist, I moved toward him.

Despite the mercenaries' claims, it seemed good warriors were hard to come by. Already, one of their own had died. The cut on his neck had bled out his life.

"Search the forest!" Gaiden shouted to his men, leaving the dead man behind.

Gathering the Skills to me, I prepared to involve myself. It had been a mistake trusting they would be able to handle the situation. This time, I would use the Skills to subdue Ikaru and his friends.

The thick forest and the steep mountain slope slowed our pursuit. It would slow down Ikaru and his friends too, but my speed was no match for that of the mercenaries, who seemed to be having an easier time navigating the fallen trees and loose soil.

I tripped and fell, pine needles piercing the skin of my hand. While the wound on my leg had healed, it still impeded my movement.

"If we head farther up the mountain," Saitou said, holding out his hand to me, "it will be easier to traverse."

We climbed higher, reaching a place in the mountain where the slope leveled out. By then, the mercenaries' shouts and jeers rose in a chorus. It seemed they had spotted our target. Through the trees ahead, I saw Ikaru. He was on his knees, and blood was smeared across his face. Farther off, Ikaru's friends continued to run. I hesitated on the edge of the mountain, gripping a tree for support as I slid down on the loose pine needles. Saitou skidded down on one leg, using the slope to gain momentum. He glanced back at me, steadying himself against a tree to stop his descent.

I waved him off. "I'll catch up."

Saitou nodded and continued down the mountain, his hand already on his sword. Keeping myself close to the ground, I found a more accessible place to descend the mountain. My foot slipped on a patch of loose dirt, and I slid down the hill. My heart raced, and I threw out my hand, snagging a low-hanging branch from a tree to stop my fall, but the branch snapped and slapped me across the face. As I rolled down the mountain, pine needles and rocks cut into me. My back hit against a fallen tree, and the force of my impact caused me to break through the rotting wood.

Dirt and bark fell on top of me.

Coughing, I spat out dirt and pushed myself up onto my elbows.

I took a shuddering breath.

When the pain in my back subsided, I stood and continued forward. As I got closer, I heard shouting and the clash of steel. I stood back to observe. A mercenary grabbed Ikaru's hand and then pulled sharply away. His hand appeared black, almost as if it had been frostbitten.

"Leave already!" Ikaru shouted, leaning on his sword for support.

Shenrae and Akio faced off against the other mercenaries, holding their own.

"No!" Shenrae shouted, but Saitou began to approach her from the other side. Although she and her companions were strong warriors, they were outnumbered

Akio lifted his gaze from the mercenaries and met my eyes.

"Shenrae, we have to go, or none of us will escape." Calmly, he held out his arm and backed up, blocking Shenrae from making a move. Gaiden, Saitou, and the other two mercenaries closed in.

Ikaru placed his hands on the blade.

He was going to do the same thing he had before.

"Don't let him—!"

A white light flashed, and a rush of cold air blew over me. I tried to keep my eyes open to see where they were heading this time, but the wind and the ice in the air kept me from trying.

After a moment of shouting, all became quiet.

Shenrae and Akio were nowhere in sight. Ikaru lay on the ground, facedown.

Gaiden shouted, "Split up and search— "

"Don't bother," I said, cutting him off. We had already lost enough time chasing them. Standing over Ikaru, I looked down at him. "Once he wakes up, we'll have all the information we need."

Saitou knelt next to Ikaru and placed his fingers against the side of his neck, giving me a small nod. Ikaru still lived—at least for now. We only needed to keep him alive long enough to question him about the Phantom and his plans.

Whatever Ikaru could tell us, it might just be what we needed to turn the tide

part six

KILO

chapter forty-three
The Ancient Phantom

The ground shook under my bruised knees, rumbling in waves as cobblestone pavers groaned at the strain of moving earth. High stone towers crashed, causing plumes of smoke to engulf me, pelting my skin with rocks and debris. Holding my breath, I kept my eyes closed until the chaos passed.

I did not need to see the destruction to feel the emotion.

Children, men, women—their screams pierced through my body.

"Still your mind, and in time the ancient Phantom will speak with you."

The Guardian who watched over Konro village had told me this almost a season ago. Day in and day out, I came to this place, to the moment of Zenkaiko's destruction, in hopes I would be able to transcend the memory and speak to the ancient Phantom.

I forced my hands open, letting my stiff fingers uncurl as I willed my mind and body to let the moment pass. There was nothing I could do. Nothing but wait and see if the ancient Phantom would find me worthy enough to speak with me. The Skills had allowed me to be here, and I had to trust it was for a purpose.

And so, I waited.

For whatever clarity the ancient Phantom would bestow on me.

An unsettling silence took hold of the memory. With my palms on my knees, I breathed in and opened my eyes. It was like a bad dream, except the cold reality of death touched the atmosphere as sadness permeated the air.

The ancient Phantom's emotion choked the scene.

And I struggled to breath.

Dust settled across the ground, raining down on the destruction wrought by the Phantom. The ancient Phantom's sword scraped against the dislodged cobblestones. In earlier meditations, I had tried to draw his attention by moving into his line of sight or by calling out to him, but today, my mind was calm. My vision blurred at the edges as a shift in the memory touched my spirit. The ancient Phantom turned his head. Remaining still, I allowed the Skills within me to relax, not daring to get my hopes up.

Be patient.

Bear witness to the moment.

The ancient Phantom balanced the weight of his blade on his shoulder. At this distance, it seemed he wore a plain overcoat, but as he came closer, the black of his armor stood out. Broken into sections, the leather armor was affixed to his shoulders and shins, but his chest was unprotected. The sleeves of his robe draped down on either side, bunching up around his waist.

When he stopped before me, I bowed my head to the ground, my hands resting on the dirt, showing him the deepest form of respect his position merited.

"Who are you?" the ancient Phantom asked.

"A servant to the people, as you once were."

It was a sentiment he would understand.

Lifting my head, I watched as he surveyed the ruins he was responsible for. The feeling in the air—his emotions—seemed to dissipate, as if the frozen memory could at last move forward.

"I see after all this time, nothing has changed."

"Phantom?" I asked, unsure of his meaning.

With a deep frown etching his face, he slid his sword from his shoulder. The crumbled ruins quaked at his summons. He made a sweeping gesture with both hands, and the ruins and rocks shuddered and cracked. The memory world shifted beneath me. Ruins and rubble were replaced by paneled walls of delicate rice paper, which softened the light from the sun. The Phantom pushed open the divider, the aged planks creaking as he crossed over them to a wooden balcony

Rain plinked against the stone pavers on the roof overhead.

The ancient Phantom sat cross-legged, his back straight as his palms rested on his knees. Motioning in front of him, he indicated I should sit on the cushion opposite him. A tray of tea rested in the middle.

Kneeling, I sat back on my heels.

"I am Takezo, one of the Phantoms of Zenkaiko," he said, looking at me expectantly. "What is your name?"

I set my palms on my knees. "Kilo. A Shadow and once a Phantom of Vaiyene."

The ancient Phantom reached forward and poured a cup of tea before handing it to me. Sipping at the bitter contents, I watched him closely. He seemed to have pulled himself out of the memory and was fully conscious of my presence.

Phantom Takezo raised his own cup and paused, gazing into the tea.

"Becoming a Phantom requires taking an oath one cannot dismiss; even into death you carry it. Being a Phantom is what brought you here and what your actions reflect. Do not let go of that which is a part of yourself so lightly."

I bowed slightly to him, acknowledging his words.

He was right.

Even though I had left Vaiyene against the wishes of the other Phantoms, effectively giving up the title and status, the action had still been done in service of the people, thereby being Phantom-like at its core.

I held tighter to the cup in my hand, letting go of the past. This was the moment I had waited for. Finally, the ancient Phantom's reason for destroying Zenkaiko would be clear.

"Speak whatever is on your mind, Kilo," Phantom Takezo said. "The only way for this meeting to have occurred is through dedicated meditation and willpower. You came with a purpose in mind. What was it?"

Meeting the Phantom's eyes, I sensed his anticipation.

Why had the ancient Phantom destroyed the knowledge of the Skills? The longer I stayed in Konro, the more I began to wonder how he had not been aware people aimed to sabotage his decision. Instead of asking my original question, I sized him up, seeing a man who was perhaps more clever than I had initially thought him to be. His eyes were calculating, watching me with a subtle intensity.

Setting my cup down, I fisted my hands on my knees.

"Did you really intend to destroy all knowledge of the Skills?"

The ancient Phantom sipped at his tea. "Are you referring to Konro?"

"I find it hard to believe you would not have known about the girl and the books she left with."

The ancient Phantom smiled. "It pained me to destroy the knowledge of the Skills and the people I cared for, but I believed it was what must be done. Still, in the end, my heart was weak. As you suspected, I allowed the young girl and a handful of others to leave Zenkaiko before I destroyed it." He took another sip of his tea. "But, as you may have learned, knowledge is not all that is necessary to understand the Skills. It is a difficult concept to grasp from the written word. It is not something one can easily learn without experiencing it firsthand, so the act of saving that knowledge may not be as helpful as they had hoped."

I frowned, getting the sense he was less than pleased by the question.

Or that he was testing me in some way.

"You seem sure of yourself," I commented cautiously.

"I was the one who wrote the books that way."

Phantom Takezo watched me closely.

Somehow, he seemed hostile now, like he was reluctant to speak of what we both knew had happened. If he had resided here since Zenkaiko's destruction, how long had he sat with his own thoughts?

Regretted his own actions?

Wished there had been another way?

"What happened to the people who did not leave Zenkaiko?" I asked.

"Ah." He raised his head and looked at me like a master would a student. "I wonder how much you have begun to realize about the Skills. Are you certain you don't already know the answer to that question?"

He waited for an answer.

I hesitated. "The Skills seem to be more of a presence than something to manipulate. When I walk through the forest in Konro, the trees, the water, the rocks, everything feels alive, as if there is an energy and a will to them."

A small smile returned to the ancient Phantom's face, and he nodded. He held out his hand, palm raised toward the sky. A silver light sparked to life in the center of his hand, and he watched fondly as the shape wavered and sent smaller lights playfully into the air.

"They are the caress of the wind, the dampness of the rain, and the scent of the flowers. They are the rocks, the trees, and the river. They are life and death. Perhaps it is better to not think of Zenkaiko and its people as 'gone,' but 'different.' The people, the buildings, and everything about it exist as we do, but not in the same way."

Zenkaiko still existed in some way?

The Reikon Tree in Vaiyene, the place where the Shadows were laid to rest, had always had an otherworldly feel to it, even before I had known about the Skills. Walking among the weapons stuck into the ground made one feel as if they were not alone. It was a place many of the Shadows frequented because it comforted them and helped remind them of their purpose. A sacred place, one where the spirits of the Shadows lingered.

The protection of the Shadows never faded, even after death.

I remembered fondly the talks I'd had with Phantom Atul years ago about philosophy and the meaning and purpose of being a Shadow. Lately, I had been so wound up about the False Shadows and Kural's involvement that I had forgotten the teachings of my Phantom. It was not always important to put things into words or to understand them fully. Dealing in absolutes was what caused divisions among people. The Skills were neither good nor evil; Finae had shown me that. The ancient Phantom had made a decision, and it had neither been the correct one nor the wrong one. It was only one path that had been taken, and it was clear from his expression he had a genuine love for the Skills. Becoming a Phantom and then sacrificing that which he had sworn to protect had cost him a great deal.

Setting down his tea, he raised his ancient eyes to me. The hostility within them seemed somewhat lessened, as if my words had somehow resonated with him.

I stood up and walked to the edge of the balcony, gazing out through the bamboo stalks into the garden. The rain continued to fall from the roof in streams.

Somewhere, sheltered in the trees, a bird began its song.

"Lately, there's something that feels *off* with the Skills," I said, speaking aloud my thoughts. "When I meditate, I can feel the Skills strongly, but something about them feels almost..." I tried to put the feeling into words but I could not find a way to describe it.

The ancient Phantom walked across the balcony, passing me without a glance.

"There is something I need to show you."

Following him, I felt a shift in the memory. The rain lessened, and the wooden planks beneath our feet disappeared. Off in the distance, mountains rose high into the sky, the clouds hiding their peaks. Below them, an expansive valley shimmered with numerous rice fields. We stood amidst a snowy meadow—or what looked to be snow; our footsteps shattered the white grass where we walked. I tried to keep my steps light to prevent breaking any more. A small crack had split the dirt and shifted the ground not far from us. Bending down to the earth, I rested my hand on it, feeling a faint pull from within—the Skills.

"What do you make of it?" the ancient Phantom asked.

"It almost seems dead. Like—"

"The Skills are no longer with it?"

I nodded.

"Not long before I destroyed Zenkaiko, we became aware of an imbalance in the world. We thought by removing our knowledge of the Skills and allowing the world to be without our interference, the Skills would be able to repair the damage we had done." He glanced over at me. "But it seems my actions did nothing but delay the inevitable. From the blackened skin on your arm, I can tell the cycle is repeating itself."

Hesitantly, I lifted my right hand, looking at the slight discoloration of my skin. The metal threads around my arm were supposed to counteract the Skills to keep me from becoming poisoned.

"The bond on your forearm will negate some of the effects of the Skills," Phantom Takezo said, "but a balance needs to be maintained within the Skills themselves. One needs to ensure the health and vitality of that which they use to retain a healthy relationship. Because there is an imbalance, the Skills are beginning to pool within you, as they will soon be doing across the lands."

Standing, I began to walk around the area, gazing at the dying grass and the sickened earth. "How were the Skills kept in balance before?"

Phantom Takezo remained silent.

From what I knew, Zenkaiko had been destroyed sixty years ago, but something about the Phantom's silence made me question the timeframe. This place, this world, the Phantom's memories, all of this *was* the Skills. From my meditations, I had been able to reach a place, a void where the Skills flourished. There was no sight, no scent, no sound, only the vast, infinite possibilities.

Walking away from the Phantom, I headed toward one of the trees. My fingertips scraped against the rough bark. The Skills were a cycle. A flow. Like the tide, it ebbed and waned. It was nothing we could control, but I was beginning to understand the dynamic of coexistence, the balance between all things.

"Has this happened before with the Skills?" I asked.

The ancient Phantom turned his eyes on me, a deep crease running across his forehead. "I grew up in Zenkaiko, and like many, I never left my hometown, so my knowledge is limited in terms of what happened outside it. Within my village, we were taught the Skills were the 'breath of life,' the life of the earth. There were many festivals and rituals dedicated to the Skills and their well-being. While all knew about the Skills, few ever directly dealt with them. Only a select few learned how to placate them and keep them in line."

Phantom Takezo looked at me pointedly.

"The Shadows?"

He nodded. "A Shadow's duty was to purify the imperfection from the Skills. To be able to assist with the people and to smooth out that which lingers in the land. To protect and nurture the relationship between all things was the Shadow's purpose. Over time, you forgot it."

Lifting my head, I saw the ancient Phantom's form waver.

The amount of strength it took for him to maintain his form all these years in this place must have been immeasurable. At once, a part of me realized that perhaps this wasn't the ancient Phantom at all but the very will of the Skills themselves. His desire to remain and the Skills' desire to speak of what had happened in Zenkaiko pervaded this place, rupturing the Skills and allowing this Phantom to wait for someone to come.

The Skills.

The ancient Phantom *was* them.

"What is it that I must do?" I asked.

My heart, my mind, and my spirit were ready. If the land itself and the power within it had made this meeting possible, what had I been brought here to learn?

The ancient Phantom's gaze remained on me. "I can sense growth in your heart—an understanding and a desire to do what is best for all people and for the Skills in a way that differs from my own. You must choose for yourself."

Phantom Takezo began walking into the void, where the images of the dying trees and grass disappeared into darkness, reflecting onto a glass like surface. There was no sound as he walked across the blackness, but ripples shrouded his reflected image upon the ground.

"A Phantom ascends from being a Shadow because of who they are," the ancient Phantom continued. "The extant Phantoms strongly hold to their ideals. Do you know why Phantom Atul chose you?"

I tried to keep my mind from wondering how it was he knew of Phantom Atul.

The Skills transcended time, and with my Phantom's death...

"It was something your father could not understand," the ancient Phantom said as he gazed out across the landscape that was now Zenkaiko. The world we walked in shifted from nothingness to the ruins of Zenkaiko before blurring into the Miyota Mountains and the peaks I loved.

My heart yearned to return.

To walk among the paths of the Miyota Mountains.

"What Genzo believed to be your greatest weakness is the exact reason why you became a Phantom—your desire to understand and the delicate way you approach such matters. Your father never understood your kindness. To see a person's true heart and their purpose… That is why you were chosen to be a Phantom. The gentle soul is one that is tormented. But do not allow the world to change you, for your gentleness is what makes you strong."

With a smile, I glanced up from the mountain path.

"Thank you, Phantom Atul."

The ancient Phantom's form remained the same, but his words were very same ones my Phantom had spoken to me in another time, and I was certain it was his will that spoke to me.

The pain of losing Phantom Atul in the fires set by the False Shadows had been eclipsed by witnessing Phantom Kural behead a man and forsake the Shadow's Creed. I had allowed the anger and resentment to grow in me, ignoring the pain in my heart. Phantom Atul had shown me there was more to a person's life than their own family, and he had come to me after my father had rejected me.

Kindness was something the world desperately needed more of; that was something I now could see. Kindness had stayed my hand with the False Shadows, and kindness had led me to protect not only Vaiyene and my own people but others across Kiriku.

"Before we part, let me leave you with something," the ancient Phantom said. He seemed to have regained himself and was now walking with a different air about him. "You are already beginning to understand, but what will help is to be able to see that which you must protect."

As the trees and mountains and all sights and smells faded, we were left again in total darkness.

Phantom Takezo stepped toward me, raising his hand. "Close your eyes."

As I did so, the ancient Phantom pressed his fingers lightly against my eyes. His touch was warm, and the feeling blossomed against my eyes, spreading across my head and into my heart.

"May the goodwill of all people and all things go with you."

chapter forty-four
A New Direction

Something pulled on my mind, and the vision and the ancient Phantom blurred. The memory of Zenkaiko faded around me. Breathing in deeply, I became aware of the breeze brushing against my face and the scent of cherry blossoms. Rays of sunshine warmed my shoulders, and I relaxed my fingers, placing them on the grass, which was still damp with dew. When I opened my eyes, the grove of bamboo trees was dancing in the wind. The sun filtered through the stalks, dirt, and pollen, creating a haze.

Standing, I surveyed the grove.

Konro.

The village of the Skills.

Starting into the forest, I walked along the shore of the Yagoi River. My bare feet sank into the sandy riverbed, leaving behind footprints in the mist. Sitting not far from where I had been meditating was Finae. She was hunched over a painting, her face close to the canvas as she delicately added the last details with her brush. Engrossed with her work, she was not even aware of me being there. Smiling, I watched as her eyes scrunched tighter while she added the remaining lines. When she sat back and tilted her head to look at her painting, she noticed the shadow I cast in the grass beside her.

"Were you able to speak with the ancient Phantom?" Finae asked, standing. She raised her arms to the sky, interlocking her fingers and stretching out her back.

"I was. We had an interesting conversation."

Moving in front of Finae's work, I gazed curiously at what she had been painting. The trees and the lakeside were the same as the area in which we stood, but there was a person—or what seemed to be one—in the painting. The form was depicted in black and outlined in silver.

Finae rarely painted people.

"Who is this?" I asked, scanning the rest of her work. There were flecks of silver over the entire piece that seemed to have a texture to them, indicating it was not paint she had used.

"Finae, is this metal?"

"It might be?"

Sighing, I hunched down to see better. There were no details on the face or body. Finae bunched up the bottom of her robes and tied them back with a ribbon before she stepped into the water and began washing her brushes.

"I've seen the trees here in Konro outlined in silver light before," Finae said, swiping her hair out of her face with the back of her hand.

"And the person?"

Finae stopped washing her brushes, hesitating. "Don't be weird about it, okay? But sometimes I see people walking in the forest. I don't think they're alive like you and me."

Considering, I looked at the trees around us. "There is a lot we do not yet know about the Skills. Being able to see the spirits of those who have passed does not seem unusual."

Finae lifted her gaze to me for a moment.

Indeed, I had just come from speaking with an entity who *was* the Skills.

From within the forest, Rin came toward us. She came to my side and tilted her head at the painting.

"I see Finae is at it again."

Her voice had an edge to it.

I raised my eyebrows.

"The metal," Rin said, nodding toward Finae, "do you know where she found it?"

Finae said nothing. Instead, she began scrubbing her fingers to try and get rid of the ink stains that had spread up her arms.

I bit my lip to keep from smiling.

"Finae?" I asked, struggling to keep a straight face.

Heaving an exaggerated sigh, she came back to the shore. Without a sound, she dried her inkstone and placed her brushes in the bamboo roll, carefully tucking them inside a large wooden box.

"It just appeared," Finae said at last. Upon seeing Rin's frown, she sighed again. "I was in the middle of painting when I noticed a flower nearby. I thought it was a drop of dew, and my water had run dry, so..." Shrugging, she shot a glare at Rin. "It wasn't exactly water like I was hoping it to be, but it worked just the same."

I laughed—more because Rin was annoyed by Finae's actions than anything. It was not the first time Finae had found something odd to paint with, and it would not be the last.

Still, it was strange.

I looked over at Rin, trying to maintain my composure.

"Have you asked the Guardian about it?"

Rin shook her head. "Not yet. When I went to talk to her, she wasn't in her house or in the library. No one in town has seen her either."

"I have an idea where she might be," I said, recalling the silver lake where we had first met her. It was a place she frequented, and one where I often went to talk to her.

"Are you coming, Finae?" I asked.

She nodded, putting away the last of her supplies into the wooden box I had made for her. Slinging the box over my shoulder, I headed back toward Konro. We walked along the lakeshore and through the forest until we came to the stone archway leading into the village. A giant, twisted rope hung from two stone pillars, with thin metal charms hanging down from it.

A calmness came over me as I passed under the gate.

It was the presence of the Skills.

Instead of heading down the main path into Konro, I cut through the forest, leading Finae and Rin to the silver lake outside the village. Fog settled over the ground, making it hard to distinguish what lay ahead. My connection to the Skills gave me a better sense of direction than my eyes did, leading me along the familiar path.

I sensed two people ahead.

Squinting, I caught the faint outline of a white robe.

"Guardian?" I asked, raising my voice slightly.

Another person moved toward us. He was tall, with a thin build and deep-set wrinkles across his forehead. Pockmarks scattered across his jawline, partially hidden by a long white beard that hung down over his chest.

On his left forearm was a bond.

I bowed to him, curious about the meaning of his appearance and his bond. He did not seem like a False Shadow, but rather someone who knew the Guardian and, as such, was familiar with Konro.

"Forgive our intrusion," I said, straightening. "I hope we have not interrupted anything."

"I was just leaving," the man said, brushing past me.

"Would you mind answering a question?" I asked.

The man looked back over his shoulder. He had a faraway look in his eyes. Even as his gaze passed over me, it did not seem like he saw me physically, but something in the Skills shifted around him. "I am a Shadow no longer," he said, his words carrying an icy tone. "I have no desire to be associated with the Skills or anyone who utilizes them."

He gave us a small bow before turning back around. Finae opened her mouth to say something, but I caught her eye before she could, and she bit back her words. Lady Chiyori, Guardian of Konro, walked toward us, the fog around her disappearing enough for me to make out her white clothing and features. She still carried herself with a quiet elegance, but a part of me had begun to sense her fragility.

Her life was coming to an end.

"Ah, Phantom Kilo," she said, a smile brightening her face. "It is a pleasure to see you. I was thinking about you and your companions earlier."

"Who was that?" I asked, curiosity getting the better of me.

The Guardian's smile faded. "Someone I had hoped would be willing to show you more about the Skills. His name is Emiko. His father taught him how to use the Skills back when Zenkaiko still stood. He is one of the last remaining former Shadows."

Finae inhaled sharply behind me.

"I did not want to get your hopes up," the Guardian continued. "It took me quite some time to locate him, but it seems the years have only continued to darken his feelings toward the Skills."

My heart sank.

Like the ancient Phantom had said, it was challenging to learn the abstract concepts of the Skills from a book, if there was someone who knew how to use them, it would have been more beneficial. The Guardian had been a young child when she left Zenkaiko, so she and the villagers knew little about the Skills themselves. They had only preserved the knowledge in the books they fled with, but most had not even practiced them.

"Why does he hate the Skills?" Finae asked.

The Guardian gave her an understanding look.

"It's hard losing something you care about," she said.

"Are there others?" I asked, watching as Finae's lips puffed out in a pout. She would have enjoyed getting to know about the Skills from someone with real knowledge of them, but at the same time, she was enjoying exploring them in her own way.

"There were a handful of people from Zenkaiko who knew how to use the Skills, but most have passed on from this life. Those who were taught about the Skills have forgotten about them or want nothing to do with them. I've always thought it was the residual desire from the Phantoms—to see the knowledge forgotten—that has led us to turn a deaf ear toward them."

Her eyes seemed unfocused, her attention drifting back to another time.

There were things she did remember about the Skills though, like how to forge a bond in the silver lake we stood next to. Rin was now able to use the Skills again without worrying, because of the Guardian's help in forging a new bond, but there were other things she did not remember about the Skills or know the meaning behind.

"Lady Chiyori?" Rin said, stepping forward and bowing slightly. It was a mannerism she had started adopting from me. "We've noticed the Skills turning to liquid on the flowers around Konro." Rin hesitated, as if unsure of how to phrase her question.

The Guardian's attention returned. "Ah, yes. When there is an excess amount of the Skills, they can take physical form." She spread her right arm out toward the lake behind her. "This is one spot where the Skills have begun to pool. From time to time, the land seems to be thrown out of balance and produces an excess amount of the Skills. I do not believe it is something you should worry about."

"If there is anything we can do to help alleviate the burden, let us know," I said, being mindful that our questions and presence drained her. "Thank you for your assistance, Guardian."

I bowed before taking my leave.

Rin and Finae lingered before they caught up to me.

It seemed the more we tried to unravel what was happening with the Skills, the more we learned how great a mystery the Skills still were. Even after speaking with the ancient Phantom, they remained so.

"How were your meditations?" Rin asked.

Finae ran ahead, shouting, "I'm going to set up the barrier for you!"

Opening my mouth to reply, I then stopped. Finae was long out of range to hear me. Rin and I walked in companionable together before I addressed her question.

"I was able to find the clarity I've been wanting about the Skills," I said, trying to describe the experience for Rin. "The ancient Phantom seemed at peace with his decision, but I believe he wished there had been another way."

I glanced over to see a frown on her face. Most of her time she spent going between Konro and the trading post, helping us keep in touch with General Mirai, Asdar, and our other allies. When she was in Konro, she helped Finae and me by reading through notes, but she always seemed unhappy about it. To me and Finae the prospect of learning more about the Skills excited us, but Rin remained uncertain.

"What makes you nervous about the Skills?" I asked, mildly.

Rin turned to me and raised her eyebrows.

Finae fully embraced them, seeing the Skills as an extension of her creativity. To her, they were an empty page waiting for color. But to Rin, there was something that always made her hesitate when using them.

"A part of me dislikes the Skills," she admitted, "because of Hitori's obsession with them. I know what you and Finae hope to do is different, but it makes me nervous when I think about others finding out about the Skills."

Her implications were obvious.

There would be others like Hitori.

When I had first encountered the Skills, that had been one of my fears as well. And it had, in fact, been Rin who had made me aware of the Skills' existence, back in Vaiyene. Back then, it had been a means to an end for Rin. It had been a way to spread fear to protect the lives of the people in Vaiyene and in other places, sabotaging Hitori's plans by lessening the damage of each False Shadow mission she took part in.

"It is inevitable there will be those drawn to the Skills for undesirable reasons," I said, considering my words carefully.

"But as long as we continue to keep an eye on the Skills and be mindful of others, I think we should place our trust in the people. If given the opportunity, most only would wish to do good."

Rin nodded slowly, brow creased. "I want to believe that, but being around Hitori has taught me differently. The Skills have only brought destruction."

She looked down at the bandages covering the blackened skin on her forearm. Even after getting a bond, the damage from the Skill poisoning had not reversed.

"According to the ancient Phantom, before Zenkaiko was destroyed, the Skills were the Shadows' duty," I said, speaking my thoughts out loud. "It's something the Shadows have forgotten how to do. Like how the Shadows had forgotten what the bonds were for. He seemed to imply there was something we could do to maintain a better balance with the Skills."

"What did he mean?" Rin asked.

I shook my head. "He was reluctant to tell me any specific details. I think he fears we will repeat his decision if he tells me too much and that it would be best for us to find our own way to approach the Skills. He also confirmed we will not be learning much from the books about the Skills. It is a shame Emiko wanted nothing to do with us. I will have to see if I can speak to the ancient Phantom again if we have specific questions, but for now"—I looked up at the acorn-shaped building entwined with an enormous tree—"there's something less serious I want to discuss with you. Finae will have the patience to wait a short while."

Rin's eyes narrowed suspiciously at me, and I nodded in the opposite direction of the building, leading us away from the path.

In the pit of my stomach, a fluttering of emotions surged in anticipation.

"Where are we going?" Rin asked. Her voice had a touch of amusement to it—a tone I had grown fond of hearing. Throughout our travels, her demeanor had softened. She no longer was as anxious and guarded as she used to be, and sometimes, she seemed to be able to forget the weight of the duty she carried. Seeing her begin to enjoy things and allow herself to smile warmed my heart.

I stopped under a wisteria tree, pushing aside the nerves that had begun to rise. Bees were buzzing at the edge of the trees, visiting each flower with a gentle touch. Rin's attention drifted toward them, and for a moment, her appearance shimmered in the sunlight. When her gaze shifted back to me, I could not help but smile at the glow surrounding her.

From within my robes, I pulled out a small object wrapped in paper and a longer one rolled in a mat I had made from bamboo. Holding them out for Rin, I swallowed, my throat too tight to say anything.

Rin smiled and tilted her head before she took the smaller gift.

"What's this?" she asked. She raised her eyes briefly before she pulled the strings securing the paper. Inside was a wooden charm wrapped with silk threads. The color I had chosen was a purple hue, made from the last buds of the tree towering over us. The flowers were now gone, but the sweeping cascade of the leaves swayed in a gentle breeze.

"In Vaiyene, and in a few other towns across Kiriku, charms are given to those who are important to us." Glancing over at Rin, I noticed her curiosity was piqued. She did not seem familiar with the custom.

Rin's fingers rubbed against the purple threads, and I hesitated slightly before explaining, feeling a slight heat rising in my cheeks. Other than giving a charm to Finae, from brother to sister, I had never made one for anyone. It was more significant of a gesture if one knew the custom, and I struggled to word it the right way for Rin. I wanted her to understand the gift without being too forward, and thereby rude, with my intention.

"It's customary for family to exchange charms between one another," I said quietly, "as well as for a person to give it to someone they have a developed a fondness for."

Rin's cheeks flushed slightly, and I dropped my gaze.

"What do the characters mean?" Rin asked after some time. Glancing up, I noticed her cheeks were still tinged with pink, and

I cleared my throat, trying to pretend nothing had change between us.

"The characters in the center are 'love' and 'protection,'" I said. She had become precious to me, and I found myself wishing for her protection more than anything of late. "The dye came from the last flowers of this tree, though it's a subtle hue. The color would have been stronger using the first flowers, but —"

"Thank you."

Rin's green eyes shimmered, and I found myself smiling without being able to restrain myself. Handing her the second gift, I watched as she unrolled it, her eyes widening slightly. This one had taken me quite some time to make, as I could only work on it when Rin was not around and the process was much more in-depth than the charm had been.

Rin held the thin tapered wood in her hand, gathering her long raven hair up at the back of her head. She tried to keep the charm in her hand at the same time, but after she started struggling with it, I held my hand out, holding the charm for her while she secured her hair back with the wooden ornament. It was dark wood, also from the same tree, painted with tiny wisteria flowers. Silk threads decorated with purple beads hung down from the end of the decoration.

Her hair looked elegant pinned up loosely in a knot.

I handed the charm back.

"Where does it go?" Rin asked.

"Some tie it around the sheaths of their swords; others sew it into their robes."

Rin thought for a moment before fastening it around her sword. She wore all black, though her robe had a slight grey pattern to it. The pop of purple on the charm stood out, drawing attention to it.

"May it keep you safe," I said, looking upon Rin fondly before remembering Finae was waiting for us. "I suppose we should go see what trouble Finae has gotten into."

Rin tried to restrain her smile, but instead it became even wider as she laughed.

"Yes, I suppose she will come find us soon if we don't," she said.

Finae would be Finae.

A few of the villagers nodded to us as walked through the village. They had been kind to us, providing us with food and supplies as we needed them. In return, we had done what we could for them. A few days prior, Rin and I had gone hunting in the forest, bringing back a young deer for the villagers. We had also gathered herbs in hard-to-reach places for them to use in medicines and food. Finae had brought back some wildflowers and had painted innumerable intricate paintings on the doorframes of houses. Everything in Konro seemed to reflect the great tree it was built around—even the spiral of the vines and the blossoming flowers. Finae had taken to the aesthetic immediately, adding her creativity and color to everything in town.

When we neared the building, we sidestepped the crack in the ground and walked under the stone archway built into the giant tree. Had the tree's roots not been so prominent and thick, I might have worried about the balance of the building, but the land itself seemed to take care as it cradled its precious cargo.

Inside the tree, we headed to the staircase affixed to the interior of the bark, climbing until we reached the room where we had collected all of the information on the Skills.

As we approached, the faint smell of smoke reached my nose.

Internally, I groaned. Now what had she done?

Rin and I were about to turn the corner into the room when Finae burst toward us. Coming to a halt, she shoved her hands against me, pushing both Rin and me back toward the staircase.

"Get back!" Finae shouted.

I stifled my annoyance as I tripped over a discarded book in the hallway. "Finae, we already know you are experimenting with the Skills in there."

"Move. *Now.*"

Out of the corner of my eye, I caught something shimmering. A flash ignited in the room, shining into the hallway, followed by a large *booooom*. The ground shook under us, and I steadied Finae as she tried to stay on her feet.

Finae kept her face straight. "That wasn't supposed to happen."

I clamped my mouth shut. We had all agreed to pursue using the Skills and to try to master them, but Finae's explorations were a little too enthusiastic at times.

"I think I've almost gotten the concept down," Finae said, brushing off what looked to be soot from her robes. "It seems a little unstable though."

A twitch of a smile broke my composure. "A *little* unstable?"

Finae waved off the comment. "Do you want me to teach you how it works?"

"Of course," Rin said, walking past me.

I looked after her, stifling a sigh. Rin's enthusiasm for the Skills seemed to have returned. Heading after them, I smiled wryly.

"I hope you are not interested simply because something caught fire."

Rin glanced back at me with a grin on her face.

I sighed. When either Finae or Rin got carried away, the other seemed to encourage their mischief. Still, the last few weeks had been some of the best of my life, and we had been productive in our own time. It was hard to know what to research and test about the Skills without knowing what our purpose was. But we had been working on creating a barrier in hopes we could better understand the barrier Hitori had used. It would be something we could use to defend ourselves with as well.

Taking a deep breath, I entered the room, prepared for the worst.

Stacked with books and assorted papers, the small alcove in the corner of the room seemed mostly intact, though a small puff of smoke rose into the air under Rin's foot. She had smothered whatever had caught fire, smiling at me sweetly as if nothing had happened. I tried to ignore her and the room, forcing myself to not complain at how messy the space had become since I had last straightened it out. I was about to tell Finae it was no wonder there had been a fire with all of the papers lying about when a crude drawing caught my attention. Kneeling, I picked it up. It was not a sketch, but rather some sort of a diagram of a person's body with a line drawn around it.

"Finae, what's this?"

She turned, a dagger held precariously in her mouth. Her hands were occupied with four more blades, her fingers spread apart in an awkward grip as she held them all.

I raised my hands and froze. "Tell me later."

Picking up more pieces of paper, I gathered a collection of similar-looking diagrams. Each appeared to map out the locations of the veins in a person's body.

Were these drawings Finae had deciphered from Hitori's notes?

Frowning, I placed the stack of notes on a pile of books crammed against the wall to get them out of danger.

"Kilo, can you place this dagger on the other side?" Rin asked as she handed me a silver blade. "Stick it about the same distance away as I've placed these."

Taking the dagger from her, I walked a few paces away, noting the distance between the blades in the ground. Finae and Rin had placed them in a rectangle, with one blade still held in Finae's hand. I pushed the tip of the dagger into the wooden floor just as they had with the others.

They should have been doing this outside...

"Now step back," Finae said.

Doing as she wanted, I moved out of the way, leaning against the wall with arms crossed, watching as Finae stepped into the center of the circle and knelt. Rin took cover on the other side of the room, shooting me a rather sly glance. Finae did not seem worried about the same thing happening twice. I pushed the concern away and instead concentrated on what she was doing. There was a slight disturbance in the air, like something—the Skills—was shifting.

Finae's eyes closed, and she rested her hands in her lap, one folded over the other. Silver lines sprouted from the blades, twisting and snaking to form a perimeter around the daggers.

They spiraled out, circling back around, burning a pattern into the wooden floor. Once the spirals touched the daggers, they wound their way around the blades as a white mist appeared where the burn marks were.

The air slightly shimmered.

Curious, I held out my fingers, encountering a feather-light resistance. The tips of my fingers burned at the same point I had seen the shimmer—the edge of the barrier? I inhaled a breath of singed flesh. As I pulled back my hand, a white mist rose from the floor.

"Finae, get out!"

But she could not hear me in her meditative state.

I glanced around, yanking a dirty cloth covered in paint from the floor before throwing it over Finae. Her barrier exploded, and I threw my arm in front of my face to protect myself from a burst of energy.

Coughing at the sharp, acidic air, I squinted against the smoke. Finae sputtered, throwing off the cloth as she pushed herself to the ground. Her hair was now smeared with blue paint, and she picked at the edge of the fabric, the ends of which were smoldering.

"Did it work?" she asked.

A tuft of burnt paper fell next to her.

Rin and I stomped on the other bits of burning paper around the room, taking care to assess any further danger that needed tending to. In the center of the room, the burn marks on the floor glowed.

"No," I said, "but"—Finae's gaze snapped to me—"I did experience some sort of resistance. You might be onto something."

I winced at the markings on the ground. Finae had left nothing untouched in her time in Konro. I kept my tone flat as I spoke.

"You should paint the marks to make them decorative,"

Finae glanced back over to where she had created her barrier.

"What marks?"

I pointed back to where she had been kneeling, but she raised her brows. Rin shook her head. Could they not see them? I ran my fingertips over the mark, expecting to feel an indention in the wood, but there was nothing there.

"Did either of you see a shimmer in the air?"

Both of them shook their heads.

"What is it?" Rin asked.

Before I had left the Skill world, the ancient Phantom had said something about helping me see what I should protect.

Had he done something to allow me to see the Skills?

Footsteps came from the other side of the library, and we turned to see one of the teenagers from the village. In his hand, he held a rolled up piece of paper. Standing, I brushed off the dust from my pants. He handed the letter to Rin, who untied the string securing the scroll.

"Hitori's False Shadows have attacked a town close to Leiko Gulf," Rin reported, handing me the letter so I could read it myself. "Some of General Mirai's men tried to intervene. It seems all of them were killed."

Skimming the letter, I looked for any additional details. The False Shadows had never been strong enough to defeat the general's men before. They were growing stronger, becoming bolder, and were more of a threat now than ever before.

I blew out a long breath.

We had run out of time.

I needed to put an end to the False Shadows and Hitori before things became worse. While we had learned a little more about the Skills, it was not as much as I would have liked before having to face Hitori directly. But the only other person who knew about the Skills seemed unwilling to help us. I frowned, contemplating the looming danger beyond the False Shadows. With what the ancient Phantom had told me, it might not be a bad idea to see if Hitori knew anything about the effects of the Skills upon the land. Was she aware of the consequences of using the Skills? Did she know of a way to combat them? And what was the purpose of her experiments with the Skills?

A small smile spread across my face. Rin and Finae would be thrilled at the idea of what I was planning.

"I'm going to join the False Shadows," I said.

Rin did not miss a beat in her counter. "You can't be serious."

"I am."

"There's no way Hitori is going to allow you near her. You do remember what happened the last time we encountered her? If it hadn't been for Finae, we all would have died."

"I know."

In different circumstances, I might have laughed, but Rin's distress was sincere and the mission came with a very real danger. I glanced over at Finae, who seemed unfazed by the conversation.

"Finae," Rin said, her voice exasperated, "talk some sense into your brother."

Finae began picking up the daggers she had put down to create the barrier, not pausing in her task. "I think it's a good idea."

Rin opened her mouth as if to continue protesting, but instead she groaned, placing the fingers of one hand over her face and pressing down.

She glared at me through her fingers. "What's your plan?"

"There are concerns I have relating to the Skill poisoning and how it might spread to affect the land. I might be able to barter information about the Skills with Hitori."

Rin continued to glare at me, and I tried to soften my tone as I continued.

"If Hitori and I can come to an understanding, no one needs to die. We have never tried talking to her."

Rin threw out her arms. "Because she doesn't want to talk! If Hitori was the kind of person you could have a conversation with, don't you think things would be different than they are now?"

"We did steal her notes," Finae said, standing up and folding the cloth I had used to cover her with. "I wouldn't feel like talking to someone if they stole from me."

"I'm going," I said.

Rin's shoulders drooped.

She had been around me long enough to know that once I was set on something, I would not change my mind, especially when it came to matters of others' safety.

"Hitori would immediately shut down if I were to come with you," Rin said, dropping her gaze. A deep crease ran across her forehead.

"I promise not to do anything too stupid," I said with a slight grin. It pained me to do something that worried Rin so much, but there was no other way. "I need you and Finae to continue learning about the Skills. If you can figure out how to use the barrier, we may be able to use it in future confrontations."

"Finae," I said, leaning over to catch her attention. She glanced up from jotting down some notes on a scrunched-up piece of paper. "I'll be back later this evening. I have a few things to do in town to prepare."

"Mm-hmm," she said, dipping her pen in a well of ink before drawing a rectangular shape.

Nodding toward the door, Rin followed me out.

I waited until we were outside of the library and well away from the building before speaking. "Stay close to Leiko and Magoto if you travel. I have more hesitations about this than I want to admit in front of Finae. While I believe it is the right thing to do, it does not mean I have to become isolated from those who are supporting us—nor would it be good for me to do so."

Rin nodded. That at least seemed to bring her some relief.

"I'll continue going between Konro and the trading post," she said. "I will also let General Mirai and Asdar know what your plans are and try and send you updates when I can."

"I would appreciate that."

"The spy network does not reach as far as Magoto normally, but with you being in the area, I will see if there are any people General Mirai can send. There are a few new recruits we've been training who might be up for the task."

"You seem to be enjoying working with General Mirai's spy network," I said as we began walking back toward the village.

She shrugged. "It's not much different than what I used to do in the False Shadows. It's fun in a way, being the go-between from one place to another. At least, it's better than having to pretend to kill people." Rin tried to smile. "Don't underestimate her, Kilo."

"I'll be cautious," I said, giving her whatever reassurance I could offer. "Will you watch over Finae for me?"

"You know I will. I've become quite fond of her."

Rin made a straight path toward a house where they made sweets. "We'd better stock Finae up on her favorites so she doesn't run out when you're away."

A smile returned to my face. "That sounds like a good idea."

Unlike the times I had left her back in Vaiyene, Finae seemed truly happy here. Sighing, I looked up at the sky as Rin entered the building, watching the clouds move across the sun. I would have preferred not to leave Rin and Finae at all. It would be easy to allow myself to forget about the outside world—to stay here without worry. There was a peace in Konro that soothed my heart, one that had been missing in my life for many years. Since being cast out from Vaiyene, that world, that person who I used to be seemed so distant to me now, and a small part of my heart desired for this life in Konro to remain untouched. With Rin by my side, it felt as if what I had always desired was here in Konro, with her.

And with Finae, we had created a sort of family here.

Smiling, I found my heart aching.

How I wished the burden of my people did not rest on my shoulders. Would it really be so bad for me to settle down here? After all, Phantom Lunia had cast me out, and the Shadows surely would question my return. Even after stopping the False Shadows, there would be no place for me to return to.

Something touched my hand.

"What is it?" Rin asked, stepping closer to me. The sun was shining from behind her, rimming her raven hair with a bright light. Her eyes held such concern it nearly undid me.

"Just thinking," I said, taking her hand in mine and placing my other hand around hers. "If I were free to do as I wanted…"

My brow creased, and I shook my head slightly. But I had given up that choice when I had sworn my Shadow vows. Before my own happiness, before Rin's and Finae's, came the people who depended on me back in Vaiyene. Squeezing Rin's hand, I lifted my eyes to find the same grim smile on Rin's face that was on my own. Her expression reflected it all.

"Come on," I said, suppressing the bitter emotions rising within me. "We'll go get Whitestar from the stables so Finae can spoil her. I'll leave in the morning, so at least we'll have tonight."

Together, Rin, Finae and I spent the night eating sweets, sipping on warm tea, and watching the stars before I left at sunrise.

chapter forty-five
A Chance Meeting

The sickening scent of rotting fish welcomed me to Leiko's shores. Pausing at the edge of the ocean, I waited for the call of gulls to breathe life into a town ravaged by tragedy, but none came.

Unease crept over me.

A thin layer of ice had formed on the sand, freezing a slight reddish hue in place. Pulling the edge of my mask down, I inhaled. The fishy, dirty waters hid the metallic tang of blood. I let out a slow breath, watching the mist creep over the seas. The last time I was here, fishermen had been out on the water, the voices of traders had been heard throughout the marketplace, and residents walked through town with neighbors and friends. Now, not even the sound of a scavenger's caw broke the silence. Only the lapping of the waves kept silence from permeating this place.

I dropped Whitestar's reins and clicked my tongue for her to follow as we walked along the shore. The tide came up to my ankles, spreading a thin white foam over the sand. Something dark drew my attention. When the water receded, I crouched down. A crack in the sand had developed, with black liquid—

oil?—oozing from the fracture. I curled my forefinger through the loop of my dagger and pulled it from the pouch at my thigh. Using the tip of the blade, I nudged the black liquid, and a jolt of energy shot up through my arm.

The Skills.

"What has happened here?" I whispered against the chill.

Removing the dagger, I stood as the tide came back in, noting a few rocks that seemed discolored. Using my boot, I pushed against one of the rocks; it crumbled like ash.

I drew in a sharp breath.

It had begun.

As it had in the ancient Phantom's time, the land was dying. How far had it spread? Solving this was a pressing matter, but if I did not put an end to Hitori and her False Shadows, the chaos she had created would destroy all of Kiriku. Dealing with Hitori seemed more of an immediate threat than Skill poisoning, and if I could gain her cooperation, I might be able to make progress with both.

Leading my white mare forward, I turned away from the town, heading north to the Kinsaan Forest. Whitestar's ears were pinned to her head as if she, too, knew we headed into danger. Reaching up, I stroked her muzzle to reassure her. If there was anyone I could have left her with, I would have done so.

We headed into the forest, the dark shadows engulfing us. The smell of damp bark wafted through the air. There was a hint of decay on it, like leaves still decomposing from the fall.

Someone coughed up ahead.

I paused.

It sounded guttural and wracked with phlegm.

Removing my hand from Whitestar, I slid the staff from my back and held it at my side, using the end to part the thick brush. My light canteen illuminated a small area around my horse and me, but the dimness of the forest slowed my movements. I squinted into the darkness, wishing I could manipulate the light as the ancient Phantom had.

Another guttural cough echoed.

Holding out my hand to signal Whitestar to stay, I used my staff for balance and traversed a patch of roots suspended above the ground. Pausing, I waited, hearing the sound coming from a large tree to my right. Its bark was twisted and malformed, and split open in the middle by massive tree roots. Nestled at the base was a man whose arms were wrapped around his stomach.

Metal encased one of his forearms.

The makeshift bond hid a gruesome mess of dried blood.

At my approach, he jumped, and I held up my hands out in front of me. The whites of his eyes were bloodshot, and sweat beaded his brow—signs of fever and little sleep. I heard no other movement in the forest, but I circled around the tree and peered into the distance to ensure we were alone. After confirming we were, I leaned my staff against the tree and knelt in front of the wounded man.

"Are you one of the False Shadows?"

He groaned as he tried to shrink back against the tree. His eyes appeared to focus on my face, but they did not seem aware of what they saw. At best, he would last another day in this condition.

Clicking my tongue for Whitestar to come to me, I unpacked a roll of cotton strips from one of the saddlebags and untied the bamboo canteen of water to offer it to the man.

"Drink," I said, watching his eyes widen slightly.

He reached out with a shaky hand for the canister, and I helped him hold it as he drank. His eyes were brimming with tears when he lowered the canister.

It seemed his emotional state had been shattered.

"I am no doctor, but I do have medicine for a fever." I set the canister next to me, trying to keep his attention. "If you'll allow me to, I can tend to your wound as well. It'd be best to make sure the fever isn't from an infection."

He gave a small nod.

Keeping my movements slow, I raised the man's right arm, trying to see the wound through the silver threads. The skin seemed inflamed on the edges where the arm had tried to heal, leaving behind red and puffy skin. Letting go of his arm, I withdrew a rolled-up piece of leather from inside my robes, as well as a pouch of herbs. During my time away from Vaiyene, I had not been able to find the same herbs as I was used to, but I had found some with similar properties.

"Swallow this," I said, holding the ball of herbs out for him to see. "It will dull the pain and give you a boost of energy."

He took it from me and placed it on his tongue, grimacing as he swallowed it.

I unrolled the leather next, exposing a thick, colorless paste.

The man's eyes focused on the bond on my arm.

"Don't worry," I said, keeping my tone light as I began to dab and smear the ointment onto his skin. "I'm one of the people trying to stop all the fighting. What's your name?"

"Tenmo."

"What happened here, Tenmo?" I asked, laying the bandages across his arm.

He cleared his throat before he spoke. "A group of people wearing this"—he raised his arm slightly and eyed the forest behind me—"attacked the village to the east. One of the fishermen warned us, but by the time he did…"

His voice trailed off, and I nodded my understanding.

"Do you know where the townspeople fled?"

"North, if any survived."

"And the people who put this metal casing on your arm? What did they want with you?"

"I was held in a camp not far from here. They put this metal on my arm, saying if I cooperated and helped them with this power, they would let me go." He grimaced as I pulled the bandage tight. "The first chance I had, I ran."

I tried to ignore the growing anger in my heart. So the False Shadows had turned to gathering people for the experiments here in Leiko, using the commotion of battle to hide their real intention. Offering my hand to the man, I pulled him to his feet. The clarity in his eyes had returned, and he seemed less emotionally fragile than he had before.

Somewhere in the distance, voices shouted, and their tone seemed urgent. Judging from Tenmo's calm demeanor, he had not heard them yet.

Handing Whitestar's reins to him, I asked, "Do you know where Tarahn is?"

Tenmo stared at me, then nodded.

"Ask to speak with Lord Kefnir. He will offer you protection. If there are others you find on the way, tell them the same."

I placed a hand on my mare's shoulder to keep her steady as Tenmo mounted. Already, his demeanor had changed, and there was a fire in his eyes.

Hope was a powerful thing.

"There's some food in the packs," I said, pushing Whitestar's shoulder to turn her back the way we had come, "as well as some more medicine and bandaging. The weather should hold up for another day, though a storm seems to be coming in from the gulf. I would ride as fast as you are able to in order to stay ahead of it."

"Thank you," Tenmo said, seeming a bit flustered at being rushed off. "I don't know how I can ever repay your kindness."

I bowed slightly. "Take care of yourself."

The voices became louder.

As Tenmo and Whitestar started into the forest, I picked up my staff from against the tree. There were at least two voices, maybe three. If they ended up being the False Shadows, I might be able to speak with them before engaging, and if they were those who resented their circumstances, perhaps they could be persuaded to rally to me. While I had not forgotten those who had turned on Rin back in Magoto, in order to make a change, one needed to be willing to give others a chance.

Even if that meant being betrayed.

I slid behind a tree as two people appeared from behind a large outcropping of rocks. They moved with intent, bending over and peering behind trees and around bushes. Were they looking for Tenmo? They spoke too softly for me to hear their words, but their tone and hushed whispers sounded anxious.

Each had a single sword belted to his hip. I could see no other signs of weapons, but they could have others concealed—as I did.

"Haru, over there!" the taller man said, pointing past me and in the direction Tenmo had gone. I leaned over and stifled a groan. From my position, I could still see the faint outline of horse and rider.

The man named Haru started after them.

Leaping from my hiding place, I swung my staff in an arc, blocking Haru from going after the man I had saved. Instinctively, he blocked my attack with the edge of his sword, stepping into a defensive stance. The tall man moved to the side, trying to split my focus and get behind me. Before he could, I kicked my staff up from the ground, jabbing the tall man in the stomach. He recoiled, his sword dipping to the side. With haste, I twisted the staff in my hand and cracked it against the man's wrist. He dropped his sword, and I turned to face Haru.

He had yet to make another move.

Haru eyed the staff in my hand. "What's your name?"

There was little point in hiding who I was.

"Kilo."

Haru sheathed his blade.

But the tall man reached for his sword on the ground.

"Leave it, Seiji," Haru said, glancing over at his companion with a wry smile. "This is the Phantom Hitori is obsessed with."

Seiji froze at the words, his gaze turning to me.

"What do you want, Phantom?" Haru asked, seeming amused. "If you came here to kill Hitori, she has not yet returned."

"I have no intention of killing Hitori."

Haru's eyebrows rose. "Oh? So it's true then? You value even the life of your enemy? I had thought the rumors about you were a lie."

"If you are aware of my character, stay your hand," I said, shifting my attention to Seiji, who seemed to shrink under my gaze. "I did not come here to kill any of you, but to learn what it is that Hitori plans to do with the Skills. I intend to ask her to allow me to join her False Shadows."

"A bold plan," Haru said.

I looked back toward the town. "What happened in Leiko?"

Seiji's eyes narrowed. "Don't tell him."

"Stop worrying so much, Seiji," Haru said, his smile fading as he became serious. "What happens to the Phantom will be decided by Hitori. Do you really think you could defeat him in a battle if Hitori could not?"

Haru started walking away and motioned for me to follow him. "Let me show you where the encampment is."

"Haru!" Seiji's face had all but drained of color.

I had not expected to be invited in without resistance, but Haru seemed to be a man unwilling to fight for the sake of fighting.

I respected that.

With a slight nod, I followed after him, leaving Seiji sputtering behind us.

"You're quite bold yourself," I commented, keeping my distance as I trailed after Haru. "Allowing me inside the camp seems like a risk."

"Unlike most of the False Shadows," Haru said with a shrug, "I joined by choice. The way I see it, we both wish to prevent bloodshed. Therefore, you and I are not enemies. Besides, my father is the commander of the guards in Magoto. He speaks rather fondly of the Phantom who does not kill."

"I see."

"As for what happened here, Hitori and Saitou went to negotiate trade deals with the neighboring town, but the town had hired mercenaries in anticipation. From what I heard, Hitori and her group wiped out most of them. When the people of Leiko heard what happened, they fled. The ones who stayed behind were the fishermen, though a bad storm took out the last of them a week ago. We finished dumping the bodies in the ocean yesterday."

I cringed.

Yet again, Leiko had been struck with tragedy.

"And the man you were tracking?" I asked.

"He was one of Hitori's experiments. She'll not be happy we lost one of them, but after escorting the Phantom she loathes into her camp, I don't think she'll care all that much."

He glanced over at me. It was a calculating look, one that could have said many things. I tried not to read too much into it, sticking with my initial gut reaction that he and I were not direct enemies and that there was hope for me to make allies in the False Shadows.

As we continued through the forest, we came upon a thin trail worn into the forest floor. Like most of the Kinsaan Forest, the ground was overgrown and crowded. The trees slanted diagonally, twisting and gnarling in an attempt to find light amidst the thick canopy. Even with my trained eyes, it took some time to notice the many structures of wood built in the forest, as they were covered in moss, with trees surrounding them. Broken branches and roots lifted the earth, making the ground unstable for walking. We passed by the buildings, toward an area that seemed somewhat cleared of trees, with stumps remaining in the ground.

Haru stopped in the middle of the clearing.

Seiji lagged behind, keeping his distance. His distrust made me uneasy. It seemed Seiji respected Haru's opinion, but it was difficult to predict how he would react moving forward.

"There's not much to show you," Haru said, gesturing to the building we had passed. "That's one of the buildings where we sleep at night. It's nothing much, but it's better than sleeping with a root in your back."

Haru glanced over at Seiji, then into the forest. There was a slight tremble to Seiji's hands, and judging by the way both of them froze, something was about to happen.

"Hitori is coming," Seiji said, his gaze fixated into the forest behind us.

I took a deep breath, steeling my resolve. There was no turning back from this moment. I had come here for a purpose; all that was left was to see what happened.

Two people on horseback rode into the camp.

The first person I recognized as Hitori. Her blonde hair was pinned against her head in an elegant topknot, and the silver circlet around her head rested just above the scar I had given her during our last encounter. But the man beside her I did not recognize. He was tall, with a long face and narrowed auburn eyes. After dismounting, he held the reins of Hitori's horse while she descended, her long flowing robes gliding off the back of the painted mare.

"That's Saitou, Hitori's bodyguard," Haru said quietly at my side. "He was picked up by the previous lord and has been at Hitori's side since she was young."

I eyed Saitou's neutral stance while he waited for Hitori.

Was he protecting Hitori out of duty or loyalty?

It took a moment for Hitori to realize I was there, but when she did her expression immediately changed from exhaustion to anger. She clenched her fists as she came toward me, her eyes flashing with rage. Pressure in the air weighed down on me from all sides. She was using the Skills, either consciously or subconsciously, to try and strangle my breath.

I stood my ground.

If I needed them, the Skills and my staff were within my reach.

"What are you doing here?" Hitori demanded. Her voice was low, deadly.

Saitou wrapped his fingers around the hilt of his sword.

Giving a short bow, I addressed her. "I've come to ask permission to join your False Shadows and to learn about the Skills."

Hitori's lips curled into a sneer. "You must think I'm stupid coming here with such a flimsy lie."

"It is a serious request," I said, meeting her gaze.

She laughed. "You know, you remind me of someone. Another Phantom if I recall." Hitori circled around me, tapping her lips with her forefinger. "What was his name again? Kural? And how did that end...?" Glancing over at me, she increased the pressure at my throat, then stopped circling as she stood close to me. She was a head shorter than I was. Her green eyes blazed up at me. "I suggest you leave now, while you still have your life."

"I would reconsider my offer," I said evenly.

Hitori snorted. "And why's that?"

"You need an ally, Hitori. Who else has offered to stand by you? Magoto's long-lasting alliances have failed, and your town is in need of assistance."

"You know nothing!" Hitori said through clenched teeth. The pressure against my throat and mind intensified.

Pushing back against the Skills delicately so to be able to breathe easier, I allowed my sense of calm to permeate them. There was a slight lapse in Hitori's composure—and in the Skills.

"You have nothing to lose but your ego," I said, testing her. "You're not the only one who knows how to use the Skills, Lord Hitori."

She clamped her mouth closed.

"Will you allow me to join?" I pressed.

Silence.

I readied myself for a confrontation, but to my surprise Hitori relented.

"Do whatever you want," she said. A deep shadow had been cast over her face as she surveyed the area. During our conversation, her False Shadows had begun to gather. "But if you interfere with what I need to do, I will kill you."

"I would expect nothing less."

"Haru," Hitori said, "take his staff."

I offered no resistance, handing over the staff at my back. Asking me to do so seemed like a pointless play of power, but if it made Hitori feel better, I would surrender it.

"Oh, and Seiji," Hitori said, a thin smile spreading across her face, "since you've allowed the Phantom into my camp, it seems only fitting you and Haru be held personally responsible for his actions." She turned and waved. "I expect a full report later today about what you show the Phantom and your conversations with him."

Her bodyguard dutifully fell in place as Hitori turned her back on me.

My blood boiled as she walked away. She intended to use Seiji's and Haru's lives to keep me in my place. It was not my intention to put the False Shadows in a position of fear because of me. Hitori had controlled Ikaru and Rin the same way.

I would not be as easily controlled.

"Seiji," I said, waiting for him to look at me. His skin was so devoid of color, it seemed as if he were already at death's door. "I do not need either of you endangering yourselves on my account. Do whatever is necessary to not upset Hitori. Tell her everything truthfully."

Seiji stared blankly ahead.

"Seiji?" I could not tell if he had heard me.

"Don't worry about us," Haru said, keeping his voice quiet. "By now, we're all used to Hitori's threats. She acts as she pleases, without reason, threatening all those around her."

Somehow, Haru's words did not make me feel any better.

If anything, it made the situation seem grimmer.

Not letting it distract me from what needed to be done, I looked up at the canopy, trying to judge how much light was left before nightfall. I needed to send a letter to General Mirai and let him know what I had found out. In the event something happened to me, hopefully the location of the camp and what little I knew about it would be of help.

"There's something I need to do," I said, turning and hesitating. "It would be best if you did not follow me."

Haru and Seiji exchanged glances, and before they decided anything, I hurried back the way we had come, using the faint trail to navigate my way outside the forest. When I reached the edge of the trees, I was disappointed they had followed me.

It would have been better for them to have not seen.

After withdrawing a brush and paper from inside my robes, I breathed on my fingers to warm them and began writing letters to General Mirai and Asdar. Inside each letter was the location of Hitori's camp and a description of my plans for joining the False Shadows. I also wrote a letter to Rin, asking her to look for places where the Skills pooled, or where the land appeared to be dying. When the letters were complete, I rolled them up and secured them each with a length of thin cord.

I set out to find the tallest tree in the area, tying the leather straps of my light canteen together before affixing the letters in the pocket of it. Standing under the large oak tree, I threw the canteen high into the canopy

It caught on one of the higher branches.

When nightfall came, the light would be visible to the spy network.

"He's going to get us killed," Seiji said, his voice coming from somewhere behind me.

I let my eyes linger on the surrounding trees before returning to Haru and Seiji.

"You are more than welcome to let Hitori know I have sent letters," I said to calm Seiji's nerves. "She would not be surprised. Besides"—I caught sight of a silhouette moving in the distance—"you were the ones who decided to follow me."

Seiji glared at me, but a wave of amusement came from Haru.

Before either of them noticed the silhouette getting closer, I entered the forest, leading them back toward camp. The mood became unbearable as we walked. I tried to brush it off, but out of the corner of my eye I noticed that Seiji's gaze was fixed on me, his eyes like daggers on my back. Finally, I stopped walking to address it.

"Is there something on your mind, Seiji?"

"I don't trust you," he said, his voice low and agitated.

"You are already aware of my intentions. Relax."

Shadow training had taught me how to control my anxiety and find peace in the moment. To focus on what could be done instead of fixating on the infinite possibilities of how things could go wrong. It had also taught me how to work as a member of a team and the importance of setting differences aside before they had time to fester.

"Seiji," I said, closing the distance between us. When he did not acknowledge me, I stepped into his line of sight, commanding his attention. "I am sorry you were forced into this. You are free to talk to Hitori about whatever you deem fit. All I ask is that you—"

Seiji snapped suddenly.

"Are you really in a position to ask anything more of me?"

Puffing up his chest, he sidestepped me to storm away, but I threw out my arm to stop him from leaving. We needed to settle things before his distrust in me became a poison.

That was, after all, what Hitori wanted.

"What is it that Hitori controls you with?" I asked, keeping my tone indifferent. "I can help you."

"There's nothing you can do," he said, his jaw tight. But his voice grew quiet as if he'd realized his outburst might have drawn others from the main camp. He relented as I continued to maintain eye contact. "Someone I respected became caught up with Hitori and her plans. In the end, his talents were taken advantage of. When he found himself powerless to stop what she was doing, he"—Seiji looked away—"took his own life."

I lowered my arm, feeling a pit in the bottom of my stomach.

Seiji's expression became vacant. "There is nowhere else for me to go. Do whatever it is you wish to. I have already resigned myself to this fate."

Without another word, he passed me, heading back toward camp.

Seiji was a tall man, but until now I had not noticed the bend of his spine and the way his feet seemed to drag behind him.

"You have to understand," Haru said, his voice pained, "Magoto did not always used to be how it is now. It was once a great town, and many of us aspired to greater things. Now our only escape from death is to join Hitori's False Shadows."

With a frown, I turned my head sharply. I had not realized Magoto had been so stricken with poverty and grief that their people would tolerate Hitori's cruelty in such a way. To place oneself in such a position of pain for the slightest hope that it would be better...

"Is it that bad?" I asked.

Haru nodded. "It is why we placed our hope with Rin when she left to find help. Hitori once listened to Rin until her anger and bitterness got the better of her. Now we place our remaining hope in you. For Seiji's and our people's sake, I hope you are as capable a Phantom as my father and the rumors make you out to be."

With a slight bow, Haru left me on the edge of camp.

I paused for a moment, lifting my head to the overgrown canopy where the light did not shine. There were many things I had accomplished in my life, but doubt crept into my heart. The circumstances here were grave.

Would I actually be able to help the False Shadows?

———

Sleep did not come to me that night.

My thoughts churned in an endless cycle over what Haru and Seiji had said. While I knew things in Magoto were bad, the extent of the pain the False Shadows endured went far beyond what I had initially suspected. If they had reached the point where they had lost hope, it would not even matter if Hitori was no longer around. Without the desire to endure and better one's circumstances, nothing would ever change. It did not matter who was in control if the people had already given up.

I turned over, pushing the blankets off and rolling the bamboo mat up before returning both to the supply building. Despite Haru's invitation to sleep inside one of the houses, I stayed by the campfire, not wanting to cause Seiji or the others any further anxiety by remaining near them.

Wandering among the campsite, I walked between the trees and around the perimeter of the camp, pausing for a moment near the building Hitori slept in.

A figure stood outside in the darkness.

Saitou raised his head at my approach and watched me with a curious eye.

I bowed slightly to him, feeling no hostility in his gaze.

Although the sun had not fully risen, it was light enough for me to make out the shapes and details of the tress and rocks in the area. Were I back in Vaiyene, the mountains would have been my companions, but today, the perverted atmosphere of the

Kinsaan Forest took their place. The twists and gnarls of the trees—silhouetted against the lightning sky—created distinctive shapes.

The darkness, somehow, almost seemed to make the forest more welcoming.

Keeping my eyes on the path before me, I followed the sound of rushing water. A creek was nearby, a river that provided clean water to the camp. While I was uncertain if any herbs or flowers would be there, it wasn't uncommon to find them growing with other plants next to water. Some tea or medicine might be a small comfort I could offer the False Shadows.

If anything, it would help warm them.

After finding the river, I walked beside it for a time surveying the plants. Dark shadows below the water's surface darted to and fro, and a slight smile spread across my face. Using the long grasses next to the riverbed, I wove together a makeshift net, draping it in the water and securing it in place with rocks. Once that was finished, I moved upstream, finding a mint plant and some small white flowers. Both were good for tea. Picking the stems and a handful of flowers, I secured them in a pouch at my side before returning to the net and pulling up a modest catch of fish. With a lighter heart, I headed back to camp, starting a fire and sorting through the available cookware in the storage building. By the time I was ready to start cooking, the False Shadows had begun to stir. A few wandered between the buildings, their heads swiveling to see what I was doing. Filleting the fish, I started frying it, adding a few of the mint leaves to the pan, along with a handful of salt I had found in storage.

The smell began wafting into the air, and out from the gathering crowd, Seiji appeared. He glared at me for a moment before Haru came up behind him, placing his hand on Seiji's back to push him forward.

I plated one of the fish and held it out toward Seiji.

Stopping, he eyed me warily.

"Please, help yourself," I said, raising my eyes to meet him. He seemed nervous, and when he continued to hesitate, I gave him a sly smile. "I didn't poison it."

Seiji's lips twitched into a smile then, and he accepted the plate.

"Thank you."

Haru knelt next to the fire, taking the chopsticks from my hands and nodding toward the kettle of boiling water.

"Are all Phantoms like you?" he asked.

He plated a fish and handed it to one of the nearby False Shadows who was brave enough to come close. She was a young woman who seemed timid and frail. I kept my eyes down, allowing her to interact with Haru instead; the people seemed to trust him. After pouring the tea into cups, I set them beside me for the False Shadows to take as they pleased.

"Is it strange to care for the people around you?" I asked, addressing Haru's earlier comment.

"Yes," Seiji answered as he balanced his plate in one hand before lowering himself into a seated position opposite me. "Most people around here don't want trouble, so they keep to themselves." He took a bite of fish and grimaced. "It's dry."

I laughed. "I admit fish has never been a specialty of mine."

"It might as well be poison," Haru said with a grin. "Seiji normally does the cooking. Maybe he can teach you something during your time here."

"If you are willing," I said, inclining my head toward Seiji.

Seiji took another bite of fish and mumbled something as two other False Shadows came over and sat beside us.

"This is Daichi and Riku," Haru said, nodding to the twins. "A lot of people seem to have trouble telling them apart, but once you get to know them, it's not that hard."

Both had black hair and green eyes with freckles covering their faces. Their skin was uncommonly dark, and while they did look similar, already I could tell the two apart by the way they carried themselves.

Daichi seemed to be more confident and assertive.

Riku seemed more withdrawn and quieter.

As I poured them some tea, Haru handed them a plate of fish.

I nodded slightly at the twins. "It is nice to meet you."

"Likewise," they said in unison.

When the line of people disappeared, I focused on Seiji and Haru. "Thank you for everything you've done. It is encouraging to find people of like mind."

Haru nodded and handed me a plate, taking one for himself. Seiji said nothing, finishing his food. The twins eyed me curiously as I took a bite. They had to have been around the same age as Shenrae and Syrane. Maybe nineteen or twenty?

"Where are you from?" Daichi asked.

"Vaiyene," I said, an image of the snow-capped peaks coming to mind. "It is a small village in the Miyota Mountains east of here."

Riku glanced up from his food.

"What do you do there?" Daichi asked.

I raised my eyebrows, wondering how to explain what it was to be a Shadow to someone who had never heard about them. Did they even know their group had been made to impersonate mine?

"I look after the people of my village," I said, keeping it simple. "Lately, I've been working outside of my hometown to extend that protection to others across Kiriku."

Riku inhaled slightly. "How many places have you been?"

Though his voice was quiet, there was something in his timid nature that spoke of great curiosity.

I paused to think. "Quite a few. Actually..." I set aside my plate and pulled out my journal from the pocket within my robe. While it did not have as many detailed notes as the earlier editions I had penned, it still contained sketches and notes on the places I had been. Flipping through the pages, I stopped on a drawing of the Kinshi Post. The crooked building, which was somewhat of an oddity, was always something people were interested in seeing.

I held it out toward Riku.

His eyes grew, and he took it, flipping through the pages. Daichi leaned over, appearing interested as well.

"There are many places over the years I have been able to visit," I said, leaning on one elbow and propping up my head with my hand. "Although most do not have the same beauty or grace of my homeland."

Still eyeing the pages his brother flipped through, Daichi sat up straighter and pointed. "Look, Riku! It's the Kinsaan Forest." They leaned in closer, their heads bumping as they read the notes I had left about the terrain and the possible causes for the twisted tree.

Smiling, I looked around for something to continue the conversation. Something that would bring the people together. There seemed to be an interest in who I was now, and if I could take advantage to show I meant no harm, it would be good opportunity to get to know the False Shadows better.

Near the edge of the camp, I spotted a fallen branch with a distinct flat edge to it. Standing, I picked it up, using a nearby axe to split it in two, cutting it into a rectangular shape and then formed a long handle. On my way back to the group, I picked up a rounded pinecone.

Handing one of the paddles to Daichi, I stepped back while I held out my own paddle to the side.

The False Shadows in the area stared at me.

I coughed, trying to contain my amusement at their confused expressions.

"It's a game we have in Vaiyene," I said.

To demonstrate, I threw the pinecone into the air, batting it with the paddle to keep it in the air. Daichi reached out with his own paddle when my aim went awry, saving the pinecone from hitting the ground. He rose from where he was seated, eager to play. Walking over to Riku, I handed the paddle to him and Daichi hit the pinecone toward his brother.

Sitting around the campfire, Haru and Seiji both watched the twins with slight smiles on their faces, and soon, more people began to gather in the audience. I headed into the forest and returned with more branches. They were not as flat as the branch I had found before, but that only made the game more challenging.

I held out a branch to Seiji next, a pinecone in my hand.

To my surprise, he took it.

Haru clapped his hands together and cheered, inciting a few of the other False Shadows to gather and applaud. Passing off the pinecone to Seiji, I allowed him the first serve. He threw the pinecone up, hitting the branch with a powerful stroke.

It was also a good way to work out tensions between people.

Haru returned with more branches, passing them out to the others. Before long, most of the False Shadows were diving to save pinecones, and those who were not seemed to at least be enjoying the spectacle.

Standing in the crowd, the young, timid woman from before seemed nervous to join. I sensed she only needed a small bit of encouragement to boost her confidence.

Waving her over, I handed her my stick before getting Riku's attention.

"He'll be gentle," I said, giving him a pointed look. The girl laughed sheepishly, and Riku threw the pinecone toward her.

Stepping back to watch, I smiled.

Sometimes hope began with the smallest of gestures.

chapter forty-six
Aventon

The sound of shouting startled me from my meditation. Swords clanged and armor rustled as the camp frantically began preparations. I left the tree I had been resting under, glancing around for the cause. One of the False Shadows rushed past, and I held out my hand to stop her.

"What's going on?"

She seemed anxious as she tried to fasten her sword into her belt. "Saitou came to wake us up. We are heading out to a village south of here."

After dusk?

I frowned. It seemed unexpected—unnecessary even—to leave at such an odd time. In less than an hour, the sun would be fully set. It was not a time to travel unless there was a dire reason to.

"What town?" I pressed her, but she shook her head.

I set off to find Haru or Seiji in hopes they would know more. Instinctively, I reached back to where my staff had been—only to find empty air; I had forgotten Hitori had taken it. While I had other means of attacking, it was a loss I would not quickly get over.

From out of the forest, leading two horses, came Saitou wearing a set of full leather armor. Next to him was Hitori. Most of the False Shadows already had gathered their gear and were mounting.

"Hitori!" I called, watching a pair of False Shadows who remained immobile by one of the wooden buildings. Some were being left behind. "What is happening?"

"We're heading south to pay one of our allies a visit." She seemed annoyed by my question.

"What town?" I asked.

"Aventon."

"Aventon does not produce its own food. The land is infertile."

"I'm aware."

"Then why?"

"As I'm sure Haru has already confirmed for you, none of our allies will uphold the agreements they have sworn to Magoto. We go to take what has been promised so that other towns do not think to do the same."

Hitori placed her hands on the horse next to her, swinging her leg over the horse's girth. I reached out my hand to take the reins.

"Let me mediate for you. I can talk with the lord there."

"I don't need your help."

"Would you rather people die, or would you rather get what you want?"

Hitori's back stiffened. "Do not tell me how I should and should not lead, Phantom!" She yanked the reins from me and tried to usher her horse forward. Reaching up to the horse's bridle, I placed my other hand on its muzzle to calm it.

"What would you have me do?" Hitori asked, her voice rising. "Allow them to disregard their oaths and turn their back on an ally they swore to protect? If they do not give us what they promised, I will take it by force. Then maybe they will reconsider their honor."

Hitori dismounted and stood before me. Her head came up to my jaw, but I did not feel as if I looked down on her. For the first time since I had come here, her warrior spirit stirred. I understood the battle she wrestled with: the duty that bound her. She had been pushed into providing for her town, with no love from her people, and she was failing them.

But her desperation blinded her.

"While intimidation may get you what you want," I said with an even tone, "it will not last. Allow me to mediate on your behalf with your allies."

Hitori's lips spread into a thin smile. "If you think you can, then by all means use your sweet words and charm. You have until we arrive to convince them to abandon their town." She glanced around at the False Shadows who had gathered. "We will give Phantom Kilo a one-hour head start, and then we proceed as planned."

Even if I had a fast horse, it would not be enough time.

Turning away, I sought out Seiji and Haru. Maybe they would have some advice or some way to help me. Seiji stood in the crowd, his arms crossed. As I approached, he uncrossed his arms and nodded his head into the forest. He was close enough to have heard the conversation between Hitori and me.

"Haru is readying the rest of the horses," Seiji said, keeping his voice quiet as he led me down a different trail than the others we had taken previously. "There's one stallion who may be suited to arrive in good time."

Haru turned as we approached the stable. All of the horses had been saddled already and were laden with small packs.

"Give the young stallion to Kilo," Seiji said. "He's riding to Aventon before Hitori."

Haru inhaled sharply before he set down the saddle pack in his hand. Coming back from the inside of the stable, he held a young stallion with a tight grip. The horse pawed the ground, its ears pinned back to its head as it snorted wildly.

Reaching out my arms for his bridle, I chuckled and took the reins from Haru, unafraid of his temper. This stallion reminded me of another spirited horse I knew.

"We have not yet fully broken him," Haru admitted, "but he has spirit."

Seiji moved forward with a saddle, but the horse bayed his anger.

"It's fine," I said. "I don't need it."

Backing up, Seiji kicked open the pen's gate, standing as a group of horses raced out into the forest. Haru made an attempt to grab for the reins of one of the horses, then sighed as understanding came over him.

It would take some take to track them down.

I inclined my head slightly to Seiji. It was a small gesture on his part, but it encouraged me to know he was willing to trust me, even a little.

Returning my attention to the horse, I placed both my hands on the sides of its muzzle, allowing the reins to hang unrestrained. He snorted at me, and his brown eyes seemed keen on what was to come.

"Quite the same, aren't you?" I said, feeling him relax under my touch. "What do you say, Blackstorm? Can we outrun the wind?"

The metal hills of Aventon sparkled as the first morning rays illuminated them. Blackstorm's enthusiasm had not wavered throughout the night, and he panted heavily. Walking beside him, I laid a grateful hand on his neck before heading into town. He plodded after me, free of his reins and bridle, seemingly pleased with himself.

Red flames mirrored the rising sun, casting long, deep shadows as we approached the blacksmith's house. The sun had not yet fully risen, but already Orin stood over an enormous furnace. He drew his hammer back and smashed it down onto an iron sword, folding the metal into itself. Sweat beaded his brow, and Orin wiped his forehead with the back of his arm.

It was then he noticed me.

"Kilo! What a pleasant surprise to see you again." He looked behind me. "Your sister is not with you?"

I shook my head, feeling a weight growing in my chest. "Orin, I need to speak with the lord here. It's urgent."

Orin's usual good humor disappeared, and he set down the hot iron on the anvil. "Follow me then. I will take you to see Lady Hiroshi."

"Thank you," I said, pausing in the doorway as a young boy appeared from around the corner. His hair was tousled and unkempt, and his eyes were unfocused from having awoken before he should have. The boy picked up the fan next to the billows.

"Leave it for now," Orin said, motioning him away.

As we left the house, the warmth from the stove faded. It was more than a physical warmth that left me as Orin's company and his shop remind me of happier times—when the villagers had taken care of Finae and me, allowing us to stay with them. I wanted nothing more than to sit near the stove and listen to Orin talk about the weapons he had forged in the past. About the warriors he had given them to and what feats they had accomplished. Instead, it had come down to this: if the people of the village did not adhere to the agreement the old lord of Magoto and the village had, Hitori would kill them.

Hardly the reunion I had hoped for.

As we passed by the statue in the center of town, the jewels set into the figure winked at me. I needed to protect this town. And the people here. Orin's pace was quick but slower than my own. Because of my long legs, I had to purposely slow my gait. Glancing back at the horizon, I tried to make out any signs of Hitori's False Shadows.

We still had time.

Orin paused in front of a weathered house before he turned his body sideways and pressed himself between two buildings— one more intricate and larger than the other. Somehow, he managed to maneuver himself through the thin alleyway despite his sizable belly. "You wanted the quickest way to the lady, didn't you? If we go through the front way, we'll be delayed by pleasantries."

I ducked down and slid into the alleyway.

He was perceptive, as always.

When we reached the other side, Orin raised his arm out to the side and pointed. A lady dressed in all black clothing stood in the middle of a garden. Her robes were short, her feet clad in open-toed shoes. Soot was smudged across her hair.

Finae would have liked her.

"This is Lady Hiroshi. When her husband died in one of the mine collapses, she took over managing the affairs here." Orin seemed comfortable around the leader of the town. His casual demeanor appeared to reflect the lady's own preference. "This is Phantom Kilo from Vaiyene."

I bowed to her. "Forgive my bluntness, but with your permission, I would like to skip further introductions. I have an urgent matter to discuss with you."

Lady Hiroshi nodded and waved for me to continue.

"What is your agreement with Magoto?" It was rude of me to ask this question, having not spoken to her before, but she did not seem surprised at the inquiry.

"My husband's father made an agreement that Aventon would supply arms and provide men for war if the time ever came." She paused, turning her full attention to me. "Hitori has already contacted me, and I have denied her request. If you are with her in this matter, you are our enemy, Phantom. We will not offer our assistance to a ruler who feels entitled to something she does not yet deserve."

Their agreement was for weapons? And men?

I had hoped it would have been for something more tangible, something I could have actually negotiated for. Hitori had sent me ahead on a futile mission, knowing full well the people would not meet her demands and that I could not press them for it. On the outside, Hitori seemed conflicted, unsure and angry with my questions. But on the inside, she remained calculating and full of distrust. She had allowed me to believe her desire was for resources, items needed for her people's immediate survival.

Despite her intentions though, Hitori *had* given me time to warn the villagers.

We needed to make the most of it.

"I am not with Hitori," I said, trying to formulate a reply that would keep me a neutral party, a mediator, as the Shadows had always been. "What's important is to save the lives of your people and to endure the hardship that will follow."

Lady Hiroshi's stance remained rigid. "This is a ravine blessed with rich minerals and held for generations. We will not surrender it to Hitori."

I grimaced.

They would not win.

From spending time with Orin and the villagers before the winter, I already knew the population was low. Most of the people here were aging miners who knew nothing about combat. And given Hitori's acquisition of mercenaries who did know how to fight, these villagers would stand little chance. Though I had not seen them yet, I expected Hitori to have sent a message to her mercenaries to meet her here.

Orin cleared his throat next to me. "It's okay, lad. We would rather die than hand over the town to Hitori."

Their words humbled me. To face death without fear. The people of Vaiyene would have given the same answer in the same situation.

"I will stand with you until it is over," I said.

Lady Hiroshi headed back toward the house and waved over one of the attendants, who seemed surprised to see us but asked no questions. "Wake the people. Prepare for battle. Tell them to gather in the center square if they can fight. Those who can't fight, tell them to flee north."

Lady Hiroshi's attendants swarmed around her, bringing pieces of leather armor to fasten to her body. A few others ran from the house to wake the people, and an additional set of armor was brought for me.

"You do not need to—"

Lady Hiroshi's eyes fell on me.

"Thank you," I said, amending my refusal of her offer.

Orin helped fasten the pieces of leather around my chest and shoulders.

"Do you have a plan of action?" I asked Lady Hiroshi, watching as armor was brought for Orin as well. Her lips were pressed thin as the attendants slipped the leather chest piece in place and began pulling at the ties on the sides.

"We are simple people," she said. "None have formal training with a sword but me. If you have a plan you can offer—"

The boy who had been in Orin's forge burst into the house, his eyes as wild as his tousled hair. "Father! There are men mounted on horses not far away."

"Eiji," Orin said, "go and bring me the sword I finished the other day and give it to Phantom Kilo." The boy glanced back and forth between us before scampering away.

I returned my attention to Lady Hiroshi. "Barricade all the streets except for the main one and lay down oil around the town. If we can funnel Hitori's forces into a manageable number, we may be able to slow down the attack."

While the Shadows desired peace, we studied warfare during our training, and we were taught to be prepared for anything. To be ready to take a stand and fight when necessary was one of the core aspects of being a warrior.

Eiji returned, his breathing heavy as he panted. He held out his father's newly forged sword to me, and I slid it into the sash tied around my waist. My displeasure at once again having to use a sword rose within me, but I pushed it aside, focusing on the present. With deft hands, I untied my light canteen and handed it to Eiji.

"Hang this in the highest place you can find."

The flames from battle would be enough to alert General Mirai of trouble, but if his spy network was able to warn him before the fight started, it could be the difference between life and death for many.

"I will try and convince Hitori to stop, but I am uncertain if I will be able to," I said, my heart already heavy. I had little expectation of being able to dissuade Hitori from attacking the town. Already, she had come all this way with that very intention.

"Whatever will happen, will happen," Orin said at my side.

A Shadow does what he is capable of; no more can be asked of him.

I moved toward the door with my own resolve.

"Finish the preparations," I said. "I will speak to Hitori one final time."

From outside Lady's Hiroshi's house, smoke rose. An open barrel of oil burned, waiting in preparation for the attack. I picked up one of the torches beside the barrel and held it over the open flame.

On the horizon, the sun had fully risen.

The torch in my hand became the focal point of all of the villagers in the area.

Blackstorm shied away from the torch in my hand, but I cooed gently to him, reaching out a hand, and his trust in me overcame his fear. Throwing my leg over his girth, I sat tall upon him. The townspeople looked up as the stallion galloped through the streets. They had begun dragging metal sheeting and barrels to create barricades.

Hitori rode at the front of her company. As I suspected, the mercenaries she had hired were with her. Saitou's eyes flicked to me, then to the town, but he, along with the other False Shadows, seemed resolute in their endeavor. Haru and Seiji refused to meet my eye. The mercenaries, on the other hand, seemed eager.

Blackstorm came to a stop before the group.

"Did they surrender the town to me?" Hitori asked, one side of her mouth twitching up into a smile.

It sickened me; she still thought people's lives were a game. I bit back my anger, replying evenly, "The people have refused to give you weapons and men to provoke war. I ask you to reconsider your actions, lest more of Kiriku turn against you."

Hitori's smile widened. "I'm not afraid of an uprising. Gaiden! Take the town!"

One day, I hoped she understood the depth of her actions.

Briefly, I caught sight of a man with grizzled scars across his skin. He responded to Hitori's command with a sneer. Clicking my heels into Blackstorm's sides, I threw the torch down to the ground as we neared the town, racing ahead of the mercenaries and their horses. Flames burst forth upon impact, circling behind us and forcing Hitori's army into a smaller force.

Eiji had left a small opening in the oil barrier on this side, while someone had lit the oil on the other side of town. Flames were now rising around the town, cutting off all entrances but Eiji's. Blackstorm's hooves clattered, shaking the metal houses and barricades as we passed. Not far behind were the mercenaries. In the center of town, the people were gathered with pickaxes and other make-shift weapons. Lady Hiroshi drew her sword. Orin and his son each held an extraordinary sword—a pity they would now be used for battle.

Pulling up on Blackstorm's reins, I dismounted, leading him to the edge of town. The flames had not yet made it to this side. I raised my hand to pat his muzzle.

"Battle is no place for you," I said.

His eyes focused on me, and I yelled, thrusting my arm out, "Go!"

The stallion ran.

I hoped that somewhere across the plains of ReRiel, others were waiting for his return. His spirit seemed to have great purpose, and I thanked him silently for having helped me in my time of need.

Steeling my nerves, I went to Lady Hiroshi's side. "There are those who follow Hitori who do not wish for this to happen, but they will do it because it is what their leader demands. It is honorable to fight for one's homeland, to dedicate one's life to protect it, but without the survival of its people, there is no meaning left in saving it."

I glanced over at her, seeing her nod with understanding.

"We will fight until the town is taken and no longer," she said.

It was a fight to keep one's honor.

Some might have insisted the people needed to die for their homeland to keep their honor, but the Shadows saw merit in relenting, bending with the change and flow of the world. Life was a sacred thing, and as long as one was alive, one could find meaning in a new way of life.

Still, this battle was pointless. The amount of ore and weapons in Aventon was inconsequential. Certainly not worth waging a war over. The very men she wanted to claim for her army would be killed by her hand. This was nothing more than a petty way to bolster Hitori's ego. The people of Aventon saw Hitori for what she was: a scared ruler trying to force others to respect her. The voice of justice was becoming louder than the people's fear, and it would not be much longer before all of Kiriku joined together to eliminate Hitori.

Orin came to my side and handed me a pickaxe with a long handle. "This might work better for you."

I nodded and smiled gratefully. "I will aim to knock the riders from their horses, try to disable them by any means necessary."

"We'll get it done."

The first riders charged down the main street, and I stepped away from the others, placing myself before Orin, Eiji, Lady Hiroshi, and the townspeople.

I bent my knees to brace myself for the first attack.

Just like in Shadow training, the goal was to read where the rider was weakest in their form and strike at that spot. The first rider to come into my sight held the reins tightly, keeping the horse in check—which spoke of the horse's flighty nature. I shifted my right foot forward and twisted my body, bringing the pickaxe around in an arc inside the horse's blind spot to spook it.

As the horse reared, the rider failed to stay upright, falling to the ground in a heap.

Moving forward, I focused on two riders coming toward me at the same time. One of the horses tried to outmaneuver the other one, speaking of competition between them. I dug the pickaxe into a pile of metal flakes on the side of the street. Holding my breath, I kicked up a plume of smoke. The particles hung in the air, catching the light from the flames and blurring the street from the horse's vision. Hunching down to the ground, I held the pickaxe steady as the horses tripped over the wooden post. The momentum from the attack broke the axe, and I released it, flattening myself against one of the metal buildings to avoid being trampled by more horses.

"Light the oil!" I yelled.

Air whooshed past me as a line of flame snaked along the ground, crisscrossing and engulfing the street in a maze of fire. I pulled the scarf up from around my neck and sank lower, hiding in the smoke.

A loud *booooom* shook the ground, rattling the metal houses and sending unease through my spine. Smoke billowed near the center of town as screams pierced the air. Silhouetted by fire, Lady Hiroshi and the townspeople pulled on ropes attached to wooden scaffolding. They gave one final heave before the entrance to the mine collapsed. Smoke and dust rose into the air, the flames rising higher.

This was their last defiant stand against Hitori.

She would not have the mines without a fight.

Their courage moved me.

Leaving the main street, I circled around the center of town and scanned the area. Some of the mercenaries who had fallen from their horses were dead. Another few were tied with ropes and had been set against the iron statue of the town's founder.

As I passed them, I noticed a figure hunched down in an alleyway. I kept my sword lowered, squinting against the smoke to make out the details of who it was.

Eiji.

I rushed to his side. His leg was outstretched. The bottom of his pants was seared from the fires, the skin underneath singed and burned. Sliding my arm under his shoulder, I hoisted him up.

"Agh!"

He seemed out of it, dazed from the battle and smoke.

"Eiji, you need to get out of here," I said, half-carrying him through one of the barricades the townspeople had set up. He shifted against my grip, and I steadied him on his feet. In the distance, the gleam of silver alerted me to the presence of the

False Shadows. I stiffened as we approached, then relaxed slightly. It was Haru and a few others. Their hands were wrapped with leather to protect them from the fires as they moved objects in their path. One of the False Shadows struggled with a barrel, attempting to create an opening between the main street and an alleyway.

Haru threw his weight against it before he nodded toward the opening and wave us through. "We've made an escape route for the townspeople. Hurry."

The wind pushed a thick wall of smoke over us, and I closed my eyes until it had passed. Another one of the False Shadows came around the corner with a group of injured people. His clothing was torn and burned, but he shepherded the people to the exit with little regard for his own wellbeing. It seemed like most of the False Shadows had used Hitori's arrival to intervene and help the townspeople.

"Get him to safety," I said, pushing Eiji forward.

Haru nodded shortly.

I rushed back to the center of town, as the pressure in the air intensified. Hitori had arrived. A new group of False Shadows made their way through the flames. They were slower, more cautious than Haru's group, with swords held in their hands as they approached Lady Hiroshi's group. The townspeople gathered in the square defended against the oncoming mercenaries with pickaxes and iron poles while others threw wadded-up rolls of cloth, producing a cloud of minerals as they impacted. Many of the False Shadows in the area were those I had met the previous night. They were making little attempt to actually use their swords unless they were in Hitori's line of sight.

I had laughed with the False Shadows. Joked with them. But the screams of pain came from the townspeople who had provided shelter to Finae and me not long ago. I placed my hand on the hilt of my sword but hesitated.

Who here was the enemy?

While I had a greater affection for the people of Aventon because of the longer amount of time I had spent with them, some of the False Shadows had welcomed me and shown me kindness—like Daichi and Riku.

We were comrades now.

Grimacing, I drew my sword, forcing myself to act, to defend, to put myself between the two opposing sides. Bringing my sword down to protect the townspeople and the False Shadows, I tried to do as little damage as I could, wearing the people's resilience down on both sides. Neither would back down. This battle would come down to endurance, and whoever was the last one standing would get to decide the course of action.

Despite knowing how the battle would go, a sudden tightness in my chest strangled my breath, making it hard to raise my sword. I struggled to act, to do anything more, but my limbs and heart were heavy.

It all felt so pointless…

Smoke blurred my vision, making my eyes water. Through the chaos, a familiar voice screamed nearby. Orin's voice. It was guttural and full of pain. He had turned away from defending Lady Hiroshi and had drawn his sword against Saitou.

Behind them, Hitori stood, looming in front of a pillar of smoke.

A weight descended onto me, and my feet became heavy.

Others fell onto their knees, their hands at their throats.

I closed my eyes and ignored the sounds of battle, reaching for the Skills and allowing them to be drawn toward my spirit— a spirit of calm. The crushing weight of the Skills dispelled as I exerted my will across the area. I moved to intervene between Orin and Saitou, but Seiji blocked my path. He appeared to be straining as he held his weapon as if he fought against himself. A glimmer of red surrounded the blade, emitting a subtle red glow. As he slashed down, I raised my sword to stop him.

I had encountered both before: The red hue indicated Hitori had used the Skills on the blade. The hesitation in Seiji's actions meant they were not entirely his own.

Pushing against Seiji, I forced him to retreat. I removed one hand from my sword and grabbed the hilt of Haru's sword. A surge of the Skills shot into my arm, the skin burning where they touched.

"Fight her for control," I said to Seiji, the heat from the blade searing my skin. "You're stronger than this!"

Seiji's eyes widened as the sword fell to the ground. The realization of what was happening to him was enough to break Hitori's control. I touched his shoulder, dispelling the Skills left inside him.

Around us, few were left standing.

I stepped over bodies on the ground and headed toward Saitou.

Orin lay at his feet.

As I approached, Saitou kept his sword point at the ground. Hitori, standing behind him, watched me with keen eyes. I knelt next to Orin. Blood dripped from the corners of his mouth, and he sputtered and gasped for air. His lungs had been punctured. Though his eyes were closed, they flickered as I lifted his head. He turned his unseeing eyes in my direction.

"Eiji is safe," I said quietly. "I will do what I can to protect the people who have survived. Aventon will be rebuilt on the bravery you have shown today."

He grunted his acceptance, his eyes focusing on the blade in my hand.

I hesitated.

Meeting his end with his own sword seemed a fitting end.

With steady hands, I gripped the blade Orin had forged and stood up. His eyes locked onto mine, acceptance and relief passing over his face. I held the sword steady above his chest, and before my will could waver, I drove the blade through Orin's heart.

It was quick.

Merciful.

And as much kindness as I could show him in his final moments.

I withdrew the sword, watching as a small skirmish persisted between both sides. Not far away, another of the False Shadows, in as bad of a condition as Orin, lay on the ground gasping for breath. Blood oozed from his side where a blade had been thrust into his torso. On his face was a deep gouge, like that from a garden rake.

"Order them to stop," I demanded of Hitori, keeping my blade at my side.

Hitori said nothing.

Defiant.

Calming my anger, I knelt before Hitori, laying my sword down in the mud as I bowed low. The screams of dying people rang through my ears.

"Please, order them to stop. Continuing beyond this point is cruel."

When I raised my eyes, Hitori wrinkled her nose in disgust.

"To think you would placate yourself so low…"

"A leader must intervene on the people's behalf," I said, evenly. "I am honored to be the one to stand between you and the people here."

I kept my face emotionless, watching Hitori as her eyebrows fell, creating a dark, piercing stare. How she hated me.

Saitou cleared his throat. "If you wish to return to Magoto before the end of the day, we will need to leave soon."

"Very well," Hitori said, turning. Under her breath she said, "You're pathetic."

I kept my head bowed, undisturbed by the anger she had for me. Saitou, whose clothing was bloodied at the hem, adjusted his sword. Without his interference, the battle might not have ended.

"Thank you," I said to Saitou, raising myself from the mud.

He gave me a slight nod before following after Hitori.

I picked up Orin's blade.

"Aventon is mine!" Hitori shouted, standing among those who still fought. "Take your pathetic lives and live them elsewhere. You have two days to evacuate. Any left after that timeframe will be eliminated without mercy."

The False Shadows and mercenaries lowered their swords as Hitori and Saitou left the battlefield. The mercenaries stood guard while the False Shadows began to move. The people from Aventon hesitated, their strength and spirit worn down. Haru and

Seiji came from somewhere in the crowd, looking tired and exhausted from battle. I had not seen Lady Hiroshi for some time—perhaps she, too, was among the dead.

Wiping the blood from Orin's blade, I sheathed the sword and walked past a group of Aventon residents. An air of melancholy had befallen the town; not only had they lost the battle, they were being forced to leave their homes.

I took a deep breath.

Right now, they needed strength and direction.

"Tend to the survivors," I said, seeing a few tears among those standing near me.

The harsh reality of battle was beginning to set in.

"Gather what supplies are in town and bring them here," I continued, pausing as I caught sight of a woman on the ground. She seemed to be still be breathing. "Move the living inside away from the cold so we can tend to them."

Kneeling next to the woman, I lifted her head from the mud and slid a nearby rock under it. "Stay with us," I told her, inspecting the sword stuck into her side. She seemed out of it. Stunned.

I breathed in deeply. She would not be out of it for long. Seiji came to my side, handing me a length of fabric. I pulled the blade, removing it from her body, and the woman screamed. Placing the folded-up material against the wound, I leaned against her, applying my body weight to the injury with steady pressure.

In the distance, others shuffled among the dead.

I narrowed my focus, concentrating on the task at hand.

One person at a time.

It was the only way to manage.

Seiji knelt next to me, his gaze on the woman's wound. Hanging over his shoulder was a saddlebag that gaped open. It was filled with vials, bandages, and an assortment of leather pouches. He pulled a needle out from a glass vial.

"You seem to know what you're doing," I said.

"Before the False Shadows, I worked with my father as a traveling medic. I know how to sew stitches, what herbs will help fight infection, how to brew sleeping aids—" He stopped talking while he threaded the needle with some form of sinew.

I was impressed with his knowledge. "Is Hitori aware of what you can do?"

Seiji shook his head. "We help in the aftermath of the False Shadows' attacks. I have no interest in Hitori perverting what I do like she did with my father."

I kept the pressure on the wound, suspicion creeping into my mind.

Hadn't he said his father was forced into something?

"What do you know about the Skill poisoning?" I asked.

"We should see if the bleeding has stopped," Seiji said, keeping his eyes on the woman in our care. *Another time* was his meaning. I removed my hands slowly, letting Seiji peel away the cloth, hoping the wound had stopped bleeding.

It had.

I let out a long breath and relaxed.

"I can take care of her," Seiji said as he leaned over the woman and began pushing the needle through her skin.

Briefly, I placed my hand on his shoulder before rising from the ground. The False Shadows who remained walked among the townspeople, checking for any left alive. Any who could be saved were being tended to. This was how they were able to live with themselves, how they slept at night. It was a small way to counteract the damage forced upon them by Hitori.

I left Seiji and the woman, stepping over the bodies of the fallen. The smell of blood and iron was still thick in the air, and when my eyes came to rest on Orin's dead body, bile rose. I wiped my hands on the sides of my robe, pushing away the memory of the blade sliding into his chest between the bones.

"Phantom Kilo!" someone shouted.

I looked up to see Haru waving to me from the other end of the street.

"I could use your help," he said. "We're sweeping the town for any who are hiding." Nodding, I walked toward him, keeping my eyes unfocused on the scene before us.

Thunder rumbled overhead, and rain began to fall, the drops tanging against the metal roofs. The oil and flames hissed as the water fell on them, but the fire would not be extinguished for quite some time. Even if it poured, the fire would remain until it burned itself out.

Walking along the streets with Haru, we began checking inside the buildings, ensuring there was no one injured inside who needed help. Daichi and Riku joined in on our search. When we reached the end of the street, other False Shadows continued past us into town, carrying supplies. I circled back toward an alley when a noise caught my attention. It almost sounded like loud breathing or muffled crying.

Stepping forward, I sank low to the ground, peering around the corner of the alleyway. Behind a metal barrel, a tuft of black hair poked up.

I hunched down to the ground and cleared my throat.

The sound of crying hushed.

"The fighting is over; you can come out now."

Silence.

"We'll begin preparations for food shortly. There's going to be some fried rice and chicken. I've heard there may even be some sort of sweet rice porridge."

The tuft of hair moved sharply.

"If you'd rather stay here, I can bring a bowl for you. You will have to leave in a couple of days, though. There will be a caravan leaving to take everyone somewhere safe."

From behind the barrel, a small boy emerged. His face was covered in what looked to be dirt, making his reddened eyes more prominent. He held his hands in front of his stomach, locked together, his knees turned inward.

"I am not here to hurt you," I said, keeping still as he looked me over.

As I waited for his response, he stared at me with concentration, his eyebrows knitting together as his lips puckered.

Laughing, I stood up and motioned for him to follow me.

"Come on, everyone is waiting."

I started back toward the camp, away from the town, glancing over my shoulder to make sure the boy followed. The farther away from town we got, the closer he walked to me until he finally reached up and took my hand. Squeezing his hand to reassure him, I lifted my eyes to the sky, silently hoping his parents were still alive.

As promised, I led him to the pot where the rice was being cooked. His eyes grew wide as he saw the size of the giant kettle. Leaving him in the care of the False Shadows, I sought out Haru. When I found him, he was giving directions to some of the townspeople. A distraught-looking couple was talking with Seiji off to the side. The father had unkempt black hair, with a similar cowlick on his forehead. The same as the boy's I had found.

When I approached them, I caught the last of their conversation.

"...missing."

"Sorry," I said, drawing their attention to me as I stepped to the side and pointed back toward the False Shadows. "There's a young boy who—"

The mother's eyes widened. "Tsumo!"

The young couple ran toward their son, scooping him up in their arms and hugging him.

Haru came over to me, a slight smile on his face. "Despite everything we do, sometimes we're able to do good."

I nodded, feeling, at last, a small measure of relief.

chapter forty-seven
Aventon Aftermath

That evening I kept watch on the edge of the town, upwind from the smoke and fires. Though it was late, well after midnight, I was not the only one still awake. Seiji remained vigilant with his patients, completing his rounds with devotion, and Haru kept watch on the other side of camp. A few of the other False Shadows kept watch around the camp, creating a perimeter to protect the remaining townspeople from any further threats.

Resting my chin on my kneed, I gazed out across the plains. The breeze blew the dirt and tall grass, creating a sea of motion under the moonlight. It was peaceful, the land continuing its cycle of life without pausing for the tragedy that had fallen on Aventon.

We were but a passing breeze in life.

A fog rolled in, skirting across the ground before it fell into the deep ravine next to Aventon's borders. I let out a deep breath. Watching. Waiting for what would come.

Back in Vaiyene, one of my favorite times to climb the mountains was when a fog settled on the peaks. Something about the white nothingness reminded me that even though I could not always see the people I protected, they were always there.

My purpose, though unseen, lay within me.

Idly, I held out my hand, looking at the calluses and scars that had developed over the years—reminders of the time spent in battle. All that I did, I did for the people of Kiriku, and for the people I had left behind in Vaiyene.

For the Shadows, whose friendship I cherished.

For my Phantoms, who shared their wisdom and teachings.

For Shenrae and Syrane, so they may never need to carry this burden.

For Rin, so her sacrifices would have been in vain.

For Finae, so her vision of the future would come to be.

And…for the False Shadows, so they might know freedom.

Since leaving Vaiyene, the way I lived my life had been on my mind. The Shadow's Creed did not consider the lives that could be saved by sacrificing a single individual. During many encounters there were times when killing would have made it easier to save more people. Times when I tamped down my own abilities to be merciful to one without a thought for the other lives that could be saved if I used more force.

Relaxing my fingers, I allowed my thoughts to shift to the ancient Phantom, to Takezo, the man who had wiped out his people and his homeland to give Kiriku another chance.

I had sensed regret when we met.

But his decision had been made in an attempt to do good.

Did not the action and intention also come into play?

I had made an oath as a Phantom to do what I needed to protect my people. I left Vaiyene for that belief, and I could not waver now. The thought tasted bitter in my mouth, and already nausea and guilt seeped into the back of my throat, making it hard to breathe.

If I could not find a way to convince Hitori to stop attacking villages...

Could I really do it?

I swallowed, forcing my breathing to return to a steady rhythm—one life for a hundred. Even taking one life to save a few seemed to justify the action on the surface. If the Shadows were greater in number, if we had more people, perhaps it would be easier to spare more lives. Maybe we could save more of the False Shadows or turn those involved with Hitori away from their path, but as we were now, the more people we were up against, the more we needed to defend those who could not protect themselves. How many had to suffer because of my reluctance?

And how many already had?

The girl and the countless people buried in the Kinsaan forest.

The people in Vaiyene who had been poisoned with grain.

The people of Leiko Gulf.

The village of Mashin.

And now, Aventon.

As the turmoil inside of me became too great to bear, I opened my eyes, hearing the beating of my heart in my chest quicken.

It had become colder as the mist now rolled across the camp.

Shifting my weight, I held onto the sword in my sash with one hand, standing. Orin's sword was a reminder of the townspeople who had accepted Finae and me. That fondness would remain even after his death, though I wondered how the people of Aventon now saw me—was it as the man who failed to protect their town?

From within the fog, a figure walked toward me.

The person seemed to be alone, but I was uncertain if anyone was there at all. Sometimes the mist played tricks on a person's mind, and I was tired and weary enough to believe its lies.

I paused.

Waiting.

A white glow illuminated the fog. Subtle at first, the white tendrils crawled like lightning from its source. Not long ago, I would have called the light unnatural as I tried to understand it, wondering about the dangers it possessed. Now I knew the Skills were as much a part of the world as I was.

Like me, they were neither good nor bad.

They only were.

A memory of a different fog and a figure silhouetted came to mind. It was in Vaiyene that I had first met her and seen the power she possessed. Even before a break in the fog revealed her, I knew who had come.

Rin.

She smiled as she approached. Happiness warmed my heart, but then the light canteen in her hand brought reality back into focus, and guilt rose in me.

I had failed the people of Aventon.

Fisting my hands, I tried to ignore the kindness in her eyes. I felt unworthy of that kindness. What was a Shadow without the ability to protect their people? The chance to stand against Hitori had finally come, and I had not even been an obstacle in her way.

Rin crossed the remaining distance between us.

And I looked away from her, not wanting to see the affection in her eyes for me.

"You got your hopes up, didn't you?" Rin said.

It was not really a question, but a statement of understanding.

I swallowed against the knot in my throat.

Seeing her now brought the emotions I had been ignoring to the surface. I had thought I would be able to make a difference, that I would be able to stop Hitori from killing the townspeople and forcing them from their homes. I had allowed myself to be blinded by the desire to do good, never stopping to think that perhaps—as people had told me—there was nothing I could do. Would Hitori have been able to scare the townspeople into leaving if I had not interfered? Would Lady Hiroshi have abandoned the town if I had not come? They were impossible questions, and I recognized my guilt for what it was—shame.

"You did what you had to." Rin's voice was distant compared to the burning emotion inside me.

I had done what I had to, but had I done the right thing?

Should I have fought Hitori instead?

Tried to kill her to spare the town?

Rin took a step toward me; I fought the urge to back away, and instead of remaining silent, I voiced the pain we now shared.

"I think I finally understand what it is you have gone through," I said, blowing out a long breath to steady my racing heart. "The False Shadows are a tragedy. No matter what they do, they will suffer for it. I had thought most were blackmailed by Hitori, forced to serve her, but some have begun to gather by themselves. They have chosen to be a part of her group. To kill and take from others because they have nothing. They do not believe there is anything left for them but this broken existence, and so they do not struggle for anything more."

Did they even feel they deserved more?

Rin reached a tentative hand toward me. She hooked her finger around the leather cord at my neck and slid out the wooden sword hidden inside my robes.

"We do what we must," I said, reciting the characters carved into it.

It had been given to me by Rin in Magoto last winter.

"Ikaru made it," Rin said, a touch of a smile on her lips. "Back when Hitori and I were friends. Ikaru understood the pain I was going through and made it to remind me of my conviction. I tried to be Hitori's friend, even after she crossed the line with the Skills."

I closed my hand over Rin's. "You were friends?"

"She wasn't always like this."

I held her hand tighter, squeezing it before letting go.

That was why Hitori had never been able to kill her. Even though Rin had gone against her, Hitori could never bring herself to eliminate a friend. There was a sadness—a tragedy—to Hitori as well as her False Shadows. One that had not yet been fully revealed. It confirmed my growing sense of Hitori's character. If Hitori was as cruel as people believed her to be, none would have stayed by her. Saitou was one of them, but even Haru seemed to hold onto hope in regard to Hitori. Did he stay only to undermine her plans? Or did he hope for something more?

And hadn't Hitori stopped her attack when I had asked her to?

Was there something more to Hitori?

"After the death of Hitori's father, it all changed," Rin said, crossing her arms and looking up at the sky. "None believed in Hitori's authority or her ability to rule Magoto. The lords pulled back their support, and Hitori was left with nothing. Her father had tried to teach her how to lead, what needed to be done as a lord, but the people hated her because she was different. As a child she wanted to know how things worked. She tried to create things for the townspeople, but most of them failed because she didn't have the support she needed. All she was ever seen as was an oddity, and she was shunned because of it."

"It is her greatest strength," I said. Her fascination with the Skills was an innate gift. She walked the line between right and wrong, but the way she saw the Skills made her an asset to this world.

The conversation was eclipsed by thoughtful silence.

"General Mirai is on his way," Rin said after a while. "I saw him when I was tracking you. There have been uprisings in some of the other towns nearby. People have begun fighting one another. The general and his men encountered Hitori not long ago."

Pressing my fingers against my eyes, I gently rubbed them. "Hitori wiped out General Mirai's mercenaries there, and the people of Leiko fled after that encounter."

Somehow, we needed to find a way to stop Hitori.

And soon.

"You should get some sleep," Rin said. "Let me keep watch for the rest of the night. The general should arrive by then, and we can see what we can do for the people here."

Reluctantly, I nodded, feeling the cloud of exhaustion on my mind.

With Rin here now, perhaps sleep would be possible.

———

The ground rattled with the approach of horses, breaking my morning meditation. Drawing in a final breath, I let go of my state of calm, rising from the ground. It had been a full day since the attack on Aventon. The deadline for the evacuation was tomorrow. Somehow, we had gathered enough supplies to move the people elsewhere from the town so as not to become a burden on the general and his men.

"General Mirai has arrived," Rin said, standing up from the rock she had been sitting against. We were outside of Aventon, near one of the crevasses. We headed back to town, climbing over one of the barricades on a side street. Most of the spilled oil had finally burned away, but there were a few places, like on the main street, where the flames still burned. We had moved the camp farther away from town after the first night to get away from the nauseating smell of tar and death.

As we passed the statue of the town's founder, I took a moment to admire the colorful gems at the base, trying to find beauty, like Finae did, in the most unwelcome of places.

At the southeast edge, where the remainder of the pyre still smoldered, General Mirai and his men slowed their horses. Their green banners quivered in the wind as the general dismounted from his horse.

I bowed, straightening with a relieved smile. "It feels as if it's been a very long time since we have seen one another, General."

His eyes were rimmed with dark circles, and he looked as tired as I felt. Giving me a small smile, he bent slightly at the waist in return. "Phantom Kilo. I wish it were under different circumstances we were meeting. There is much we need to talk about."

I nodded, already knowing part of it from what Rin had told me.

"If your men have not eaten," I said, gesturing toward the makeshift camp to the north, "there is plenty of food. The False Shadows have been keeping the people well fed as they finish their final preparations."

"Help where you can," General Mirai said, addressing his men behind him. "We'll leave in a few hours. Relax while we have the time."

Extending my arm toward town, I led the general into Aventon.

"What is it you wish to speak to me about?" I asked.

"The people are becoming anxious across Kiriku. Supplies are dwindling between towns. We're doing what we can to alleviate the shortages, but I'm not sure how much longer Tarahn will be able to continue." General Mirai paused, his hand going to his sword. He glanced over at me. "If we don't do something soon, there will be war. My brother has no desire to involve himself in such bloodshed. While I maintain a certain amount of freedom with my mercenary group, if things continue as they are, I'm not sure how much longer I can support you and the Shadows."

I frowned. "I see."

Withdrawing his aid did not mean the general was afraid of getting involved. It was a calculated move to try and slow the fighting, as well as a means of self-preservation for his men and Tarahn. If he involved his men and the only outcome was death in battle how could he justify continuing to fight?

How could any leader ask that of his men?

Back in Vaiyene, the Phantoms had refused to involve themselves. While they did not have the resources Kefnir and Mirai did, Lunia and Asdar had made it clear they wanted nothing to do with the outside world. Even if they did, the Shadows were still rebuilding their strength after the devastating fires. Their number was close to two dozen, hardly a formidable force. But General Mirai could not continue risking the lives of his people if there was nothing to be gained. Nor could Lord Kefnir continue to involve Tarahn if he was the only one fighting. If I managed to stop Hitori and the False Shadows, we would need help repairing the damage that had been done.

Alliances needed to be repaired.

Trust reestablished.

And anger smoothed.

I bowed with my right hand over my chest. "Please give me a little more time. Continue to watch over the people of Kiriku until I am able to stop the False Shadows."

"I have always trusted your judgement, Kilo," Generali Mirai said, a note of sincerity in his voice. "I will do what I can to maintain the peace for as long as I am able to."

As I straightened, I met Rin's intense gaze.

She eyed the general with intent. "Konro's land is fertile. I will see if they will allow us space to create a reserve of food to be redistributed between the towns. With spring upon us, we will be able to plant new crops in anticipation of the need."

General Mirai nodded. "I would appreciate whatever help you can offer."

"I will send word in one month detailing my progress," I said with a heavy heart. "If nothing has changed within that time frame, I will take more extreme measures to ensure it does."

"We're counting on you," the general said.

"I will do my best."

The words seemed hollow against the amount of work still left to do, but they were the only ones I could offer.

When we returned to the main camp, Rin grabbed bowls of rice, handing one to me and one to the general before she dug her chopsticks into her own bowl.

Across the camp, Haru bustled through the crowd of people, seeming disgruntled about something.

"There are a few of the townspeople who are refusing to leave," he said tersely. "They insist when Hitori comes back, they will fight her."

"They'll be killed," Rin said without emotion in her voice.

As I glanced down at the rice inside the bowl, my appetite dwindled. I sat down on a log next to the campfire, setting my chopsticks across the bowl.

"They would rather die than leave behind what they have known," I said, looking closely at the people gathered around the other campsites. Uncertainty was hard to face, especially when the course of action was not of person's own choosing.

General Mirai sat down across from me. "They'll leave," he said, taking a bite of rice, sounding certain in his answer. "They will take their memories and grief and find another place to call home. If they are lucky, they will find happiness there."

Through the wavering flames of the campfires, Seiji's form appeared as he returned from seeing a patient. His pack of medical supplies hung across his chest.

He seemed so exhausted he could barely stand.

I stood up and offered my seat and bowl to him.

He accepted both.

Resting my hand on my sword, I watched as two children, their figures blurry from the fires, ran through the camp. They chased one another, knowing nothing of worry—only that tomorrow would come again.

"I will return Aventon to its people," I said. "The town will be remade by the people's desire to return. It will take time, but I believe the people here have the courage and will to see their homeland lives on."

Haru leaned forward, propping his head on his hand.

"And what do you believe for Magoto?"

Rin lowered her chopsticks. She, too, was keen to hear the answer. Like me, she had left her homeland in pursuit of doing something to help her people. From what I knew of Magoto, most of the people there had given up and no longer desired to fight for their survival. But there was still hope for Magoto. Some still chose to fight against Hitori, and those actions would become a catalyst for others.

"Like Aventon, it is up to the people to save what is important to them." I held Haru's gaze before I focused on Rin. "It will not be saved by me or a change of heart from Hitori. The power has and always will lie with those who choose to defend their home."

When I looked back at our surroundings, there was a change in the camp. We were sitting not far from a large group of townspeople, and when I focused on them, a few averted their eyes, pretending they had not been listening to our conversation. I walked over to them, seeing a mix of ages, but most seemed to be in their late teens and twenties. A few I recognized as the last to lay down their swords during the battle.

I crouched down on the balls of my feet, to talk to them at eye-level.

"Leaving Aventon is not the end," I said.

A few snorted, dismissing my words as a routine phrase said after a tragedy. It was too early to talk about the pain of defeat. I understood, but what they were not aware was how the world would move on without them. Without action, they would become like a flame. Dim and forgotten. Extinguished before it even had the chance to burn at its brightest.

As I stood, the edge of my robe brushed the embers of the campfire. Fire flared up, and the Skills in the air carried them into the sky, illuminating it in a myriad of colors.

The people's attention fell on me.

Drawing in a breath, I addressed them. "Today will forever be the day *they* forced you from your homeland. Going forward, bitterness will make you act in ways you never thought you would. We are at the beginning of a new era in these lands. Whatever you choose, wherever you go, you have the power to shape what is around you. Hold your head high, knowing others will look to you for courage."

One of the teenagers sitting by the fire stood out to me. He had a fierce look in his eyes. A look I was all too familiar with.

"Tell me, what is it that you feel right now?" I asked him.

"Anger," he said. A bandage was wrapped around his forehead. A wound he had likely gotten from battle.

The others nodded their agreement.

"Why?"

"Because we couldn't stop them from destroying our town."

I nodded. "General Mirai?" I called, seeing him watching from where he remained seated. "What do you make of these six warriors?"

All of them sat up straighter at the mention of "warrior."

"They have potential. Each seems strong enough to endure training. Lord Kefnir is always looking for recruits," General Mirai said, giving it some consideration before he continued.

"They could also join my group, but we seem to be doing more fighting than we usually do. It might not be as safe for them."

"I'm not afraid to die," the boy said. He stood up and glanced around at his companions. "I say we set a trap for them when they come back! And take back Aventon now!"

I frowned, feeling a tension in the air. "Battle should not excite you. Learn the sword, but do so that you can protect life, not take it. Perpetuating this cycle of hatred will do nothing but bring sadness to you and those around you."

He glared at me, his anger growing.

"Stand down, Naiki," someone said from behind me. I turned to see Lady Hiroshi limping toward the campfire. She leaned against a wooden pole, using it to support most of her weight.

I let out a relieved breath.

She was alive after all.

Lady Hiroshi drew herself up as best she could considering her injuries.

"I would rather it take years for us to regain ownership of Aventon than to watch more of you die in battle," she said. "Go with the others and learn how to use a sword so next time you will be able to protect the people you love."

Naiki hesitated. In the presence of his lady, he did not have the same confidence.

"Be patient for now," I said, watching as his anger redirected toward me. "I will be working with the surrounding villages and towns to create an alliance, and then—"

"What do you know of loss!" Naiki yelled.

Standing up, he spat at the ground and took a step toward me, his arm swinging back. One of his companions leaped forward and caught his arm.

I met Naiki's gaze, unflinching. "Do not forget you are not the only ones who have suffered!" I said, allowing my anger to break through my usually calm demeanor. He knew nothing of war but the injustice he was feeling now.

"Your friends and family died to defend Aventon so that you may live to see another day." I clenched my fingers into a fist at my side. "Do not dishonor the lives of the dead by throwing away your life on some meaningless act of revenge."

Naiki threw off his friend's hand and stormed away.

The mounting tension in the air made those in camp restless.

"He's not the only one," General Mirai commented, setting down his empty rice bowl and coming to stand beside me. "They lust for vengeance because they haven't experienced what we have." The general spotted one of his men who had seen the encounter and jerked his head toward Naiki, saying, "Go see if he will join us. Maybe we can temper his hatred in training."

I stifled a jolt of shame, noticing Lady Hiroshi's clenched jaw. This was hard on everyone.

"I appreciate your intervention," I said, letting out a deep breath. "It is easier to allow ourselves to hate what hurts us than it is to try and understand how we must live with it. I regret that I was not able to do more for you."

"Orin held you in high regard," Lady Hirohi said. "He was my grandfather, did you know? The little boy he always had with him was some villager's child he adopted. I will look after him now and the rest of the orphans."

I nodded, trying to keep my mind from spiraling back to such matters.

The best way to move forward was to take action.

It was time to move on. Before Rin left, I had something to give her. I also wanted to talk to her about how Finae was doing and see if she had found anything unusual with the Skills.

"General, Lady Hiroshi," I said, bowing slightly to both of them, "if there is anything more I can do, do not hesitate to ask."

Lady Hiroshi nodded shortly.

She still seemed upset about Naiki and was most likely uncertain if she and her people would ever actually return to Aventon.

"Things will change," I said to her, "but the people here have a certain charisma to them. A certain rugged flexibility and stubbornness. I do not doubt that, when the dust settles, Aventon will grow stronger because of it."

Lady Hiroshi fisted her right hand. "I look forward to the day we can return."

"As do I," I said.

I gave a passing glance to the general before going over to Rin.

She let out a long breath as we walked away from the camp and into the isolation of the trees. Away from the general's men and the townspeople, at last, we could let down our guards.

I tried to mentally brush away my exhaustion so I could be there for Rin before we parted ways.

"How are you feeling?" I asked.

She was quiet.

Which meant she, too, was drained.

"I'm ready for this to be over," she said, finding a fallen tree to sit down on. "Days like these are beginning to wear me down. I've seen so much of the False Shadows' aftermath you would think it wouldn't bother me anymore, but…"

She looked down at her hands.

"It wears on me too," I said, kneeling on one knee in front of her.

Only a short time ago the bandages on her arm only went up to her elbow. Now they were almost to her shoulder. As I reached out a hand, Rin tensed, knowing I had noticed the difference.

I rested my fingers on her forearm, searching for the end of the bandages. "You should stop using the Skills until your body has had time to heal."

Rin smiled slyly. "You know I can't allow Finae to endure them alone."

I sighed.

Sometimes, she was impossible to deal with.

"I asked Seiji to make a medicine that might help." Withdrawing a small cloth from within my robes, I raised my eyes to her as to ask for permission to proceed. "It has some properties of pain relief, and he said there's something in it to promote faster healing."

She hesitated but gave a short nod.

Peeling the cloth away from her arm, I exposed the blackened skin underneath. In some places, her skin seemed almost red, as if it were so thin it was about to tear.

"It's gotten worse," she admitted.

I tried my best not to let the ache in my chest keep me from breathing, hoping my concern was not showing too much. "There is a river not too far from here. We need to soothe the skin with cool water before applying the paste."

Rin opened her mouth and took a breath to say something, but when she looked up at me, the words died out, and she relented.

Perhaps I was not as good at hiding my concern as I believed.

I started into the forest with Rin, navigating through the dense trees. The trickle of water flowed over the rocks, dropping minerals and flecks of gold. Not too long ago, gold had been a source of wealth for Aventon, but from what Orin had told me, the majority of it had already been collected. Most of what was in the water now was not worth their time and effort.

The memory of Orin's laugh came to my mind.

Aventon would not be the same without him.

I allowed the sadness to seep through me. Accepting his loss would be difficult for many. It would be for me. He'd had a personality not easily forgotten and one that would be sorely missed.

While my thoughts were on Orin, Rin had taken the lead, and tracking the river, she led us to a spot where the water flowed the cleanest. She knelt next to the water and brushed her fingers over the surface of a small alcove. Rocks were wedged at the top, creating a slight drop-off where water pooled.

It seemed as good a spot as any.

I sat in front of Rin, and she held out her arm over the water.

"In Vaiyene," I said, cupping my hands and scooping up the water, "near the highest peak, there is a cavern lit by crystals. The water there can purify and heal a person's spirit."

Allowing my thoughts to drift to the cavern and Vaiyene, I drizzled water over Rin's arm. My fondness and desire to take away Rin's pain was at the forefront of my mind.

"The Shadows wash their weapons in the water whenever we are forced to draw blood. It helps cleanse the mind and allows you to put what has been done in the past. When you kneel in the waters, there is a resonance you can feel. A pulse like the earth's heartbeat."

I held my hand on the surface of the water, watching intently as the ripples disturbed the stillness of the small alcove. My fingers dipped into the water, and I breathed in deeply, holding onto the feeling I knew lay deep below the earth's surface.

The Skills fluttered around me, humming with the connection. Silver light scattered across the surface, and when I scooped up the water and drizzled it over Rin's arm, an innate peace flowed through me as thought of the love I had for her. As the silver light caressed Rin's skin, I held the request to heal Rin in my mind, allowing the Skills to resonate with that desire. A touch of color returned to her skin, the dark black tint fading into a grayer tone. She inhaled slightly, and I glanced up to find tears brimming her eyes. Her lips spread into a small smile, though they quivered with emotion. The Skills flowed from me into Rin. They were pure, resonating with words we did not need to speak.

Gently, I cupped my hands around hers, feeling a lightness to my heart.

Rin's eyes seemed to sparkle, and her voice was quiet as she spoke. "I've heard so much about Vaiyene. I hope one day I can see it for myself."

"I will take you there," I promised.

I had not intended for it to happen, but little by little, day by day, her presence had become a constant in the stream of uncertainties. Her strong will and courage inspired feelings I had not wished for—but feelings I was grateful for all the same. With the danger and chaos of the world around us, we knew nothing of the future. It made it hard to hold onto any sort of promise that tomorrow would be a better day. In my heart, I knew it was foolish to become involved with someone who, like myself, was not guaranteed a tomorrow, but my affection for her had only grown since the first time we met.

There had been no stopping it.

Perhaps the best course of action was to simply enjoy one another's company and not take for granted the small moments that made life worthwhile.

After all, what was it we fought for?

Safety for the people we loved.

Hope for those who relied on us.

And a world where people could live without fear.

I removed my hands from Rin's, withdrawing the leather pouch Seiji had given me. Untying the cord around the leather satchel, I used two fingers to scoop up the thick paste, rubbing the medicine into Rin's skin. A thin patch began to bleed. I tried to be gentle, but my hands were rough and calloused.

I hesitated. "Sorry." Picking up a clean square of cloth from the satchel, I pressed it to Rin's skin, and the blood soaked into the bandage. I began wrapping her arm with new bandages, being mindful of how tight I wound them.

"Thank you," Rin said.

I finished wrapping her arm and sat back on my heels. Drawing in a breath, I waited for my heart to still as I sat down beside Rin, leaning my back against hers. The Skills had made the connection between Rin and me so strong I could almost feel her own heartbeat racing alongside mine.

"How's Finae?" I asked after some time.

Rin chuckled and leaned her head back against my shoulders. "She is still fascinated by everything in Konro. The water, the trees, the flowers. Even the rocks and air. She spends all day 'talking with the trees.' She says she can feel them and that some even hold memories."

So Finae had also found a deeper connection.

I recalled the first time Finae had used the Skills to show me memories of Konro, remembering clearly the quiet disbelief in my mind. Since that day, I had stopped trying to understand the mysteries of the Skills and allowed things to be as they were.

"It is similar to a state of mind you can achieve through meditation," I said, watching as small orbs of light rose up around us. "Through the Skills, a person can experience things they would not have been able to otherwise. Because I met with the ancient Phantom, I have begun to see the Skills across our land."

Rin was quiet.

"Can you see them?" I asked, feeling Rin lay her full weight against me.

Her breathing became slower.

"No," she said, "but it sounds like it would be beautiful."

I smiled. While the Skills were certainly beautiful, they were nothing in comparison to Rin's own beauty.

chapter forty-eight
Kilo and Hitori

Three days after the battle in Aventon, I parted ways with Rin, General Mirai, and the refugees. Hitori and Saitou had come to inspect Aventon after their departure. Haru, Seiji, a few of the other False Shadows, and I traveled back to Leiko, to the main encampment.

We left in the morning, arriving at the camp in the late evening.

Whatever Hitori's true plans were for Aventon, they involved leaving behind some of the mercenaries and a handful of False Shadows, most likely to comb the town for anything she deemed useful and to ensure no one took the town from her. While we had been preparing the caravan for the refugees, we had taken advantage of the collapsed mine, burying Orin's swords and stores of metal. It would take them some time to find them, if they even bothered to try.

Swinging an axe overhead, I brought it down, splitting a length of wood in two. The bitter memory of Aventon still clouded my mind. The False Shadows had gone their own ways in camp, needing—as I did—time to process what had happened.

Wiping the sweat from my forehead, I began arranging various pieces of wood I had cut, interlocking the notches together to create a bench. It was not much, but it would replace the rotting logs the False Shadows used now. It was the third piece of furniture I had created that day.

It was a small catharsis, but it was better than stewing in my thoughts.

When dusk was close, Hitori and Saitou returned.

Crimson light from the setting sun broke through the thick canopy, casting the camp in a disconsolate atmosphere. I stayed on the edge of the camp, calming my lingering anger toward Hitori. While I knew she had done terrible things before Aventon, witnessing those events firsthand weighed heavily on me.

A Shadow does not condemn,
searching for the truth with unclouded eyes.

To withhold judgement until one understood was to be a Shadow, but after Aventon, it was clear Hitori had her own dark motives for what she did. My sympathy toward her had waned. A part of me wanted to avoid the confrontation, but nothing would be accomplished if we ignored one another.

With a quiet sigh, I approached Hitori's horse.

Bowing to her, I reached out to take the horse's bridle as I straightened, keeping the mare steady. It was something Saitou often did for her.

"I see you're still here," Hitori said mildly.

"I am," I replied with forced politeness. "How are things in Aventon?"

"It's under control."

Restraining a smile, I kept my face emotionless as Hitori dismounted and strode past me, Saitou, as always, a step behind her. I had not meant anything beyond pleasantries. She seemed irritated as I was.

"Lady Hitori, do you have a moment?" I called, catching up to her. "There's something I want to speak to you about."

"What is it?" she asked, exasperation heavy in her voice.

"With your permission, I would like to start training the False Shadows."

Hitori stopped and turned to face me, her eyebrows knit together. Behind her, even Saitou seemed surprised.

I continued. "The Shadows train together daily. It is a way to deepen our understanding of one another as well as a way to keep our skills sharp."

She stared at me. "You want to train the False Shadows?"

"Yes."

She considered for a moment, then nodded. "Do as you like."

"Thank you," I said, bowing slightly.

Her gaze was piercing as she continued to stare at me. Then she tilted her head, the corner of her lip pulling back into a sneer. "If you're doing it in hopes of turning the False Shadows against me, I'm afraid you will be disappointed. They know what I do to those who betray me."

I said nothing, allowing her to believe she had the upper hand.

Hitori had been too absorbed in her own delusions to see what had been done in Aventon. She had not noticed how regret burned in the False Shadows' eyes, nor their hesitation to comply. The False Shadows were beginning to tire of her, and with the growing distrust and anger across Kiriku, it was only a matter of time before people began to rise up.

Hitori waved me off and continued into the forest with Saitou behind her, her footsteps quick and agitated. Even though she was cross, she seemed more open today, more willing to listen.

I could not let the opportunity pass by.

"There's something else," I said.

Hitori continued walking away, ignoring me. She used silence as a means to show her displeasure, but she had not yet commanded Saitou to stop me.

Curious to see where they were going, I kept pace with them. Saitou kept himself between Hitori and me—an obstacle should I try something—though I did not sense any agitation or distrust from him. He seemed to act on duty and routine more than anything, seeing me as only a mild threat.

As we continued walking, the trees in the forest became more twisted and a deep, putrid smell permeated the air as thick as blood. The source seemed to be the trees themselves; their bark openly weeping with sap. Since connecting more deeply with the Skills and becoming more aware of them, the forest seemed more alive than I previously had thought. The impression it gave off was as unpleasant as I remembered it to be, but it was as if the forest had done what it could to adapt, using the gnarls in the branches and the festering sap as a way to soothe the pain it had experienced.

Somehow, the trees had found a way to survive.

I could not help but feel a measure of admiration for their endurance and their desire to live. When I was free from the conflict with Hitori, it would be enjoyable to return to this forest and study it further. The forests in Konro and the Miyota Mountain were ancient and beautiful, full of the Skills and life, but the Kinsaan forest had a different feel to it. Was it because of what had been done here with the Skills that made it the way it was? Or was there something else that had happened?

Was there not beauty in how it was now?

Hitori changed direction, cutting off any further musings as I scrambled over a fallen tree, heading south, toward the sound of a distant stream. We stopped at the edge of the creek, where a small sliver of water ran parallel to the more substantial steam. A small trickle of water flowed through rocks and pebbles, wandering under tree roots and becoming a source for moss and algae to grow. The water looked cloudy, either from the sediments in the rocks or something else. With a curious eye, I watched as Hitori knelt beside the creek. She opened a leather pouch slung around her waist and fanned out a collection of thin silver blades that lacked distinct handles. They were very similar to the ones Rin had made for Finae to play with the Skills in Konro.

Hitori's blades, though, were stained red.

After dropping the silver blades into the water, she acknowledged my presence.

"What is it you want, Phantom?"

"I have a few questions regarding your involvement with the Skills and Vaiyene."

Hitori's attention returned to her daggers. "Ask your questions so I can be rid of you."

She wanted me gone, but—I glanced over my shoulder to find Saitou still apparently unfazed by me—it also seemed she had not given orders to keep me from approaching her.

Did that mean she was more willing to talk with me than she let on?

I crossed over the creek to the other side, being mindful of the rocks slick with algae. Sitting down on the edge of the riverbank, I rested my elbows on my knees and leaned forward, watching Hitori closely.

"There's no reason for you to be so angry," I said. "Other than Saitou and Haru, I am the only one who does not fear and avoid you. We can have a conversation, even as enemies."

Hitori grunted her annoyance.

To the point then.

"Why did you send Skill poisoned grain to Vaiyene?"

"I didn't," Hitori said, picking up one of the daggers from the water.

"The only one who knows about the Skill poisoning is—"

"I never said the False Shadows were not responsible," Hitori said, cutting me off. Her grip tightened around the dagger in her hand. "I find it amusing you believe I have time for such elaborate matters or that I am interested in doing such negligible things. What I meant was *I* was not personally the one who did so. There are others who act against you, both inside the False Shadow group and outside."

She held the dagger tightly in her hands, running her fingers along the dull edge of the knife as her eyes narrowed.

I knew she was cunning, but her anger at my assumptions was real.

As if it had hurt her pride for me to accuse her of such an act.

"Who sent the grain then?"

"One of the False Shadows stole a vial from me. It was part of an ongoing experiment with the Skills to see how they affect the human body. She thought it would be amusing to stir up trouble with you."

"And those outside the False Shadows you mentioned?"

Hitori turned to meet my gaze. "They operate independently, following where my False Shadows have been to take advantage of the villages we weaken." She dipped the dagger into the water and began rubbing the dried blood from the blade. "Saitou knows more about them. I only asked to be informed of the most important details."

Behind Hitori, Saitou kept his attention on the forest as he spoke:

"They are a group of thieves who call themselves 'The Silver Foxes.' They follow the turmoil left behind by raiders and natural disasters, using the commotion to make off with anything valuable." He turned to me, regarding me with mild amusement. "With General Mirai's spy network, I'm surprised you hadn't figured it out."

We had been blinded in our hatred for Hitori.

If they had been imitating the False Shadows and following after them, we would not have second-guessed who they were. This information alone made being here worthwhile.

I leaned forward on my knees. "How was Phantom Kural involved with you?"

It was the piece of the puzzle I had yet to figure out, and the one question that burned inside of me.

"Phantom Kural came to me, the same as you," Hitori said, her voice tense. Agitated. "He had heard a rumor about a strange power and wanted to learn more about it. At first, he seemed excited about the Skills, but the more he learned, the more he withdrew from our experiments, saying it went against his creed and that the Skills were an abomination to this world." Hitori clenched the dagger tightly in her hand, cutting into her own finger. She swallowed; her jaw clenched before her voice became louder. "He sought to destroy my research, threatening me, he—" Hitori stopped abruptly and stood, cocking her head to the side as a flash of rage threatened to break free. "But Phantom Kural forgot one crucial detail before he betrayed my trust."

I held her gaze. "And that was?"

"I asked him for Vaiyene's location when he first approached me." Hitori's eyes narrowed as she lowered her head, a shadow darkening her eyes. "It was done in good faith, an exchange of information on the surface, but the significance of the act was precautionary. I knew your precious Phantom would betray me. Before he even had the chance to act, I smelled it in the air. And even you, Kiriku's beloved 'Phantom who does not kill' will betray me in the end. They all do…" For a brief moment another emotion—sadness?—came over Hitori before her back straightened, and it was gone sooner than I had time to believe it. "I've grown tired of waiting for the inevitable betrayals, becoming more proactive in my dealings of late." Hitori's sneer widened. "Why is it do you think I destroyed Aventon? Do you really believe I expected Aventon to surrender men to me to start a war? Or that I cared about the pathetic amount of ore and iron there? No, the sole reason was to ensure they suffered for sheltering you. It was a statement so that they did not feel emboldened and rise up against me."

I stood, stunned by her sudden change in demeanor.

She had always seemed distant and bitter, but her lust for vengeance now came to the surface. The image I had formed of Hitori shattered. I had been trying to hold on to the hope I could become her ally, but she had broken that hope as if she had spat upon me. Every action had been a careful calculation on her part.

A careful play of power and restraint.

"You are a fool!" she said, throwing the dagger into the river; the blade slid between the pebbles, quivering as it remained upright. "Give up the idea of befriending me before more people are killed by your misplaced kindness."

She met my eyes, unwavering, a storm building within her. Withdrawing a scroll from inside her robes, she threw it at my feet. "Send word to General Mirai and your precious homeland. If you continue to oppose me, Phantom, you'd better be ready to kill me."

Turning, she left in a flurry. Her robes whipped over the underbrush in her rage, tearing where they caught. Saitou kept pace with her heated departure. I stared after her, unmoving as she left me by the creek. My eyes dropped to the letter.

Already, I recognized the red seal of the Phantoms on the scroll.

Bending down to retrieve it, I unrolled it.

To the False Shadow leader,

Kilo is working on his own.
Neither Vaiyene nor its allies condone his actions.

Phantom Lunia

I crumpled the letter in my hand, feeling a reluctance settle around my heart. While it was for the best, Phantom Lunia's statement left a bitter taste in my mouth. One of the Phantoms I had served and trusted for years was so displeased by my actions she had disowned me before our common foe.

It was like salt upon a wound.

Although Lunia and I almost always saw eye to eye, she had always been more cautious than me. More hesitant in her actions and reluctant to take a stand. She would rather dismiss the danger outside our boundaries and live a lie, only confronting trouble if it came directly to Vaiyene.

It was the difference that defined us.

Whether Lunia wanted to believe it or not, Kural had inspired Hitori's wrath and because of it, Vaiyene would always be a target. Before all this was over, Hitori would see Kiriku burn to spite it.

I ripped the letter into pieces, dropping the remains into the river. Staring at the place where Hitori had left, I steeled my resolve and returned my attention to the present. The dynamic had changed between the False Shadow leader and me.

It was a battle of wills. A test to see who could outmaneuver the other.

In the end only one would remain.

Hitori was willing to do whatever it took to remain in power, and I was willing to give up everything to stop her.

part seven

SHENRAE

chapter forty-nine
Return to Vaiyene

Breathing deeply, I looked out from the top of the Miyota Mountains. The scent of Sakura blossoms was heavy on the wind. Rays of light pierced through the clouds and illuminated the valley below. There were deep, black scars from the fire that marred the beautiful landscape, but my heart still soared.

I was home.

Phantom Asdar reined his black stallion in beside me, glancing over at me. "We've been working hard to repair the damage. Most of the people now have a place of their own again, and the new fields are almost ready." He pointed north of Vaiyene. "The land above the Phantoms' house has proven to be the most fertile. We'll begin planting as soon as the danger of frost subsides, although we have already started experimenting with planting a few crops to see if they can survive the cold temperatures."

"That's good to hear," I said, not sure why he was telling me.

"Your brother has been in charge of the fields."

I smiled. So that was what Syrane had been doing. Months had passed since we had last seen one another. Our parents had always planted a small garden beside our house, and Syrane had enjoyed it more than I had. It hadn't occurred to me that he might be drawn to agriculture, but I was happy he seemed to have found something that called to him.

While Syrane had spent his time working the fields, I had been training and learning from one of the Shadows' most important allies, General Mirai's mercenary group. Throughout the winter, my fondness for the general's group had grown. By chance, I had also been able to learn about the Skills from one of the False Shadows—who may or may not still be alive. On our way back to rejoin the general's group after a scouting mission, Akio, Ikaru, and I had run into Hitori. To escape, we had left Ikaru behind. After a few more weeks with the general's group, spring returned, and as promised, when the Miyota Mountain passes were navigable, Phantom Asdar came to escort me back home.

Akio had stayed with the general.

"Has General Mirai sent any messages about that False Shadow?" I asked Phantom Asdar, trying not to be too anxious about any news.

"He hasn't, but I will remind him in my next letter to keep looking."

It was one of my only regrets about coming back to Vaiyene. Akio had promised to keep an eye out for Ikaru as well, but I couldn't shake the feeling I should have done more for him when I'd had the opportunity to do so.

I sighed, missing Akio's light-hearted smile and joking manner.

He would have known what to say to lighten the mood.

Phantom Asdar's stallion snorted as he passed by me, and I pushed away my reminiscing. My own stallion, Greymoon, followed eagerly behind his sire. It had taken us quite some time to make it back to Vaiyene, but the horses seemed to still be in high spirits. Nightwind picked up speed, disappearing behind a dense cluster of trees. As Greymoon's ears flicked this way and that to catch the murmurs on the wind, I reined in his excitement. Patting his neck, I cooed to him. "Patience."

We passed the clearing of trees, and Greymoon's head lifted. Villagers stood on both sides of the road. They cheered and waved to me, their delight overwhelming as I drew closer.

"Welcome home, Shenrae!"

"You've returned!"

"We're happy you're safe!"

Standing in front of those gathered was Asdar. He had dismounted and now held Nightwind's reins lightly. He bowed at the waist with his arm across his chest, and when he straightened, a rare smile was upon his face.

"Welcome home, Shenrae," he said.

My eyes brimmed with tears, and I slid off Greymoon. I was about to return the bow when Syrane and Torey ran from the crowd. Torey threw her arms around me and squeezed me hard, choking off my breath.

My throat constricted with emotion.

I hadn't realized how much I'd missed her.

Grabbing Torey's arm, I pried her off.

Phantom Asdar raised his voice over the noise. "I expect you at Shadow training tomorrow. Early, at our usual time. We'll see how well the general's men have taught you."

"I'll be there," I said, taking a deep breath as Torey released me.

Asdar led his stallion away. A child came running up to him, and he passed the reins off to the boy, placing a hand on the child's head. A few moments later, the villagers disbanded and headed off in different directions.

It hardly seemed possible they had gathered for me.

I wasn't even a Shadow yet.

Syrane stepped forward, seemingly self-conscious or maybe embarrassed as he approached. He gave me a quick hug before he stepped back.

"Did you miss me?"

I laughed. "Of course."

"I was hoping you would return in time for the festival!" Torey blurted out, her eyes already aglow with excitement. "I worried you wouldn't make it. Phantom Lunia insisted we hold the festival, even though there's still a lot to do with restorations."

"I wouldn't miss it," I said with a grin. Since becoming friends with Torey, Syrane and I had never missed a festival with her. Even the year when I became ill, Syrane and Torey had come to spend the night with me, bringing sweets and pinwheels to cheer me up.

"We've made a lot of good progress rebuilding the village," Syrane said as we began to follow the path that led to the Phantoms' house and stables. "It's taken a while, but we've finally managed to rebuild enough to move the people out of the Phantoms' house."

The wood of the new buildings stood out against the trees and rocks of Vaiyene's forest. Many of the old houses had been weathered by the elements, with moss and vines growing over the structures to obscure them.

"So, how was it?" Syrane asked.

I raised my eyebrows at the question, taking longer than I should have to realize what he was referring to—the general and his men.

"It was a good experience," I said.

"See! I told you it would be," Torey said, turning on her heels and walking backward. "Lunia has been keeping the Shadows busy with the preparations for the town's survival. She says it's important for the Shadows to be more involved in the village itself."

Only half-listening to her, my interest drifted to the burned trees and the soot that led north. It was where our parents' house had been.

Nothing seemed to be growing there yet.

"How was it really?" Syrane asked, letting Torey walk ahead. She continued to mumble about festival preparations, pointing at different places with different ideas for decorations and foods.

I thought about telling him about the False Shadows and the Skills, but a part of me wanted to enjoy this moment a while longer.

"I trained with a bunch of mercenaries, and…" I said, puffing up my chest to look fierce, "I can hold my own now in a fight."

Syrane raised his eyebrows, a grin returning to his face. "Oh? I guess we'll find out tomorrow, then, won't we?"

I laughed, relaxing my chest. "Do you have some time?"

Whenever our parents came back from Shadow missions, they always made time to do something with Syrane and me. Even on nights when they came back long after dark, they would always wake us up to spend time with us.

Syrane's gaze turned north, to the fields.

"I'll cover for you," Torey said, finally realizing we had not been listening to her. She grinned from ear to ear and pushed us both forward with her hands. "No one wants to deal with you sulking because you were stuck working."

A smile crept across my face. "Thanks."

"Where to?" Syrane asked.

"The gardens?"

We settled into a quiet companionship as we walked down to the river and into the bamboo grove. Tall stalks grew around a large pond, standing like sentinels. On the edge of the pond was a cut piece of bamboo being filled with water at the end of a long row of bamboo chutes. Once full, it tilted over, emptying the water into the pond with a hollow *thunk*. Spanning the river, a wooden bridge led to the Phantoms' gardens. On the opposite side, cherry blossom trees were planted in a row, the flowers of which were in full bloom. They created a cloud of pink and white against the rich green backdrop of the Phantoms' garden and the mountain peaks.

We slowed in the middle of the bridge. Syrane relaxed against the railing, and I leaned forward to look at the creek below. Pink petals floated down from the trees, landing in water. There were so many blossoms that piles of flowers collected at the sides of the stream.

I had missed this.

Keeping my gaze on the water, I laid my head down on my arms to watch the petals float by. "How have you been?"

When he didn't answer, I glanced up, finding Syrane staring off into the gardens.

"Syrane?"

He sighed. "It's been different. Not because of your absence. I did miss you, but…" He hesitated before continuing. "Being a Shadow is not what I thought it would be."

Though his words were unexpected, I tried not to seem too surprised. Did Syrane not like being a Shadow? Back when we had both asked to be sponsored, he was the one most excited about it.

"You always seemed to enjoy sparring and training," I said.

Syrane shrugged. "It's something to do. With the preparations for rebuilding Vaiyene, Phantom Lunia has been trying to keep the Shadows busy with other matters. We've made good progress with replanting the orchards and rebuilding the houses, but it never seems to be enough. No matter how long we work, it seems things never go as planned."

I raised my eyebrows.

"Disease killed off a quarter of the trees we planted. It dampened people's spirits. We worked hard to keep the saplings alive through the winter, but for some reason, they contracted a disease and died off a few weeks back."

"But the fields are ready to be planted soon, right?"

"They should be, although we'll have to wait for most of the vegetables. The ground is too cold at night, but we're planning on starting the ones that can withstand the temperatures in a few days." He turned around and leaned on the railing beside me, gazing down at the waters. "We're trying to make sure we're not rushing things. We can't afford to have the harvest jeopardized."

A smile crept across my face.

Syrane seemed to be enjoying some aspects of his Shadow duties.

When he saw my expression, his eyes narrowed slightly. "What is it?"

"Nothing." I shrugged. "It's nice here in the gardens is all. I'm glad the False Shadows didn't ruin it when they came."

A pang of sadness crept over me.

Spring had been our mother's favorite season.

This was the first year she would not get to see the Sakura trees bloom. Our father had always picked her the first wildflowers he saw too. Now that I was back in Vaiyene, the sadness of losing my parents had returned. It had been easier to not think about them when I wasn't here.

Sighing, I laid my head back down on my arms. A pink petal fell from the tree closest to us, floating in the air for a while before it landed on the calm waters, sending ripples across the surface.

"Do you miss them any less?" I asked.

"No." Syrane's voice was quiet.

I raised my head and stood back, suddenly not wanting to talk about our parents anymore. "Will you show me the new gardens you've started?"

Syrane's eyebrows rose. "Sure. I didn't know you would be interested."

I grinned, smothering the feelings of loss as best I could.

"I want to hear all about it."

The first genuine smile I had seen today appeared on Syrane's face, and inside, a part of me sighed in relief. While I was gone, something had happened. Something about Syrane was different. Although, my own heart had been heavy since returning, so it was hard to tell if I was merely tired and worrying about something that was not there.

We left the Phantom's garden, heading toward the edge of the valley and higher into the mountains. The old fields were on the other side of the village. I thought about asking to go back to the old areas, to see the damage for myself, but I knew it would do nothing but upset me.

Following the curve of the mountain, Syrane led me up a new trail. The trees were thick, and without knowing the fields were ahead, I would not have known to look here.

Had that been intentional?

Syrane pushed back a low branch, holding it for me while I passed him. He watched me closely, as if nervous, but he didn't need to worry about my reaction. Cut into the mountains were plots of various sizes. The dirt was plowed in rows, with stones decoratively marking the edges. It reminded me of the way they marked off different sections of rice paddies.

"We spent a few weeks separating the plots into different areas. The plants that grow well together will be planted in the same plot, taking advantage of the space we have. It was one of our goals to maximize our time and effort by researching ways to produce more effectively."

I nodded, admiring Syrane's dedication. "You've done a good job."

My eyes were drawn to the stones. Something about the arrangements of rocks reminded me of Syrane—a memory of our childhood. When we were younger, we had often played in the rivers around the village. Syrane liked to stack and arrange pillars of rocks for fun. He had the utmost patience in finding the balancing point. While these stones were not set upon one another as they had been in the river, their arrangement seemed balanced somehow, as if he had placed a part of himself into their design.

"It's nothing too special…" Syrane said, moving on to the next plot.

"It's wonderful," I said, cutting him off before he could dismiss it. "Is it weird it reminds me of you?"

He laughed. "How?"

"That's because Syrane designed the entire area," someone shouted from above us.

Squinting, I raised my hand to block the sun as I looked up.

A man jumped down from one of the higher garden plots, landing lightly on his feet. When he stood up, he gazed over fondly at Syrane. His short hair was a light brown color, but in the sun, it seemed to have an almost golden tone to it against his pale skin. He was slightly taller than Syrane, with a warm and bright smile. The sleeves of his kimono were tied at the waist. Typically, the Shadows wore earthy tones, but he wore a radiant white robe that suited his appearance. He was one of the older Shadows, and if I remembered correctly his name was Kai. I had seen him around during Shadow training, helping Phantom Asdar set up for drills.

"It's good to see you're back safely, Shenrae," Kai said, bowing slightly at the waist. "Syrane has missed you a great deal. He's been keeping himself busy though. We just finished breaking ground on the newest area of the gardens where the more delicate plants will be growing." He glanced over at Syrane. "I had Mei help me with tilling the ground, so all you'll need to do is adjust the soil to the plants' liking."

Syrane nodded. "Thanks. I'll make sure to get to it before the rain comes today."

"Anytime," Kai said with a grin. "If you need anything else, let me know. I'm always happy to help."

Kai's gaze drifted up toward the mountain where another person stood, her white hair tousled from the breeze. When she saw me looking in her direction, she raised her hand and waved.

Bowing his head, Kai turned to leave. "Mei and I said we'd help Phantom Asdar with drills this afternoon, so we'll see you both later."

Syrane nodded, then hunched down near the perimeter of the plot we stood in, adjusting one of the rocks.

I glanced up at the different levels of the garden, up to where Mei and Kai had been. "Since we still have some time, I can help you with preparing the soil."

Syrane held his hands steady and then removed them when the rock fell into position. He stood, looking up at the sky. "Sure, if you don't mind. It'd be better to get it in before the rain. That way, it'll soak into the ground."

For the rest of the afternoon, I helped Syrane pour and mix different soils together, crushing up eggshells and dead plant matter into the loose dirt. When the sun began to set, he showed me around the newly constructed areas in Vaiyene, stopping before a wooden building that safeguarded the plants he had started from seed. Inside the building were saplings he had separated from the shoots of an older tree and grafted onto a different root system.

As he showed me around, Syrane beamed. His pride in his work was obvious in the care and attention he had shown each plant. Somehow, his enthusiasm made me feel better, reminding me there were still things precious to me here.

I inhaled and let out a long breath.

It was good to be back home.

chapter fifty
Shadow Training

Phantom Asdar stood with his arms crossed over his chest, leaning against a tree. His eyes were fixed on the rising sun, and his breath was visible in the frigid air. After spending the winter months at lower elevations where it had been warmer, the brisk morning came as a shock to me.

Shivering, I headed toward him.

Upon spotting me, Asdar uncrossed his arms and walked into the center of the arena. At his hip, he wore two swords. There was also an axe resting in a holster at his back. He picked up a wooden staff lying on the ground, moving his hands across the surface. Deftly, he twirled the staff from one hand to the other, then rolled his shoulders and stretched out his neck.

I began my own warm-ups, feeling a strange sense of normalcy fall over me. Phantom Asdar had been the first one to teach me how to use the staff. It felt as if I had gone back to that time, like nothing had happened with the general's men and Akio, like I had been in some strange dream.

I looked down at the staff in my hands.

It had been a gift from Akio.

"What did you think of the general and his men?" Phantom Asdar asked. He rested one end of the staff in the dirt, his eyes keen on me.

Shaking off the strange feelings, I held my staff loosely in my hands.

"I miss them," I said, surprised at how much it hurt to admit.

Being with the general had opened my eyes to how others trained and how they thought, and it had made me realize there was more to the world than just Vaiyene. There were others out there who were trying their best to survive.

People like Ikaru who could use the Shadows' help.

It was something I would never have understood without leaving Vaiyene.

I knew now that had been Asdar's intention.

"Ready?" Phantom Asdar asked.

I nodded.

Asdar held his staff to the side and bowed to me. I did the same, feeling more at peace than I ever had facing my Phantom. He had been the one to sponsor me, believing in my desire to become a Shadow. Shortly after Shadow training, I had asked him to help me learn how to fight, as it was not an ability that came naturally to me. We had trained in the early mornings, before the other Shadows, and by the time I'd left to join the mercenaries, I at least knew how to use the basic strikes.

This would be my first time to show Asdar the flow Akio had taught me.

Excited, I shifted my staff, holding it securely with both hands. Phantom Asdar held his own weapon loosely in his hands, his feet spread apart in a defensive stance. His eyes were narrowed as they analyzed my form, looking for any weaknesses. I crossed the distance between us, bringing my staff up diagonally, aiming at Asdar's left leg. Without hesitation, he moved his weapon down, blocking it as I shifted the other end of the staff in the opposite direction, bringing it toward his head. This he blocked as well, but instead of retreating, I stepped closer to him, stepping to his side and bringing the staff around in one fluid movement.

Nimbly, he shifted to block me.

"I see you've learned how to use the staff beyond two strikes," he said, a note of approval in his voice.

Stepping back, he began a series of diagonal moves and swings. I blocked each, keeping my eye focused on his hands and feet rather than the ends of the staff. Akio had taught me how to focus on the direction and possible lines of attack to anticipate an opponent's movement rather than be distracted by the movement of the staff.

After testing my defenses, Phantom Asdar lowered his weapon. He lifted his head and nodded, his eyes becoming less calculating. "You should be proud of how far you've come, Shenrae. Your abilities have improved beyond what I had expected given the short time you had to train. He held his staff out to the side and bowed, keeping the position for a few moments.

"Forgive me for doubting your drive."

My eyes widened, surprised he would apologize. "I was uncertain of it myself. If not for the men in the general's ranks, I'm not sure I would have learned to enjoy it."

Phantom Asdar straightened. His usual calculating eyes had softened. It almost seemed as if he were content—happy even?—to be speaking with me. "There's something else I'd rather spend time on this morning than testing your abilities," he said, crossing the arena and heading to the cliffs where a large waterfall hid the rugged trail. We were close enough to the water for a slight mist to waft over to the large boulders and rocks in our path. Phantom Asdar pressed himself against the walls of the rock, following the edge of the mountain until it widened.

"How much did you learn about the Skills?" he asked.

His question surprised me. I was unsure of his reasoning for asking. The roar of the water made it hard to hear, so I stepped closer to him, feeling as if the location had been strategically chosen.

"I know a little about how to use them."

"Good. I was hoping you did. It's what I want to talk to you about." Leaning back against the wall, he crossed his arms. "As you know, when Kilo left, it was Phantom Lunia who was the most anxious about it. I've been sharing what Kilo and the general have been sending me with her, but it's reached a point to where she no longer wishes to speak about anything outside of Vaiyene. As far as Lunia is concerned, Kilo no longer has a place here. She sent a letter to Hitori saying as much."

My throat became dry. "She did what?"

Asdar raised his hand to silence any further questions. "Don't worry. When Kilo is ready to return, he will be able to take his place as a Phantom. Her intentions were to protect Vaiyene in the eyes of our allies. Once they find out he has gone not to kill Hitori but to try and befriend her, there will be misgivings from many of them. My intention in telling you this is not to upset you, only to inform you and ask you to not speak too openly about the Skills to the other Shadows." He paused, thinking for a moment. "At least, for a time. Kilo may be able to calm Lunia's nerves in regard to them. I have done my best, but if there's anyone who can calm the Shadows' anxiety, it is him."

"Aren't you worried?"

He appeared calm. Unperturbed. I found it hard to believe he was not more upset about the matter. After all, it was Phantom Lunia who had forced Kilo to leave.

Asdar smiled slightly. "No. I saw what Kilo could do when he was younger. It's because of him that the Shadows have such strong camaraderie. He was able to unify them, bringing them together to rally around a shared purpose. I have never met someone who has the same amount of patience and empathy as he does. There is little doubt in my mind that Kilo will find a way to bring a peaceful end to both Hitori and the False Shadows. Somehow, he always finds a way."

There was a sort of pride as Asdar talked about Kilo.

"You always seem so moody around Kilo," I said, trying to figure it out. "I find it hard to imagine you were friends when you were younger and that you look up to him."

Laughing, Asdar pushed himself off from the wall to stand at the edge of the cliff. He glanced up at the sun briefly before turning back to me with a wide smile. "Unfortunately, there's not enough time to tell that story before training begins." Down in the arena below, a few of the Shadows had begun to gather.

"We should head back," Asdar said.

I tried to hide my disappointment. Phantom Asdar was always reserved when it came to personal matters, but it was hard to be upset when he seemed to be in such good spirits. His calmness in relating the news about Kilo made me feel better, and I was happy he had trusted me with the information.

By the time we returned to the arena, all of the Shadows and those in training were warming up and stretching. Daily practice began when the sun had risen and, on most days, didn't end until around midday.

The cheerful mood Asdar had been in faded as he walked down the center of the arena, assuming his usual weapons-master demeanor.

"Line up!" he shouted, laying his staff off to one side.

Across from me, one of the other Shadows in training—a boy about my height with freckles spanning across his face—readied his wooden sword. A scowl rested upon his face. It was Yu. He was friends with one of the Shadows who had been expelled shortly after we all began training. He drew his sword, and I held my staff in front of me, feeling uneasy as we waited for the signal.

"Begin!"

Twirling my staff, I jammed the end into my opponent's legs. Yu sucked in a breath as the wood connected. Instead of pulling back, he swung at me with teeth bared. I blocked the swing of his sword and nailed him in the chest, restraining the power behind my attack.

We disengaged, each of us stepping back as Phantom Asdar walked by.

Yu narrowed his eyes, holding his sword so tightly his knuckles turned white. Each breath he took seemed punctuated with rage. He kept his eyes locked on me. His hair was slicked across his head with sweat. Suddenly, Yu sprang forward, beginning a flurry of movements, slashing with his wooden sword. Moving back, I dodged the end of his sword, gliding out of his reach. When he raised his sword, I moved into his attack, sliding my hand across my wooden staff to brace for the impact.

Before the weapons collided, Asdar's arm shot out, and he grabbed the wooden sword to keep Yu from executing his attack. Phantom Asdar's eyes narrowed. Yu tried to withdraw his wooden sword, but Asdar didn't let go of it.

"Grudges from the past have no place here."

Yu's lips pressed into a thin line.

Asdar let go of the sword. "Take a walk in the gardens to clear your mind. Losing control of your emotions makes you weak on the battlefield."

Yu stiffened and gave Asdar a short bow, his jaw becoming tight. When he turned to leave, he had schooled his emotions enough to not glare at me, though his back was rigid as he strode away. It seemed he still had not gotten over Meyori's expulsion from the Shadows, and he still blamed me, even though the fault was not mine. Meyori had taken advantage of my weak self-confidence, seeing me as unworthy of becoming a Shadow. So much so that she had gone out of her way to make her annoyance of me known—doing what she could to hurt me both physically and emotionally in order to try and get me to quit. Because of that, Phantom Asdar had expelled her from the Shadows.

I relaxed my grip on my staff, noticing Asdar studying me. The other Shadows continued to spar with one another, and I was left without a partner.

"They still don't like me," I said.

Phantom Asdar laughed. "If I remember correctly, not too long ago, you didn't like me."

I opened my mouth to protest but knew Asdar was only teasing me. When I first met him, he had intimidated me, but over time, I'd begun to understand his bluntness and rough manner, and when he'd started training me one-on-one, I'd developed a deep sense of respect for him.

"Give them time," he said, watching the Shadows sparring. "Many of them are envious because I chose you to train with the general. Being strong comes at a price. Often, that breeds envy and bitterness among peers. It's something you'll have to endure."

Asdar drew one of his swords and pointed it at me, becoming my opponent in Yu's place. We sparred for some time, growing familiar with one another's movements again as we fell into a sort of routine in our match. I came away with bruises and sore muscles, but I felt better because of it. After our intense bout was complete, I blew out a long breath, trying to return my heart rate to normal. Phantom Asdar lowered his sword, wiping a bead of sweat from his forehead with his arm.

He turned his attention away from me, sliding his sword into this belt.

"Kai, Mei, Genshi!" Asdar shouted, motioning for them to follow him. "Grab the straw mats and set up for the drill."

I relaxed my staff at my side as Torey and Syrane came over to me.

"You've gotten so much better, Shenrae!" Torey said.

"I learned a lot from the general and his men," I said, my breathing returning to normal. "I'm grateful for what they and Phantom Asdar were able to teach me."

Syrane nodded absently. "You've definitely improved."

"Thanks," I said, feeling as if his heart was not in his words.

Syrane handed me a sheathed sword before going to line up with the others behind the straw mats. Looking over at Torey, I slipped the sword into the sash tied around my waist.

"Is he always…" I gestured toward Syrane's back.

"He gets like this sometimes. He's one of the best with the sword in terms of skill, but some days"—Torey shrugged—"it seems he'd rather be somewhere else."

I frowned.

Yesterday he had mentioned that being a Shadow wasn't what he had expected it to be, but he had also said he was excited to see how my skills had improved. Today, however, he seemed distant, as if he didn't care about being here.

Following Torey, I stood behind the others gathering in a circle. The oldest Shadows paid little attention to Torey and me, their focus fixed on the rolled mats before them. The Shadows still in training watched me warily. Yu had returned from the gardens. He turned away at my approach, moving to the opposite side of those gathered to get away from me.

Something stirred inside me then.

Not anger to prove myself, but annoyance at their petty judgement. Leaving Vaiyene had not been my choice. They had no right to be bitter about it. Asdar had commanded me to go— as my Phantom. I'd been thrust into a situation I had not wanted, and I'd made the best of the circumstances.

Leaving the line of those waiting, I approached one set of the straw mats in the center. One of the older Shadows made to stop me, but Asdar held out his hand.

"Let her be."

Drawing in a deep breath, I unsheathed the sword Syrane had given me and dropped the sheath onto the ground. Shifting the sword in my hands, I held the hilt firmly but without locking my fingers, thinking of the weapon as more of an extension of my arm than something I needed to control. With another deep breath, I slid my right foot forward and sliced diagonally across the rolled-up mat, following it with successive slashes. The mat split cleanly into three pieces, the chunks hitting the ground with soft thuds.

The Shadows in the arena were suddenly quiet.

All eyes were on me.

Bending down to pick up the sheath, I froze as someone shouted in the distance.

"False Shadows!" a young boy yelled at the edge of the arena. Sheathing the blade, I retrieved my staff.

The boy ran toward us, breathing heavily, his words coming out in gasps.

"They're…almost…at the…caves!"

Asdar stiffened, sweeping all of us in his gaze. "We move! Now! Bring your weapons and your resolve."

Not waiting a moment more, Phantom Asdar ran into the forest. There was a slight hesitation from the Shadows, a collective breath before we raced after him. Asdar headed north, toward the Reikon Tree, meaning to take the path to the mountain overlooking Vaiyene. Syrane and Torey ran beside me, the others not far behind.

Asdar stopped momentarily at the top of the trail and waited for everyone to group up. "Kai, Shenrae, Mei, Daisuke, Syrane, Torey, come with me. The rest of you, head to the edge of town and spread out. You will be the last line of defense between the False Shadows and Vaiyene. Shoji, you're in charge."

"Understood, Phantom!"

"And, Shoji," Phantom Asdar said, a grim resolve deepening his voice. "They cannot step foot in Vaiyene. Do whatever you must."

Shoji nodded, turning to leave. "Let's move!"

From what I knew about those in my group, Asdar had chosen the ones who were most skilled in combat to be on the front line.

Butterflies rose in my stomach, but I steeled my resolve. Working with the general and Akio had prepared me for this.

I could do this.

Syrane ran a few steps ahead of me, his brow furrowed and his lips pressed tightly together. With white knuckles, he held onto the sword he had been using in practice. During the last and only Shadow mission he had been on, he had frozen.

Did it still worry him?

"It'll be fine, Syrane," I said, giving him a reassuring smile.

He glanced over at me and nodded shortly.

Phantom Asdar led us up to the upper trail, one of the steepest in Vaiyene. It was a challenging climb, but it was the shortest path to the cave. When the entrance was in sight, he held up his hand for us to stop.

"Are all of you familiar with the cave system?"

We nodded.

"Good," he said, drawing the axe from his back before he continued with his orders. "Break into pairs and scout out the tunnels. We need to stop the False Shadows from entering Vaiyene. Even though we have a second line of attack, don't rely on it. We stop them here." He glanced over at me. "Shenrae, you're with me. Syrane and Torey, the two of you pair up with the older Shadows."

I let out a breath. It eased my mind a little knowing Syrane and Torey would be with someone who was experienced and not with each other.

Glancing at Syrane one last time, I followed Asdar into the caves. A rush of wind howled through the tunnels, creating an eerie wail that caused hairs to stand up on the back of my neck. An old legend said the howl was from a child lost within the caves. Syrane and I had ventured into the caves when we were young, as had most of the youth in Vaiyene. While no one had ever seen the missing child, as it was likely made up, walking into the caves still gave me chills.

I crept after Phantom Asdar, moving soundlessly, taking note of the other groups shifting throughout the caverns as we moved deeper into the caves. Even with Phantom Asdar beside me, my breath was constricted. Not knowing what lay ahead or how many people we would be up against made my palms cold and clammy. From within my robes, I dug out a small bag of chalk and rubbed it between my hands. It was a trick Akio had taught me to keep my hands from slipping on my staff.

Phantom Asdar shifted beside me. "You're ready for this."

I nodded.

A clank of metal halted our movement. It had a different type of ring and tone than a sword would. I furrowed my brow, and Phantom Asdar nudged me with his elbow, pointing at a crystal wedged into the ceiling of the cavern. A figure stepped forward, reflected in the crystal shard; at least one person had entered the cavern. Asdar kept his gaze fixed on the reflection, watching and allowing one, two, then three men into the caverns.

Holding my breath, I remained still, waiting for Asdar to make the first move.

The other Shadows did the same.

A metal-plated foot dislodged some rocks next to our hiding place. The plates on their foot shifted as the person continued into the cave. If not for Phantom Asdar's stoic demeanor and his air of confidence, it would have been hard to remain immobile with my growing nerves.

I kept control of my instincts through sheer willpower.

Breathe in, breathe out.

Breathe in, breathe out.

Wait.

Phantom Asdar glanced back at me. "They're mercenaries. Stay close."

He left our hiding place and stayed low, removing his axe from its sheath as he trailed one of the mercenaries. There was a moment's pause as Asdar nodded to one of the Shadows near us—Mei—before he struck the man's exposed neck with the handle of his axe. The mercenary dropped, and Mei caught the man and lowered him to the ground.

There was no sound except for a slight *ting* of metal.

None of the other mercenaries appeared to have noticed.

Asdar and Mei tracked another mercenary, and I moved between piles of rocks to stay close to them. In the shadows, the others did the same. Mei slipped her hand into a satchel tied to her thigh, and a slight burst of powder left her hand. With a serene grace, Asdar hooked the mercenary's neck with the axe's handle, and Mei pressed one hand over the man's mouth as he drew in a breath to warn the others. The man sagged in Asdar's grasp, and he lowered him to the ground.

Poison.

We had learned about the effects of some of the herbs the Shadows used. Mei, it seemed, was a skilled user of them. Likely this one was something that paralyzed or sedated them, as the Shadows used no poisons that had a deadly effect. At least, not intentionally. It was of course possible for a person to die, if too much was used on the victim or they had a bad reaction.

A streak of black shot toward me from the right. Metal glinted in the darkness, and I raised my staff, blocking the attack.

My hands were spread out across my staff, and I sprang forward from my crouched position, using the momentum to push back against the mercenary. Shifting into an offensive stance, I waited, wanting to take advantage of when the mercenary repositioned himself. Before I could, however, another mercenary charged at me. Phantom Asdar rammed into the second man, knocking him to the ground.

His head hit a stalagmite, blood oozing out.

"Shenrae, move!"

Asdar's words jostled me from my momentary daze. The first mercenary I had engaged with came at me, his sword slashing out. Scurrying back, I pressed myself against a pillar of rocks as Phantom Asdar shielded me with his axe. He pushed the man back, overwhelming him with his strength before disengaging. Asdar sliced through the thin gap in the man's armor at the neck, leaving behind a shallow cut.

I fell into place at Phantom Asdar's back, my staff raised and my eyes sharp. Asdar let his axe dip toward the ground. There was the slightest discoloration on the tip where blood slid off the blade.

He had poisoned the edge.

The first mercenary Mei had poisoned lay on the ground, his companions not giving him a second glance as they continued inside the cave. Instead of showing concern for their own, they turned their anger on us.

Five mercenaries closed in, surrounding us with swords drawn.

Phantom Asdar attacked first, using his swiftness to engage the three opponents facing him. I hesitated, waiting for the two on my side to make the first move. They exchanged glances, sizing me up before they attacked together.

Sneers curdled their faces.

If they thought to underestimate me, they were mistaken.

The man on my right raised his sword over his head, exposing his torso. The other slashed out in an arc—a swift attack. Holding my staff steady, I braced one of my hands on the back of it to block the attack. Then, using the other end of my staff, I jammed it into the second man's rib cage.

Phantom Asdar moved behind me, swinging his axe to engage with one of the mercenaries. He paused and drew back. "Move to the entrance with the others," he said, drawing out a small pouch from within his robes and raising the scarf from his neck. "Hold your breath until the clean air blows in."

Dutifully, I obeyed, placing my own scarf over my mouth and nose. I glanced back to see Asdar toss the satchel into the air. With a quick slice, he split the bag open, releasing a plume of poison into the air. Sheathing my sword, I maneuvered myself back to the entrance of the cave. On the other side of the entrance, hidden in the darkness, Mei noticed me and held up her hand, acknowledging my presence. Behind her, another Shadow lay in wait, though I could not see who it was.

A single mercenary squinted as he entered. He kept his head high, mistakenly assuming the enemy would not be crouched low. I now understood why Asdar had concealed himself in the darkness and waited to attack when he did. After entering the cave, there was a brief moment when the mercenaries were blind as their eyes adjusted to the darkness.

Mei shot out from her hiding place. She swung the blunt edge of her sword into the mercenary's jaw. Bone cracked as the sword connected, and the man crumpled to the ground. I darted forward into the light to help Mei pull the unconscious man into the shadows.

We waited for the next one.

A shout came from outside, and more mercenaries stormed the caverns.

"Fall back!" Asdar shouted, charging the group. He swung his axe in a broad arc, using it the same way I used my staff to keep enemies at bay.

The Shadows shuffled around, positioning themselves to make use of the terrain.

The mercenaries hesitated before Phantom Asdar.

"Go find Syrane and Torey," Asdar said. "They were headed to the other side of the tunnels." He took one of the swords from his belt and handed it to me. "You'll know if you need to use it." I closed my fingers around the sheath, feeling the weight of steel in my hands.

"We'll take care of this group," Asdar said, throwing his right leg forward and swinging his axe up in a diagonal strike.

Nodding, I slipped the sword into the sash around my waist and ran back into the tunnels. The air still shimmered with the poison. Even the surfaces of the rocks seemed to have a different sort of shine to them. Crouching close to the ground, I dragged my staff across the cave floor, unsettling the powder there. When I was sure it was coated in a reasonable amount, I continued through the cave system, taking the most direct way that led into Vaiyene.

The clash of metal echoed behind me, but the farther away from the entrance I traveled, the quieter it became, which meant the mercenaries had not made it this far.

But where were Syrane and Torey and the Shadows who had gone with them?

Peering into the tunnels and around the towering stalagmites, I walked quietly, ready should anything be waiting. Water dripped in a steady rhythm from the stalactites hanging down from the ceiling. Pausing, I closed my eyes and listened to the sounds of the cave. The faint sounds of fighting echoed across the walls but seemed to be coming from the tunnel behind me.

I stayed still and quiet, and after a few moments, I honed in on the shifting of metal. Opening my eyes, I pressed myself against the wall of the cave and began to circle the area, looking for any trace of the mercenaries or Shadows. In front of one of the tunnels, drops of blood dotted the ground.

It was the tunnel leading to Vaiyene.

My heart beat faster in my chest.

Had they reached the village?

I rested my hand on the wall, leaning around the corner to make sure it was clear. My fingers brushed against something sticky and wet, and I withdrew my hand, startled. After wiping away the blood onto my robe, I wrapped both my hands around my staff. A shadow passed across the tunnel opening, backlit by the light coming in from the cave's opening.

Metal shone in the sunlight.

A mercenary.

I rushed after the figure, mimicking Asdar and Mei's earlier stance. When the mercenary paused at the edge of the cave, I yelled, "Hey!" He turned around, and I jammed the end of the staff against the side of his face. The mercenary held his nose and groaned, momentarily stunned before he rounded on me, drawing his sword. I took a step back, holding my staff steady to block his swing. His nose was broken and bloody, and his lips curled back into a grimace.

"You piece of…!"

Judging by the bruise on his face, it appeared one of the other Shadows had tried to bring him down and failed. Which meant he was hardier than the other mercenaries we had faced. I hoped the poison on the end of the staff would be enough to slow him down.

I waited, holding my weapon across my chest.

Out of the corner of my eye, I noticed a figure clad in dark clothing—one of the Shadows—was lying against the cavern wall, a dark patch of blood staining the rocks behind them. I moved toward the Shadow, keeping the tall mercenary in view.

When I drew closer, I saw that it was Kai.

"Syrane and Torey fled back into the tunnels," Kai said as he coughed. "I tried to protect them, but we were separated."

He had a cut across his forehead, but his eyes focused on me without drifting. He pushed against a stalagmite pinning his leg to the ground. Somehow, the rock formation had been broken off at the base.

Behind me, the mercenary fell to his knees, seemingly dazed.

The poison was working.

"Help me lift this, would you?" Kai said.

I laid my poisoned staff down on the ground and slipped Asdar's sword out from my sash. Wedging it into the space between the stalagmite and the earth, I stepped onto the hilt, pushing the stalagmite up.

"Just a little more," he said, straining.

As I pushed my full weight against the blade, the rock shifted, and Kai pulled his leg free. Slowly, I stepped off the sword and wrestled it out from the rock. Kai braced himself against the cavern wall as he stood up. Next to him was a patch of blood and a body slumped on the ground.

"Don't worry. The blood isn't mine," Kai said. He smiled when I looked at him, then placed his hand on my shoulder. "You did well, Shenrae."

I returned his smile.

"Ijijou headed after Torey and Syrane, but I don't know if she found them."

"Thank you," I said, giving him a small bow.

The tall mercenary remained still, almost as if he had fallen asleep on his knees. From the main tunnel, a group of three enemies came toward us. Skirting the edge of the wall, I hesitated. If I stayed in the shadows, I might be able to sneak past them.

Kai nodded. "Go. I can take care of them."

I didn't want to leave him to fight the mercenaries alone, but someone needed to make sure Syrane and Torey were okay.

"I'm sorry," I said, stepping over the armored mercenary on the ground and racing through the tunnels.

All thoughts of stealth left me as the weight of panic gripped my heart. When I came to the center of the cave system, I turned to the left, where the tunnels began to shrink. Darkness slowed my progress, and I hesitated to ignite my light canteen, evaluating the cost of doing so against the need for stealth. A few rays of light reflected naturally from the crystals in the walls, so I decided against it, progressing slowly by using the wall of the cavern as a guide. An archway had formed in this tunnel, connecting the stalagmites to the stalactites. I crawled under it, being mindful of any sharp edges.

From ahead I heard movement.

Ducking under another archway, I followed the tunnel into darkness. Fire swayed ahead, illuminating an armored figure.

Shadows flickered across the cave's surface, making it hard to discern the position of the mercenary. I kept close to the wall, slipping out of sight and staying well out of sight. Something grabbed at my leg, and I jumped, pointing my sword…at Ijijou.

We both froze.

I let out a long breath, my heart pounding in my chest.

Ijijou sat against the cavern wall, her leg turned at an awkward angle. She grimaced and nodded toward the mercenary. In a low voice she said, "She's weak on her dominant side. Syrane and Torey headed back into the main tunnels. If you go back the way you came, you should be able to meet them from behind."

"What about you?"

Ijijou became serious, a shadow coming over her eyes as she lowered her head. "It would bring the Shadows shame if Syrane and Torey died before they became full Shadows. Besides"—she splayed out the daggers in her left hand and smiled—"even with a broken leg, I can protect myself."

The Shadows cared more for those under their protection than they did their own lives. But without the older and more experienced Shadows, we would become weakened as a group. We looked up to them, and if they were going to sacrifice themselves for us, why couldn't we do the same?

"Hey!" I shouted, my voice echoing in all directions.

The mercenary whirled around, raising the torch high to spread its light.

Ijijou hissed at me. "Don't!"

Running toward the mercenary, I brushed the edge of my staff against the open wound on her right arm. She came after me, the light from the fire jumping across the rocks, casting a disorienting array of shadows. Quickly I ducked under a stalactite and raced through the tunnel, following my instincts to choose a path that would lead me back to the main cave system. On the wall to my right, crystals glowed, and I redirected my path, recognizing the tunnel.

The woman still pursued me, though the light from her torch was a comfortable distance back. I scanned the ground, noting a few bodies that had not been there before.

"Syrane!" someone shouted nearby.

It sounded like Torey's voice.

I moved toward the sound, or where I believed it to be coming from, walking along a large pool of water. The ground leveled out, with sheets of rock stacked one on top of the other, creating an almost platform-like arena. Rocks from the ground reached up from the water, creating a large archway that separated the expanding lake.

Standing on the opposite side of the raised layers of rock was Syrane.

He was backing away from a mercenary, climbing over a section of rock to retreat further. Though his right hand was on the hilt of his sword, he had not yet drawn it. Torey fought against an enemy on the other end of the cavern. Her attention was split between defeating her opponent and trying to get to Syrane.

No wanting to waste time, I ran through the water, splashing and creating ripples across the still lake. Swiftly, I jumped on to the platform, watching in horror as the mercenary slashed out at Syrane, catching the side of his clothing with his sword.

"Draw your sword!" I yelled.

The mercenary turned his blade to cut across Syrane's chest. Panicking, I scooped a rock up from the ground and threw it at the man, hitting a pile of stones near his head. He paused, momentarily distracted. I lunged at the mercenary, swinging my staff when I was within range. He turned and blocked me, and my staff shattered. When the top half flew off, I grimaced. I had but a few inches left to fight with. Tossing the remainder of the staff onto the ground, I reached for the sword Phantom Asdar had given me.

The mercenary dragged his sword across the ground, scraping the metal against the rocks before slashing upward. I drew Asdar's sword and blocked the mercenary's sword near the hilt, sliding the blade forward and cutting into the man's side. Had he not been wearing armor, my attack would have done more damage. I disengaged, stepping back and looking for any sort of weakness in my opponent. It didn't seem like he was injured or favored either side. Narrowing my focus, I scanned the terrain instead, noting the length and width of the platform, the piles of rocks, and the slight drop-off into the water.

A shadow moved near the edge of the cave.

Another mercenary.

Upon spotting me, the newcomer charged, and I noticed it was the same mercenary I had encountered before. She had a slight wobble to her step, which was new, but it seemed the poison was having little effect beyond that.

Turning my attention back to my current opponent, a plan came to mind. I stepped back, leading him away from Syrane. His eyes glinted with amusement at my retreat, and I did my best to seem fatigued. When he swung his sword, I glided back further, my left foot teetering on the edge of the cliff. The mercenary slashed down, and I grinned. Shifting my weight onto my right foot, I dodged the blade and rammed my shoulder into the man's back. He tripped over a small stalagmite on the ground and fell into the water, hitting his head against a rock.

At the sound of armored plates behind me, I turned.

Raising my sword, I blocked the woman's attack, catching her blade in the center of my own. She pressed down, and my arms shook from the effort. The extra weight of Phantom Asdar's blade was taxing my muscles.

Behind me, something shuffled, and I turned my head to see Syrane running toward me. He drew his sword from its sheath, aiming for the woman's exposed neck. The mercenary blocked Syrane's attack with her armored forearm. The sword clanged against the metal, leaving behind a significant dent. She rounded on Syrane, bringing the sword high over her head and then down. Syrane tried to block it, but the tip of the mercenary's blade caught his shoulder.

Blood oozed from Syrane's wound, and panic gripped me.

Rounding on the women, I slashed my sword into the space between the armor on her arm and torso. The blade plunged deep into her skin, and I pulled it back, releasing a stream of blood. She stepped back from Syrane and pressed a hand to her wound. I tightened my hands around my sword and positioned myself between her and Syrane. She took an unsteady step and half of another, before falling to the ground. Her sword clanged uselessly across the rocks, and I kicked her weapon away, lowering Asdar's sword.

Syrane's eyes were wide, and there was a strange expression on his face I couldn't place—almost disgust or horror. Torey came running, removing the sash from around her waist to wrap it around Syrane's shoulder. She pulled it tight, and Syrane grimaced.

I felt faint at the sight of Syrane's blood.

"It looks worse than it is," Torey said, watching me out of the corner of her eye. "Syrane managed to stop most of the attack."

I knelt next to Syrane, hot tears falling from my eyes.

"I'm sorry it took me so long to find you."

Syrane looked away from me. "It's nothing serious. Don't cry, Shenrae."

Nodding, I tried to regain my composure. A cut ran across Syrane's right leg. Reaching up to the scarf at my neck, I untied it and wrapped it around my brother's leg. No blood soaked through the makeshift bandage, and Syrane didn't seem to be feeling lightheaded.

I let out a breath of relief.

No one else came from the tunnels, and from where we were, I could hear nothing save the erratic breathing of Syrane, Torey, and me.

Was it over?

Were Kai and Ijijou still alive?

Shifting Asdar's sword, I curled my fingers around the hilt to try and keep command of my muscles. I wiped the blood off the blade using the bottom of my robe. While I had trained with swords before, I had never had to earnestly fight against others who wished me harm. Not since my first Shadow mission. My body ached, but I stood up, forcing the weariness away. Training had taught me I was more capable than I believed.

After standing, I wiped my forehead with the sleeve of my robe, surprised to find blood on the fabric.

My blood?

I didn't remember being cut.

"Where are you going?" Torey asked. Her voice trembled. "Shenrae, you're bleeding. Stay here and rest for a while."

Ignoring her, I surveyed the area, looking for any tunnels that led to this part of the cave. It seemed the only way to get to this particular location was to use the tunnel I had come from, which meant I would be able to keep watch over Torey and Syrane while still being able to search for Kai and Ijijou—as long as I didn't pass any other tunnels where someone could sneak past me.

"Watch over Syrane for me," I said to Torey, looking back at her.

Torey seemed about to say something, but instead she nodded. "Be careful."

Leaving my friend and brother behind, I used the fingers on my left hand to trail over the walls of the cave. They were cold, wet, and rough against my fingertips, and there was a slight amber glow reflecting across the surface.

My light canteen was not lit.

I turned, looking for the source of the light, but found nothing.

Tilting my head back, I looked up at a collection of yellow crystals hanging from the ceiling. They had an ochre tint to them, with a slight white rim that seemed to radiate. It almost seemed as if they produced their own luminescence. Upon closer inspection, I could see thin strands of what looked to be something similar to silk. The threads illuminated the cave ceiling, creating a rippling wave of light.

It was beautiful.

I took a step forward, then another, feeling a little less drained. When I reached the end of the tunnel, I paused. Voices echoed throughout the cave.

Pressing my back against the wall, I waited, listening to the sounds of voices grow louder. There were at least three, maybe four of them.

Instinctively, my hand went to the hilt of my sword.

From across the way, Phantom Asdar, Kai, and Mei emerged.

I breathed a sigh of relief.

They were okay.

Kai was the first to rush over to me. "Were you able to find Syrane and Torey?"

"They're at the end of this tunnel. Syrane's leg and shoulder are injured, but he and Torey are both fine. It doesn't seem to be anything serious."

With a quick glance at Phantom Asdar for approval, Kai headed down the tunnel.

Fatigue suddenly caught up to me. It felt as if I had run into a wall, so sudden was the exhaustion that came over me.

"How are you feeling?" Phantom Asdar asked.

"Tired."

Mei laughed. She reached out her hand and put it on my shoulder. "You did great. Kai told me about how you helped him free his leg from the stalagmite. And Ijijou owes you her life."

My head snapped up. "Is she all right?"

Mei nodded. "We moved her to the entrance. She is doing fine."

"We'll send the other group of Shadows through," Phantom Asdar said, "to ensure no one is hiding and to help us carry the wounded out. We may need to enlist some of the villagers to help, but for now, it seems Vaiyene is safe."

Asdar's eyes were focused behind me, and I turned. Torey headed toward us. Kai, not far behind her, was helping Syrane walk.

"Are there any survivors?" Phantom Asdar asked.

"One," Kai said. "I bound his hands and legs as best I could, but I doubt he will wake up any time soon. The wound to his head should be treated immediately."

My throat became dry.

That meant the mercenary I had cut with Asdar's sword had died.

"Kai," Phantom Asdar said, "take Syrane and Torey outside the caves. Send the other Shadows when you see them, and keep an eye out for any possible mercenaries who may have gotten through the caves. We don't know for certain none escaped. Mei,

survey the remainder of the caves. Shenrae"—I looked up—
"walk with me."

I stayed next to Phantom Asdar while the others left. He was
silent for some time before he walked down the tunnel leading to
where Syrane and Torey had been. My stomach clenched at the
thought of returning to where the women had died. To give
myself something to do while we walked, I fiddled with my light
canteen until it ignited, welcoming its warm glow.

When we approached the lake, Phantom Asdar examined the
area. It didn't take him long to find the dead body at the edge of
the area.

My stomach sank as he headed toward the mercenary.

When he spoke, it was quiet yet firm. "I am proud of how
much you have grown as a warrior. Without your actions today,
Syrane and possibly Kai and Ijijou would have lost their lives."

Asdar knelt next to the mercenary I had killed, turning her on
to her back. He pressed her eyes closed and arranged her arms
next to her sides. "Kilo has never let go of the first person he had
to kill to save your father's life. While it is not my story to tell, I
played a small part in it. I've watched Kilo suffer from that guilt
for years. What you did today saved not only your comrades' lives
and your brother's but possibly the villagers' lives as well."

He raised his eyes. "You did nothing wrong."

His gaze was firm, as were his words.

My eyes drifted to the woman. I felt an odd mixture of anger,
regret, and sadness. She had come to hurt Vaiyene and its people.
I understood that, but I also felt sympathy toward her, for her
life having ended like this. While I was angry—she had, after all,
come with the intent to hurt us—I wondered what had pushed
her to do it in the first place.

And would I have done the same thing if I'd been in her
position?

"Shenrae."

I looked up.

"Spend some time reflecting, but do not allow yourself to fall
into the same prison Kilo has created for himself." His voice

became softer, more rugged with emotion. "Not being able to help him is my greatest regret."

Within Asdar's eyes, I recognized the same pain I had seen before in Kilo's.

Guilt and shame.

It flickered across his eyes briefly before he turned his back to me.

"We'll talk more later, but for now, focus on the good that has come from your actions."

chapter fifty-one
The Way

Dew slid down the curved edge of my mother's sword, the sun's light reflecting off the blade. I closed my eyes, feeling a tear roll down my cheek. My parents had died protecting Vaiyene. It was their duty, and I was proud, but at times like this, all I wanted was to be able to talk to them—to ask them questions and hear stories of how they, too, had felt lost as Shadows.

I tried to recall any of the stories they had told me, but none came to mind.

Usually, the hike up to the Reikon tree helped me feel better, but today the journey seemed empty and hollow. Coming to the tree was something I used to do with Kilo after finding out he came here every morning.

All those times, I had felt the protection of the Shadows fall around me.

But today I only felt sadness.

"I thought I would find you here," a voice said.

I jumped, startled from my thoughts. The voice had come from beside me. I swallowed my emotions and drew in a deep breath before glancing over at Phantom Asdar.

Hastily, I wiped my tears away with my sleeve.

Asdar walked past me, his black and gold Phantom's robe splaying out over the large tree roots of the Reikon tree. The paper ornaments hanging from a rope around the trunk rustled in the wind. Asdar rested his hand on the bark of the tree and closed his eyes, tilting his head down in silent prayer.

He was quiet for a long time.

When he opened his eyes, he turned his head to see me watching him. "I know I am not the person you had hoped to speak to, but I am here if you need me." His voice was gentler than it usually was. "It sometimes helps to speak with others who have experienced the same things."

Typically, Asdar wore leather armor and plain robes, choosing, like all the Shadows, to wear what allowed for a full range of movement—unhampered by elegance and weight. The golden embroidery and extravagant robes were a reminder of Asdar's Phantom oaths.

"I…" The words died even before I began to form them.

Leaving the tree, Asdar walked among the Shadows' weapons, touching a few swords and an axe, lingering for a few moments at each one before he moved on. Though I had trained with him, I knew little about him. Both my father and mother had been among the Shadows serving with him, as had Kilo, but I'd heard no stories of Asdar.

Who was it he had lost?

What had been his purpose for becoming a Shadow?

"There's a place I want to show you," he said, heading to the trails above the Reikon tree. He paused and waited until I followed after him. The path led to the lake where Syrane and I had purified our parents' swords before laying them to rest.

A lump of emotion caught in my throat.

We hiked for some time, up the mountain and through the alpine landscape. There were no trees to maneuver around, but streams were hidden underfoot by wiry brush. When we had attempted to traverse this path before, Syrane and I had not known which way to go. We had struggled to find our way, getting caught in the maze of undergrowth, our feet becoming soaked from the icy waters.

I stifled a chill as the wind whipped against me, grateful when we descended the peak of the mountain and climbed down into the small ravine below. The lake spread out across the gorge, with water so pure you could see to the gravel at the bottom. I remembered kneeling in the water, washing the blades of our parents' swords. The ritual had released their spirits from their service.

Phantom Asdar stepped into the lake, turning his body and slipping in between two large rocks. Wincing at the cold, I stepped into the lake too, squeezing into the crack in the mountain. The damp cavern walls pressed against me, and darkness engulfed us. I reached for the light canteen at my side, but Asdar stopped me.

"Wait. Allow your eyes to adjust."

We listened to the trickle of water until our eyes became used to the darkness. My vision became clearer, and the cave illuminated as small lights—white with a slight yellow hue around the edges—floated up from the water. Water sloshed against my legs as we moved over the uneven surface.

Asdar walked with long strides, light blossoming under each footstep.

"What is this place?" I asked, looking around.

The water had an almost silvery quality to it, and something about it seemed peaceful and otherworldly. An innate sense of calm came over me as if a gentle caress had wrapped around me.

"This is a sacred place for the Shadows," Asdar said, standing in the middle of the cavern. "The waters, like the Reikon Tree, are a part of who we are. You will find the answers you seek here."

"How?"

He slid his hands into the folds of his robe, his eyes wandering the caverns. "Meditate on what it is that troubles you. Focus on why you feel such unrest, and allow the emotions and thoughts to come to you as they will. This is a place of healing where the waters cleanse the mind and rejuvenate the spirit."

Spreading out his hands, he indicated a raised rock in the center of the lake.

I hesitated.

"I wouldn't recommend standing the entire time," Asdar said with a note of amusement in his voice. "There are matters I need to attend to, but I will return in a couple of hours."

He bowed, and I returned the gesture before he left the cavern. Drawing in a lingering breath, I knelt, sitting back on my heels. I folded my hands in my lap and closed my eyes to begin to focus on my breathing.

Water dripped from the ceiling into the lake, creating a rhythmic atmosphere similar to the Phantoms' gardens. The familiarity of it put me at ease. When I inhaled, I smelled the damp, earthy air and the pure, sweet smell of water.

I exhaled.

After drawing in another deep breath, I meditated on my misgivings about returning to Vaiyene. While I was happy to see Torey and Syrane again, somehow everything seemed different. Changed. As if I no longer belonged here, or it had been a mistake to come back. There was a lingering bitterness inside me about being back in Shadow training. I felt accomplished in my progress and proud that I had stuck through the times when it was hard, but all those feelings were not what bothered me the most.

It was something else.

What was it?

I recalled the fighting and the mercenaries, the woman who had died after I cut her with Phantom Asdar's blade. The moment she had fallen to the ground came back to me.

The blood that pooled around her.

The look on Syrane's face.

His horror?

At the time, I'd brushed off the feeling, too worried about Syrane to think about the consequences of what I'd done. Seeing Syrane hurt had stirred something inside me. He had frozen again in battle, and I had rushed to intervene. If I'd not shown up when I did—with the resolve to do whatever it took to protect him—would he have been the one to die? The mercenaries had been sent for a purpose. Whether it was to set fire to our fields again or to kill our people, we couldn't sit by and let that happen. How could it be wrong to defend against that? If any of them had escaped the caverns, the people I cared for, the people I had grown up with and who were like family to me, might have died because of it. In my heart, I felt little remorse, except for the guilt of not feeling the regret I should have.

Did that make me a bad person?

If I had continued to pursue the Skills instead of coming home, would anything have changed? I had not tried to use them since coming to Vaiyene. A part of me was afraid they were beyond my control, but why did I feel like I had failed by giving up on them?

Squeezing my eyes shut tight, I tried to push away the feelings of worthlessness that rose inside me. All my meditations seemed to do was confuse me further. Frustrated, I shifted my legs, bringing them around and crossing them in front of me. The lights reflecting in the water seemed to have disappeared.

Somehow, it darkened my mood.

Pushing myself onto my feet, I walked the perimeter as uneasiness grew inside me.

It was then Phantom Asdar moved from the shadows into the light.

How long had he been there?

I tried to keep the frown from spreading across my face, but Asdar raised his eyebrows. "You don't seem happy to see me."

"Just uncertain."

Asdar nodded. "And why is that?"

In the reflection at my feet, I saw blood on my hands. Asdar moved to stand beside me, and panic gripped me.

Could he, too, see the reflection?

"Taking a life is something I've had to learn to accept." Asdar's voice was quiet as he moved away from me. "It weighs on me, as it does Kilo. Your actions were in accordance with the Shadow's Creed. Defending the life of your brother, as well as that of Torey, was the right action for you to have taken."

Killing: it was my deepest fear.

I feared becoming like the False Shadows.

Lost.

Imperfect.

Without direction.

Phantom Asdar knelt in the water.

He looked up at me and reached out his hand. "Let me see the sword."

I drew Asdar's curved sword and knelt in the water, facing him, holding the sword in the palms of my hands. He took the blade, lowering it into the water. Darkness seeped out from the sword, pooling around me and clouding the once pure water. Asdar raised the blade and drizzled water over its surface, and a slight glow emanated down the surface as the water moved over it.

"Being a Shadow means upholding the Shadow's Creed, but that is not all it means. It is to follow the way laid before us. If you feel compelled toward something, if something speaks to your soul, it is your duty as a Shadow to pursue it and accept whatever comes from it. Until now, the Shadows have never had to rethink their ideals. We've never needed to change. We served our people. It was simple. Uncomplicated. But now that Kilo has begun to pursue the Skills and involve himself in others' lives, the Shadows will become responsible for more than just Vaiyene."

Scooping up another handful of water, he paused. "It is something we all must figure out for ourselves: what does the creed we live by mean? And how do we live in peace with the things we must do?"

Images of blood, of men and women, rose in my mind. The black coloring from the sword's edge continued to spread around me, engulfing me and closing in from all sides.

Panic began to rise in my chest.

The cave.

The False Shadows.

Death.

All of the memories seeped out from me, mixing with the black water from the sword, spreading like a disease. I could never be rid of it. I could never make things right again. Struggling, I tried to shut off the images, to break away from the thoughts overwhelming my heart.

It was too much.

Too painful.

"You need to accept what you've done."

Terror rose inside me, and I swallowed, raising my head.

Phantom Asdar held my gaze. He dipped his hand into the water again, spilling a handful of water over my blade. It hissed, and the blackness that seeped from it darkened and clouded even more.

"What do you feel at this very moment?"

"Fear."

"Why?"

"I don't feel bad about what happened."

Asdar nodded for me to continue.

"They came here to do harm, and I feel..." I hesitated, and Phantom Asdar waited. I sighed, reluctant to voice it. "I don't feel as bad as I should that the mercenary died. I feel sad it happened, and I wish it hadn't, but Syrane and Torey are alive, and Vaiyene is unharmed."

"And you fear this makes you a bad person?"

I looked away.

"The change in yourself, the restlessness you feel, the desire to be more than who you are, trust it. Trust in yourself, Shenrae. You have always doubted yourself too much. It is your biggest flaw."

Tears welled at the edges of my eyes.

"But do I even have a right to be a Shadow?"

"To question oneself *is* to be a Shadow. Did I serve the people wholeheartedly? Did I act in accordance with myself and my beliefs? Did I use my strength as a means of protection? All of these questions help us to find our way. Finding your path is something you will struggle with all your life. No one can tell you what you have to do, but once you find your way—embrace it. Hold onto it and never let it go. It is the heart of why we are Shadows and why we endure this pain."

Asdar's eyes blazed as he stared into the water, as if he too could see his own uncertainties as he faced them.

Something inside me stirred then.

A desire to find my own resolve.

After all, wasn't that the reason I had joined the Shadows? To find meaning in my actions? It was the one thing I wanted more than anything: purpose.

The blade in Asdar's hands pulsated.

Its coloring returned to normal as the water surrounding it began to clear.

"A Shadow's weapon is a reflection of their spirit," Asdar said as he looked up. "The sword was blackened because of your pain. Your parents may have taught you the customs and beliefs of being a Shadow, but understanding what it means to be a Shadow is something you will have to experience for yourself."

Asdar held the blade across his palms and handed it back to me.

I hesitated. "I'm not sure I want it."

"Hand me the sheath," he said. I passed it to him, and he slid the blade inside before holding the sword back out to me. "Keep it with you for now. You don't need to draw it again, but let it serve as a reminder of your resolve."

Nodding, I took the sword from him, letting my fingers trail over the engraved decorations in the sheath.

"Phantom?"

"Hmm?"

"What is your purpose as a Shadow?"

"I have always found happiness in training others. During my early Shadow years, I helped Kilo learn how to use a sword. He had a talent for it, and before long, his talent with it was equal to my own. We pushed each other to our limits, seeking a level of mastery few have ever achieved. My methods may be harsh at times, but it has allowed me to separate those who do not have the drive, focusing my attention on those who have an unwavering desire to be strong."

Standing, he bowed fully at the waist, remaining in the position as I raised myself from the ground. "Thank you for rekindling that part of my spirit."

His words and the deep gesture of gratitude moved me. I had never heard that level of sincerity in his voice before, and I felt humbled by his words. Sliding the sword into the sash around my waist, I looked up at him as he straightened, a smile on my face.

It made me happy knowing Asdar had enjoyed our time training. When I had first asked him, I thought it might be a burden on him, but now I finally knew how he had felt.

My mind wandered back to the Skills, to General Mirai and Akio. I knew why I was unhappy about being back in Vaiyene, and what I needed to do.

"I can't stay in Vaiyene," I said as my conviction solidified. "I have unfinished business with General Mirai and the False Shadows. I feel it's more important to be with them than it is to be here."

Phantom Asdar nodded, seeming pleased at the decision.

"I will support you in whatever way I can."

chapter fifty-two
The Rift Between Us

I stood before Syrane and Torey with a heavy heart. From their expressions, I could tell they were already unhappy with me. I blew out a long breath, rubbing my left arm absently as I tried to find the right words.

Syrane broke the silence first. "Why do I always feel like I'm not going to like what you have to say?"

I bristled at the comment, not sure how to answer. I *was* here to tell them I was leaving Vaiyene—again. It wouldn't be what either of them wanted to hear, especially Syrane. His anger seemed misplaced though, and I hesitated to answer him, looking to Torey in hopes she would at least understand.

"It's been nice seeing you again," Torey said. Like always, her tone was warm.

She, too, knew I had come to say goodbye.

I sighed. "Is it that obvious?"

Leaning over the railing of the bridge, I gazed down at the water. Birds sang in the trees nearby, creating a colorful melody. The flowers that remained on the trees filled the air with the sweet scent of spring. Hesitantly, I glanced over at Syrane, who looked sullenly off toward the fields. They were beginning to dig rows today. The danger of frost had passed, allowing the sowing of seeds.

It was peaceful in Vaiyene, but not in my heart.

I tried to swallow the guilt.

It hadn't even been a full month, and already I was anxious to leave.

Torey smiled at me. She was too kind and understanding sometimes. It made me feel even more guilty, knowing she had been excited for us to spend some time together. Tomorrow the village would hold the spring festival to celebrate the coming of new life. The people would come together to begin planting and readying the village for the new season.

"I'm sorry I'll miss the festival," I said to her.

"It's okay."

The people here could enjoy the peace and the festivities, but even if I chose to stay one more day, it wouldn't alleviate the fear in my heart. The only way to stop the False Shadows and to protect the people's happiness was to stop the False Shadows before they become too great a force to deal with. General Mirai's men were stretched thin. Their resources were becoming depleted. I knew I was only one person, but someone needed to be there to fight for Vaiyene and its people.

Syrane and Torey faced me as I pushed away from the railing.

If I could keep the False Shadows from engaging with Vaiyene and keep my brother and Torey from getting mixed up in the fighting, I would do it. I had never thought myself capable, but it seemed my resolve had been growing. If any of us had to confront the False Shadows, I would rather it be me.

I searched for the right words to express my feelings.

How could I explain it?

"I joined the Shadows to find my place," I said, being mindful of Syrane's emotions. "While I was happy to train with you both, I—"

"Found other people you like more?" Syrane snapped.

"You know that's not true," I said, trying to keep my voice even.

How could he even joke about that?

Syrane averted his eyes.

I took a step toward him, drawing back his attention. "I can't wait around for the False Shadows to come back. What General Mirai is doing, what I was doing, was making a difference. I…"

Fumbling, I struggled to express what I needed to. I missed Akio and the general's group, just as I had missed Syrane and Torey, but a part of me would always long to be back in Vaiyene.

It was, after all, my home.

"Shenrae is trying to do what she can," Torey said, eyeing Syrane, then back to me. "Even if it's outside Vaiyene, she's still doing what a Shadow should."

I flashed Torey a relieved smile.

Syrane's lips pressed into a thin line.

Reaching out, I touched his shoulder. "Syrane, please."

He brushed my hand off. "You don't get it! You don't understand what it's like being here." Gesturing behind him at the village, he said, "We're weak, Shenrae! When you and Kilo left, it was like a piece of Vaiyene had been torn out. Phantom Lunia has been trying to repair the village, and Phantom Asdar does what he can to prepare us for battle, but we won't be able to hold our own if the False Shadows come again. We're lucky the damage from the mercenaries was not greater!"

I clenched my jaw. "And that's why we're doing what we are! I've been working with General Mirai to prevent the False Shadows from growing, from gaining too much power. You do know that's why Kilo left in the first place, right? To learn about the Skills and the False Shadows to protect us?"

Syrane shook his head. "Whatever these 'Skills' are, it doesn't concern us."

"We can't ignore them," I said. "They're dangerous!"

"And none of our concern!"

Anger sparked within me. He couldn't seriously be dismissing them; he didn't even know anything about them. None of them understood the danger we were in.

"I've learned how to use them," I said, curling my fingers into my palm.

Resting my hand on the wooden railing of the bridge, I willed the wood to grow cold. It had been a while since I had summoned the Skills, but the flow of energy spread over the wood without much effort. Tiny crystals of ice spread out in a fractal.

Syrane took a step back, his eyes widening in horror.

Maybe now he would understand the danger.

"You shouldn't be learning to use something like that," he said, his hands clenched into fists at his sides. "It's unnatural."

I pointed to the bridge where the ice had already begun to melt. "*This* is what Kilo is afraid of. I have no talent with the Skills, but in the hands of someone who knows what they're doing, they're a force that cannot be stopped. If we leave this power unchecked, I am certain they will come to Vaiyene. There is no more hiding and wishing this away. We have to take action." Taking a deep breath, I attempted to calm my frustration. "I have to leave."

Syrane became silent. It made me even angrier. He was harboring resentment toward me but refused to tell me what was actually bothering him.

Was he upset about the Skills?

My leaving?

Kilo?

"If you have something to say to me, Syrane, say it."

After a prolonged silence, Torey cleared her throat. "Shenrae is going to leave regardless of what you have to say. You might as well make peace with it."

"I have nothing to say to her," Syrane replied. He walked to the edge of the bridge and looked over the railing. "Except both you and Kilo have betrayed your own people. You've betrayed our parents, our way of life, and you've betrayed me."

He turned on his heel and stormed across the bridge. Syrane had always been quick to anger, and he often used that rage to build a wall between himself and others.

And I didn't want him to shut me out.

I went after him.

The water reflected the amber light of his canteen, mixing with the sun's fading glow. Lining both sides of the path through the bamboo forest were lanterns that one of the Phantoms would soon come to light. Closing my eyes for a moment, I attempted to ignore the overwhelming fear that I might lose sight of Syrane in one of the many alcoves or hidden places in the landscape of the garden. But in fact it had been designed that way—to be a place of solitude in which one could seek comfort.

When I had nearly reached the end of the stone bridge, I yelled, "Syrane!"

My heart ached. Syrane stood with his back facing me, looking down into the lake.

His hands were fisted at his sides.

Too afraid to look at his reflection, I kept my eyes on his back.

Drawing in a steadying breath, I tried to collect the words necessary. Syrane needed to know I still cared for him. Deeply. There were other matters at stake here, but talk of the Skills and the False Shadows seemed to have caused him to withdraw. There were others outside of Vaiyene—a whole world—that Syrane was afraid of. He had been scared ever since our first mission.

And he needed to stop running from it.

I illuminated the canteen at my side, shaking the container that released flames to create more light. "This is something I need to do, Syrane. Now that I know what the Skills are, what Kilo has been pursuing, I can't wait around and pretend I don't know what's happening outside Vaiyene. Learning about the Skills and how to combat them is something I've dedicated myself to. But more than that…" I struggled to find the right words, as I didn't fully understand it myself. "I don't want to fight any longer than I have to."

I looked around, admiring the trees and the flowers in bloom—at the beauty that could be created by Syrane's hand. Stepping forward, I looked into the reflection of the water to see sorrow in Syrane's eyes.

"Syrane, please, I don't want to leave like this."

His sadness lingered but for a moment. With the passing wind, his expression darkened, and Syrane's robes whipped back. The strands of his hair revealed his vacant eyes.

It was at that moment I knew he had shut me out.

He had made his decision.

"By the time you have finished 'doing what you need to,' there will be nothing left of Vaiyene to save. What you loved will be gone." His voice became ragged and strained. "You're losing yourself, Shenrae, and I never thought you would. Our parents taught us what it was to live like a Shadow. To love our homeland and to honor it." Pausing, he shook his head. "You're the farthest thing from a Shadow now."

I wanted to close the distance between us, to fill the widening gap, but I stayed silent, unmoving, watching as Syrane drove the wedge deeper between us.

My chest remained tight, and I tried to breathe, feeling his words gut me, hitting the uncertainty growing inside me. Had I really strayed from the Shadow path? Phantom Asdar had encouraged me to find my own personal truth. Was Syrane's rejection of me because he could not see beyond his own beliefs and Asdar could?

Or was it something else?

My hand went to the sword at my side.

No.

I was a Shadow *because* I was doing what was best for Vaiyene.

Even if it meant leaving Syrane and Torey behind, even if it meant—a small smile spread across my lips—leaving Vaiyene to save it. Syrane saw what I was doing as endangering Vaiyene, and I saw it as the only way to protect our home.

We had reached a crossroads.

One we could not settle with words.

I took a deep breath after his continued silence. "I'm sorry, Syrane, but I have to follow what I believe."

"As do I."

His words reflected neither anger nor sadness. They were calm, quiet, and full of acceptance. I turned away from him, the gardens losing their beauty and color.

Torey ran toward us, out of breath.

But it was too late.

Bitterness coated my tongue. Not because Syrane and I disagreed, but because he didn't see the value in my actions. He refused to see how my efforts would help Vaiyene and how they would protect him. He refused to think of the possibilities, instead denying everything to create the perfect, absolute mindset that anyone who acted outside of his own desires was in the wrong.

It stung.

When I looked back over my shoulder, he had disappeared from sight.

"He hates me, doesn't he?" I asked.

Torey shook her head. "He misses you."

I sank onto my knees, the weight of choosing to follow what I believed in too much. How did Kilo bear it?

Torey sat down next to me, placing her hand on my back and rubbing it. I tried to remind myself how to breathe.

Finally, I managed to speak, raising my head.

"Does no one see the danger but me?"

Torey thought for a while before answering. "It's easier to believe we're safe here. I don't think many of us want to believe the danger is real. Even the attack today will be minimized to not cause panic. It's not that Syrane doesn't believe there's a threat; he just refuses to involve himself because he believes it will make the problem worse. Phantom Lunia feels the same."

They were lying to themselves.

Pretending that if they forgot about the outside world, they could live in peace, and that my actions disturbed what they had created. But I hadn't thought about what happened outside of Vaiyene before I became a Shadow, before Asdar had sent me to

General Mirai for training. So a part of me understood Syrane's anger.

Torey smiled, her head tilting to the side. "Do you think you can keep the False Shadows from attacking Vaiyene again?"

"I'll try." After getting to our feet, I embraced Torey tightly. "Watch over Syrane for me, will you?"

She held on for a moment before she released me. "Take care of yourself."

Giving her a nod, I left the gardens and headed toward the Phantoms' house, allowing my thoughts to quiet and my resolve to harden. The wooden deck creaked under my feet. I searched for Phantom Asdar as I walked the perimeter of the veranda.

Phantom Lunia came around the corner and stood in my path.

"Phantom," I said, bowing.

When I straightened, a few of the Shadows who had been training with wooden swords stopped to watch us. It seemed as if they were waiting for something. I swallowed, uncertain why Phantom Lunia no longer seemed welcoming.

"Where are you headed?" she asked.

Someone moved behind her, and I shifted to see who it was.

Syrane's eyes were narrowed as they connected with mine.

He had warned her.

"I have business with Phantom Asdar," I said.

"I'm sure you do," Phantom Lunia said, her voice unusually tense. "We've been working hard to rebuild Vaiyene in your absence. It would be a shame if a single person were to undo everything."

"It would be," I replied, keeping my tone polite.

Her words were a threat.

Phantom Lunia's calm demeanor dropped like a mask. Within the blink of an eye, her eyes blazed and her fighting spirit came to the surface. "I will say this once and only once, Shenrae. I have no intention of letting you leave Vaiyene again. I made the mistake of allowing Kilo to leave. What you and Kilo are doing will bring ruin to Vaiyene, and I will not allow that to happen."

I froze, unable to believe what I was hearing.

Was she going to try and keep me here?

I forced my hands to remain away from the sword Asdar had given me. I hadn't seen Lunia wield a weapon before, but as she was in fact a Phantom, she undoubtedly had a considerable amount of skill. She wore no sword at her hip, but daggers could be hidden, and Syrane and at least four other Shadows were close enough that if something happened, they could easily take me.

I swallowed my rising nerves.

I never fought as well on my own as I did with someone else.

Cold sweat beaded on my brow, and I began analyzing possible routes for escape. If I could head back the way I'd come, perhaps I could lose them in the mountain passes.

"Do not try it." Phantom Lunia's voice brought my attention back to her.

A blade winked in her hand, and I dodged to the left. I removed the sheathed sword Asdar had given me without drawing it, holding it at my side.

My heart beat so fast I could hear each pulse in my ears.

"With all due respect, Phantom Lunia," I said, attempting to keep my voice calm, "my direct orders as a Shadow come from the Phantom who sponsored me."

Lunia drew another blade from the folds of her long-sleeved robes, flinging it at my head. Ducking, I slammed the end of the hilt into her hand, causing her to drop the dagger.

"I will not allow you to endanger Vaiyene!" She lunged, skirting past the end of my sword and ducking low.

I sidestepped as another dagger flew past my face. Crossing the sword over my chest, I shoved Phantom Lunia back and retreated, holding the sword between us to keep her at a distance. When she froze, I glanced over my shoulder to find Asdar on the veranda.

His gaze flickered between Phantom Lunia and me. "What is the meaning of this?" he shouted. "Are we so shortsighted we attack our own now?" When Lunia did not answer him, his attention snapped to me. "Shenrae, what is going on?"

Breathing hard, I seethed, keeping hold of the sword in my hand. The daggers embedded in the wooden posts caught the light of the falling sun, apparent to all. Phantom Lunia wouldn't admit fault though, and there were no witnesses who would reveal what they had seen. With her rank, she had the power to turn what had happened against me.

I drew my shoulders back.

Asdar would not believe her over me.

"I came to talk to you about leaving Vaiyene," I said, keeping my eyes on Phantom Lunia, whose face showed none of her earlier anger. "We have differing opinions on the matter." I phrased it in a way to not be accusatory, to shroud it in a bit of mystery so as not to directly call her out in front of the others. I didn't know if the others had been close enough to hear everything that was said, but by now, more of the Shadows drew near.

"What you are and are not allowed to do is up to me," Asdar said without emotion. "It's archaic to be dragging up the duties of the Phantoms and their Shadows, but as you are under my sponsorship, the final decision is mine."

Lunia slipped the dagger in her hand away and straightened, brushing off her robes as if she had merely been involved in a scuffle and nothing more. "I was just explaining how pleased I am peace has returned to Vaiyene and how good it is for Shenrae to be back. Her brother and friend have been so thrilled to see her. Wouldn't it be a good idea for her to stay for a while?"

My skin crawled as Syrane and Torey were drawn into this.

How low would she stoop to get her way?

"Shenrae, come with me," Asdar said, turning his back on Lunia and the lingering Shadows. His strides were quick and forceful, and I hurried to catch up to him. "There's something I've been meaning to talk to you about. Something in regard to what has just happened, and…" He trailed off, veering away from the training grounds and the arena, heading deeper into the wood.

After I spent a few moments trying to keep up with him, he stopped. He checked to make sure we were alone before speaking.

"I didn't expect Lunia to come after you so openly. I knew her wishes were to keep you from leaving Vaiyene, but I didn't understand the extent of her desire to ensure you stayed. It's been a while since her calm demeanor has broken. Not since she demanded Kilo's exile. I was able to leave Kilo's status open-ended on a technicality she overlooked, but she is much more adamant about stopping you than she was with Kilo, and being that you're not even a Shadow yet…"

He didn't need to explain it.

"Why doesn't she want me to leave?"

"She is afraid," Asdar said, glancing back toward the Phantoms' house. "We've been through so much, and she does not want to believe we will soon be under attack again. She would rather believe Kilo's involvement with the False Shadows is the cause of recent attacks than accept we have no control over what happens. Change is coming, and a new world is on the horizon. Lunia is afraid of it, and her influence over the Shadows has swayed some of them, but…" He flashed me a smile. "Why would we not want to take part in creating a new world?"

I returned his smile.

Deep down, it excited me too.

Walking farther into the forest, Asdar diverted from the trail, stepping over rocks and fallen trees. Our feet crunched the wood and bark on the forest floor. The high peaks of the Miyota Mountains jutted up before us. The last remaining sunlight was blocked by the mountainside, casting us into dark shadow and sending chills over me. Asdar motioned to a group of rocks, settling himself down onto one and leaning back. Gazing up at the sky, he waited for me to seat myself on the rocks before he spoke.

"I will escort you through the Miyota Mountains tonight, but you will need to make the rest of the journey on your own. Now that Kilo has made his move with Hitori, the conflict with the False Shadows will be decided soon. It won't be long before all of us are tested in the final phase."

Tears welled at the corners of my eyes, my mind overwhelmed by all that had happened. Kilo was risking his life to stop the False Shadows. And Phantom Lunia and Syrane hated him for it.

And now, they hated me.

"It's going to be okay, Shenrae," Phantom Asdar said. His words were gentle. He kept his eyes on the sky, and I appreciated that he said nothing more on the matter.

I sniffed loudly, letting the tears fall down my cheeks.

We sat on the rocks until the sun had fully set, the stars becoming visible as the magenta and orange sky faded into darkness. Two people on horseback started up the trail toward us. I stiffened and glanced over at Phantom Asdar, who seemed undisturbed. The moonlight cast them in dark shadows, outlining their hair and shoulders with a silver light.

Asdar stood up and walked toward them.

"Thank you both for coming," he said.

One of the horses snorted, and I recognized the white stripe and black coat of Greymoon. I rushed toward my stallion. My light canteen cast enough of a glow for me to see Mei. She dismounted and handed the reins to me, giving Greymoon a pat on the neck.

"He was nervous, but I think he knew we were bringing him to you."

I grinned.

Kai dismounted, letting go of Nightwind's reins as the stallion crossed the distance to his master. "There are enough supplies for both of you in the packs," Kai said, smiling at Phantom Asdar and me, "as well as a few other things we thought you might need." He reached behind his back and handed me a long staff. The wood seemed to be cherry or oak. Silver threads were wrapped around the exterior.

Mei bumped against Kai's shoulder and winked at me. "We reinforced it with metal around the outside. It should hold up better to a sword, should you have to face one."

"Th-thank you," I said, stunned they had done all this.

Mei became serious. "Asdar asked us to bring your horses and supplies, but we wanted to let you know you have friends here in the Shadows."

"Please be careful," Kai added. He gave me a warm smile before his attention shifted to Phantom Asdar. "We'll keep Phantom Lunia and the Shadows in check if anything happens."

Phantom Asdar nodded. "I'm counting on you."

We mounted our horses and left Kai and Mei behind, riding swiftly through the night. By morning, we stood at the base of the Miyota Mountains.

As the horses drank deeply from the river, I stretched out my back, glancing back up at the peaks of the mountains.

Phantom Asdar came toward me, carrying something lumpy wrapped in a thin piece of cloth. He handed it to me, and I pulled the thin cord holding the wrapping in place, exposing the leather armor inside. Running my fingers over the chest plate, I admired each piece and how it was sewn together flawlessly.

I looked up at Asdar, not knowing what to say.

"Be careful," he said. "If you find yourself in trouble, hang your light canteen upon the highest branch of a tree to signal General Mirai's spy network. They are working with us to expedite letters between Kilo, me, and the general. I'll send word you're on your way."

I held onto my new staff and bowed low. "I'll do my best."

chapter fifty-three
Tarahn & Meetings

Reining in Greymoon's excitement, I looked up at the black spire jutting across the horizon. The young stallion's unrestrained joy at being able to run for hours made the journey quicker than I had anticipated. My thighs were less enthusiastic, but traveling with Greymoon, seeing him happy, made me less nervous about being alone.

I dismounted and began leading Greymoon toward the gates of Tarahn. He nibbled my ear, and I pushed him off, but he continued to pester me. With a sigh, I dug inside a saddlebag and pulled out one of the many carrots Mei and Kai had packed. He crunched it happily.

It seemed he had gotten used to being spoiled.

"Needy horse," I mumbled fondly.

On either side of Tarahn were towers made of light-colored stone. Rocks of different colors were intermixed across the towers, and the mismatched design seemed to carry into the houses and cobblestone streets. Akio had described the guardhouse to me once, saying it was situated at the back of the town. It was the most recognizable building in Tarahn, being the source of the black spire.

Greymoon and I navigated the streets cautiously. We kept to the edge of the road and out of the way of bustling tradesmen who pushed carts with their wares, shouting as the wave of people traveled through town in search of goods.

"Shenrae!" a voice called.

Knowing it was Akio, I scanned the cluster of people in search of him. I pulled Greymoon down one of the alleyways, removing us from the flow of traffic. After some time, I spotted Akio's red hair bobbing toward me. When he managed to push through the horde of people, he held out three doughy-looking balls skewered on a stick.

"I thought you might be hungry," he said with a grin.

Taking the pastries from him, I bit into one, enjoying the sweetness. His smile and happiness brought warmth to my cheeks.

I had missed him.

"It's good," I said, pushing away Greymoon's snout.

"They were my favorite when I was little," Akio said. He pointed down the alleyway. "If we head to the other street, it will be less busy. We'll have to take your horse to the stables before meeting up with the general anyway."

Relieved, I led Greymoon after Akio, pulling off the final dough ball from the skewer and eating it.

"How's everything in Vaiyene?" Akio asked, pausing at the end of the alleyway and holding out his hand before motioning us through. "I heard from the general there were mercenaries who attacked."

"No one was seriously hurt," I said, trying to keep myself from thinking about Syrane and Phantom Lunia. "We managed to disable most of the mercenaries, although…" I paused as Akio glanced back, and I tried not to seem too bothered by stating the facts. After all, what I had done was nothing to be guilty about. "A few of the mercenaries didn't make it."

Akio's gaze lingered before he put his arms behind his back. "From what I hear, we might be at the point where we won't need to worry about the False Shadows or the mercenaries any more."

He stretched his legs out and ambled forward, half-jumping, half-skipping across the cobblestone to a box positioned against a wall. Leaping up, he stood upon it, reaching around to his back to unhook the spear there.

"Before all this, I was a street performer of sorts." He paused for dramatic effect and bent his knees, giving me a wide grin. "What you're about to see will be nothing less than a great feat of human skill!"

Akio jumped off the wooden box, flipping forward and landing on his feet.

I glanced over at Greymoon; he seemed as unimpressed as I was. Laughing at the stallion's expression, I covered my mouth while Akio flipped and twirled his spear around. When Akio bowed, I slid the reins onto the crook of my arm and began clapping.

Akio seemed to swell with pride at the gesture.

"Thank you, thank you. You're too kind." He walked back over to me, his smile and his playfulness fading as he became more serious "When all this is over, I'd like to do something that makes people smile again. It's hard being the one who decides if a person lives or dies."

I could sense there was more to his words than I knew.

"Why did you join the general then?" I asked, eyeing him curiously.

Akio shrugged. "I couldn't make enough money to buy food and shelter. I was lost and didn't know what to do with myself. Most days, I tried to wrangle up some coins for food by performing, but usually I came up short and spent my time in the alleyway feeling sorry for myself." Akio started walking again in the direction of the spire. "The general found me one day after watching me spin my staff. He told me it could be used to help people and spent a few months teaching me how to wield the staff for battle. Most of the general's men came into his group the same way. It's why we have a deep fondness for him."

I smiled, hearing the gratefulness in Akio's voice.

The general was a kind man.

Akio headed right and circled around the two-story building with the spire, motioning toward a large stable in the distance. There was a large wooden pen and arena next to it, with a few people working the horses.

A woman came up to us, her eyes immediately going to Greymoon. She reached out her hand toward him. Greymoon hesitated a moment before pressing his nose against her palm. She stroked his muzzle, a small smile on her face.

"This is Shiori," Akio said, turning to me and giving me a nod. "She has a gift with horses and is one of the horse masters here. She'll look after your stallion and make sure he's taken care of."

Greymoon stepped toward her and nuzzled her ear. I tried not to be too jealous that he liked her already. After handing over Greymoon's reins, I followed Akio back to the guardhouse.

"We received some new reports earlier this morning," Akio said, heading up to the guardhouse, "which means we might be leaving earlier than you were expecting. I wanted to let you know in advance."

I nodded, appreciating the warning.

The two-story guardhouse, it seemed, was made from the same stone as most of the buildings in Tarahn, though unlike the other structures, it didn't have any of the colorful rocks in its architecture. It did, however, have a large window at the top, with a smaller window on either side. The spire I'd seen from a distance was enormous—nearly a third of the size of the building. From up close, it looked more like an elongated sword tipped on its end.

Waiting outside of the guardhouse was General Mirai. Standing next to him was a person clad in dark blue garments. A letter changed hands, and the person bowed before racing off.

Most likely, it was someone from the spy network.

General Mirai turned toward us, a smile appearing on his face when he saw me.

"It is good to have you back with us, Shenrae."

I bowed. "I am honored to continue working alongside you."

General Mirai bowed briefly before he pushed open the doors to the guardhouse and motioned us inside. A long, dark wooden table spanned the interior. At least two dozen chairs were set around the table, many of the seats filled by the general's men. All eyes fell on me, and my stomach dropped. I remembered the hostility of the Shadows, and my self-consciousness came back to me.

"Shenrae!"

"You're back!"

"Look, Shenrae's here!"

Akio bumped into my shoulder, giving me a wink. "See, it wasn't just me who missed you."

I waved sheepishly at the men. As General Mirai stood at the head of the table, the friendly greetings came to a close. Whatever they were speaking of, it seemed to be urgent. Akio pulled out an empty chair for me, motioning for me to sit while he stood behind me against the wall.

"A group of mercenaries is heading to the Orem Cliffs," General Mirai said, raising his voice so all could hear. "According to the reports, these men seem to have been sent by Hitori, but with the information Kilo sent me, we now know there's a secondary group working independently from the False Shadows. Regardless, the village contains knowledge on the Skills, and it's something we cannot allow to be destroyed."

"How many of them are there?" Akio asked.

"Our initial reports estimate at least two dozen."

One of General Mirai's men poured steaming liquid into mugs before began passing them out down the table.

Two dozen trained men.

Rays of light spilled down from the ceiling, and my eyes unfocused watching the play of dust in the air as it glittered. I had told Phantom Asdar I wanted to make a difference and to do something to help Kilo, but was I prepared for it?

A mug was place in front of me.

Akio leaned down and whispered. "Ginger tea. It's the general's favorite during war meetings. He says it settles his stomach, and over the years, despite its taste, we've all grown to actually like it."

Cautiously, I brought the mug to my lips, inhaling the unique aroma. It was spicy, but there was a hint of honey, giving it just the right amount of sweetness.

Akio placed his hand on my shoulder.

"General, Shenrae and I can head out now." He withdrew his hand and grabbed his pike from against the wall. "With only the two of us, we can be there within a day to give them warning."

The general pushed himself up from the table, the chair scraping against the stone floor. "Follow me then, both of you."

We left Tarahn's guardhouse behind, heading down the main cobblestone street. The crowd parted around the general, Akio, and me, allowing us to pass without needing to fight against them.

We wound swiftly through the cobblestone streets, away from the market, the noise, and the crowds of people. Small houses were situated in the delicate landscape, with yards decorated to reflect each owner. We slowed before a modest home with a painted blue exterior. General Mirai opened the door, peered inside, and headed into the back where a small gathering of men conversed. Judging from their elaborate dress and posture, they seemed to be people of importance.

"Kefnir, I need to speak with you," General Mirai said, interrupting the conversation. "It is an urgent matter."

A tall, lanky, dark-haired and dark-skinned man with freckles spanning his face broke through the circle of men and came to the general's side. "What is it?"

"We need your fastest horses and any medicinal supplies you can spare. The village of Konro is about to come under attack. We're hoping to get there before it happens, to warn them. And…" The general glanced over to me. "Kilo's sister is still there."

My stomach dropped.

Finae was there?

"Take what you need," Kefnir said, raising his eyebrows at me. Beside me, Akio gave a short bow, and I threw my right arm over my chest, bowing deeply. When I straightened, Kefnir turned to the general. "Ah, is this the Shadow who has been training with you?"

General Mirai nodded. "Shenrae, this is my brother, Kefnir. He is the lord of Tarahn."

Kefnir gave a short bow before he stepped back inside the house. "A pleasure to meet you, Shenrae. I apologize we have not yet had the chance to speak." He held out his hand, summoning one of the people in the house to him. "Have Umei pack a bag of our most potent medicines and wound-dressing supplies. Take them to the stables immediately."

The woman nodded and left.

Kefnir returned his attention to Akio and me. "Good luck to both of you. We are honored to continue working with the Shadows in such a matter."

I bowed again.

"I'll take you to the stables," the general said, leading us out of the house and back through the town to the stables.

I held my hand out as we passed by Greymoon's stall. He pressed his nose against my side, and I gave him a quick pat before catching up with the others. I was sad not to be taking him with me, but after our journey he deserved his rest.

"Konro village is located near the base of the Orem Cliffs," the general said. "We are in a good position for you to ride straight there, without having to circle around the cliffs to reach it." He handed a folded-up piece of paper to Akio. "We will head out shortly, with a larger force to intercept the mercenaries. I don't know if they ride as one unit or if they will come in waves. Whichever it is, we will try and take the brunt of the attack."

"And our directive, General?" Akio asked. He had unhooked the spear from his back and was now holding it at his side, his back rigid and straight.

"Consult with the Guardian. Preserving the knowledge of the Skills may be more important than saving all the villagers. Either way, abide by the Guardian's wishes."

The woman Kefnir had spoken to earlier, Umei, ran toward us, a large bundle in her arms. A young child shuffled after her with another pack. "Supplies and rations, General Mirai," Umei said, handing over the first bundle, then the one the child was carrying.

The general gave her his thanks and headed into the paddock as a stable boy approached. "Your fastest horses, by order of Lord Kefnir."

It all seemed to be happening too fast.

Drawing in a deep breath, I closed my eyes momentarily to re-center myself. Akio would be by my side, which made me less nervous, and Finae and the villagers needed our quick action.

The stable boy brought out two white horses, handing one set of reins to Akio. General Mirai took the other and placed his hand on the horse's muzzle to keep him steady while I mounted.

The general stepped back, bowing his head. "Ride swift and true. You carry the goodwill of all our people."

―――――

As soon as we entered the forest near the Orem Cliffs, a damp mist rolled over us. Light from the moon had helped us find our way, but nothing had prepared me for the thick fog.

"Stay close," Akio said, reining his horse in until I caught up with him.

Removing my canteen from my side, I shook it until the light grew. It would help should we become separated. I drew my outer robe tighter around my shoulders, peering uselessly through the thick fog. Even though Akio rode beside me, his features were shrouded, fuzzy, and distant.

It made me nervous.

"Do you think we're lost?"

I knew we were, but I wanted to hear Akio's voice.

He chuckled. "It's hard to be lost when we don't know where we're going. The map the general gave to me isn't complete, but I have a feeling we're close."

He guided his horse to the left until we reached a wall of rocks. Dismounting, he began to walk on foot. I started to dismount as well, but he held out his hand.

"Stay there."

His hand crept toward his stave.

My stomach soured at the thought of a fight in this fog. The people of the hidden village had the advantage of knowing the landscape. They undoubtedly had some other means of navigating it.

"We're being watched," Akio said.

"What do we do?"

I dismounted, against Akio's warning, leading my horse forward. Despite not being able to see into the mist, Akio didn't seem as nervous as I was. It eased my mind somewhat, but I couldn't help feeling anxious about who waited for us.

Akio nudged my side with his hand. "Hand me your light."

I untied the canteen and handed it to him.

Akio peered into the mist, his eyes fixed on something. He covered the light with his cloak, then removed it, repeating the same gesture three times. Short, then slow, then fast again. This was a sort of greeting among Mirai's mercenaries.

Who was he signaling to?

And would they be able to understand?

"It'll be okay," he said, handing the light back to me. "If they're not allies, we can disappear back into the fog. No one can see in this dense mist. Keep your light exposed until then."

Water sloshed ahead of us, and we slowed. When we were close enough to see it was a lake, Akio stepped into it, testing its depth.

"It's pretty deep. We'll have to swim with the horses to cross it."

I wasn't thrilled by the idea.

We stripped down to our undergarments, packing our clothing in the wax-coated saddle packs. I held onto the reins of my horse and walked into the water, encouraging the horse as I went. The water rose above my knees, then my chest, and when my feet could barely touch the bottom of the lake, I looked nervously at my horse. Surprisingly, she didn't seem to mind the water. Both of the horses seemed to have been desensitized to it. Relieved, I held onto the mare's mane, kicking my legs out behind me and gliding alongside her as we followed after Akio and his horse.

We navigated around tall stone pillars that seemed natural in their formation but unnatural in their placement. Every so often, out of the corner of my eye, I saw them glow. It was subtle, but the farther we swam, the stronger the silver light began to emanate from them. Below the surface of the water, lights glowed as well.

My horse found her footing on the bottom of the lake and together we walked out of the water, following Akio and his horse. The mist lessened as we moved away from the lake, and soon, sand and bedrock gave way to a forest with trees taller than any I had seen before.

"Well, shall we?" Akio asked, gesturing at a slight path worn into the dirt.

I nodded. Already the sight of the forest lifted my spirits.

It reminded me of home.

We walked in awe of the towering trees, reveling in the warmth of the sun as it leaked through the canopy. There was a slight breeze in the forest, for which I was grateful, as it dried my white robe. After a short time, Akio and I were able to put the rest of our clothing back on. This provided a little more protection as we navigated around bushes and over rocks.

In the distance, a light came into focus.

A second light joined the first.

Akio raised his voice. "We seek the village of Konro."

The light wavered and took shape as two people dressed in white came toward us. They blended seamlessly into the fog around them. If not for the lanterns they carried, they would have remained hidden in the thick mist.

Hairs on the back of my neck rose.

How many others were hidden?

"Who are you?" the taller of the two men asked. He had a thin frame and a long white beard that flowed down his chest. Two swords were belted at his hip.

"Messengers," Akio said, not hesitating in his answer. "We bring word of a threat to Konro."

The tall man eyed Akio, then glanced over at me. "We have been tracking your progress through the mist for quite some time. To what town does your loyalty belong?"

"Vaiyene," I said. "We're friends of Kilo and Finae."

The man with the long beard waited for Akio's answer.

"To General Mirai of Tarahn."

This seemed to satisfy the man, who then gestured back toward the forest and stepped back. "We will lead you to Konro. I am Emiko, and this is Jitarou. Although most just call him Jita."

Jita was shorter and stockier than his companion. He had a collection of pouches tied around his waist, with a short sword hanging down from a rope. When he walked, the sword swayed side to side, although his walk was more of a wobble compared to his companion's elegant gait.

Emiko walked with his hands clasped behind his back, his posture perfect as he followed his partner. They seemed an odd pair, but they had a sort of cadence to them, as if they had a friendship that spanned many years.

The fog vanished, and the earthy smell of decaying leaves held a hint of sweetness. Trees on the edge of the trail had tiny buds, with sprouts of orange flowers emerging.

In another few weeks, this forest would be a beautiful sight to behold.

Akio had his eyes on the trees and blossoms. He picked one of the open flowers and came to my side, dropping it into my hands with a mischievous smile. The white petals were delicate in my palm. Fragile. When I brought it closer to my nose to smell it, I could see silver rivets in the leaves. They were not veins but something else.

When the trees began to thin out, the slope of the ground tilted. Stone stairs were built into the mountain to make the climb easier. Emiko and Jita came to a stop, bowing slightly before they began to ascend.

Curious, I asked about it. "Why did you bow?"

Emiko looked back at me with a small smile upon his face. "The place you walk is a sacred one." He gestured toward the two stone pillars at the top of the hill where a large rope hung suspended between them. "This archway is an entrance."

As I crossed under it, the tension in my body dissipated as if there were something indeed otherworldly about the place we entered.

I drew in a sharp breath, the realization coming over me.

It was the Skills.

This place was alive with them.

Jita and Emiko paused for a moment, standing to the side of the pathway as two people clad in white robes approached us.

Emiko nodded toward them. "They will look after your horses for you."

Akio took my horse's reins and handed them off. "Take care of them. They've had a long journey."

The two caretakers bowed. "We will make sure they get the attention they need," one of them said. She had a light voice, reminding me of a bird's song.

We continued into the valley where tall grasses swished in the amber sunlight. The view made my heart soar, feeling as light as blades of grass as they danced. Holding my hand up, I let the breeze take the flower Akio had given me. It floated across the field, shimmering as it was swept away. On the horizon, a large, round building rested atop a tangle of vines. Large flowers sprouted from the top of the building, with smaller leaves and buds dotting the vines around the structure. It almost seemed as if the structure itself had merged with the landscape, becoming one with the vines and rock.

As we drew closer, the building towered over our company.

Our escort led us through an area thick with bamboo. New sprouts poked through the ground, and I walked with care to not disturb them. A group of children with hoes in their hands huddled around a shoot. One of the taller boys swung the tool, overcompensating, and fell backward. The others burst into laughter. I found myself smiling, remembering how Syrane and I used to dig up bamboo shoots and bring them home to prepare for dinner.

Akio touched my arm and pointed ahead. "Look at that."

A large lake, its water as still as glass, spread out across the bamboo forest. The mist rolled across the landscape, brushing the edge of the water. Standing in a path cleared of bamboo was a woman who turned at our approach. Around her eyes and forehead were deep wrinkles showing years of experience and telling of her great wisdom.

"This is Lady Chiyori, Guardian of Konro," Emiko said as he bowed to the woman.

Akio stepped forward, bowing his head as he knelt on one knee. "We bring news of an attack from the False Shadows. There are at least two dozen mercenaries on their way. My general has sent my companion and I to offer our help while he and his men try and cut off a possible second attack."

I crossed my right arm over my chest and bowed at the waist.

"Raise your heads," Lady Chiyori said.

Straightening, I saw her attention was on the lake. "I knew by allowing Phantom Kilo into our village, it would come to this. No matter what we did, this could not have been helped." She turned away from the water, focusing on me. "Are you a Shadow?"

I was surprised by her question. "I have not yet sworn my Shadow vows."

Lady Chiyori nodded and then motioned me over to the lakeside. "I can feel the Skills being drawn to you, yet you do not have a bond on your arm. It is dangerous to practice the Skills without one."

It seemed like a trivial thing to be discussing now.

Especially since I didn't use the Skills that much.

She seemed unhurried, calm, and collected at the mention of mercenaries coming to her village. Was she not worried?

"With all due respect, Lady Chiyori, while I appreciate your concern for my well-being, I cannot help but feel anxious to prepare. We've come to help defend Konro. There is little time for other matters."

Lady Chiyori looked at me with kindness and nodded slightly. "Another time then. I will take you to your companions so you may prepare for the coming conflict."

From out of the forest, as if he had been waiting for the conclusion to our conversation, a man came toward us. Like the Guardian, he, too, was clad in all white. He extended his arm toward Lady Chiyori and walked by the Guardian's side, moving away from the lake at a slow pace. As we left the silver lake behind, the bamboo stalks clacked together in the wind. Wooden houses were hidden throughout the forest with paper doors slid open to let in the fresh air. Birds sang overhead, and insects chirped. It was an atmosphere so similar to Vaiyene that tears appeared at the edges of my eyes. I longed to return home, to a time not long ago, when my parents and my brother waited for me. Where the people of the village smiled, giving me flowers and peaches ripe from the orchards.

But that wasn't possible.

At least, for now.

Akio slowed down. His brows knit with concern. I wiped the tears from my eyes, and he grabbed my arm, pulling me closer to him. Taking my hand in his, he smiled.

"Soon, things will be better," he said quietly.

With all my heart, I hoped so.

At the base of the acorn-building, the roots dug deep, reaching into the earth with such force the ground had been broken, creating deep chasms. Stone arches were nestled inside the roots, reinforcing the entrance into the building.

We walked under the arch, maneuvering around the trees and flora to enter a half-stone, half-wood interior. Small stone pieces were inlaid in the floor, creating intricate patterns. So entwined were the stone archways and design that I was unsure if it was the natural inside of the great tree or if some architect had made it to look like the tree had been flayed open to create the structure. The inside of the building was vast and dimly lit and triangular in shape. Windows had been cut into the bark, with branches and leaves living off the tree's shell. In the ground, the stonework converged toward the center, leaving a place where a tree with golden leaves grew. Silver strands of metal wrapped around the tree's branches, and lanterns were hung from a thin rope. As we passed the tree, the fire in the lanterns seemed to waver peculiarly, and I doubted whether it was actually fire that lit them.

I lifted my eyes to the ceiling, craning my neck back to see the different platforms built into the walls. Bookcases rested against the different levels and platforms, and slits were cut into the ceiling, allowing light to spill in.

A white-haired man with ruddy skin came from across the building. His eyes were bright and youthful, and he had a small brown birthmark over his nose. He bowed to the Guardian.

"What may I assist you with, Guardian?"

"Please let Finae and Rin know they have visitors. We'll be out on the terrace." The Guardian climbed a short staircase and walked out of the building. The terrace, if you could call it that, was created from a large branch of the tree with wooden boards affixed to it, forming a platform for us to stand it. Jutting out from the main trunk, the branch had vines wrapping around its circumference. I stopped at the edge and peered down. The roots of the tree extended so far into the earth and chasms I couldn't see the bottom. There were chairs on the terrace, with vines holding them in place. They were not ordinary chairs but ones made from small branches wrapped together with a curved shaped that reminded me of a crescent moon.

Moving with an elegant grace, the Guardian sat down on one of the crescent-shaped chairs. The silver spirals of her robe mirrored the movement of the vines of her chair.

"Shenrae!" someone yelled.

I turned to see Finae running toward me. She threw her arms around me, and I braced myself, not expecting such an enthusiastic greeting. Behind her, a tall and slender woman approached. She wore a wrapped top with oversized pants tucked into shin guards and boots. Her black, hip-length hair was tied up in a simple ponytail adorned with a wooden ornament, and her green, elongated eyes set into dark skin.

She watched me with interest.

Finae released me and stepped back. She grinned, her nose wrinkling as she did so. Her personality had always been carefree—a stark contrast to Kilo's more reserved nature. She wore a white robe similar to the Guardian's, except hers was stained with large splotches of different colors of paint. Over her shoulder, a bag draped down past her thigh.

She was almost as tall as I was now.

"It's good to see you again, Finae," I said, bowing slightly to her.

After returning the bow, she motioned back at the woman. "This is Rin. She's been helping Kilo and me learn about the Skills."

Rin's attention shifted to Akio, who slid his arm over my shoulder and leaned against me. "I'm Akio, one of General Mirai's men. I'm also Shenrae's trainer and bodyguard."

I nearly choked at the addition of bodyguard to Akio's list of titles.

Amused, I slipped out from under him, a smile appearing on my face.

"It's nice to meet you," I said, starting to bow to Rin.

"I've heard a lot about you from Kilo," Rin said with a smile, which seemed to soften her appearance. "It's a pleasure to finally be able to meet you."

Sneaking a glance at Finae, I saw her smiling wryly. There was something she knew about Kilo and Rin that I didn't. Judging by the fondness in Rin's voice and her lack of formality when referring to Kilo, it seemed they must be close.

Akio cleared his throat, shifting slightly. As much as I wanted to continue with the introductions, we didn't have the time for it.

"A group of mercenaries is headed here," I said, watching as Rin's mood changed. What kindness was in her eyes faded at the mention of the threat. "We came to warn you while General Mirai attempts to cut off the larger force. It's not much, but Akio and I can help fight against them."

"There are a few warriors who were taught in Zenkaiko who may be able to help," the Guardian said. Her eyes roamed the terrace, flickering slightly as if they couldn't focus on anything. It was only then I realized she was blind.

Finae plopped down, sitting cross-legged on the wooden boards. "We don't need to fight them," she said, reaching into the bag to withdraw a drawing stick. "If we place daggers around Konro in multiple locations, it may be possible to enclose the village in a barrier and keep the mercenaries out."

She sketched outlines of silver on the terrace's planks, depicting the main tree and the surrounding houses we had seen earlier. The silver she drew with, what was it?

I bent down next to the drawing. "Is that—?"

Finae grinned. "The Skills. It'll absorb into the wood after a while."

"How long can you hold the barrier?" the Guardian asked.

Finae chewed her bottom lip and sketched another silver line, drawing a circle around the building. "If we situate the anchors as close as we can—"

"The library will be sufficient."

Finae considered for a moment. "With a barrier that size, we can hold out for maybe a few hours. We'll need two people to maintain it though."

"I know a little about how to use the Skills," I said, almost not saying anything as I remembered the times my use of the Skills had gone awry. "Is creating a barrier difficult?"

Finae brightened. "It's not that hard. Let me show you."

She pulled out a bamboo canister from her bag and pulled the plug at the top, handing the container to me.

"Pour the water over me."

I stared at her. "What?"

Rin covered her mouth while she tried not to laugh at my confusion. Not sure what to expect, I drizzled the water from the container over Finae's head. But instead of touching her, the water hit something I could not see and slid off.

"It's taken Finae a few weeks to get the hang of it," Rin said, straddling one of the chairs and sitting down. She rested her elbow against the chair's back.

"Can you also use the Skills?" I asked.

"To an extent. Not as well as Finae, though."

Finae crouched down, adding silver circles onto her drawing. "We'll need to place daggers in a circular pattern to allow the barrier to be erected. Ten should be enough."

Akio leaned over Finae's drawing. "I'll place the daggers in the right locations. The sooner we finish preparations, the better. Will any dagger do?"

Finae pulled out a rolled-up mat of straw from her bag and handed it to him. "They need to be infused with the Skills or be made from them. These I'm familiar with."

Akio nodded. He looked down at Emiko and Jita, who stood at the building's entrance below.

He turned to me, saying quietly, "I'll find you when I'm finished."

Anxiety tightened my chest. I stood silent, watching Akio appear down below before he, Emiko and Jita disappeared into the forest.

"We should start our own preparations," Rin said, moving to exit the terrace.

Finae stopped in front of the Guardian.

"We will protect the village; don't worry," Finae said.

The Guardian smiled. "You have our gratitude and thanks."

I gave a short bow to the Guardian, then hastened to catch up with Rin and Finae. We passed through the library and headed back through the forest and bamboo stalks, to the silver lake, where Finae stopped at the edge of the water.

"You need a bond," Rin said, "before you even think about maintaining the barrier. The bond will negate some of the negative effects of the Skills when you use them and protect your life."

She walked to the other side of the lake, looking out across the forest.

I hesitated. "But I'm not yet a Shadow…"

I realized she might not understand my reluctance. How much did she know about what it meant to be a Shadow? To go against tradition and pretend I had ascended to a Shadow with a bond seemed dishonorable.

"Both Finae and I have bonds to counteract the Skills," Rin said, holding up her right forearm. Though I could not see her bond under the bandages, I did see a slight indentation of what could be one.

Finae pulled back the sleeve on her left arm, exposing her bond.

"Even though we are not Shadows," Finae explained, "Kilo insisted we both have one. He would want the same for you."

The Shadows back home would not understand.

Syrane would not understand.

He would see it as a betrayal, one more thing to add to my list of grievances.

I drew in a breath, remembering Phantom Asdar's words. The traditions and customs we observed were changing. If a bond kept a person safe while using the Skills, if they had more meaning than symbolizing being a Shadow, we needed to change the way we thought about the bonds. Sooner or later, Vaiyene and the Shadows would have to accept the Skills. This was my duty, to preserve the knowledge of the Skills and to protect the people.

"What do I need to do?" I asked.

Finae looked down at the lake. "Reach your hand into the water."

I raised an eyebrow. "That's it?"

"The Skills will do the rest."

Kneeling at the water's edge, I peered into the depths. Up close, it didn't look like water but like metal. Squashing my hesitations, I reached out my hand.

The cold water engulfed my hand, and my consciousness slipped...

———

Nothingness engulfed me.

There was no sound, no smell, and no feeling in the darkness.

My heart rate began to rise, the void intimidating me as I tried to find something to brace myself with. I breathed out, feeling—hearing—the air move in and out, which only made my growing anxiety more pressing.

Turning inward, I recalled where I was and what my purpose was.

I was in Konro, and I was trying to forge my bond to use the Skills.

With that purpose in mind, I took a step, finding the plane I walked on to be without texture or variation. With everything in darkness, the only thing I could make out was my own reflection in the mirror-like ground. Bending down, I splayed my fingers out, trying to feel something that would indicate what kind of terrain it was, or if it even was tangible.

As I moved my hand across the cool glass-like resistance, a small light trailed where my fingers dragged like ripples across a lake. A gentle presence hung suspended around me, similar to the atmosphere of the lake in Vaiyene, where Phantom Asdar had taken me.

I stood quietly, my hands outstretched.

Small lights, tiny orbs of the Skills, began to rise from below, illuminating as they swayed and meandered to create shapes in the air. The more I reached out to them, the deeper my sense of *knowing* became. The Skills made it feel as if I were connected to the Skills, myself, and everything else. So strong was the feeling that it nearly overwhelmed me, giving me a sense of profound understanding words could never express.

Silver light collected from every direction. It spiraled and wound before my eyes, snaking over my forearm as the lights melded together.

The scent of morning dew wafted over me, and the void shifted.

I walked through a forest of aspen trees laden with snow. Sunlight shined, warming the air as the snow melted and dropped from the branches. Leaves and buds replaced the snow, and soon delicate white and pink flowers bloomed. It was not long before the leaves turned golden, then red, falling to the ground.

Breathing in deeply, I caught a hint of smoke in the air.

Fear gripped me, and the ground gave way.

My vision blurred, and I coughed at the onslaught of smoke, my eyes burning.

Vaiyene was on fire!

My heart clenched, but then I forced myself to be rational. It had been almost half a year since the fires had razed my homeland. Ignoring my misgivings, I took a step forward. The smoke's grasp on me faded, and in the shadows of flames, I saw two figures. Their identities were distorted as I approached, but a sense of knowing who they were sprang up in my heart.

It couldn't be...

I prepared myself for some delusion, searching for any way to understand what I was seeing, but I found nothing that could make me believe the people standing before me were not my parents. The flames blew over me—the fire licking at my side, burning my clothing, and searing my skin. I winced and pulled back, seeing the figures distort.

No!

I pushed through the fire, casting aside all doubt.

Why did it matter if I indulged in this fantasy, this memory, this dream the Skills were showing me? For I was sure the Skills were behind it. Why should I deny whatever this moment was meant to show me?

Clamping my jaw tight, I gritted my teeth, fighting against the tears in my eyes as I tried to reach my parents in the flames.

Did they hate me for leaving Vaiyene?

Did they approve of me joining General Mirai's group?

Were they disappointed with Syrane and the rift between us?

Their figures swayed in the flames as they disappeared into them. My chest tightened, and I swallowed thickly against the knot in my throat.

"Wait!" I croaked.

Their figures blurred, shuddering against the onslaught of wind. The smoke barreled me over, and I fell to the charred earth.

Summoning my remaining strength, I yelled, "Don't go!"

The flames and smoke vanished in a burst of wind. My head was dazed, but I continued—toward the figures who shimmered in silver light. My mother smiled and looked at me with kindness in her eyes. My father smiled too, though it was more of a smirk, as if he had known I would be worried I couldn't reach them.

I moved closer, not genuinely believing it was them.

It couldn't be, could it?

Placing my right arm over my chest, I bowed at the waist before sinking to my knees. My legs had lost their strength, but my respect and reverence for them was nothing short of the reverence a Phantom deserved.

"That surprised to see us, huh?" my father asked. He chuckled, his smile spreading as he looked over at my mother.

My mother tilted her head at me. "Don't look so surprised. You were raised by Shadows. You should understand, Shenrae."

I blinked my tears away, feeling them stream down my face. The Shadows believed those who died still watched over Vaiyene and the ones they loved. Their duty and protection never ended. But what got to me was how I had forgotten what my father's voice sounded like and the way he laughed. He looked the same as I remembered him, but hearing him speak made me sob harder. My mother knelt next to me and threw her arms around me. I tried not to remember the night I'd said goodbye to her.

The night of the fires.

"Enough. It is passed," my mother said, hugging me tighter.

Drawing in a deep breath, I lifted my head and wiped the tears from my eyes.

"I've missed you."

Time seemed not to have passed since we were last able to speak. The day I asked to be sponsored sprang up in my mind. This was the moment I had longed for them to see since becoming a Shadow, and now, I had the opportunity to say what I wanted.

"Phantom Asdar has sponsored me as a Shadow," I said, scraping my foot against the rough dirt and standing. I brushed off my Shadow garb to look presentable.

My mother stepped back as my father wrapped his arm around her.

Their eyes were filled with pride.

"Congratulations, Shenrae," my father said.

"We always knew you and Syrane would do great things," my mother said. Her voice was soothing and gentle. She always listened when I was upset, speaking words that calmed me.

My father grinned, his chest puffing up with false bravado. He winked at my mother. "You are, after all, our daughter."

My mother and I laughed.

He always knew how to lighten a mood.

My heart was soothed, warmed by the love and pride of my parents. In this place, within the Skills, their love had a feeling to it, like their emotions were so strong they created an atmosphere around me.

My eyes fell to the bonds on their arms, a question resting on the tip of my tongue.

"What is it, Shenrae?" my mother asked.

"Were you...did you ever feel uncertain about being a Shadow?"

My father's chest remained puffed up, and I became nervous.

"Of course," my mother said. "There was a long period where both of us wondered why we had wanted to become Shadows. When I first became a Shadow, I spent my time alone, keeping to myself and working hard on my studies." She smiled a little sadly. "It was my parents who wanted me to spend my time studying so much, so at first it was mostly to please them. But then..."

She sighed, eyeing my father.

"She met me," he said. He rubbed the back of his head and smiled a half-smile. "I never took Shadow training seriously until I met Kilo. For a lot of us, it was something we wanted to do together because it seemed fun. Training every day, going on missions, studying warfare and the arts. For most of us, that was enough, but—" My father shifted his feet, his eyes turning upward as he contemplated his next words. "For Kilo, it was different. He had a purpose. He didn't want to become a Shadow because it would make his parents proud. He wanted to become a Shadow for the people."

Phantom Asdar had said much the same. That there was a reason to become a Shadow. A purpose that ran deeper than duty or will.

"What was your reason?" I asked my mother.

She grinned, her eyes crinkling with her happiness. "I wanted to be able to protect your father. And Kilo's desire to make a better Vaiyene also inspired me."

My father nodded. "Kilo inspired all of us. The Shadows would not be what they are today without Kilo's influence."

"And?" My mother looked over at him pointedly.

His eyes narrowed, and he pushed out his lips. "And Asdar."

Covering her mouth with her hand to hide her smile, my mother looked over at me with knowing eyes. I had always known there was tension between my father and Asdar. It was probably because my father had disliked him that both Syrane and I had been so cautious of him.

Uncovering her mouth, my mother continued. "Asdar and Kilo were a pair who encouraged one another. Without each other, they would not have risen to be Phantoms. Asdar always saw your father as too much of a prankster to be friendly with him. He always used to say if your father spent more time practicing with his sword, he would have been a better Shadow."

My father waved off the words. A touch of red appeared in his cheeks as he muttered, "Narcissistic sword freak."

My mother laughed.

"It will take time to find your reason, Shenrae," my mother said, steering the conversation back to my main concern. "Be patient. Over time, your heart may change, and you might find you were worrying about things that never were important. Keep your eyes and your heart open. It will come to you in time."

The redness in my father's cheeks faded, and he crouched down in front of me, holding out his hand. "Let me see your hand."

Unsure of his plan, I complied.

He rubbed the burn mark on the back of my hand with his thumb, scrutinizing it as he turned my hand. "Do you know what this symbol means?"

I shook my head.

"This is an ancient symbol of the Phantoms. While the design itself has no name, it represents the way of the world and our journey to understand it. The most important things in life are not 'what' or 'who' but 'why' and 'how.' It's the meaning found in our everyday actions that matter the most."

Running his thumb over the symbol again, he looked up. "Follow your heart, Shenrae; it will not lead you astray."

My father wrapped his arms around me, drawing me tightly to his chest. My mother came over and hugged both of us, speaking softly. "Whenever you feel the Skills, know we are there too."

Her coloring faded, as her form took on a silver hue and translucence. She hugged my father and me tighter.

"We love you."

"And we're so proud."

An aching sadness came over me, but my heart remained warm when they were one with the Skills again. Silver metal and light converged around my arm in an intricate design. My bond encircled the burn mark Syrane, Torey, and I had given ourselves with the daggers Kilo had passed on to us.

It was a good reminder.

All this time, I had been worried about not being enough. About not having the strength to help Finae, but I had forgotten one of the core aspects of being a Shadow: we were never alone. I had never entirely understood it until now—why Kilo and Phantom Asdar visited the Reikon Tree and the cave above it so often. I had thought it was merely a routine, but was it because they were able to experience the same thing I had?

Were they able to talk with the people they loved?

The Shadows who had passed?

The bond on my arm felt warm—a gentle reminder of the memory. There was a strength within me, around me, and across Kiriku. At the edge of my mind, I became aware of my surroundings—the smell of the damp air, the trickle of water, the wet grass under my knees— and the vision before me faded.

Pushing myself up from the ground, I glanced over at Finae. Rin's silhouette could be seen against the fog. Finae drew a blade from a pouch at her side and held out the blunt side to me.

"Are you ready to learn how to create a barrier?"

chapter fifty-four
Konro

The Skills awakened in the air as Finae stepped close to me. She handed me a thin, silver dagger, identical to the ones she had given Akio to place around Konro.

"What do I need to do?" I asked, feeling an energy around the blade.

Finae walked back into the bamboo forest, leading me away from the silver lake. Rin sat cross-legged on the ground, a whetstone at her feet. She scraped her curved sword across the rough surface in a steady rhythm. Finae joined Rin on the ground, and I sat across from both of them, folding my legs underneath me. I thought back to the techniques Ikaru had taught me.

"I never fully learned how to control the Skills," I admitted, feeling my chest tighten. What if I couldn't help Finae like she believed I could?

Rin glanced up from her work. "After reading through the books the Guardian saved from Zenkaiko, I've come to understand that the Skills exist as we do and how to use them remains abstract. There are varying theories and approaches. The technique I taught my brother involved senses of hot and cold, but lately, I've adopted more of Finae's and Kilo's way of thinking."

I stared at her and blinked. "Is Ikaru—"

"My brother, yes." She chuckled, returning her attention to the sword.

Ikaru had never said anything about having a sister. Restraining my questions, I waited for Finae to explain. There would be a better time to get to know Rin.

"Will there be enough time for me to learn how to use the Skills?"

Finae nodded. "Don't worry, there's enough time. Already, you should be able to feel the Skills through your bond and in the dagger I gave you."

"The bond and the dagger *are* the Skills," Rin clarified. "They're the purest form of the Skills, distilled down into tangible objects. Just being in contact with them is enough to make a connection."

"You'll be able to use the Skills easier in Konro as well," Finae said, continuing on as if she had not been interrupted. "The Skills are alive here. Other towns and villages don't have the same atmosphere, so learning how to use them here will be easier." She paused for a while, considering her words. "It almost feels like a warm blanket."

I laughed at the comparison.

As a matter of fact, I did feel the comforting presence in the air.

Finae grinned and withdrew four daggers from a pouch tied to her ankle. She slid each blade into the dirt, spacing them evenly around herself in a square. "I'll create a small barrier, and you can help me sustain it."

I dug my fingers into my palm, the fear of the Skills crawling back into my mind.

What if I lost control again?

"Shenrae?"

Shaking the momentary panic from my mind, I looked from Rin to Finae, realizing I didn't know who had said my name.

"Sorry," I said.

Embarrassment choked any explanation for why I was apologizing.

"Don't be nervous," Rin said, wiping down her sharpened sword with oil before she sheathed it. "Finae knows the ins and outs of the Skills. There's nothing you can do that she won't know how to work around. She's walked me through how to use the barrier and quite a few other experiments with the Skills as well. You can trust her."

I nodded.

Finae pointed at one of the daggers. "These blades are the anchor points where the Skills will be channeled to. You'll feel a pull from the Skills. Sort of like a current in a stream or the wind in the air." Her hand hovered over the dagger. "Ready to try?"

"Yes."

Finae's hand closed around the handle, and she stayed still for a few moments before she withdrew her hand and placed it in her lap, her eyes closed.

I raised an eyebrow to Rin, who held out one of her fingers near Finae.

"You can't see it, but…"

She pressed as hard as she could against an invisible wall, splaying her fingers out where there was resistance. Reaching out with my own hand, I let my fingers explore the smooth, cold surface beneath my palm.

"Finae will need to focus on maintaining the barrier," Rin said, kneeling next to me, "so I'll walk you through how to connect to it."

"Okay."

"You'll want to clear your mind first, allowing any worries or concerns to fade away. Concentrate on the movement and flow of energy around Finae. Let the Skills reach out to you."

Letting my thoughts dissipate, I closed my eyes, finding it was easier to calm my thoughts than it had been a few months ago. I breathed in and out in a deep, rhythmic pattern, waiting for whatever was going to happen. After some time, a breath of wind brushed against my arm. There was an ebb and flow, like the swell of the tide, or a heartbeat, as the energy moved toward a single location. My awareness grew as I slowed my breathing to match its movement.

I opened my eyes, surprised that even with them open the feeling persisted.

"I can feel them," I said, grinning up at Rin.

"Good. Can you feel where they are going? And what their purpose is?"

Their purpose?

I almost voiced the question, but instead, I shifted my focus back to the Skills to see if I could understand what Rin meant without her having to explain it. The Skills were moving like a wave toward Finae, toward the silver blades she used as anchors.

They had a destination, but how could one determine their purpose?

"There's a current to the Skills," I said, tilting my head as I spoke. "They're being drawn to the barrier, but I don't understand what you mean by a 'purpose.'"

"The Skills have a will of their own. Originally, I had thought they were something to be controlled or used, like weapons, but they have a consciousness. From our experience working with them, we've determined that when we do something they desire, we're able to feel their power more within us than if we do something they are averse to."

Rin placed a hand on Finae's shoulder, then bent down and whispered something into her ear before extending her hand toward me. I let her pull me up, following as she walked me to another area.

"The Skills become exhausted the longer they're in use. You'll need to be able to guide the Skills from a different location to strengthen the barrier when you're helping Finae. All you need to do is hold out your hand and feel for the Skills."

I almost laughed at the simplicity. Using the Skills was that simple? After everything I had gone through with Ikaru, after all the careful meditation and planning. Just hold out my hand, and the Skills would come to me?

Rin's eyes never left me, and after my amusement died down, I held out my hand, palm up to the sky, to humor her.

I waited, staring at my hand, reaching out to feel the Skills. But nothing happened.

"Wait," Rin said.

Concentrating, I allowed my expectations to fade. After some time, there came a wind. Not a physical wind, but a pull—to where Finae controlled the barrier. An orb of light appeared in my hand, and I almost dropped it before it streaked across the area to where Finae maintained the barrier.

Laughing, Finae opened her hand and stood up.

"Finae's learned how to create a light," Rin said, offering an explanation.

Amazed, I stood with wide eyes as the orb of Skills followed Finae's hand in circles as she moved. The light wavered, then stretched into a rectangular shape before disappearing. Finae came toward me, keeping her palm facing the sky.

"Try to move your hand above my palm."

A shimmer of colored light flickered at the edge, where my hand pressed against it.

"You'll feel the same pull you did before," Finae said, dropping her hand and releasing the Skills.

As she did so, a breath of air caressed my face, almost as if someone had exhaled.

Rin paced the edge of the forest, her hand wrapping around the hilt of her sword. "I will leave the barrier to you and Finae. I'll work with the scouts and warriors from Konro to ensure no one makes it past the barrier."

"And what if they do?" I asked.

Would she kill them?

Before she could answer, leaves crunched behind us.

Rin crossed in front of Finae and me, sword half-drawn as she looked intently into the forest. Akio and the two guards,

Emiko and Jita, appeared. Akio carried his spear in his hand. He had unwrapped the blade, which indicated he had either used it or was ready to.

"We found scouts," he said, placing the pole of his spear on the ground. "A group of two dozen is not far behind them. They're traversing the cliffs down into the valley. If we meet them there, it'll allow us to pick them off before they're able to find the village."

"That's a good plan," Rin said, glancing over at Finae and me. "Does that sound good to both of you?"

We both nodded.

The Guardian had said she wanted to protect only the library, but if we made our stand near the cliffs it would give us two chances to stop the mercenaries. Once at the cliffs and the other around the library. If we only used the barrier around the library, it would leave the houses and other places of the village vulnerable.

I rubbed the bond on my right arm, the metal cool under my fingers. I had wanted this, to be involved and to make a difference, but could so few of us really protect the village?

A Shadow serves until he is no longer able, his life freely given to the people.

Death was a part of life, and for the Shadows, it was our duty to freely give our life in defense of those who could not protect themselves. If I died defending Konro and its people, I would have fulfilled my duty.

"Let's hurry," Akio said. "Emiko and Jita—will you tell the others?"

Emiko placed his hand on a nearby tree, focusing intently on a patch of silver that ran lengthwise along the trunk. I helped Finae pull the daggers from the ground, and after a few seconds, Emiko looked back at Akio. "The others will meet us there."

"Good."

I eyed Emiko curiously before following after Akio and Rin. There was something about him that seemed odd, something familiar. Only, I couldn't put my finger on what it was.

Brushing the thought away, I focused on keeping up with the others. We ran through the forest, past the meadow, and under Konro's gate. When we neared the lake, we crouched down, hiding in the thick brush of the forest. The mercenaries would have to swim across the lake like Akio and I had—which would leave them vulnerable to attack. And if they were like the mercenaries who had come to Vaiyene, they would have metal armor that would need to be removed before entering the water.

"Is there another way around?" Akio asked, addressing Emiko and Jita.

Jita pointed ahead. "This is the most direct path. However, if they descended the cliff from the north, there is a way to circle around Konro. The water is too high to use it after the snow fully melts, but the path is open now if they find it."

Something splashed across the lake.

They were coming.

Glancing around, I analyzed the small strip of land we stood on between the water and the forest. The barrier Akio and the others had set up was placed around the library. It was farther back than we were, leaving us vulnerable here.

"Can we create a smaller barrier to keep them on the shore?" I asked.

Rin and Akio exchanged glances.

"We might still have time," Akio said.

He turned to Finae who unrolled her daggers and handed three to Akio and two to me. "Place them in a circle around us as best you can. I'll keep one for the main anchor point."

Rin drew her sword, her eyes keen on the lake. "Hurry," she whispered.

"One hundred steps in each direction," Finae said, pointing to the forest. "Then halfway between where I'm standing and the shore. Hide the ones near the lake in the water."

"Understood!"

Akio ran south, and I headed north.

I kept my attention on the lake, counting one hundred steps in my head. At the right location, I waded into the water and slid the dagger in between two large rocks, wiggling the blade to ensure it was secure.

Air whirred near me.

Letting go of the dagger, I snatched my hand back as an arrow skidded across the rocks. A mercenary stood farther down the lakeside, his bow drawn back and an arrow nocked. With haste, I ran back to shore, reaching the forest as another arrow whistled past me. Branches whipped against my arms, but I ignored them. The most important thing was to set the barrier. If we had to retreat, we would not get another chance to make a stand unless we pulled back to the first barrier we had set.

And that meant endangering the lives of the villagers.

Keeping my eyes on the ground, I jumped over fallen logs and navigated around rocks and bushes. Finae stood not far ahead, waiting. I counted fifty-three paces from the first dagger I had placed. Judging from where Finae stood, this seemed about halfway. Bending down next to a bush, I pushed the blade inside the tangle of branches.

With the daggers set, I sprinted back to Finae's side.

"Did Akio manage to place his?" I asked.

"He did," she replied, pacing back to the shore.

Our other allies had begun to gather in the area—five of them, with long black hair, braided and tied back at the shoulders. They wore long white robes similar in design to the Guardian's. Each carried two swords. These were the warriors the Guardian had spoken about——the ones trained by the descendants of Zenkaiko.

How much did they know about the Skills?

A fog rose from the ground in thick waves, rolling in on itself and expanding across the forest. It collided with the mist on the lake and plumed skyward before floating back down. I eyed the warriors. Their expressions were calm, but was it possible they were the source of the fog?

Hidden among the trees, Emiko and Jita each held a bow.

Rin and Akio stood at the edge of the forest.

Finae touched my shoulder and nodded toward a grove of trees. After finding a good position, I settled in a sparse area to ensure I could see the shore. Finae sat cross-legged, the dagger resting between her palms. She closed her eyes, and the air shifted around us. A gentle wind rustled my hair and robes.

Collectively, a silence settled over us.

Every bird, insect, and person waited on the precipice of the moment.

Then came a whirring.

"Arrows!" Akio whispered.

They sank into the ground at different angles and locations. Emiko and Jita kept their bows at the ready, waiting for a target, but the fog hid the mercenaries from our view.

"Should we take the fight to them?" Akio asked, turning to Rin with a rather wolfish smile on his face.

She drew her sword, returning his smile. "I'll cover you."

"I can expand my reach to protect you," Finae offered, her voice carrying to them.

"Save your strength," Rin said. "The fog will work to our advantage."

Silently, Akio and Rin disappeared into the mist.

I hesitated.

"They'll be fine," Finae said.

Her eyes were closed, but she was conscious enough to recognize my fears without seeing me. Or perhaps, she'd said it to reassure herself as well.

Closing my eyes, I sank into the Skills, feeling their resonance. Finae's presence was with them, and distantly, I could sense the daggers Akio had placed around the library and the town.

Something hit the barrier, and I flinched.

My eyes flew open at the impact of an arrow.

Beside me, Finae remained undisturbed, too lost in concentration to react. Another group of arrows fell from the sky, clinking against the barrier's edge before falling onto the sand. I peered through the fog but saw nothing. There was no glint of metal, nor silhouettes framed in the mist.

Had Akio and Rin engaged with the mercenaries?

The next impact on the barrier was stronger, but it felt more distant than the first. I tried to pinpoint the feeling, tilting my head as I followed the flow of the Skills past Finae and to the daggers placed on the other side of Konro.

"They've split forces," I said, the realization coming to me, and I glanced over at Finae to see her grimace.

Something hit the barrier again.

This time, the force seemed weaker, almost as if they were testing it. We had gambled on the main group coming down the trail, through the mist and the pillars, but they must have split when they reached the bottom. They had dispersed into the forest and circled around the town, finding the pathway around the lake.

I scrambled onto my feet and hurried over to Emiko and Jita.

"There's another group on the other side, near the library."

Emiko let out a deep breath. "The few who came here were likely a distraction."

Finae shuddered as something hit the barrier.

The Skills pushed against me.

"I don't know if I can hold it at this rate," Finae said, her voice strained as she spoke. "It's too far."

From the mist, Akio and Rin came running toward us.

"What's happening?" Akio asked, panting hard. A stain of blood was smeared across his arm, but he looked fine otherwise. He glanced over at Finae, then at me, his eyes narrowing as both Finae and I flinched against another impact.

My chest constricted, and I wrapped my hand in the folds of my robe against the pain. "The barrier is going to give out if we don't get to the other side."

"I'll stay with Finae," Rin said, holding tight to her sword.

Akio nodded. "Let's go, Shenrae."

We ran back to Konro, through the forest and to the top of the valley. As we passed under the gate, a surge of the Skills awakened under my feet; a sensation of knowing I was not alone descended over me. My parents and the wishes of the Shadows, Tarahn, and Konro were with me.

At my side, Akio kept pace with me, and I remembered training with him, the fun we'd had while in General Mirai's ranks. We'd sprinted as a company, motivating one another to become quicker and stronger together, making it more of an experience than a chore. The rest of the company had been in much better shape than I had been, and Akio had often stayed behind to encourage me.

Now, we ran at full speed, and I found joy in knowing I no longer held him back.

My feet seemed light under me as the Skills filled my body with new energy, whisking away my weariness.

"I can feel them," I breathed, a smile spreading across my face. It was as if someone had slid a piece of me into place. Something I never knew had been missing.

Akio glanced over at me. "I knew you could do it."

I drew in a breath, reveling in the Skills.

Then a weight slammed against me.

A splitting crack rippled across the barrier. My breath fell out of sync as I gasped for air and stumbled. Akio grabbed my arm and pulled me close to him as I fought a sudden wave of dizziness. Through the blur and the fog in my mind, I saw figures up ahead, moving in and out of my vision. There were at least a half dozen mercenaries, if not more. Their swords hit against the barrier, one after the other, each with greater force.

Like a drum against my mind.

I blinked and focused up ahead, seeing the edge of the village through a thick mist. Akio helped me take a step, but the closer I got, the more my head pounded against my skull. When I became too weak to move, I sank onto the ground.

Akio knelt next to me, his hand still under my arm.

"Is this close enough?" he asked.

I squinted my eyes, searching for the metal dagger tied to the barrier. "The dagger..." My words came out pained, and Akio pointed to it—a few paces from where I had fallen. I could make it that far. Leaning against Akio, I relied on him to take my weight and carry me forward.

The fog here was not as thick.

Through the mist, I could see the mercenaries.

"Let me go," I said, slouching against Akio. Reluctantly, he did so. I fell onto all fours and reached out a hand toward the dagger. A surge of the Skills rushed into me. My hand blackened, and I smelled the pungent odor of my skin burning. Through my palm, the Skills surged inside me, down the dagger and into the barrier. Multiple streams of energy fed the barrier, and I adjusted and strengthened the ones where I saw the mercenaries standing. The Skills responded to my request, and the flow around me affirmed they were moving. Finae had not taught me how it was done, but I felt the Skills guiding me.

Their will to protect Konro entwined with mine.

"Shenrae, they're carrying a large tree," Akio said.

I struggled to split my focus between maintaining the barrier and discerning Akio's words. His voice sounded urgent, and I heard him, but it took a while for my brain to process what was to come.

A tree?

Then the realization hit me.

They were going to slam it against the barrier.

"I can hold it," I said.

I had to.

If the barrier came down, we would have to fight against a dozen mercenaries. I knew Akio was strong, but those odds did not fill me with confidence. Better to hold out for as long as I could with the barrier. Drawing myself up, I folded my hands in my lap allowing my senses to narrow. I could hear nothing save for the beating of my heart and Akio's steady breathing. The mercenaries yelled and screamed, but the noise faded away. The taste of blood at the back of my throat reminded me I still breathed and had the strength to protect Akio and the people of Konro.

The mercenaries swung the tree against the barrier.

I recoiled from the force.

Akio placed his hands on my shoulders. Through the connection to the Skills, I felt Finae's presence with me as well.

Her belief and trust I would be able to hold the barrier gave me strength.

Another impact came, and the Skills stirred.

They moved, anticipating where the next strike would be, shuffling and rearranging themselves to reinforce specific areas. The mercenaries rammed the tree into the barrier again. The impact, this time, was lessened. Finae was right. The Skills had a consciousness of their own——a will and a desire. What they needed was a person to help them, to guide them. They humbled me, trusting in an outsider like me to defend this place. The Skills were truly incredible. I now understood what Kilo fought for and why Hitori was so desperate to possess them.

Forcing out a breath, I grimaced as the mercenaries slammed the tree against the barrier again and again. After some time, they set the tree down and glared at us, conversing amongst themselves.

The Skills in the barrier were weakened.

In an attempt to compensate, I shifted the barrier, drawing in more of the Skills from the surrounding area and redirecting them. At the edge of my awareness, I felt something waver, like the barrier where Finae and Rin were had become faint.

"How are you holding up?" Akio asked, his eyes resting on the bond on my forearm. The skin around the metal had begun to turn grey, almost black, where the metal touched me.

"It doesn't hurt," I said, knowing he worried about me.

"You have to let me help."

"No." I didn't even want to think about it. "There are too many of them."

Akio shifted his spear. "You can't hold this barrier forever. We should use it when we need it, not as something to hide behind."

"I can hold it."

Akio let out a deep sigh. "I can hear your breathing, Shenrae. Your hands are shaking from your efforts. You can't keep this up. Neither of us want to kill them, but I'm not sure we can dissuade them by any other means."

I balled my fists in my lap, a defiance building inside me. What had I been training for, if not for this moment? I couldn't stand the thought of allowing Akio to confront the mercenaries while there were still other options. The Skills were a powerful force and part of every living thing. Surely there was a way for them to help in this situation, behind the barrier.

Akio took a step forward.

"Wait," I said, pleading with him. "I have an idea."

It seemed beyond my limited capabilities, but perhaps the Skills themselves had found a solution. Without hesitation, Akio nodded, and I reached out to the dagger thrust into the ground. The barrier hummed in my mind. Withdrawing the barrier, I pulled the perimeter closer to where Akio stood next to me, ignoring the jeers and whoops of the mercenaries as they realized the barrier was retreating.

I restrained my smile.

They thought my power was fading and that they had won.

They didn't even consider they were falling into my trap.

"Don't move," I said under my breath to Akio.

His foot lifted, dislodging dirt and rocks underneath him. From what I could feel, the Skills were not as concentrated in the rocks, soil, or dead foliage upon the ground. There was a line of grass at the edge of the boundary where the Skills were very much alive.

I reached out and touched my fingertips to the blades of grass. One of the men swung his sword at the barrier, against my hand, causing me to flinch.

They laughed.

Gritting my teeth, I ignored their taunts, feeling Akio's quiet, barely restrained anger and his low growl. He didn't shift his stave or move, but should the barrier come down, I knew his spear would be through the man's chest in an instant.

Pushing the thought aside, I placed my hand against the barrier and closed my eyes to be rid of the distractions. Lying in wait, the Skills reached out to me. One of the mercenaries cut against the barrier, the impact jostling my hand and mind. Their taunts brought me back to my Shadow training days and Meyori's bullying, back to the anger I felt then. The stream of the Skills grew more turbulent as the memories swirled within me. The Skills were sentient enough to match the user's will. I didn't need to force them to do anything. If I allowed them to do what they wanted...

Another presence rose at the edge of my mind. Unlike Finae, who was full of happiness and good nature, this presence had a bitterness to it—harboring a deep regret. It covered my mind, creating a blanket of darkness.

I recoiled at its touch.

When I opened my eyes, the grass wavered with an unnatural wind. I lowered my gaze, ignoring the mercenaries, a sudden wave of fear rushing through me. Near the outside of the barrier, the Skills seeped up from the ground. The grass withered as if parched, and the ground cracked and ruptured, creating a chasm that swallowed two people.

They screamed.

A bubbling movement in the earth orchestrated by the Skills shot across the ground, and my stomach clenched.

"What's happening?" Akio said next to me.

With a frown, I shook my head, a growing horror weighing down my stomach. I had done nothing. "The Skills are acting on their own."

A mercenary hung from the ledge of the earth, clawing at the edge with his fingers. His companions dragged him up, and he gripped his leg, pulling off the armor affixed to it. Underneath, his skin had turned a sickly gray.

Skill poisoning, or something else?

The man screamed as the Skills slithered over his body, turning his fingers, then his hands, an ever-darker shade of grey. Another man began screaming. His body brushed against the barrier. As he stumbled away, the clothing on his back burned as if on fire. Smoke rose from his backside, and I winced at the sight. The barrier had become deadly to the touch, as had the ground in front of it.

I dug my fingers into my palm, watching as another man succumbed to the Skill poisoning. This wasn't what I had wanted!

"This is harder to watch than running them through with a spear." Akio's voice seemed strained. His fingers were wrapped so tight around his spear, his knuckles turned white.

Agreeing, I swallowed my own horror.

It seemed wrong, sneaky and underhanded, to hide behind the barrier. The Shadows would never hide like this, nor would they use the Skills to disable their opponents in such a way.

I had only wanted to help.

To defend and to protect.

"I don't know if I can do this anymore," I said, feeling on the verge of tears. I needed to feel right about this, about defeating the mercenaries and defending Konro.

Akio blew out a long, unrestrained breath. "We both knew this wasn't going to be easy." He balanced his staff against his chest. "They will not show us mercy when they reach us. I can try and disable them, but—"

"I know."

If it were not so ingrained into me that every life had value—would things have been easier? Would I have not felt their pain as my own? The mercenaries would not hesitate to kill us, and yet I didn't want them to die, and I hated they were suffering because of what I had done. Knowing Akio felt something similar didn't lessen the burden of my emotions, but it did allow me to see that the Shadows were not alone in this matter.

Life was precious, and too many people disregarded it.

Was money so prized by them that they would destroy the very lives of the people who lived here? Did they even know what it was they were destroying? Did they know anything about the people they'd been sent to kill?

I pressed my hand against the dirt, feeling the Skills vibrate under my touch. The earth itself seemed angry, upset and in turmoil. It pained me to think that perhaps it was my inflection of despair and hopelessness that had caused the Skills to respond in such a way. As my fingers scraped the ground, the rough earth cut into my skin and stained the rocks with blood.

Akio reached out a hesitant hand toward me, resting it on my shoulder.

I smiled at him before I walked away.

This ended now.

"Wait here for me," I said, taking a step outside the barrier. The black liquid oozed under my feet, creating a pool separating me from the mercenaries. They turned on me and raised their weapons, but I kept my staff lowered.

The mercenaries touched by the Skills continued to wail. I did my best to draw my shoulders back and maintain a level of authority in front of them.

"Turn back and leave this village," I said.

A broad-shouldered man, about the same height as I was, pushed through the circle of mercenaries. A large fur was draped over his shoulders, hanging down to his waist. The corner of his lip raised into a sneer. "You talk big for someone who can't even hold their hands steady."

I curled my fingers into fists. I wouldn't let him get to me. So what if I was afraid of him? His arrogance and privilege astonished me. He thought his life was worth more than the people who lived here—that he had a right to kill and take what was precious to them. All because he could use a sword and had been paid to do so.

Defiantly, I lifted my eyes to meet his. "I might be afraid of you, but I will never respect a man who values coin above a person's life."

The man's smile disappeared.

"Your men will die if you try and harm this village," I continued, ignoring the creases of anger appearing in the mercenary's face. "Only those with no ill will can enter."

"Is that so?"

I took a step away from the barrier, walking over the black liquid that bubbled and seeped from the earth. The more I walked, the farther the blackness spread. Though the mercenary leader had seemed self-assured and fearless, he stepped back when the Skills slithered toward him. He was afraid of them.

Probably more so than he let on.

And why wouldn't he be?

His lips curled into a half-smile, half-grimace.

Turning his back on me, he began to walk away. Then he spun on his heel, drawing his sword and lashing out at me. I threw my arm out to catch his blade, not even thinking as I did so. The man's sword connected with the bond on my forearm, the impact jolting my entire body. From my bond, black liquid oozed, snaking across my arm and onto the mercenary. Across his hand and forearm, the skin blackened. The fur gauntlet tied to his wrist hissed and burned, dropping in singed chunks. He let go of his sword and howled in pain as the Skills continued to eat into him.

I stepped back, horrified as his eyes rolled back into his head.

A blur rushed from behind me. Akio thrust his spear into the man's chest. As he crumpled to the ground, Akio yanked his spear free.

"I'm sorry, Shenrae." Akio's eyes were cold, focused, and without emotion.

At the corners of my vision, the world dimmed.

How had it all gone so horribly wrong?

"Shenrae!"

Akio grabbed the staff in my hand and yanked. Instinctively, I held onto it and snapped to attention, blinking away the daze. Akio sprang forward with his spear and drove the end into another man's chest. Another blur rushed past me. An arrow struck the barrier as a needle-like pain hit my heart. I leaned against my staff to support myself, clutching my hand over my heart as I struggled to breathe.

"What's wrong?" Akio said, shuffling back to my side. He kept his spear outstretched, pointing the tip at the other mercenaries, who now seemed hesitant to attack.

Gasping for air, I looked back at the barrier.

The arrow hung suspended in the air. Around the edges of the barrier, a light shimmered, and my mind was pulled into the Skills...

———

Water splashed over me, and I choked and sputtered, coughing up liquid as it filled my lungs. A trail of red seeped out from the bond on my forearm, coating the silver casing and dripping over the sides.

I inhaled a shallow, ragged breath.

My body ached.

I turned my head, looking down to where my blood had mixed with the black liquid under my feet. Ripples moved outward as I shifted one foot, seeing my reflection on the surface I walked.

What was this place?

"Hello?"

There was no echo.

Glowing orbs floated before my eyes, and I froze as they danced before me. I had seen them before, but the connection of when and where faded before I understood it. Carefully, I walked forward, my feet creating no sound as the water and black Skills moved under me. Though I didn't have a destination, the movement calmed me.

A noise came from ahead.

The sound was hard to place, indistinct and garbled. The orbs of light flared and distorted, creating some kind of pattern around me.

They were showing me something.

A form.

A memory?

Silver light spread across the area and came into focus. Someone sat on the ground, cross-legged. Nearby, dark shadows were held at bay by an invisible force.

A barrier.

Finae!

A pain in my chest caused me to double over. The Skills rushed at me from Finae's direction. She seemed peaceful, unaware, or perhaps oblivious as the Skills shattered. Pieces burst from the barrier, shimmering in a rainbow hue around the sharp edges.

I fell onto my hands and knees and wiped the back of my arm across my mouth.

Blood.

Spitting out a mouthful, I pushed myself onto my feet, stumbling forward.

"Finae! Hold on!"

Her head bobbed up, and I caught the slightest smile before a wave of shadows engulfed her. My stomach dropped, and I opened my eyes against gritty eyelids. I blinked and rubbed at my eyes, finding my hand covered in blood. My clothes were damp—soaked by black liquid and blood. Swallowing the bile at the back of my throat, I wiped my nose and face with my sleeve.

"Shenrae!"

My mind remained dazed, but I recognized Akio's voice.

"The barrier broke," I said, wishing I could still see what was happening on the other side. "Finae is in trouble."

Or was it already too late?

"I know," Akio said gently.

He threaded his arm under my shoulder and pulled me upright, then handed me my staff. After an uncertain step, I remained upright.

"Can you walk?"

I nodded, feeling numb. Being here was no longer necessary as the black liquid, the Skills, would stop anyone who tried to enter while we left.

"What happened?" I asked.

Akio hesitated.

I felt a sickness churn inside me. "Akio?"

"The mercenaries are no longer a threat. I ended a few lives, but most of them were consumed by the Skills."

I turned my head to look, but Akio pulled on my arm.

"We need to get to the other side and see if Finae and Rin are okay."

Although I knew he was right, I resisted.

"Shenrae, please," Akio begged. I could tell being here was causing him pain, but I also knew he wanted to leave for my sake, so I wouldn't have to see the horror I had unleashed.

"It's okay, Akio. I need to face what I've done."

Reluctantly, he let me go.

I walked over to the dead, looking down at the leader of the mercenaries. His body had been entirely blackened by the Skills as if he had been seared by them. Whatever had happened after I was pulled in by the Skills, I couldn't remember. Had I really done all this? It had almost felt like something took control of me. Not even the Skills, but something—someone—who knew what they were doing.

I met Akio's gaze. His brow was knit in concern.

It looked as if he were going to ask me something and I panicked.

"Finae needs us," I said, steering the conversation away from it. I didn't know if I would be able to go on if he asked me to explain what I had done.

Walking away from the dead mercenaries, my head began to clear. When it did, I began running. Akio stayed at my side, every so often checking to make sure I was okay.

"Do you feel the Skills?" Akio asked.

"No."

At least, not the Skills concentrated around the barrier.

Before, I had been able to sense the Skills spanning from one anchor point to the other. Now, there was not even a distant feeling of the barrier or its protection.

We had to hurry.

The Skills and the barrier had drained my energy. I struggled to keep running. With each step, my feet seemed heavier, dragging against the dirt. The only thing that kept me running was the thought of Finae, Rin, and the villagers depending on us. If the barrier had broken, were the villagers in danger?

Were Finae and Rin okay?

"Let's cut through here," Akio said, veering off into the forest. His sense of direction was keener than mine.

I swiped at the low-hanging branches, shielding myself from most of them as we ran through the forest. As the trees thinned near the edge of the forest, I could just see the top of the library. The gate and the lake were not far. We slowed down, and I gasped for air, my lungs burning and my body growing stiff. I pressed on, sensing nothing of the barrier. When I descended the final steps leading into Konro, my heart constricted in my chest.

Dozens of mercenaries lay dead, their bodies strewn about. I walked past them, heading toward the gate.

Someone lay in between the posts.

A person with blonde hair and white robes.

"Finae!" I yelled, running the remainder of the way to her. I fell to my knees beside her and placed my hand on her shoulder. My vision blurred, and Finae was no longer in front of me but at the top of the stairway. The memory of what had transpired flashed before my eyes.

The mercenaries had gathered below while Rin and Emiko stood at the base, keeping them from entering Konro. Behind me, I felt a presence, and I turned to find Finae walking toward the gate. She smiled at me briefly—as if she saw me in the memory—before raising her hand to touch the stone post of the archway.

In the air, the Skills shifted, and I closed my eyes to better concentrate on the feeling. The barrier pulsed with energy, revitalized by Finae's touch. Another presence came to the edge of my mind. I opened my eyes, briefly seeing the Guardian standing beside Finae. Her form was translucent, outlined with the Skills in a silver light. The appearance lasted only a moment before Finae spread her hands out to the side, palms facing the ground. Her eyes seemed to shimmer with light before the Skills in the air became heavy.

A gentle wind passed through me before a weight settled over everyone in the area. My eyes drooped, and I fought against the intense feeling of sleep pulling at me.

Shaking off the Skills, I regained my focus on the present.

The last remnants of the Skill memory released me.

"They're all asleep," I said, glancing back down at the mercenaries. "Finae and the Guardian put them to sleep with the Skills."

Astonished, I looked down at Finae's crumpled form.

"Her heartbeat is faint, but she's alive," Akio said kneeling next to her. He put his arms under her shoulders and leaned her up against the stone gate.

Emiko emerged from the forest, as elegantly poised and regal as he had been in the Skill memory. His robe had been stained with dirt and blood, but he otherwise seemed unharmed. Akio went to his side, and Emiko whispered something I couldn't hear.

Akio looked back at me. "Will you be okay without me for a little bit?"

I nodded.

Akio tightened his grip on his stave before heading into the forest. Briefly, I thought I heard shouting, but it was gone almost as soon as I'd heard it. After a while, I lost interest in listening for anything.

Thoughts faded from my mind, and I stared blankly ahead at Finae's slumped-over form and the edge of the gate. Numbness blocked my emotions, keeping me from experiencing anything too intensely. I let out a deep breath as my eyes wandered down to my arm. The skin underneath my bond had turned a sickening black. It smelled charred, as if the Skills had indeed seared my skin.

Letting my eyes unfocus on the ground, I waited.

How long before Akio would come back?

It started to become cold, and I shivered, but doing anything about it seemed too great of an effort. At some point, someone stood in front of me, laying their warm hands on my shoulders. I blinked and stared at the frayed edges of a robe, annoyed because it was less attractive to stare at than the ground had been.

Akio leaned forward and looked into my eyes.

"I've found Rin. She's wounded, but she'll be okay."

My gaze shifted back to Finae.

"One of Konro's warriors also survived," Akio continued, extending his hand toward me. "She's run ahead to inform the village to expect us. They'll bring horses to carry the mercenaries to the village and decide what to do with them from there."

I continued to stare at Finae.

Emiko came to stand in front of me and nudged me with his foot. When I looked up, he nodded toward Akio, whose hand was still outstretched.

"Stand, Shadow," Emiko said, his voice firm and commanding. "There is still work to be done."

Sighing, I squeezed my eyes shut for a moment.

He was right.

I was not done here.

Taking Akio's hand, I let him help me up. Slowly, I stood, staying still for a moment to allow my head to stop spinning. Emiko walked past me, and I felt a stirring of the Skills follow him. From inside his robes, I caught the glimmer of a bond.

"You're…" I said, my voice trailing off as Emiko stopped walking.

He glanced back at me and smiled.

Rin rested against a tree not far away. A large wound gaped across her shoulder. As we approached, her hand tightened around her curved sword, and she tensed. Her eyes fluttered open, recognition filling them, and she released her grip on the sword. Akio slid his arms under her legs and held her to his chest, lifting her up.

When we returned to the gate, some of the villagers had begun to gather. Emiko scooped Finae up in his arms, and he started down the path into the village. I trailed after them, feeling conflicted by the outcome.

The Skills had protected me.

Why couldn't they have done the same for Finae and Rin?

And what had happened to the Guardian?

Slowly, I continued forward. Not because I had a desire to do so, but because it was my duty.

chapter fifty-five
Konro: Aftermath

Resting my head on my knees, I poked the black Skills with the end of my staff, sending ripples across the surface. It had been three days since the battle, and the pool had yet to sink back into the earth. The silver pond, where my bond had been forged, was the purest form of the Skills.

This seemed to be the opposite.

I flattened my cheek against my knee, considering my reflection with a mild dislike. When Finae used the Skills, they were beautiful, but when I used them, they were something else entirely.

A spear point rippled the water, distorting my reflection.

"Feeling sorry for yourself isn't going to change anything," Akio said from behind me. He softened his tone. "You've been out here for hours."

I nodded absently. "I was just thinking."

"The doctor is visiting with Finae and Rin," he said, rubbing his puffy, reddened eyes with the sides of his hands. Akio and I had been taking turns staying with Rin and Finae throughout the nights, tending to them and making sure their injuries healed.

Neither of us had slept much.

Akio laid his spear against his chest. Even when he was with Rin or Finae, he didn't put it down. He seemed on edge, restless like he couldn't relax anymore.

Sighing, he sat down next to me, crossing his legs.

"How are you feeling?" he asked.

He had a knack for finding me when I needed him most.

"Tired," I admitted, then hesitated slightly. "Not so much physically as my spirit seems worn out." I wasn't sure I wanted to talk about what had happened yet with the Skills. "Have they finished the memorial service?"

Akio nodded. "It ended not too long ago. Emiko has been named the next Guardian of Konro. From what he told me, he's one of the last people still alive who remembers Zenkaiko. It seems fitting for him to take Lady Chiyori's place."

My eyes drifted back to the black liquid. Once things settled down, we could ask Emiko what he knew about the Skills.

In the black Skill's reflection, I noticed a small sword tucked into Akio's sash.

"Where did you get that?"

He pulled the blade from his sash and handed it to me. "I recognized one of the mercenaries we fought. He was one of the men I killed after the Skill poisoning got to him. Before serving General Mirai, I wandered with mercenaries like those. We took whatever job paid the most and cared little about who was affected by it."

I ran my hands over the carved dragon on the red-lacquered sheath. One of the dragon's claws was raised, and its mouth was open as if to intimidate its opponent.

"His mother gave him that blade before he left home. I thought maybe I could return it, or maybe it would be better to bury it. I'm not really sure why I kept it, but it does make me wonder." Akio looked down at his hands. "If I had not met the general, would I have ended up like him?"

Handing the short sword back, I reached out to him, placing my hand on his arm. "I'm happy you ended up with the general and we were able to meet."

Akio smiled and placed his hand on mine. "Me too."

"Thank you for coming to get me," I said. This place was one I'd been returning to whenever I could, as if the answers I sought about the Skills would come to me by being in the presence of the mysterious black liquid.

"Ready to go back?" Akio asked.

Nodding, I stood, and we walked back to the library together. The library, as the villagers called it, was more than just a library. It had many rooms built into it that were used when people became ill, as well as other sections in which people could congregate and work.

"In Vaiyene, there's a house similar to this library," I said, imagining the Miyota Mountains and the Phantoms' house. "It makes me feel nostalgic for the happier times I spent with my family and friends."

"From what you've told me, it sounds like a nice place."

"It is. It's…"

Suddenly, I became aware he didn't have a home to return to except for the general's group. He continued walking silently next to me, not seeming bothered that I had mentioned my homeland.

Once inside the library, we took the stairs and came to Finae's room. When the doctor saw us, he rose from his seat on the floor.

"Any change?" I asked, hopeful.

He shook his head. "Her condition remains the same. I have asked my students to read through the books on the Skills, but so far they have found nothing."

"And Rin?" Akio asked.

"Her fever has finally broken, and the infection is under control. I anticipate she'll wake up soon. When she does, there's a vial of medicine next to her bed she needs to drink."

I let out a long breath and bowed. "Thank you for your care, Fujika."

He bowed in return. When he straightened, he wore a kind smile. "You both should try and get some rest. You'll not be of much use to anyone if you collapse."

With a wave, Fujika descended the stairs, and Akio and I entered the adjacent room. The walls were bathed in a delicate light, and a breeze rustled the light gossamer curtains.

A heavy scent of flowers wafted inside.

"I should probably walk the perimeter again," Akio said, his eyes focusing outside the window, "to make sure there's no danger."

"Be careful."

"I will."

Pushing the curtains open, I walked out onto the terrace, waiting until I saw Akio enter the forest before glancing up at the enormous tree that made up the library. Blue flowers bloomed across the vines covering the bark. They smelled similar to Sakura blossoms but had a distinct cinnamon-like quality that was more earthy and spicy.

The sound of sheets rustling came from inside the room, and I dipped back inside, noticing Rin's eyes were open. She stared at the ceiling, her eyes drooping.

"Rin?" I called her.

Her eyes remained on the ceiling.

Gently, I walked inside and took the rag from her head, rinsing it off in a bucket of clean water next to her bed. Once I had wrung it out, I placed it on her head. Though she had woken up before, she was never aware for very long.

"How's Finae?" Rin asked, her words quiet.

"She's still asleep," I said patiently. She always asked about Finae or Kilo, and every once in a while, she would ask about Ikaru.

Rin closed her eyes; a tear ran down her face.

Fatigued, I sat down next to her bed, leaning against the wall as I propped my head up with my knee. My forearm ached dully where the bond rested on my skin.

The blackness had yet to disappear.

Rin's chest rose and fell in a steady rhythm, and I closed my eyes, intent on relaxing for a moment. It had been calm since the battle had ended. None of the mercenaries who had been affected by the Skills had woken up either.

Focusing on my breathing, I let my thoughts slow, sleep pulling at me.

"Kilo?" Rin asked.

Startled, I awoke with a start, glancing around to find the room darker than it had been before. I must have been asleep for some time.

"He's not here," I said, rolling my shoulders back before pushing myself off from the wall. I crawled forward on my knees to Rin's side. Her eyes seemed brighter than they had been in a long time.

"Finae has not woken up yet," I said, wiping away the sleep from my eyes. Rin seemed to focus on me instead of staring off into the distance. She might finally be cognizant enough to converse.

"They've built the pyre for the Guardian and the mercenaries who died," I continued. "Do you remember anything that happened during the battle?"

Rin's brow furrowed, and her breathing seemed to catch as if the memory pained her. "The barrier broke," she said, her words scratchy. "I held them off for as long as I could, but there was a blinding light and a pain in my chest, and…" She shook her head. "That's all I remember."

I leaned forward and grabbed a small vial from beside the bed.

"Can you sit up? This is a medicine that's supposed to help with the infection."

Rin braced herself on her good arm and managed to elevate herself. I grabbed one of the cushions next to her bed and wedged it behind her back, handing her the cup.

She sipped the contents.

"After the barrier broke," I said, "we found the Guardian had died. The Skills briefly showed me a flash of what happened, but we've been waiting for Finae to share what she remembers."

Rin handed the vial back to me. "Have you heard anything from Kilo?"

"Only that he is still with Hitori and the False Shadows."

Rin leaned back against the pillows, tilting her head up as she let out a long breath.

"Do you want anything to eat?" I asked. "Or to drink?"

"I might be able to eat a little."

Standing, I went to the corner of the room. Resting upon the table was a selection of bread and fruits as well as a bamboo canteen of water. After selecting a few items, I brought them over on a tray to Rin's bedside and sat down next to her.

"How is Finae doing?" she asked, reaching for a piece of bread and tearing a small piece off.

"Physically, she seems to be doing fine."

Rin swallowed and waited for an explanation.

"She doesn't respond to anyone, but her physical injuries have been healing. Something must have happened with the Skills, but I'm not sure how to help her. Ikaru used to warn me about losing control of the Skills. That something would happen to my mind if I lost concentration…"

I let the words die out as Rin set down the bread in her hand. If she had been the one to teach Ikaru how to use the Skills, did she know what had happened?

"When Hitori first started learning about the Skills, there was someone as eager as she was to learn about them. It was the first 'experiment' Hitori ran. He didn't know anything about the power, but Hitori had found a book and shared it with him." Rin waved her hand across her face. "Anyway, this person was the first to lose themselves to the Skills. His mind never fully returned to them after Hitori walked him through how to use the Skills."

Rin's voice wavered. I handed her the bamboo canteen, pulling the wooden stopper from the end. She drank heavily and cleared her throat.

"As you might have felt," she continued, "the Skills have a presence, a will of their own. If you give yourself to them, if you lose your own grasp on this world, the mind seems to not remember how to come back." She rubbed her fingers along the bamboo canister. "Sorry, I'm not quite sure how to explain it any better."

"No," I said, thinking back to the presence and the desire in the Skills I had felt. "I think I might understand."

Realizing it had been a while since Akio left, I crossed over to the terrace, lifting the curtains to look down at the forest. The sun was beginning to set, and he had not yet returned.

"Hey, Rin," I said, looking at her from out of the corner of my eye.

"Hmm?"

"When I was maintaining the barrier, I felt someone else while using the Skills, and a black liquid came up from the ground. Is that...normal?"

Rin's eyes narrowed, and she regarded me with a cautious look for a few moments. "Kilo was able to talk to an entity within the Skills, saying that at times it seemed like he was lost to someone else. He also has seen areas where there are pools of the black Skills." She paused for a moment, pressing her fingers against the bridge of her nose. "Kilo would be able to talk to you more about the Skills and their worth."

There seemed to be a slight bitterness to her words.

"Do you think the Skills are bad?" I asked, keeping my eyes on the forest below, waiting, hoping Akio would return soon.

"Kilo believes they are a part of this world. Therefore, they belong and should thrive the same as we do. He is respectful of their wishes and their desires, knowing that we are connected to one another's fate. Finae sees little difference between herself and the Skills. With their unique spirits and perspectives, Kilo and Finae are the two people who can probably best teach us how to live and interact with them."

"And what do you think?"

Rin raised her eyebrows. "I've often wished it was something we didn't know about. That the knowledge would have remained forgotten."

I dropped my gaze and sighed, a little disappointed.

"Buuut," Rin said, stretching out the word until I looked up at her, "I have hope Kilo and Finae will uncover the Skills' true purpose and meaning in this world. If they are integral as a part of the natural order of things, perhaps it is my experience with Hitori that has soured my view of them. I am willing to keep an open mind."

Outside the window, the sky had burst into gold and crimson. Leaning close, I admired a large cloud that was rimmed with a fierce orange outline.

I turned back to ask Rin more about the Skills, but her eyes had closed. The rhythm of her breathing was slow and steady. Removing the tray next to her bedside, I crept outside her room and down the hall, slipping back into the adjacent room. Finae lay peacefully on a long futon set on top of tatami mats. A fluffy white duvet covered her. I placed my hand on hers, feeling the warmth of her skin. The Skills leaped at the connection, their energy flowing through me before they faded.

Kneeling next to Finae, I tried to hold back my tears.

"I'm sorry I couldn't do anything for you."

"She's a gentle soul, but a fierce one."

Startled by the voice, I turned to find Rin in the doorway. She stood on unsteady legs, her hands gripping the paper screen door for support. I rushed toward her and helped her settle onto the cushions beside Finae's futon.

"I thought you were asleep," I said, feeling guilty I had left her.

Rin chuckled. "Only resting."

"Will you be okay sitting up?"

Rin nodded, though her attention was on Finae. "Kilo insisted on bringing her along. I thought she wouldn't be able to keep up with us, but she's saved my life twice now." Rin's voice wavered with grief, and I found tears in my eyes. "It's hard to see her like this."

We both watched Finae sleeping.

Idly, I tried to recall the connection Finae and I had with the barrier and how it had felt with her presence in my mind. We were connected through the Skills—shouldn't I be able to reach her? I rested my hand on her head and allowed my awareness to fade away. The warmth of the sun, Rin crying beside me, the scent of flowers, all of it became distant. It still felt as if Finae were stuck in the realm of the Skills, the place I had seen the memory of the Guardian, the moment before Finae collapsed.

I breathed in and out, calming myself.

Searching.

Waiting.

Wood creaked behind me, and I sensed someone had come into Finae's room. Rin quietly murmured something, and I kept my focus on Finae, on the Skills, and on the faint beating of her heart. A slight wind, so soft and gentle I had to hold my breath to feel it, moved throughout the room.

It flowed toward Finae.

Slowly, I drew in a deep breath and opened my eyes.

The Skills were keeping her alive.

"If her spirit is strong, she will not be lost to the Skills," an unfamiliar voice said beside me. Tilting my head back, I saw Emiko.

He smiled at me.

"I've come to speak with the two of you," Emiko said, bowing slightly. "I had hoped to speak with Finae, but as she has not woken up from the Skill world, I will entrust the knowledge to the two of you in her and Phantom Kilo's place."

Rin and I eyed one another.

"Because of the death of my only child, my daughter Shizuka, I have secluded myself for the past ten years. She died learning how to use the Skills, poisoning herself daily in an attempt to master them. The Guardian asked me to come and speak with Phantom Kilo when he was here, but I refused to. Seeing the three of you defend Konro has moved me, and I wish to speak of what I know before it is too late."

He moved next to Finae, lowering his head as he looked at her.

"Before Phantom Takezo erased the knowledge of the Skills, I begged him to allow me to find another solution. He refused to listen. My daughter and I had a theory on how we could repair the land. It is incomplete, but perhaps with Phantom Kilo's help, we will be able to alter our path."

"What path do you think we are on?" Rin asked.

"One of destruction."

Rin stared at Emiko, her eyes narrowed as if she were trying to size him up. "If you've been hiding for ten years, what makes you think you know the state of the world?"

Emiko didn't waver before Rin. "Because I have not been idle with my time. I've wandered these lands, watching. Waiting. I may have become jaded with the Shadows of old, but I have not lost my reason."

Seemingly satisfied, Rin nodded. "Kilo asked me to look out for anything off with the Skills. I haven't seen many places where the land seems to be dying."

"We are still in the early stages," Emiko said, heading for the door. "Will you be able to make it to the other side of Konro?"

"I'll be fine," Rin said, pushing herself up from the cushion. She seemed steadier than she had earlier, and I admired her determination and strength.

Helping Rin down the stairs, we followed Emiko outside the library and returned to the far end of Konro, where the pool of black Skills remained.

The liquid seemed to have spread farther.

"What is that?" Rin asked.

"A manifestation of the decay of the Skills. It is an impurity of the Skills, absorbing the ill will and hatred in the world. To get rid of it, it needs to be cleansed. Purified." Emiko's eyes rested on me. "That was once the purpose of being a Shadow."

My eyes widened.

"So you are a Shadow," I said.

"A long time ago, but I have not considered myself to be one for many years."

Emiko knelt on one knee next to the pool of black Skills. They seemed to move at his approach as if they could sense something was about to happen.

"Before Phantom Takezo decided to remove the memories of the Skills, there were places across Kiriku that showed signs of this decay. This process to purify and heal was something my daughter gave her life for. She had a better propensity for the Skills, but after working through the process with her, I was able to learn it myself."

He held his hand out over the black liquid. "The impurity comes from an imbalance within the Skills. It can affect the land, plants, animals, and even people directly." As he said this, he nodded toward the bandages around Rin's arm. "Once the damage is done, the body will slowly repair itself after the top layer of skin revitalizes itself. In order to prevent the Skill poisoning and the imbalance in the world, we need to cultivate a better relationship with the Skills. Nothing in excess, everything in balance."

His right hand hovered over the black liquid, a slight glow illuminating the outline of his fingers. "The basic concept is to remove the excess Skills and restore the balance. It is not an easy thing to explain, but I would venture to say you may have both felt a presence or an emotion in the Skills before."

"I did," I said, feeling Rin's gaze on me. "It was almost as if there was anger, as if the Skills were lashing out at the mercenaries. When I reached out to them, I didn't intend for—"

"It's quite all right," Emiko said, stopping me before I could confess my guilt. "The Skills have a will of their own. They seek to exploit those who use them if they believe they can get away with it. The fault does not lie with you."

Even if that were true, guilt still remained in my heart, but I tried to quiet it, focusing on what I could learn here so I could make amends.

Emiko withdrew his hand from the tainted Skills, and a portion of the black liquid slithered over his arm where it began to coat the outside of his arm.

"While purifying the Skills, it is not unusual to be able to see pieces of what has happened. It is"—Emiko searched for an explanation—"trying on the mind. To be able to bear that kind of pain, to accept it and allow it to flow back through you, is not easy. You must have a sharp mind and an even stronger heart."

He was quiet for a few moments as he focused intently.

As the last of the black Skills sank into his arm, a subtle white light began emitting from his bond. The light seemed welcoming almost, as if the aura of pain had indeed been purified.

It was the same as when Phantom Asdar had purified the sword.

"You must allow yourself to be vulnerable to the Skills," Emiko continued. "This can be done by touching them or even sitting close to them. Once you have opened yourself up to the Skills, it becomes a matter of learning what needs to be done to soothe them. This particular spot was brought about by anger from the mercenaries. So accepting their regret and rage will calm the Skills.

Emiko motioned for both Rin and me to approach. If the Skills had already taken advantage of me, would they try to do so again?

"Do you think the Skills will try to…" I started, but Emiko shook his head.

"Don't be afraid. This is a different way of connecting to the Skills. I think you'll find they'll be receptive to your conversation."

Emiko's words were kind, understanding.

I had tried so hard to be able to use the Skills, but every time I did, nothing seemed to go as I planned. Still, I would do what I could in Kilo and Finae's place, and if Emiko thought I could, I needed to believe in that. To believe in my own strength.

Kneeling, I joined Rin next to the black Skills.

Rin's right arm hung in a sling, so she extended her left hand out toward them. Her eyes were focused on her task, and I sensed neither fear nor nerves from her. Despite her own misgivings about the Skills, she, too, was trying to do what she could. Somehow it made me feel better knowing I was not the only one who was unsure with the Skills.

She gave me a slight smile. "We're in this together."

I nodded and let my fingers disrupt the surface of the Skills as Emiko had done. The tips of my fingers grew warm, uncomfortably so. I allowed the Skills to be, to exist, and to show me what needed to be done. Warmth rushed through me and tightened my heart. Squeezing my eyes shut, I reminded myself to breathe. My purpose was to figure out what needed to be done to "restore balance".

When the barrier had been erected, there was a particular emotion to the Skills. Anger had permeated them, and as a result, my own feelings had turned that way. Even though the black Skills had been born from hatred, something about it almost made me sad. My hand relaxed, feeling the Skills slide across my arm. Withdrawing my arm, I brought my palms together, chin-level. I had asked Kilo about the gesture once, when he did it at the Reikon Tree before the Shadows' resting place. He had said it helped him to center his thoughts and to show respect to those who had passed on. It was a silent plea that they would be able to hear the words spoken to them.

Pressing my palms tighter together, I kept my intentions focused on the mercenaries—on what had transpired.

Rin's presence was within the Skills as well; distantly, I could feel her.

I exhaled slowly, feeling my mind quiet.

Faces and glimpses of people I didn't know rose in my mind, along with memories of being cast out. A lover lost to disease. A child dead upon birth. These memories and emotions washed over me, like a wave of the ocean breaking upon the shore. My heart ached for what the mercenaries had endured, what they had given up, and the moments that had driven them to be here.

Through a series of events, they had arrived here, just the same as I had.

Whether or not they had died doing what they believed was right or wrong didn't matter. What mattered was that the mercenaries' lives were over. They had been taken, and their spirits were uneasy with what they had left behind.

"Once the connection is found," Emiko said distantly, "we learn the reason why people do what they do. Through this understanding, it is easier to forgive and to let go."

Rin moved beside me, and I became aware of my own thoughts and feelings again. The warmth and the pressure around my heart lessened, and I began to feel the breeze in the air and smell the scent of the earth.

"Be at peace," Rin said, whispering beside me.

When I opened my eyes, the pool of the Skills was the same as it had been.

Black, dark, and with a malicious aura.

"How long does it take to restore balance to the Skills?" Rin asked, placing her hand on the ground as she began to ease herself onto her feet.

"Sometimes it takes a few days, even weeks for places like this to return to how they were," Emiko replied, slipping his hands into the folds of his robes. "It's one of the reasons Phantom Takezo did not believe our theory would work. He believed the world was too broken to be healed."

"Is there a way to absorb more of the Skills?" I asked.

Emiko met my gaze. "The more you become used to the Skills, the easier it will become and the more you will be able to do. But sometimes, things take time to mend, especially if there are many pieces to put back together." Turning around, he began heading back to the library. "Come, there's much for us to learn and little time for you to master it."

My fingers curled into a fist, excitement bubbling inside me. Finally, I had found something I'd be able to do to help Kilo and to protect Vaiyene.

part eight
HITORI

chapter fifty-six
An Unlikely Understanding

Gaiden ambled toward me, a group of his men dawdling after him. He had finished his first mission: to eliminate a town in the east and take the fishing port adjacent to Leiko. He'd brought five carts full of grain and rice, as well as other supplies like oil and coal. His next mission would be as crucial for Magoto's survival.

"Head to Keshlan next, in the Plains of ReRiel," I said, handing him a scroll sealed with my father's mark. This town would be the third we had formally requested aid from without the council's interference.

"And if they don't cooperate?" Gaiden asked.

"Take what we need."

Gaiden's smirk widened, and he nodded to his men as they gathered. "And when I get back, you'll show me how to use the..." He pointed at the bond on my arm.

My eyes narrowed at him. "We'll see."

Gaiden had been pestering me after every mission despite being paid a hefty sum for his work, loudly proclaiming that the highest prize would be learning the Skills. His arrogance and obsessive desire made me more adamant about keeping the knowledge from him.

"Leave the carts," Gaiden said, nodding to his mercenaries. Then he turned his attention back on me. "We'll be back within a couple of weeks."

The mercenaries finished the rice porridge in their bowls and departed with great clamor and shouting. They took little time to prepare. Whatever they needed to sustain them, they took from the travelers and merchants in other villages. They were competent and quicker than my own False Shadow group.

I drew my cloak closer to my body against the chill in the air. With my arms wrapped tight around my cloak, I moved in a billow of fabric across the campsite, eyeing Kilo, who sat next to a campfire. He dipped a wooden spoon into a large pot simmering over the flames, stirring the contents.

Noticing my approach, he spoke.

"I hope you do not intend to teach him how to use the Skills."

Bristling, I said tersely, "I will do as I see fit."

Kilo drew up the spoon and sipped at the liquid, seemingly unbothered by my remark. It irritated me how calm and collected he remained, no matter what went on around him. Even after I'd told him he would have to kill me, he had lingered. I had made it clear I wanted nothing from him. The people at Aventon hadn't followed his advice, and when the battle had begun, he'd refused to take a side, instead fighting for both the people and the False Shadows.

His benevolence remained his fatal flaw.

And I hated him for it.

Kilo filled a bowl with the soup he'd made and held it out toward me. "It will help to keep you warm. It's been cold at night, and some of the False Shadows have been feeling unwell. There are some herbs in it to strengthen the body."

Not dignifying him with a response, I stared at him.

While his offer of warm food enticed me, I wouldn't allow his kindness to sway me. I left without saying anything, noting a few of the False Shadows as they began to gather around Kilo.

"Would you like me to take care of him?" Saitou asked.

"No," I said, gritting my teeth and heading into the forest. "There is some use still in keeping him around."

He was teaching my False Shadows how to fight. It would prolong their lives and allow me to keep the appearance of my power intact across Kiriku. If I had enough control, perhaps the "allies" we had agreements with would begin to take me more seriously, and spending time on such trivial matters would no longer be my concern.

As we entered the Kinsaan Forest, the canopy overhead blocked out the light. We followed a faint trail in the undergrowth to a small wooden building containing my research notes and supplies. I flung open the door, rattling the vials and bottles lining the shelves. Saitou threw out his arm to steady the door, catching it on its hinges before it broke.

He seemed amused at my anger.

"What is it?" I snapped at him.

"He gets on your nerves, doesn't he?" Despite Saitou's attempt at keeping a straight face, a small smile broke across his face. "Are you mad because he has refused to leave, or are you mad because you have grown to respect him for it?"

Bending down to pick up one of the bottles on the stone floor, I turned the vial over to ensure there were no cracks before replacing it upon one of the tiered shelves nailed to the wall. Ignoring Saitou's question, I focused instead on turning all of the labels on the vials to the front.

"For as long as I have known you," he continued, walking behind me to the other side of the building, "you have desired someone of equal mind. You tire of most friendships before they even begin. Even when you were a child, you preferred to be alone with whatever interested you. Other than Rin, I have never seen you this worked up about any person."

I sighed and stopped aligning the labels, running my fingers over a stack of notebooks next to the vials. "And your point is?"

Saitou crossed behind me again, heading toward the door, his gaze fixed outside. "Phantom Kilo is a worthy adversary. He may dislike killing, but he has a strong will to protect those around him. Those kinds of people have a way of drawing others to them. Do not continue dismissing him."

Glancing sidelong at Saitou, I considered his use of the Phantom's title with unease. He respected him. Pushing the thought away, I reassured myself; Saitou had pledged himself to me.

"Yes, yes, I know," I said, leafing through a notebook to the last page. It was about time to check in on the experiments.

Saitou looked back at me with a pointed stare.

"I am aware of his influence in my ranks," I said, passing him in the doorway and heading back into the forest. "My False Shadows look up to him, but their fear of me is stronger."

Saitou followed after me, his voice resuming his usual indifference.

"If you are content with that."

I waved off his concern. "He is making my army stronger while damaging his own reputation. Whatever game he is playing, the advantage remains mine."

"He also has an interest in the Skills," Saitou said, keeping his voice quiet. "He did say he would tell you what he knew. It might be a good opportunity to expand your knowledge. You haven't learned anything new in quite some time."

I straightened, aghast.

New discoveries didn't happen quickly. They took careful planning, with changes to the variables in a controlled environment, to whittle down options most beneficial for research purposes. However, it *would* be interesting to speak with the Phantom about what he knew, if only to assess his abilities and find out if he even was a threat.

"Do you think he would tell me what he knows?" I asked.

"You know his creed. The Shadows are honor bound to uphold their word. He said he would exchange information, and even if he does deceive you, you will know his true character."

I considered for a moment. It did seem like an appealing way to spend the rest of the afternoon, and the experiments could wait until later.

"Very well," I said.

When we arrived back at camp, the False Shadows were practicing with their wooden swords, but Kilo was not among them. I checked the campsite he had been at earlier.

Empty.

Saitou approached the group of False Shadows who were practicing drills. "Do any of you know where Phantom Kilo has gone?"

A woman with black hair tied back with a red ribbon spoke first. "He headed into the forest a while ago to find more herbs to make medicine for those of us who are sick." She pointed to the southeast, her eyes flicking briefly over to me. There was a hint of anger and blame in her voice.

Was I now supposed to know how to brew medicine to make them well again?

Biting back any retort, I headed into the forest where she had pointed, Saitou a step behind me. There were no trails or paths, as the trees were thick and overgrown, and after some time, it became clear we were without direction.

I was about ready to turn back when Saitou motioned ahead.

"He's gathering herbs near the creek."

Balanced on a rock, Kilo was bent over toward the river, carefully plucking shoots of plants from the water. Once he finished harvesting the stalks near him, he turned to the shore, picking up a pile he had placed there.

Noticing Saitou and me, he put the herbs safely in a pouch.

I seated myself down on a nearby boulder and pulled out my leather journal.

"I want to know what you can do with the Skills."

Kilo's eyebrows rose.

I tried to stifle my impatience and anger at the delay.

Had he forgotten?

"When you first came here, you did say you would tell me."

"I remember," he said, looking at me curiously before he knelt on the ground opposite me. He sat back on his heels, not seeming bothered by sitting in such a submissive way. "What is it you would like to know?"

"All of it."

Kilo nodded. "I know the Skills are within every object, person, and living thing, and one can manipulate them at will."

"And beyond the basics?" I asked.

It seemed his knowledge was rudimentary.

Kilo raised his right arm and turned it palm up toward the sky. "I have been able to see the Skills for a short while. While it's easier to detect when it's darker, there is a faint glow around my bond and around my hand."

I glared at him. The Skills could not be seen. If he thought I was stupid enough to believe he could see the Skills, he took me as a fool.

"I can also sense the Skills when they become agitated," Kilo added, pausing for a moment. "Like how they are now."

Saitou coughed, attempting to cover his laughter.

"The Skills are attracted to strong emotions," Kilo continued, letting his gaze wander the area as if he actually saw the Skills now. "They have their own will and desire. It is why you lost control of them in Aventon. You disregard how the Skills interact with the world, infusing them with your hatred so that they able to take advantage of your weakness."

Having heard enough, I stood up.

"What you speak of is nonsense! The Skills are not something to reason with but something to command. I've spent months researching how they interact with the human body and how people are affected by them. If you think you can come here and make me believe you have some special connection with the Skills, you are mistaken! Do not forget, I have allowed you to remain here as long as you are useful. My patience, however, is running thin."

"Without me, you will be consumed by the Skills."

The arrogance!

Kilo sat unmoving, defiantly staring at me as my anger grew. The air became thick, and a black fog rolled across the river— but all of it faded from view as I focused on the Phantom. I took a step toward him, raising my right arm, but he didn't recoil as others would. Instead, a flash of anger shined in his eyes.

"You haven't even begun to understand the Skills, Lady Hitori," Kilo said, his voice emotionless, despite his apparent anger. "You're putting more than people's lives at stake with your carelessness. The Skills are the foundation this world is built upon, and if you continue on this path, we all will suffer because of it."

Reaching for the Skills, I attempted to force Kilo into yielding before me. Even though he was a *Phantom*, a leader of many people, he didn't have the right to speak to me in such a manner. No one did.

The Skills came to me quickly, the burning sensation attuned to my rising anger. All of them would be sorry for ever doubting me, for trying to control me.

The black fog from the river rolled toward Kilo, engulfing him in a plume of mist. I heard a scuffle from within. The fog grew heavy, pressing down on my arms and shoulders. It became more and more difficult to breathe, the air becoming thick like mud. I directed all my control and anger at Kilo, intent on crushing him, but something in the air rippled. Instead of obeying me and becoming denser, the Skills lightened.

Incensed, I glared into the mist.

Somehow, he was diverting the Skills to toy with me.

Drawing in a breath, I felt my lungs expand and my mind narrow. Nothing mattered more than proving my power. I pulled the Skills from the air, drawing them into me. Their energy surged. The tightness in my chest increased, but I ignored it, intent on my purpose. Doggedly, I poured every ounce of my strength into the air. The dirt under my feet shifted and buckled. A black liquid oozed from the crack, bubbling forth. It hissed as it touched my foot, and I stepped back, wincing at the pain.

My vision wavered, the details of the forest lost in a sea of black.

"Hitori!" Saitou shouted.

I released my hold on the Skills.

Drawing in a deep breath, nausea overwhelmed me. I rested my hands on my knees, staring at the ground until the feeling passed and the details in my vision returned. The rage inside me shifted to fear, and I vomited blood.

With a shaky hand, I wiped my mouth.

The fog around Kilo dissipated.

He stood, insolent.

"Leave!" I yelled.

My heart beat fast against the continued nausea. I swallowed, trying to control myself so the Phantom wouldn't see the momentary lapse in my composure. As I raised my eyes, I expected to see satisfaction from Kilo, but instead, his frown deepened, and he glanced down at the pool of black liquid writhing on the ground. I thought he would fight to stay, but he bowed stiffly.

"Whenever you wish to talk," Kilo said, taking his leave, "I will be waiting."

Saitou was slouched a few feet away, leaning against a tree and panting hard. He met my gaze, steadying himself as he tried to breathe.

The Skills had touched him.

"You didn't even realize what he was doing," Saitou said, one hand going to his temple as if his head ached.

I frowned. "What he was doing..."

Saitou pushed himself off from the tree and walked over to me. "If you desire my counsel, you will have to accept I will not always approve of your actions. Do you still wish to hear what is on my mind?"

"Speak," I said, tight-lipped.

"You need to learn discipline. It is the one thing Kilo has mastered that you are lacking. If what he says is true, about the Skills being influenced by emotion, then it is only a matter of time before the difference in your power grows."

I bit my lip to keep myself from interrupting Saitou, tasting blood in my mouth.

"You have always been too quick to anger. While it does make the people around you fear and obey you, it also makes them distrust and hate you. Your father left Magoto to you, and you—"

Saitou seemed to come to his senses then, cutting off his words.

"And I what?" I asked, daring him to continue.

Saitou hesitated, seeming to consider his words. "I took an oath to protect you, Lady Hitori, but I also promised your father I would watch over you. Forgive me for saying something I know will anger you, but you need to heed the Phantom's advice. I don't believe he is lying when he says you need his help. He knows something about the Skills you don't. You should try and persuade him to tell you."

Flaring my nostrils, I fisted my hands at my sides.

The thought of the Phantom knowing something about the Skills I didn't set my blood boiling. What made matters worse was that Kilo was also aware that he knew something I didn't, and he had deliberately angered me to prove it.

Saitou's gaze on me remained unbreakable.

Finally, I relented. "I will consider it."

Saitou sighed and began walking back through the forest toward the main camp. He was quiet, his pace brisk as he took the lead. When we arrived back at camp, Kilo had gone to train with some of the False Shadows, but a few of them lingered in the camp.

Asleep from the looks of it.

I went to wake them, annoyed they were being lazy, but Saitou stopped me.

"They're the ones feeling unwell," he said, circling around so as not to disturb them. "Let them rest."

Saitou's jaw was set, and his words were pointed. It almost seemed as if he were angry with me. Rin had sometimes gotten this way too. Figuring out a person's emotions was not something I did well. Over the years, I had tried to pay more attention to Saitou and Rin, but even knowing them for so long, I often disregarded the subtle signs until they grew so tired of me they refused to speak—or, like Rin, they left.

"I'm going to check in on the experiments," I said, watching Saitou closely.

He was observing Kilo and the False Shadows on the outside of the camp.

"There's something else I need to take care of. Take Haru with you."

"Very well," I said, not bothering to hide my annoyance.

Now I knew Saitou was upset. In the twenty years we had been together, he had hardly left my side, insisting he come with me even when I refused him.

Dragging my feet across the forest floor, I followed the pathway to the second camp—where the experiments were being held. One of the keepers, Ayame, noticed me and bowed, the journal in her hands pressed against her chest. When she straightened, she didn't meet my eye, instead looking somewhere to the side of me.

"How is number twenty-three doing?" I asked.

The last time I was here, the Skill poisoning had been affecting him: nausea, fever, coughing, even some black marks manifesting across his body.

"His condition has stayed the same," Ayame said.

I nodded. Now that I was here, I did not feel like dealing with him. Saitou's anger with me had put me in a bad mood, and as long as his symptoms had not gotten worse, the subject would be able to manage for another day.

Besides, there was something else my time would be better spent on.

A matter I had been putting off for some time.

Heading to the last building in the camp, I paused, making sure no one had followed me. The wooden planks of the cabin were stained with dried blood and worn by the elements, and the roof sitting at an odd angle. It was the oldest and most run down of all the buildings. Pushing the door open, I raised my arm up to cover my eyes. There was a hole in the ceiling where, at the right time of day, the sun blinded those who entered.

Lowering my arm, I turned to the man asleep in the corner. Ikaru.

His hands were bound with rope that was fixed to the wall. A welt marred the side of his face where one of the mercenaries had struck him. It has been a fruitless interrogation; no amount of persuasion had led to any pertinent information. He had not been in contact with the Phantom, and now that Kilo had come here of his own free will and had been here for quite some time, there seemed little reason to hold him any longer. It would only sour the relationship between the Phantom and me, and keeping him here drained the resources needed for the other experiments.

Other than the bruise on his jaw and a small cut on his cheek, he was relatively unharmed. All traces of his boldness had disappeared as soon as he was separated from his companions.

Clearing my throat, I looked down at his pitiful figure.

"You're free to go."

When he didn't stir, I nudged Ikaru with my foot. His eyes flew open, and he pressed himself back against the wall, trembling. When he noticed it was me who stood in front of him, his eyes glazed over. His head rested against the wall, and he dropped his gaze to the ground, subordinate.

Drawing the short sword from my back, I cut the rope keeping him attached to the wall. When I knelt down and placed the blade next to his wrists, he flinched involuntarily. The blade sliced cleanly through his bonds.

I stepped back from him.

He was pathetic. All of his will to survive had left him.

"The Phantom has joined my ranks as one of the False Shadows," I said, annoyed when he didn't look in my direction. "When you talk to him, let him know it wasn't me who struck you."

Though I doubted the Phantom would believe me.

I went back to the door, feeling a note of disgust at his lack of motivation. As my fingertips brushed against the door, I hesitated. A memory of Rin and her brother came to mind. We were all sitting at the edge of the cliffs, looking out into the ocean. Rin had brought us a new kind of pastry one of the guards had found in a nearby town. Ikaru had been there, though he was quiet and dismissive of me as always. Rin had been happy then. It was the day before she became one of the guardsmen—a role she had taken to stay in service to me as the lord's daughter.

When Rin had found out about the Skills and turned on me, holding Ikaru hostage had been a means to an end. Threatening him had kept Rin close. That's all it had been. I cared little for him, and our mutual hatred had always been a strain on our relationship. We tolerated one another because of Rin.

I turned my head, watching Ikaru out of the corner of my eye.

None knew of Ikaru's presence here, except for a handful of the keepers and Saitou. Not even Haru knew. But I was not stupid enough to believe I would be able to keep his being here a secret for much longer.

Turning back from the door, I knelt next to Ikaru. He was quite malodorous, with dirt covering his clothing and skin. Up close, the bruise looked even worse. It had a purplish hue to it, and the cut on his cheek seeped a sort of pus. It was better to let it air out, but the sight of it made it seem like I had neglected his care.

Hadn't I told the keepers to watch over him?

Lifting his hands, I uncoiled the ropes around his wrists. There were no indentations or red marks, which meant he had not even struggled against them.

"Get up," I said, standing back.

When he continued to stare at the ground, I grabbed his arm and pulled him away from the wall. His feet were unsteady, and I supported him until he decided I was not going to leave him alone if he didn't do as I wanted.

Walking outside, I waited for him to leave the building, eyeing him as he finally did so. He squinted his eyes and raised his hand to filter out the sun. While his eyes adjusted, I retrieved a canteen of water and a piece of bread from the supplies laid out on the table for the others.

"Here," I said, shoving both into his hands. "There's a river not far from here. Go and bathe yourself. When you're done, I'll lead you back to the main camp where Kilo is." As an afterthought, I added, "Kilo may know where your sister is."

He glanced back over his shoulder as if he were interested in at least Rin.

Waiting for Ikaru to return turned into an agonizing endeavor.

The keepers kept glancing over at me, so much so it made me suspicious of how things typically happened when I didn't come every day. Did they always have this much free time? Judging from Ikaru's condition, they were not taking their duties seriously.

While I stewed about their lack of conviction and efficiency, the sun reached its midpoint, brightening the forest. It was the only time when the sun was at the right height for light to make its way down through the thick canopy. I raised my eyes, following the twisted branches of the trees. They created a spiral, forming together to create one single canopy.

Someone came and stood next to me, and I lowered my eyes from the trees, surprised to see Ikaru had returned. A part of me had believed he would try to escape. Not that he had anywhere to go, but the expectation was there. The cut on his cheek looked better than it had before. He had washed the dirt from his skin and hair, and he now looked more alive, more alert.

We walked in uncomfortable silence back to the trail worn into the forest floor. While I rarely chose to initiate conversations, this time, it felt as if something needed to be said. Though our mutual dislike didn't need any explanation.

Ikaru seemed to feel the same in that regard, keeping his distance from me.

At the edge of the main camp, I looked for Saitou and Kilo.

Had they finished talking?

The False Shadows watched us as we came closer. Near the middle of the camp, Saitou and Kilo sat on opposite sides of a campfire. They turned their heads as I approached. They seemed to have been deep in conversation.

I felt an unwarranted concern rise in my chest.

What was it the Phantom and Saitou had been talking about so adamantly?

"Leave or stay. The choice is yours," I said to Ikaru. Gone were all thoughts of trying to explain myself or make any sort of amends.

Ikaru's eyes widened slightly at my words.

Kilo rose from his seat, motioning for Ikaru to take his place next to the fire. He seemed more concerned about Ikaru than he did me. Saitou glanced over at me, a question in his eyes, but I didn't wait for him to ask any questions.

Some things were better left unsaid.

chapter fifty-seven
Skill Trails

Days passed after the incident with Kilo, and Saitou remained distant. My mood darkened as his silence prolonged. While he still followed me, as was his duty, he stayed one step farther behind than usual. The safety that came with his protection seemed fragile.

As if at any second, he would choose to be rid of me.

Like Rin had.

A part of me wanted to ask what he and the Phantom had been talking about, but I was certain if he wanted me to know, he would have told me. So instead of asking him, I went about my usual morning routine: documenting the changes in my experiments, checking in on the human trials, and taking care of any discrepancies that arose in camp.

Moodily, I walked through the forest to check in on the experiment currently running among the local flora. It had been some time since I had last come here, and the path had become more overgrown. The ends of my robe dragged over the dirt and snagged on a branch from a bush. Yanking it free, I tripped over a raised root, stubbing my toe. I managed to catch myself from falling, but my anger sparked up when Saitou regarded me with a curious eye.

I half-waited for a witty remark about my clumsiness or the state of my distracted mind, but other than an inquiring gaze, he gave me nothing.

Breathing deeply through my nose, I tried to quell the rising anger.

Becoming angry would only push Saitou further away.

That much at least I understood.

I squeezed between two large piles of rocks, pressing my hands in front of me as I shimmied through. The boulders enclosed a small area, protecting it from the wind and elements. Inside were five different plants I had grown from seed. Some of my first experiments had to do with rats and their ability to endure the Skills, how long it would take for their skin to blacken and for their behaviors to change. It was one of the experiments that had led me to begin including humans as subjects. But this experiment focused on the plants. Like the rats, and like the humans I had cut open, the plants contained a small amount of the Skills. When I touched the leaves, the energy was palpable. At the base of each plant I had placed a metal dagger to see if proximity to the blade had any effect on the rate at which it grew. At first, it had seemed the ones closer to the daggers had grown faster, but after leaving them for almost a month, I had determined the test was inconclusive. There was no difference in growth. Their stems and even their leaves were identical in length and width.

I clicked my tongue, disappointed.

"Lady Hitori?"

Saitou stared at me from the entrance. "Why did you release Ikaru? I've been thinking about it for the past few days, and I haven't been able to come up with a suitable answer."

It was the first time he had spoken to me for a few days, and it surprised me he'd been thinking about it that much. The answer seemed obvious to me, but Saitou continued to stare at me with a strained expression on his face.

"Ikaru was no longer of use," I said, shimmying back through the crevasse. When I reached the other side, I leaned back against the rocks, sitting down on one and allowing my legs to drape over the side.

There had been many times when Saitou had come to me to question why I had done something. When we were younger, he used to ask me the strangest things. Like why I didn't cry or why I liked sitting out in the rain.

Always, he had come with the same perplexed expression.

Until this moment, I'd thought I had done something to displease him or that he was bothered by something the Phantom had said, but was it only because he couldn't figure out my reasoning?

"At first, I was using Ikaru to keep Rin close to me." I paused, trying to discern Saitou's reaction. He didn't say anything but listened intently, and I took it as a sign to continue. "When we captured him by the Orem Cliffs, we had the opportunity to learn about the Phantom and his plans. Since Ikaru had not seen him and knew nothing about it, he was no longer useful to me, especially now that Kilo came to me. Keeping him here only took up space and took resources away from the other experiments, so I released him."

"And that's all?" Saitou asked.

He leaned closer to me, waiting.

I frowned. "Why else?"

Saitou's head tilted, and his eyes became narrowed with calculation. "I think there's a part of you that still desires Rin's friendship, and knowing that Rin and Kilo are working as a team..."

He didn't go into all the details, but I knew what he referred to.

"Ikaru made it clear to Kilo that you said he was free to go," Saitou said, voicing his thoughts aloud before he questioned me. "You're not forcing him to stay?"

I conceded.

"A part of me remembered when Rin, Ikaru, and I used to spend time together. I figured Kilo might tell him where Rin is so Ikaru can be reunited with his sister."

"And your intentions beyond that?"

I had briefly considered tracking Ikaru to get to Rin's location, but chances were good that Rin was not far away from Kilo. She had, after all, sought him out specifically to fight against me. If I waited long enough, sooner or later, our paths would cross again.

But what I really wanted...

"I've reconsidered speaking with the Phantom," I said, hopping down from the pile of rocks. As I knew it would, Saitou's full attention focused on me. "Perhaps it is time to find out exactly what he knows."

———

I hesitated at the edge of the forest, watching the Phantom and the others move through a flurry of sword positions and stances. They followed Kilo in a synchronized routine before they split off into pairs to practice with one another.

"Just go ask him," Saitou said. A touch of amusement glinted in his eyes. "Unless you're afraid to."

I glared at him. "Why don't you go train with them? Your skills are getting rusty."

He laughed. "Maybe I should. You can tell he's spent many years perfecting his form and technique. He's quite skilled."

"Is he better than you?"

"No, but he would make a worthy opponent," Saitou said. His hand rested on his sword. "It's almost a shame he prefers the staff."

Kilo faced off against two of the younger False Shadows. Twins. They came at him as one force, swinging at the same time. Kilo blocked both attacks, shifting his wooden sword to counter them.

"They practice from the time the sun rises to midday. Then they do the daily chores around camp before they begin training again." Saitou glanced over at me. "In other words, unless you're going to wait there for a good portion of the day, I suggest you break up the session."

Saitou seemed to have forgiven me enough to speak freely again.

"Very well."

At my approach, all of the False Shadows lowered their wooden swords, their eyes watching me warily. I waved impatiently at them.

"Don't stop on my account. I've only come to talk to the Phantom."

After exchanging glances, they nervously began sparring again.

Kilo thrust his sword at one of the twins, dodging the second's attack. He glided backward and turned his head, catching sight of me. He lowered his sword. Seeing an opportunity, one of the twins swung his sword at Kilo's head.

The Phantom caught it with his hand.

"Nice try," Kilo said with a wry smile. "That was a good attempt at using your opponent's distraction to your advantage though." Letting go of the sword, he nodded toward the other brother. "Practice with each other for now."

"Awwww."

They groaned as they left.

Kilo slid his sword into the belt at his side and put his arms back into his robe, pulling it up to his chest and adjusting the collar.

"Is there something you needed from me?" he asked.

"There is," I said, trying to keep the tone of my voice pleasant. "I've reconsidered what you said. I would like to continue exchanging notes on the Skills to see if there is an overlap in our techniques."

A smile twitched across Kilo's face. "You mean you want to work with me?"

Remembering Saitou's warning about Kilo intentionally trying to get under my skin, I conceded to his phrasing.

"I think it would benefit both of us."

Kilo studied me for a moment before he nodded.

Together with Saitou, we walked into the depths of the forest, where we could be away from prowling eyes. Saitou began asking Kilo questions about who had trained him and how different it was to use a sword as opposed to the staff. I tuned out their conversation, finding it unappealing, instead strategizing what I would say in my conversation with Kilo. It would be best to find out how much he knew about the Skills before revealing too much. But then again, what did it matter? Most of what he knew had probably been stolen from my notes. Or perhaps Rin had taught him. She had always warned me against using the Skills and expressed her displeasure with them. Then she'd had the nerve to learn how to use them to defy me. It was probably because of her the Phantom had learned how to counter my attacks.

Then again…

I couldn't keep underestimating him. He was more intelligent than I had initially thought him to be, and even though he was passive, he analyzed all of his options.

Which made him dangerous.

Saitou hung back as we neared the river, situating himself near a small grove of trees to ensure we would not be disturbed. The water from the river had an unusual black hue to it, and I noticed the Phantom eyeing it.

I cleared my throat. "Why don't we start by comparing how we summon the Skills? Is that acceptable to you?"

Kilo's gaze softened. "It is."

Pulling out one of my thin blades, I adjusted it between two fingers. "I'll show you how I summon them first." I focused on the air in the area and sought out individual particles in the air—the ones filled with the Skills—pulling them to the metal in my hand. The blade grew warm as the Skills began to gather.

Kilo's eyes were intense.

Could he see what I was doing?

"Do you see any light on the dagger?" I tried to keep my question casual, but the smile on Kilo's face showed he knew why I'd asked.

"There is a slight glow."

I held the dagger out to him, unsure of how to explain or describe how I'd interacted with the Skills. "I felt the Skills in the air and told them to move toward the blade."

Kilo nodded and took the dagger. "I have also found the Skills seem to be drawn to metal—in particular, the same kind of metal the bonds are made of."

Not following him, I frowned, and he noticed my confusion.

He held up his arm and clarified. "The metal around the forearm."

"Ah," I said.

Taking the dagger, he turned it over in his hands. "Is this the same material as the bonds your False Shadows wear?"

"It is."

He seemed unsurprised by my answer, which meant he likely knew how I had gotten the metal and where it had come from.

Kilo ambled alongside the river, looking back at the black tint running downstream. "I call the Skills in much the same way, except they are drawn to my intentions rather than my demands. I ask, and they respond."

I couldn't keep myself from scoffing at his words. He held the same idealistic beliefs about the Skills as he did people; he thought they were something to be reasoned with, to humor and to speak with. The Skills were a tool, and they could be summoned and used as one saw fit. They were not something that had a will of their own.

Saitou coughed, and I knew he did so to caution me against dismissing what the Phantom knew about the Skills.

"And how do you know the Skills are receptive to you?" I asked, humoring his point of view.

Kilo considered for a moment. "I can sense them. I have felt their will align with my own when I have meditated with them." He handed the blade back to me. "I don't see any black marks around your bond. Does that mean you know how to reverse the Skill poisoning? Or do you not use the Skills as often as you allude to?"

"Whenever I have felt the Skills burn my skin, I pushed it into another part of my body for it to dissipate over a few days," I said, sliding the dagger into its pouch. "If a person is proactive, and builds up a tolerance to the Skills, the poisoning does not affect a person as much."

"Is that what you learned from your experiments?" Kilo asked.

His eyes were sharp, unwavering.

"Yes."

"I want to see the people you're holding captive in the second camp."

I scowled. While I knew one of Kilo's reasons for coming had been to interfere with the experiments, I hadn't expected him to confront me so openly about it, and especially not to use it against me when I was beginning to become interested in our conversation.

"Did Haru and Seiji tell you about them?" I asked.

"No. I was aware of your experiments, as others in Kiriku are, long before I came here." His gaze shifted from the water to me. "This is between you and me, Lady Hitori. I will not be cowed into submitting to your desires with threats and manipulations of the False Shadows under your control."

Trying to control my anger, I clenched my fingers into a fist.

"You have some nerve."

"Are you afraid to show them to me because you know I will be displeased?"

"I'm not afraid of you."

"I think you are, Hitori," Kilo said, goading me. "Why else haven't you killed me? You're intrigued by the Skills, and you know I have answers you haven't been able to find. That alone gives me the leverage I need to ensure my safety. It also gives me some measure of pull in getting what I want."

I hesitated because I knew he would flinch at what must be done. To learn about the Skills, one had to be willing to do whatever it took to discover their limitations. He was too kind-hearted for that. But if I didn't allow him to observe my experiments, he would refuse to teach me what he knew.

Annoyed that I needed him, I stifled a sigh.

"Fine. It's about time for me to check in on the experiments anyway." As I bent at the waist in a mock bow, I motioned him forward. "Since you know so much about it, you can lead the way."

Kilo didn't flinch at my jab; instead, he seemed pleased he had gotten his way.

As we headed toward the second camp, Saitou caught my eye. Even though the Phantom had gotten what he wanted, he wasn't going to be pleased. We needed to be prepared for however the Phantom would react.

Near the buildings, Kilo slowed his pace.

The keepers wandering the area stopped to stare. Not wanting to make a big deal out of Kilo being here, I found Ayame to get the latest reports, trying to recall what the previous conditions had been with all of the test subjects. There had been multiple tests of endurance going on the last time I was here.

"Ayame, give me your report," I said.

The girl looked back anxiously at Kilo, who lingered behind. His eyes were fixated on the building behind me, and he seemed poised to act. Outwardly he still seemed calm, but I wondered how strong his restraint truly was.

"Ignore him," I commanded.

She nodded. "Number seventeen's Skill poisoning seems to have gotten worse." Rubbing her arm with her hand, she clasped her hands in front of her. There was a bruise on her arm that hadn't been there yesterday.

"He is being aggressive today because of it," she said.

There had been a few cases when the Skills had taken over a person's mind and they'd lost control. If number seventeen's mind had started to go and he had become a danger to himself, I would need to eliminate him.

"Continue your report," I said.

Ayame gave me a small nod, her hands still wringing together. "We watched him through the night like you requested and the following days, but nothing unusual occurred. However, when he woke up this morning he was in intense pain, and he—"

Someone screamed.

It was raw and full of anguish.

It could only be number seventeen.

That amount of intense pain usually knocked a person out and sent them into a coma, but this subject had a strong will and a stubborn streak to his personality. I peered behind Ayame, my gaze locking onto the small, wooden building that contained number seventeen. It was a meager enclosure. Built for functionality and containment.

"Leave us," I commanded Ayame.

She started crying, hiding her tears with her hands before she headed back toward camp. Sighing, I pushed open the door. The man inside had his hands pressed against his head, his fingers digging into his skull. He was crouched in a corner, where he rocked back and forth.

He screamed again.

It hurt my ears.

"Be quiet," I said, approaching him.

Beads of sweat dotted his forehead. His clothing was damp and torn in places. His bloodshot eyes darted to the door, then back to me, then back to the door. He reminded me of an animal gone mad.

How had this progressed so quickly?

From my robe, I pulled out my journal, flipping to the pages where I'd noted his condition during the previous week.

Nothing out of the ordinary.

Why lose control of the Skills now?

I stood in the entrance, catching sight of one of the other keepers. "You there!" The man paused and came toward me. "Bring this one some herbs to induce sleep."

He hurried away to do as he was told.

Kilo stood silent, watching, his face expressionless.

I proceeded to the next experiment in the adjacent building, where a much more docile subject was housed. When I entered the building, there was no noise. A woman blinked and rubbed the sleep from her eyes. At my approach, she pushed herself into the corner. The mark on her arm, under the silver bond, had not faded. When I reached out a hand toward her, she withdrew, but there was only so far she could go. Ever since the first experiments, not even a groan or a whimper had escaped her lips.

Swiftly, I removed my necklace and held it out toward the woman.

The metal circle swung from the leather cording.

"Pour the Skills into it," I directed her. She reached out her hand and held her palm toward the metal pendant. The warmth of the Skills traveled up the leather cording. After a few moments, the mark on her arm remained the same color. She was becoming accustomed to using the Skills.

Nodding, I clutched the necklace in my hand.

"Good," I said, standing up to leave.

Kilo stood in the entrance, blocking me from exiting the building.

"Release her," he said.

Saitou drew his sword behind him, but Kilo paid no attention. The anger in his eyes was restrained by his desire to know more about the Skills and to win my trust. The game we were playing had reached its climax, and this was the move we each had to consider carefully. We both wanted the same thing— to maintain our strained peace for the sake of shared knowledge.

Moving slightly, I shifted to look past Kilo, noticing the same boy from earlier I had asked to return with herbs. "Souji," I called to him, ducking under Kilo's arm and moving past Saitou. "Remove the ropes from number seven."

If removing the woman's bonds would appease the Phantom, so be it.

"You have to realize this is not right," Kilo said. His eyes were narrowed at me. There was an underlying threat to his voice—a crack in his calm demeanor.

"All great achievements come with sacrifice."

"They don't deserve this."

"Life is not fair, Phantom, and to most, I have done them a great service. Those you see here are the ones who were rejected from their own hometowns. They were a burden and were left starving in the streets. When they 'disappeared,' no one cared they were gone. With my experiments, I have given them a purpose. They have shown me the limitations of the Skills and will progress my knowledge. In exchange, they are fed and given shelter."

"If you have given them a purpose, as you say," Kilo said, "it would benefit you to treat them better. They might even become grateful for what you can teach them and thank you for the improvements you've made to their lives. It seems the scales are weighted far too heavily in your favor."

I averted Kilo's displeasure by walking to the next building.

Doggedly, he followed after me, and Saitou crossed his path to block him.

"Lady Hitori!" the Phantom shouted after me.

The next experiment was number thirty-seven, a new subject we had recently acquired from the town adjacent to Leiko. When I entered the room, the boy's eyes widened, and he thrashed forward against the ropes restraining him.

"Are you ready to participate in the trials today?"

In response, he spat at me. Undeterred, I sat atop the wooden table opposite him. Focusing on the boy, I picked at the particles in the air, rearranging the Skills so they became burdensome. They weighed down his arms and legs, and he began to bend under the weight.

"Are you ready now?"

He said nothing.

The Skills accumulated, and it became harder for him to breathe. A smile crept across my face as the boy tried to pretend he was unbreakable within my presence.

Something slammed against me, unseating me. I fell against the side of the building and immediately righted myself, pressing my back against the wall as cold metal touched my neck.

Kilo pressed his blade against my skin.

"Let them go," he said, his eyes blazing with anger.

Saitou scrambled inside the building. Blood dampened his right leg as he limped forward. He froze when he saw the sword at my neck. A few seconds passed, during which Kilo breathed heavily, his hand trembling to hold the sword steady. He drew in a deep breath and exhaled loudly as he lowered his sword and clenched his jaw.

Stepping back, he glanced over at the boy tied to the wall.

"Let me take their place," he said.

My lips curled back into a sneer. "That seems like a poor arrangement. I have over a dozen experiments in place. Why would I trade all that for a single person?"

He had grown arrogant during his time in my camp. He truly believed he could best me. Smiling, I reached for the Skills, grasping at them, but they seemed to slip away from my reach.

Kilo stood defiant.

Did he have that much control over the Skills?

The realization chilled me. I had been so confident I would be able to control the Phantom, and now—I gritted my teeth, keeping an air of indifference in my words.

"I will release half of them—of your choosing. The remainder I will release if I am satisfied with your performance. Until then, you are not to interfere with the other subjects I have in place."

Kilo sheathed his sword. "Show me the others."

We left the building, and I stood back as Kilo entered the remaining structures. Saitou limped to my side. The stain of blood on his right leg had spread, but he kept his hand on his sword hilt.

When Kilo had finished, he came back to where I stood.

"Do they ever get to leave those buildings?"

I kept my voice even. "If the subjects could be trusted, I wouldn't care."

Kilo nodded, his mood less hostile after my response. "Allow me and some of the other False Shadows to keep an eye on them. They should be allowed to stretch their muscles and to see the sunlight. Respect them as people and give them their dignity. They will appreciate it."

"Did you choose the ones to be released?" I asked impatiently.

This was becoming more of a pain than I had expected.

Kilo chose the ones who were most at risk during the experiments, the ones who were either injured or were the most frightened. The loss of number seventeen, the most promising subject, stung. But with the poison progressing, he likely would not have lasted much longer.

"Will you allow an escort for the ones you've released?" Kilo pressed.

"Send Haru and one other," I said, my patience at an end. "Prepare what they need, then meet back here in the evening. There is much we need to accomplish with the Skills."

Kilo placed his right arm over his chest and bowed at the waist before rushing to help the keepers with the subjects I had released. Number seventeen stumbled from his building, doubled over with pain. With the help of one of the keepers, he and Kilo started walking back toward camp. The five others Kilo had freed clustered around him, sending me wayward looks as they walked away.

I was too used to their hate to care.

Saitou sat down on the steps of one of the buildings, pulling off the leather armor around his shin to expose a large gash.

"You misjudged him," I said, shifting my attention to Saitou, a smirk spreading across my face. "Maybe you *should* start training with the Phantom."

He frowned. "I wasn't expecting his restraint to break so abruptly."

I summoned one of the remaining keepers, sending her to fetch some medicine and some water to clean the wound. When she returned, I took the wooden bucket, shooing the keeper away. After inspecting the vials, I selected the most potent medicine.

"It's nothing more than a surface wound," Saitou said, reaching for the bucket and cloth. "It's nothing serious."

Ignoring him, I placed the bucket on the ground, out of Saitou's reach, and sat on the lowest step of the building by his feet. There was a time when Saitou had almost died from a sword wound. He had said it was nothing to worry about then as well, but an infection had developed, and he'd been bedridden for a week.

"Lady Hitori," he said, pulling his leg away from me.

"Yes, I know it is not befitting of someone of my 'status' to be tending to my retainer's wounds. Would you prefer I called one of the keepers?"

Saitou's eyes widened slightly.

"No," he said, averting his eyes from me.

"The council is not here to criticize me and tell me what I can and cannot do. You know I only accepted this status because Lord Shingen wanted me to."

He had placed that noose around my neck the day he had rescued me from the battlefield. Letting the resentment die out, I soaked the rag in the water and pressed it to Saitou's wound. He flinched at the contact but remained still as I cleaned it. There wasn't a need to explain my misgivings to Saitou. He, too, had been taken in by the warrior turned lord. We both owed our lives to him, and thus, we were bound to abide by his wishes. Our debt was to repay his kindness.

When I finished binding Saitou's leg and rubbing the medicine onto it, I stood up, watching warily as Saitou put weight on his leg.

"I'll be fine," he said, gently. "We should go check to make sure the rest of your ranks don't think you're getting soft after releasing the subjects."

Restraining a scowl, I began to walk away, leaving the rag and bucket for the keepers to deal with.

Yet again, Kilo had the upper hand.

"If it helps any," Saitou said, shuffling after me and falling into place behind me, "I think it was the right thing to do."

I slowed my pace to make it easier for him to keep up.

I didn't turn around to address him, but a slight smile spread across my face. I was looking forward to finding out how strong the Phantom really was with the Skills.

chapter fifty-eight
A New Threat

When the sun had set, Kilo returned. He sat opposite me, close to the river and away from the main camp. The moonlight bathed the area in a slight silver hue.

Like always, Saitou stood guard a few paces away.

Before we began theorizing, I wanted to measure his ability and resistance to the Skill poisoning. Removing the necklace from around my neck, I held it out to Kilo by the leather strings.

"Fill the necklace with the Skills for as long as you are able to."

Kilo took the metal ornament in his hands and laid it down on the ground before placing his hands on his knees and closing his eyes. Saitou glanced over, curious to see how Kilo would perform. I reached out a hand to touch the metal. It was not hot, but my fingertips prickled with the Skills.

While we waited for Kilo to exhaust himself, the air became frigid. Saitou left to gather firewood, and when he had a sizable pile, he knelt beside me and began building a fire.

I placed my finger against the metal again.

The Skills continued to gather.

When the fire died down, Saitou added more wood to the embers and returned to the edge of the campfire's glow. From the sash at his waist, he withdrew a long bamboo flute. He brought the instrument to his lips, a melody of contentment rising and falling as the night wore on.

It had been quite some time since he had played it.

Idly, I watched the flames from the fire crackle and sway. When the fire grew weak again, I tossed more logs onto it, surprised to find the pile Saitou had cut was almost gone.

Kilo still had not stirred.

By the time he finally did, Saitou had left to gather more wood.

"How much longer should I continue?" Kilo asked, opening one eye. His voice carried a tone of innocence, but I could tell he was pleased I hadn't expected him to last this long.

He had purposely wasted my time.

"I can do this well into the morning if you would like," he added.

Annoyed, I scooped the metal ornament from the ground and dropped it back over my neck. Kilo had already surpassed the level of all of the subjects. Most had taken a few weeks to even be able to sustain the Skills long enough for me to grow bored.

Kilo held out his arm, nodding at the metal encased around it.

"Keep your eye on my bond."

Near his wrist, the metal seemed to stop catching the firelight. Instead of red light reflecting across it like one would expect, Kilo's bond began to glow, taking on a white hue. It grew in intensity, bathing his black robe in a shimmering silver radiance.

I leaned closer. "How are you doing that?"

"I asked the Skills to allow you to see them."

Sighing, I sat back. "That's absurd."

Kilo laughed. Anger flared up inside me, and he held out his hands in front of him, as if sensing he had upset me.

"It's not speaking to them as you and I are now," Kilo explained. "It's more like imagining the moon's glow and desiring for it to come into focus. Learning to see the Skills takes a while, but the more I've become aware of them residing in everything, the easier it's become." He stretched his hand out toward the fire, the silver glow becoming red. "I imagine it has more to do with the Skills reflecting color than them actually creating light." He shrugged. "Though I'm not sure it matters."

Excitement leaped in my stomach.

It did seem as if he had a different way of approaching the Skills. If we could compare our different perspectives, it would further our understanding.

Reaching for a blade of grass, I plucked it from the ground and held it up. "The Skills can be used to push against something," I said, moving the blade as if it were being pushed by the wind. "I'm assuming you can feel that?"

Kilo nodded.

My excitement was mirrored in his eyes.

"What is it you wish to accomplish with the Skills?" Kilo asked.

"I want to know their limits and applications," I said, watching Saitou return from the forest with more wood. "To know the full spectrum of their use."

"I know another person who has been enjoying learning about the Skills for the very same purpose," Kilo said. As he smiled, creases appeared near his eyes.

He rose to his feet and wandered to the other side of the campfire, looking off into the distance. "A question keeps resurfacing in my mind. It's something I've meant to ask you, but I've been uncertain if you would take me seriously."

Saitou had begun to play his flute again. The solemn melody cascaded around us, echoing off the dense forest. Despite having been hurt by the Phantom, it didn't seem to bother him to leave Kilo in my presence.

"What is it?" I asked.

Kilo turned and started toward the river. "Let me show you."

The river again? I gave a passing glance to Saitou before leaving him. We went deeper into the forest, traveling north toward Leiko Gulf, where the ocean fed into the stream. Kilo bent down next to the water a few times, dipping his fingertips in and disturbing the sediment of the riverbed before moving on. When he found the spot he was looking for, he shook the leather canteen at his side. The light illuminated the area in a warm glow. He crouched down next to the river, where a pool of water had been trapped by rocks.

"Something is happening with the Skills," he said, disturbing the minerals with his hand when I stood behind him.

Gravel and sand floated in the water, moving downstream. A black patch seemed to spread across the bottom of the riverbed. Kneeling beside Kilo, I leaned forward to inspect it. It looked thick and sticky as it pooled from the gravel. The substance resisted the slow-moving current of the stream. I reached out my hand, feeling the Skills emanating from the ooze.

Kilo looked at me expectantly. "There is a pool of the same material on the shore of Leiko Gulf near the town. It also occurred before when you lost control of the Skills in Aventon. Do you know what could be the cause?"

Ignoring his comment about losing control of the Skills, I stuck my forefinger into the black liquid. It burned. With my fingertips, I moved the gravel around. I didn't recognize it as one of the sediments local to the area.

"What makes you think it's the Skills?" I asked, looking upstream.

"You mean you cannot feel them?"

Sharply, I glanced back to find a wry smile on Kilo's face.

He was mocking me.

I shook my head. I hadn't seen anything like it before, and I barely remembered the same thing happening when I had used the Skills in Aventon.

"I have a theory about what is happening," Kilo said, moving toward one of the trees. He extended his hand, letting his fingertips rest on the bark.

I waited for him to continue, and when he didn't, I let out a long breath.

"And that is?"

Kilo exhaled heavily, and the Skills in the air became quiet. It unsettled me. I hadn't realized they were active until Kilo quieted them. It was like the absence of noise in a forest or the complete darkness that came from a cave. It was an unusual feeling, one I couldn't put words to, but one that felt unnatural.

When the Phantom looked back at me, his eyes shimmered with an almost silver hue. He removed his hand from the tree. "There's a tree inside this forest that has absorbed the pain of many lives. Somehow, it holds onto the memory of the people who have died here." His voice grew quieter. "It allowed me to see the people here who have died from the Skills. I felt the pain they endured during your first experiments."

My throat went dry.

Kilo continued to talk, but I barely heard the words over the pounding in my head. If he had found out, why was he still talking like it didn't bother him? Was he measuring my reaction? Waiting for his chance to undermine me?

The Phantom's hand went to the sword at his side, and I stiffened.

I needed to appear like I didn't care what he had found out. He already knew I had killed people to learn about the Skills, why were his words making me falter?

A cold sweat broke out across my back.

Once he found out all that he wanted, it was only a matter of time before he turned on me. I knew this, but a part of me was enjoying our conversation about the Skills, and I felt sad by the prospect of losing the dialogue we were having about them.

The calm in the Skills changed, becoming agitated in the area.

I looked at the Phantom.

We were two opposing forces that should never have come into contact.

As my frustration grew, I turned and stormed away. I didn't need to justify myself to the Phantom! What I did was none of his concern. I had never cared about anyone's opinion before. They were all just pawns to me. Tools to further my knowledge of the Skills.

Saitou's flute droned through the forest, and I let the music drown out my thoughts as the Skills built around me. Holding onto the bond on my arm, I felt the thrumming of the energy as it warmed my fingers.

The music stopped suddenly, and Saitou came to my side. He tucked the bamboo flute back inside the folds of his robes and said not a word as we continued through the forest, the glow of the main camp's fire a beacon in the night.

It was surprising anyone was still awake at this hour.

A cart and a few indistinct figures come into focus.

I stopped.

Gaiden's men had returned.

Dread filled me. They were the last people I wanted to see. But before I had time to slip back into the forest, Gaiden noticed me.

"Lady Hitori!" he called, his ambling gait filled with bravado.

His men created a semicircle around Saitou and me. The subtle click of Saitou's sword being adjusted made me aware he, too, was anxious about this encounter.

"Where's your new friend?" Gaiden asked, a sneer curling his face. He looked around the camp, as if looking for the Phantom, before he returned his attention to me. "I hear you've been teaching that new friend of yours how to use the Skills. Are you too cowardly to give me the knowledge? Are you afraid that I will become stronger than you? Well, let me tell you something, Laaaaady Hitori…" he said mockingly. "You're not the only one who has been setting plans in motion."

Gaiden's face had begun to turn red, and a vein bulged at the top of the head. His words were slurred as he grew angrier.

He almost appeared drunk on his own sense of power.

"At this moment, the council members are fortifying Magoto against you. They, with help from a few other mercenary groups, have taken over your precious town. Soon you will be Lady of nothing!"

I fisted my hands at my sides.

The longer he talked, the less I wanted to hear his prattling nonsense. My grasp on the lands had been shaken by others who wished to take what was mine—first by the Shadows, then by the Silver Fox group raiding the villages in tandem with my chaos, and finally, by the mercenary men whose service I had employed. While others had been moving against me, I had allowed the Phantom to pacify my actions, nurturing my belief that people indeed wanted peace above war.

How wrong I had been to allow my thoughts to be swayed.

Those in my service did nothing but cultivate their hatred of me and seek to satiate their greed. It was foolish of me to think any would cooperate with me or keep their word.

"You're nothing but a coward, Hitori!" Gaiden said, reaching his hand back to the oversized sword resting on his back. "It's time someone—"

I forced the Skills around us to slam into Gaiden, pushing him down without regard to his well-being. He fell to his knees and struggled to breathe, clutching at his neck and wrapping his hand around his sword as his breath faded.

There was no going back.

The Phantoms.

The general who worked with them.

The lord in Tarahn.

The others scattered across Kiriku.

They would never extend their friendship to me. All of them waited for a convenient time to betray me. It would be the same with the Phantom.

Movement out of the corner of my eye set me into motion. One of Gaiden's men lashed out at me with his sword. The Skills rose up, creating a barrier between the man and me, but my hold over Gaiden broke, and he gasped for air. I stumbled back and steadied myself. Saitou was already locked in combat with two of Gaiden's men. The person who had broken my barrier raised his sword overhead, and I turned my hand to him, rearranging the

Skills at his feet. A torrent rose around us, my anger rising and expanding to those in camp.

Gaiden pushed off the ground with his sword.

"Hitori! Stop!" Kilo yelled, running toward us from the forest.

I glanced over at him briefly before returning my attention to Gaiden and his men. The mercenaries had betrayed me, and I refused to show weakness by allowing them to live. They could take the pitiful villages and the resources I had begun hoarding, but they would not take Magoto from me!

All thoughts and desires to work with the Phantom faded.

It had all been some elaborate dream. There had never been a way for me to survive without taking what I needed by force. Why had I thought anything would change? To survive, I had to take control.

I had to take what was mine.

And the Skills... I nearly spat at the thought they were anything more than a means to an end, a tool that would allow us to fight for the right to survive. I had been too soft, too foolish to see them for anything more. I had been hypnotized by the allure of the Phantom's words.

Turning, I moved toward the group of mercenaries, bypassing their rage. They shrank away from me; fear had returned to their eyes.

"I will teach the Skills to anyone who makes it back alive, " I said, my back straight and my head held high. "Head to the Miyota Mountains. Burn everything in your path."

Greed rose in their eyes.

Their loyalty to their commander shattered in an instant.

Gaiden's obsession and desire had passed onto his men. They cut the horses from the carts and spurred them into the night, leaving the men weighed down by the Skills to die. A low growl from my left made me turn just in time. Gaiden swung his massive sword at me.

I stepped to the right, the impact of his blade shaking the ground.

A horse cleaver.

Stepping back, I gathered the Skills to me.

I was fatigued from earlier, but I stood tall as Gaiden rushed me. He drew back the impossibly long blade and swung it down. A blur flashed past me, moving ahead of me.

Gaiden's sword connected with a sheathed blade.

Kilo's hands spread out across his sword to bear the weight. The sheath split, and metal scraped against metal. Gaiden and Kilo disengaged.

Off to the side, Saitou was still locked in combat.

Kilo threw off the sheath to his blade, bringing up his sword as he sliced across Gaiden's arm, moving with speed and deadly precision. Blood dripped from Kilo's blade, but Gaiden didn't relent. The mercenary's bloodlust invigorated him to keep attacking. The small amount of the Skills that had gathered in my defense fell apart. The bond on my arm burned, and I released the Skills. My arm had blackened from my lack of control. The ground shook and split as Gaiden's cleaver hit the ground. Dust billowed. Gaiden struggled to free the blade, but before he could, Kilo turned the sword in his hand and slammed the unsharpened edge into Gaiden's forearm. He yelled in agony as his wrist snapped, clutching it with his other hand. His oversized blade remained wedged in the ground.

Kilo slammed the dull edge of the sword against his back.

And Gaiden fell to his knees.

"Don't move," Kilo said, placing the sharpened edge to the back of Gaiden's neck.

Kilo remained rigid.

Poised.

A chill traveled down my spine as his eyes focused on me. His deadliness, his restraint, all of it spoke of someone who had been trained to kill.

Saitou came to my side, breathing heavily, his hands still on his sword.

Did he also feel the rage from the Phantom?

"He will never hold a weapon the same way again," Kilo said, his voice emotionless as he looked down at Gaiden's crushed wrist.

The Phantom surveyed the chaos around camp before putting his fingers to his lips. He whistled shrilly. Long, then short.

"I am going to stop the men you've sent to destroy Kiriku," he said, his voice and expression flat. "When I am finished, I will return to you."

Kilo flicked the sword to rid it of blood and wiped it with a rag he drew from his robe. Picking up the sword's broken sheath, he slid the weapon inside.

By now, the False Shadows had begun to wake up and gather. Seiji and Haru rushed to the Phantom, and the three walked back into camp, exchanging words I couldn't hear. I looked back at the death Saitou had wrought and the man who remained on his knees at my feet.

"Execute him," I said, bracing myself for the impact of Saitou's blade. If Gaiden remained alive, his bitterness would spread into revenge. It didn't matter if he could not hold a sword. He would find a way to exact his vengeance some other way.

Saitou's sword separated Gaiden's head from his body.

The campsite went silent.

A few moved to follow after Kilo.

The others were too stunned to react.

"Leave the bodies," I said to the handful who came forward to rid the camp of filth. "We ride for Magoto."

Saitou shouted orders. "Prepare yourselves for battle!"

The False Shadows dispersed—all except for Haru and Seiji, who stood defiant at Kilo's side. From out of the forest, a black stallion charged. Kilo threw out his arm and mounted the horse, spurring the steed into a gallop as he rode into the woods.

It was the same horse he had ridden into Aventon.

"Haru! Seiji!" I called.

Seiji withered as he approached, but Haru had a much different reaction. He frowned, creating a deep crease in his brow. The sword at his side had blood on it.

When he spoke, it was quiet. "I had hoped your actions would become less rash after bringing the Phantom under your command." Looking down at the ground, he seemed to struggle with his next words. "My loyalty has always been to the people of Magoto. I will help you retake the town, but after we are through, I will no longer serve you."

With that, he walked away.

From where he was situated in the shadow of the trees, Saitou looked to the north, where Kilo had left in pursuit of the others.

Anger swelled in me.

Did he too desire to serve another?

"And what will you do?" I asked Seiji.

"It's about time I started making amends for what my father has done." He shifted a pouch at his side. For the first time, I noticed the symbol on it—a medicinal flower. It was the same symbol one of my first research subjects had carried, a man who had cooperated to save his son's life.

"Should I send riders after Kilo?" Saitou asked.

I looked around at those who remained. "No, we'll conserve our forces. Fear will spread faster than the flames of the mercenaries. What can one man do against all that?" The False Shadows dawdled, and I snapped at them. "Ready yourselves, or you will wish you burned like Magoto."

This, at last, seemed to motivate them.

Heading toward the building where I kept the equipment for the experiments. I picked up an extra pair of knives and my short sword. My hands reached toward the leather armor, which had sat neglected in the corner for years. It was a gift from my father I had never worn.

A shadow blocked the light coming in from the door.

Saitou crossed the room and reached over my shoulder to grab the chest piece.

"Your father had a name for you when you were younger," he said, dropping the chest plate over my head. "Do you remember it?"

"Child of the Storm."

Saitou tightened the ties, securing the armor tightly to my chest. "We found you on the battlefield amid a torrential storm. Instead of taking shelter from the lightning, you stood there with your eyes raised toward the sky—unafraid. From that day forward, Lord Shingen knew your life would be a storm to those around you."

I allowed him to piece the remaining leather armor onto my body. He pulled on the ties, ensuring they were snug against my skin.

When he was finished, he bowed.

"I will follow you to whatever end."

chapter fifty-nine
Coup d'état

The sun rose behind us, casting long shadows over the Plains of ReRiel. We rode swiftly, stopping only when we needed, cutting down the usual three days of travel to two. Magoto's gate was shut tight when we arrived, with no guards on duty—or at least, none who waited for us where we could see them.

They thought to deny me entrance to my own town?

"Should I send riders to check the side gates?" Saitou asked with a small smile.

I was unamused.

While there were other ways inside Magoto, I refused to consider them.

This was my town, and I would enter through the main gate.

"No," I said, pacing before the gate on horseback. The cowards didn't even have the gall to stand up to me, to deny me entry in person. I could use the Skills to burn through the wood, though it seemed a shame as I would then have to rebuild it.

But if the cowards refused to open it, what other choice did I have?

"Let them know you will be merciful if they comply," Saitou suggested.

"Very well," I said, irritation coating my tone. I guided my horse to the side of the gate, to get a better vantage point if any chose to show themselves.

"Open the gate!" I demanded.

Saitou gave me a pointed stare.

"Open the gate, and I'll allow you to live." I waited but a moment before embellishing the request. "You have one minute until I burn the gate down and kill each and every one of you."

Saitou sighed; his hand went to the sword at his side.

Impatiently, I waited, not surprised when the timeframe elapsed.

Moving my horse closer to the gate, I shouted to the False Shadows behind me.

"Get back!"

The heat from the Skills started at my fingertips and grew, expanding to my hands and body. A rush of warmth washed over me as I collected and rearranged the Skills in the air. Sparks snapped, and I reached my hand out to the wooden planks of the gate. The bond on my forearm vibrated, and flames leaped toward the gate.

When the fire began to consume the wood, I moved back to wait.

The False Shadows fell into line behind me, and Saitou came to my side.

"We head to the castle first," I said, turning my head slightly to address the False Shadows. "Stay alert. Assume all are working against us."

If it looked like we were going to win, the people would feign their loyalty in an attempt to have their pathetic lives spared. Then again—I eyed the others—the same could be said about those standing behind me. None of them, besides Haru and Saitou, had chosen to be here.

Reluctance was in the False Shadows' eyes.

They were more withdrawn than usual.

Parting with Kilo had chipped away at their resolve.

"Let's go," I said, pushing the thought aside. It was no different than it used to be. Fear would keep them complacent. They were drawn to Kilo because of his passive heart and compassion. It was me—the one willing to get my hands dirty— who would take back their town.

The flame on the gate ate through the middle, leaving a weakened section. Saitou pulled back on the reins of his horse, and his stallion reared and kicked at the door. The wooden planks split, opening a hole wide enough for a horse to fit through. Saitou headed inside first; moments later, he called back, confirming it was clear.

I motioned the False Shadows through. "Move."

One by one they obeyed, and once we were on the other side of the gate, no one confronted us. It seemed careless to not have posted guards at the entrance. Perhaps they had fallen asleep or had drunk themselves into a stupor. It would be easy to slit their traitorous throats if that were the case. Saitou moved his horse beside me, throwing his arm out. A whirr in the air brushed my ear. Then something else shot past, ricocheting off the leather bracer on Saitou's arm.

It seemed shouting at them had indeed set them running.

In the air, warmth still floated as embers smoldered on the gate.

"Move away from the gate; scatter the men," I said to Saitou.

He gave me a curt nod before surveying the area to make his plan of action. He split the group into two teams, dividing them according to their preference and talent with certain weapons.

I trusted him to lead the False Shadows while I took out the archers.

"Team one, ready your bows!" Saitou shouted as he moved his horse in front of me. "Team two, prepare to converge."

Immediately, they spread out, engaging in combat with people I had never seen before. They had the same metal armor that Gaiden wore, so they were most likely mercenaries that had been enticed to take over the town. The guard towers on either side of the gate seemed empty, all except for… I smiled. Why not make them tremble as they watched our approach? I sneaked over to the guards' area, picking up one of the porcelain jugs hidden in a pile of straw. Liquid sloshed inside, and the scent of fermented rice rose from the opening.

With care, I dribbled the liquid across the cobblestones, creating a zigzag pattern on the ground. Saitou plunged his sword into his opponent's chest, finishing him off before he moved to my side.

He eyed my handiwork, and I felt his approval.

Emptying the final contents, I summoned the Skills. Flames leaped up and meandered around the feet of those fighting, blazing a path and separating swords. The flames rose, circling around the guards and mercenaries. They screamed, and Saitou slashed his blade into the nearest man.

"End it," Saitou said to the others, pulling his blade from the man's chest as he moved on to the next person.

I left the smell of burning flesh behind.

My heels clicked against the stone pathway as I strode past the run-down stone buildings to the castle. The townspeople hid in the shadows, and slunk back inside, no doubt wishing my anger would stay subdued and pointed at the ones who had turned against me. The people's lives were a burden to me, and I held no great love for them. Even now, they exhausted me. All along, I had been powerless to change anything, and yet, I couldn't let matters rest as they were.

I would rather Magoto burn than to come under the traitor's possession.

Off to my right, a woman emerged from her house, a basket balanced at her hip. She took one step outside and froze, her eyes widening as she saw me. Shouts from the fighting echoed off the buildings cut from the cliffside. She dropped the basket in her fright, and I felt a presence come to my side. Smoke wafted over, obscuring Saitou's silhouette. His hand was wrapped tightly around his sword; a quiver at the corner of his eyes was the only betrayal of the conflict inside him.

Saitou had helped revive Magoto with my father.

Without me, the people would not have been in this situation. They would not be suffering, and Magoto would undoubtedly have been flourishing.

"Are you still with me, Saitou?" I asked.

"Always."

Saitou never hesitated in his answer, and for that, I was grateful. His ideals aligned more with the Phantom's than my own, but loyalty kept him bound to me.

Leading our small company down the narrow streets of stone, we came to the abandoned quarter on the far side of town. The houses here were more weathered, beaten down, nearly indistinguishable from the mountain they were carved from. Near the end of the row, a narrow staircase led up to the castle. The path was small, and when it rained, it became obscured as water ran over it, but we could bypass the patrols this way.

If the council had even thought to dispatch any.

A thin layer of white moss covered the staircase, blending into the mountain. It softened our approach to the keep, squishing quietly as we ascended the multiple levels of Magoto's design. At the top, a tall man—one of the guardsmen—with a thick beard and a square jawline caught sight of us. Gai, commander of the guards.

The commander gave me a short bow. "It happened almost as soon as you left, Lady Hitori. The council members demanded we pledge our loyalty to them. They seem convinced you will surrender."

I kept my eyes focused on him. "And who do you swear your loyalty to?"

"To the lady of Magoto and its people."

I tried not to let the slight get to me. The commander's loyalty should be to me alone, but if he still believed Magoto and its people could survive and he was willing to work with me, I would accept it.

After all, his son, Haru, had said much the same.

Saitou stayed close to my side as Gai slid open the door to the west wing of the castle. Haru moved to the front to help his father ensure the castle was clear. Darkness enveloped our group. The interior had no windows, and the torches had not been lit this far from the main hallways. Father and son separated from our group, moving cat-like through the darkness. It had been quite some time since I'd been in the west wing of the castle. There was a faint smell of mildew here.

Haru came back, his eyes shining in the darkness. "The council members have situated themselves in the main wing. Guarding them is a handful of the elite guards turned traitors and a few mercenaries sent by Gaiden."

Nodding, I made a note of the details and numbers. I needed to conserve my energy for the council members, but the thought of waiting through a lengthy battle dissuaded me from inaction.

Best to get it over with.

I pushed past Gai and Saitou and turned the corner to the main hall. As I knelt in the shadow of darkness, I felt the Skills burn inside me. An overwhelming heat engulfed me, and the veins in my hands trembled.

Saitou bent down next to me. "Hitori," he dared, "wouldn't it be wise to—"

"What? Let them live so they can kill me?" Restraint had run dry in my veins. "There's no one in this castle worth saving."

They had been corrupt long before the day my father was killed. These past months had shown me the council members were unworthy to be in the positions they held.

Clenching my jaw tight, I drew in the Skills, holding them momentarily before releasing them. My awareness drifted with the mist, rolling down the stone stairs and burning the carpet, the stone underneath charring.

When the mist touched the first person; he twisted and writhed.

Then, one by one, the guards and the mercenaries dropped to the ground.

Haru and Gai entered the hall, looking at the mass of bodies strewn about. Shouts came from the other tunnels. More were coming.

"Spare only those you trust," I commanded, noticing the sword the commander wore at his side. It was one given to him by the commanding lord. The sword was a symbol of his position, passed down from the lords of Magoto. "When you're finished, clear the streets of the remaining corruption. If you do not have the stomach to do so, I ask you to return the sword my father gave you."

Trusting in my father's decision, I had left Gai in command of the guards.

What would he choose?

Next to the commander, his son's hands clenched tightly around his own sword, either from rage or from the magnitude of my actions.

Gai met my gaze without hesitation and gave a short nod. "We will see to it." The commander raised his voice. "Clear the castle!"

The Skills had welled up inside me, and I pushed them to disperse throughout my body. My legs felt weakened, but I ignored them. The time to act was now. It was time the council members answered for what they'd done.

I walked down the hall to the chamber room, pausing momentarily outside before I commanded the Skills in the area to the closed door. The wooden boards shattered across the hall, and I lifted my head high, entering. The members of the council scowled down at me from the elevated platform. A handful of guards standing in the middle of the room drew their swords. Saitou ran to meet them, slashing his sword across the neck of one of the guardsmen.

A low growl came from deep within my throat.

I turned my attention to Giichi first, whose long beard and wiry frame seemed frail against the extravagant robe he wore. His eyes were focused on Saitou, and the smugness that had been on his face transformed into fear.

When I approached him, he turned his eyes to me. "After the death of your father, I thought you would finally leave Magoto. It was a mistake to have ignored you for so long." He paused, and his smile deepened. "Although we were not idle with our time. We did try to have you killed more than once."

I narrowed my eyes.

It was foolish for them to think I didn't know it was them behind everything. Their ploys were one of the reasons why Saitou never left my side. Even as a child, and under my father's protection, they had sent assassins after me.

But their pathetic attempts were nothing in comparison to the plan they had hatched to eliminate my father.

"What kind of leader sacrifices the people they're supposed to care for to slight a child?" I asked, my blood boiling. "I know it was you who poisoned the water in the fountain I built. You not only turned the people against me, but you also took away their chance to progress as a society. You sicken me."

The other members of the council were just as guilty.

"All of you," I amended.

On the end of the dais, Reiko sat with her head propped up on one hand. She was perhaps worse than Giichi. While the others followed Giichi's lead and were more like sheep in their actions, both she and Giichi had ambitions to rule Magoto themselves.

Reiko waved off my words. "We warned Lord Shingen he was nurturing someone who would bring destruction to Magoto. He refused to listen. The consequences that followed were because you continued to live."

Giichi stepped forward, placing his hands on the table and leaning forward. "Your father was a fool. When he came to ask for you to be allowed to experiment with this new power, we knew there was no compromising. The only cure for stupidity is death."

I frowned and looked over at the other council members. Each of them was younger than Giichi and Reiko by several decades. If I recalled correctly, Ichikuro, Genma, and Hatsuhiko had all been raised to their status by my father.

"And you?" I asked. "Do you have nothing to say on this matter? No loyalty to the man who gave you a title and wealth? Or do you just agree to what the others decide is best?"

They dropped their eyes, and I clicked my tongue, disgusted. Pathetic.

"While we were all fond of your father," Ichikuro said, his voice quiet like that of a snake, "all of us agreed the prospect of you ruling Magoto was one we couldn't allow. It was a unanimous decision."

He stood and left the platform, drawing the sword at his side. Genma and Hatsuhiko joined him. In their hands they carried kama—wooden rods with short, curved blades. I glanced back to see Saitou battling one of the remaining guards. I had already surpassed my normal usage with the Skills. Underneath the bond on my arm, the skin burned, even without using them.

Would it be better to eliminate all of them at once or conserve my strength and take them out one at a time?

Retreating back, I kept the three younger council members in sight. They moved as one, from a single direction, but the longer I waited, the more time they would have to surround me.

Drawing my short sword from my back, I leapt at one of the men, slashing out at Ichikuro. He drew his blade, blocking me as he brought his sword up and slid it across the length of mine. Genma and Hatsuhiko split, coming at me from two different directions.

Having finished off his opponent, Saitou dashed in front of Genma, bringing his sword up and pressing him back. I summoned the Skills to my short blade, stepping away from Ichikuro. Hatsuhiko hooked the curved edge of his weapon on to my arm. A thin barrier created by the Skills blocked most of his attack, but when he pulled back, a small line of blood appeared on my arm.

I spread my hand out across my blade, evoking fire along the metal's edge. Hatsuhiko hesitated, and a pattering of footsteps came from the hall. Haru drew his sword, pressing Hatsuhiko back with force. Turning, I focused my attention on the final of the three younger council members. Ichikuro sank down onto his knees and sprang forward, bringing his sword up from the ground. I held my sword steady with two hands, holding off his attack. He pressed against me, causing my back foot to slide to the rear. My arms shook against the effort. He was stronger than me, but strength didn't always win a fight.

The Skills blazed hotter around my sword as embers flew off. Ichikuro's skin hissed as the ashes reached him, but he continued to press me, his lips drawing back as he clenched his teeth together.

Saitou yelled, and I glanced over to see blood on the side of his neck. He stepped back and panted heavily, sweat pouring from his forehead.

He was tiring.

Unleashing the Skills against Ichikuro, I sent him sliding across the floor. Drawing in a breath, I gazed over at Haru.

Like Saitou, he was showing signs of exhaustion.

Ichikuro rushed back at me, raising his sword up over his head. "I wouldn't get too distracted by your companions. You have enough to worry about!"

Angling my sword, I sidestepped Ichikuro's incoming attack. He shifted the angle of his sword at the last moment, but I jumped back, dodging his flurry of slashes before catching his blade with my own.

He grinned at me as I strained to hold him. "Your life has always been a plague to those around you. Why don't you do us all a favor and just die already!"

He withdrew his sword and slashed up, catching the edge of my armor with his attack. His words were an echo of the nightmares that had plagued me.

Retreating, I lowered my sword, trying to steady my breathing. The Skills stirred at my summons, creating a wind in the air. A dagger scraped across the armor near my shoulder, and I looked up to find Reiko standing on the platform. In her hand, another blade glinted. I kept my attention on her and Giichi, allowing the hatred and the conviction of their betrayal to surface in my mind.

Fighting Ichikuro was a waste of time.

He was nothing against the Skills.

"Die!" Ichikuro said, leaping at me.

His sword broke the instant it touched the barrier that hummed against me skin. I had not even summoned the Skills to make one. My lips curled back into a smile. Was this what the Phantom had meant when he said the Skills aligned themselves with a person's desires?

That they had a will of their own?

Slamming the Skills against Ichikuro, I crushed him to the ground, strangling his breath. Reiko and Giichi braced themselves against the table as the shockwave slammed into them. My heart beat faster, wanting more than anything to erase the smugness from their faces. Hatsuhiko and Genma leaped at me, their weapons like playthings against my barrier. The Skills crashed into them, and they fell to the ground, clutching at their necks as the Skills strangled them.

More than anything, I wanted to be rid of them.

All of them.

Intense heat clouded my vision, and pressure from inside my chest threatened to burst. I struggled to maintain control of the Skills as they grew, raging inside the council room like a typhoon. The windows broke, and the pressure building inside the room sent a shockwave that collided with the stone walls. The ground shook and small chunks of rock fell from the ceiling.

The Skills seared my flesh near my bond, but it was nothing in comparison to the years of hate and abuse the council had put me through.

I could hear them, shouting in the distance, their voices echoing, drowning my breath and reason:

"Go back to where you came from, filth!!"

"You're a disgrace to your father's name. Why he took pity on you, I'll never know."

"Your father should never have brought you here."

"Demon child…"

"…war filth…"

"…a living plague in Magoto."

Figures of black smiled at me from the darkness. Silver weapons glinted in their hands, and I threw the Skills out at them. Fire enveloped their silhouettes, but even as they were incinerated their eyes glowed red.

Their hatred loomed over me, closing in on all sides.

I screamed.

Pressing my fingers against my head, the Skills whipped around me, fire burning all that it touched. My vision shifted momentarily, and I felt rain upon my outstretched arms...

I stood within a thunderstorm.

It was the day Saitou and Lord Shingen had called to me.

Peace I had not felt in years settled over me. A voice spoke to me, as lighting crackled overhead. My father knelt in front of me, his hand outstretched toward me.

"Would you like to come with me?" A smile was upon his face.

Lightning struck the ground, outlining his figure in an ominous light. His body fell to the floor, a knife in his back, and blood spread under my feet.

I screamed, holding my head in my hands. Both flames and water lashed against me in a torrential storm. Trapped in the past or in a waking nightmare, I knew not where I was.

All I cared about was that it would end.

A sudden touch on my shoulder broke the Skills' hold on me, and I jerked away, but fingers clutched at the leather armor near my neck.

"Lady...Hitori," someone said, their voice strained.

They sounded as if they, too, were lost in the storm around me.

Father?

No. I tried to place the voice, feeling the grip of the Skills and the air suffocating me as it dragged me away from reality. My father would not call me as such. The voice was rougher than my father's but more welcoming.

More dear to me.

"Hitori..."

My eyes flew open, and the voice fell into place.

Saitou collapsed against me, and I threw my arms under his shoulders, struggling to keep him upright. His eyes were closed, and a touch of moisture rested at the edges of his eyes. Where my hands held him, his leather armor burned.

Afraid, I let go of him, and he sank to his knees.

His hands grasped my forearms.

I tried to let go of the Skills, to push them away, but they continued to drown me. I closed my eyes, feeling tears roll down my cheeks, and fought against the panic rising in my chest. *Be at peace*, I pleaded, remembering what Kilo had said about the Skills reacting to a person's request.

Please.

Saitou still held onto me, and I allowed myself to be pulled down by him. When my breathing relaxed, I tried to stand, but his grip tightened around my arm.

"Don't…look," he said, his voice ragged.

Saitou's eyes met mine briefly before they rolled back in his head. His hold loosened, and I lowered him down to the ground, glancing around at what remained of the guards and council members.

I had killed them.

All of them.

Their bodies were nothing more than charred masses.

Saitou gasped for air, his skin turning slightly blue.

"Saitou," I said, sinking down next to him, "I'm sorry. I didn't realize…"

I couldn't finish the words. Every wound Saitou had received, every battle he had been in—he had never been brought to his knees. I placed my hand on his forehead. It was impossibly hot. Laying his head down, I took his sword into my trembling hands and forced myself to stand.

Haru lay a few paces away, face down on the ground. Kneeling next to him, I turned him over. His breathing was slow but stable. He, too, was alive.

I stood up, clutching Saitou's sword in my hand as I stepped back.

For the first time, I was truly alone.

I had thought my control of the Skills was absolute.

Infallible.

How wrong I had been.

By using them, I had become consumed, blind to what was important.

My knees felt weak, and I sank down next to Saitou, the long length of my robes covering the stone floor. Drawing in a deep breath, I held my hand out over Saitou, feeling for the Skills inside of him. Desperately, I pulled the Skills into me. Warmth shot across my arm, enveloping my body in an unnatural heat. The skin around my bond turned a deeper shade of black. For a moment, I hesitated, fearing I would not be able to handle this concentration of Skills, but when Saitou's breathing began to relax, I no longer cared. The Skills within Saitou's body were infused with the ill will of the council members, reflecting their hatred and malice. Mixed with my own anger and contempt, all of the emotions slammed against my mind, twisting my heart and wringing my lungs. I braced myself against it, squeezing my eyes closed as I waded through the emotions and forced myself to breathe. Their hatred was nothing new to me. I had borne it since I was young. Ever since my father had brought me here it had been like a poison to me…

But now—finally—it was over.

Every member of the council was dead.

Their grasp on Magoto was removed. The plague upon the people was over. Maybe now the town would finally be able to flourish as my father and Saitou had wanted.

Tears rolled down my cheeks, and I kept my hand on Saitou's chest, watching as the skin around my bond hissed and flaked. My head began to spin, the edges of my vision becoming blurry.

None of it mattered as long as…

A sudden wave of nausea came over me, and footsteps came from the hall.

I tore my gaze from Saitou to see Seiji, Gai, and a handful of the guardsmen. Their clothing and weapons were covered in blood. They started to check on the dead and quickly came to the conclusion there was no one left alive.

Seiji was the first to come to my side.

He gazed down at Saitou, his lips pressed thin.

"He's still alive," I said, averting my gaze as the others came over. "As is Haru."

Gai knelt next to his son before he stood abruptly.

"Move them out of the hall. Find the other doctors."

I coughed violently, my chest aching. Covering my mouth with my hand, I noticed flecks of blood on my palm. Seiji leaned over to offer his hand to me. Several guardsmen picked up Saitou and Haru and carried them away. After wiping the blood onto my robe, I allowed Seiji to help me to my feet.

"Let me tend to your wounds," Seiji said, inspecting my arm. The Skin around the silver casing was black and oozing blood.

"Saitou and Haru are the priority," I said, pulling my arm away as I steadied myself. In an attempt to hide the damage, I slipped my hands into the folds of my robe.

Seiji's eyes widened slightly at my words, and he bowed, keeping his head down as I left him and the others to tend to Saitou and Haru. There was nothing anyone could do for me even if I allowed them to try.

There was no cure for the Skill poisoning.

chapter sixty
Coup d'état: Aftermath

From on top of Magoto's stone wall, I watched the smoke billow from the pyre. It had been five days since I had reclaimed the town from the council's clutches. I should have been celebrating their deaths, especially those who had manipulated the affairs here, but instead, I was uneasy.

Seeing so much death had never bothered me before.

Why did it now?

We had removed the bodies from the castle and stripped the guardsmen of their armor. A pile of shoes and clothing rested next to me, leaving a foul taste in my mouth. They were necessary supplies for the people in Magoto. Those of us who remained would survive because others had died.

At least, for a time.

Without the full strength of the False Shadows and guardsmen, Magoto was vulnerable. And with everything I had done, it was only a matter of time before the people of Kiriku would come for their revenge.

Which would happen after *he* came for me.

As he had promised.

"Lady Hitori."

From behind, Haru approached. He had taken off the more substantial parts of his armor and uniform, leaving behind a thick turquoise robe and a white inner robe. His hands were raw and bruised, and his face was solemn.

He gave me a short bow before straightening and waiting for orders.

Down below, a family set out across the Plains of ReRiel.

"How many?" I asked, watching as another person left through the open gate. Their faith in me had broken. Without the council members, they did not see Magoto surviving the season.

"We stopped counting."

In some twisted way, I was relieved knowing the people of Magoto had given up. The burden of their lives had been lifted from me. We would be able to survive with what the mercenaries had gathered, and we no longer would need to call in favors or destroy villages for supplies. For now, we would survive.

My thoughts became more sober, drifting back to the absence of Saitou at my side.

"Have you come to help me?" I asked.

We had saved Magoto, and as Haru had threatened back in Leiko, he had resigned from his position as one of my guards, though he had come at my summons.

Haru hesitated to answer.

And rightly so.

"If there were anyone else I could ask, I would," I said, fearing he would turn me down. I had not slept since the battle. My body would not handle much more of the Skills.

"If it's for Saitou," Haru said at last, "I will help you."

"Thank you," I said as a rush of relief surged through me.

Haru nodded, and we left the stone wall, taking the steps down through the watchtower and heading into the empty streets of the lower quarter. Usually, I avoided this route because of the townspeople, but it was the quickest way to the castle. We saw few people, and those we did see didn't seem to notice me or care. They looked just as I felt. Tired, worn, and beaten. By the time we made it back to the castle and my personal quarters, the sun was beginning to fade. I knelt next to Saitou's side, seeing a little more color in his face.

Briefly, Haru left the room before returning with a lantern. He lit the other hanging lamps, before kneeling down on the other side of Saitou.

"How's he been doing?" Haru asked.

"He's improving," I said, lifting Saitou's hand from his side. Though the Skills were still burning inside him. Even the act of touching him stirred the poison inside me. I nodded to the tray on the bedside table. "Seiji came by earlier today and dropped off some medicine, but Saitou hasn't woken up to take it."

There were voices in the hallway.

I let out a pained breath, turning my head to the side.

Haru didn't look up. "They've come to help."

My throat tightened as a few of the guardsmen entered the room. They gave me wary looks before their eyes rested on Saitou.

"I told them what you've been doing to help Saitou." Haru motioned to the others. "I've told them about how the Skills work, as much as I know at least, and I've explained to them what will happen and how it feels."

Nodding, I dug out the thin blades from the pouch at my side. "These metal daggers will attract the Skills. You won't need to do more than to endure the pain. With all of your help, we might be able to draw the rest of the poison out of him tonight."

Briefly, I looked around at the guards. They all gave me a small nod of approval.

"You can count on us," Haru said, reaching out for a dagger.

Passing out the rest, I took Saitou's hand in my own. The Skills leapt up at the connection, spiraling and wrapping around my arm. Feeling the daggers in the guards' hands in my mind, I began channeling the Skills. The Skills were attracted to the metal, so all I needed to do was divide up the force I pulled from Saitou.

The hardest part was being able to keep the amount consistent and small enough that I did not overwhelm Haru or the guards.

It would have been difficult with only Haru, and now, with four additional locations to maintain, it taxed my mind in ways the Skills never had before. Sweat beaded on my brow, rolling down the side of my face. I concentrated, adjusting the flow of the poison with careful, meticulous adjustments.

One of the guards groaned, and I hesitated, feeling the connection weaken. Haru exchanged words with her while I kept my focus on adjusting the outpouring of the Skills. I squeezed Saitou's hand tighter, feeling the heat from him beginning to subside.

"Only a little more," I said, straining to speak while maintaining the Skills.

Through the connection came a surge of strength from the guardsmen. I directed the last remainder of the Skill poisoning, dividing it up between the six of us. Then I exhaled slowly. A bout of nausea and dizziness came over me, and I set Saitou's hand down as I walked away from the others, placing my hand on the wall to steady myself.

The stone darkened at my touch.

"He's awake!" one of the guards yelled.

I glanced over my shoulder to see Saitou's eyes open. He struggled to sit up, and Haru pressed his hand onto his chest until he stilled. Saitou turned his head in my direction, spotting me against the wall.

Recognition filled his eyes.

I rushed to him, falling to my knees. My vision blurred from the tears in my eyes as he smiled at me. He was conscious for only a moment, but it was enough.

"Thank you," I said to the guards, squeezing my eyes shut as more tears fell.

Relief rushed through me. The kindness the guards had shown me tightened my throat. I knew I did not deserve it. But without Haru and the others, I wouldn't have been able to draw the poison quickly enough from Saitou's body and he would have...

Haru placed his hand on my shoulder. "Let me stay and keep watch over Saitou while you sleep." He nodded toward the futon by the corner of the bed. "It doesn't seem like you have slept much since the battle."

Haru held out his hand, and I accepted his help to stand. The other guardsmen began to rise as well. Some looked drained, while others seemed not to have felt the effects yet.

"Let me know immediately if any of you feel side effects from the Skills," I said, pushing my shoulders back and regaining my composure. "It's normal to feel fatigued after experiencing the Skills, but if you start to feel a pain in your chest or prolonged dizziness, come see me no matter the hour."

I slipped my hands inside the folds of my robe to hide the black, flaking skin.

The guards bowed to me before they left.

Haru walked over to the window, gazing outside at the night sky. He kept his back turned as I took off the outer layers of my clothing and settled under the blankets.

As I closed my eyes, I felt a surge of happiness that Saitou would survive. It would take some time for him to heal, but the immediate danger had passed.

Now that the corruption in Magoto had been purged, there was one remaining piece in play.

My mind churned back to our last encounter and the person who knew something about the Skills that I didn't.

Had the Phantom been able to stop the mercenaries?

I had motivated Gaiden's men with the lure of the Skills, knowing it would be unlikely any would return alive to claim their prize. It was an action done in retaliation to Gaiden's betrayal and to reestablish my power over those in my company.

I was not foolish enough to believe the Phantom would not hold it against me. After all, I had sent them for his hometown this time; a direct threat to what he held most dear. When Kilo returned, his judgement would pass and our uncertain friendship would come to an end.

part nine
KILO &
SHENRAE

chapter sixty-one
To Vaiyene

Shenrae

The smoke was so thick, it made it hard to breathe. The red sun, blurred on the horizon, shone down through the haze, darkening the area in an eerie aura.

I sat with my legs curled up to my chest, leaning against a tree near Konro's border. Akio sat next to me, his head resting against my left shoulder. Judging from his deep breathing, he had fallen asleep.

After failing to contact the spy network, Rin had gone to the trading post in search of information from General Mirai, Kilo, and Phantom Asdar. She had not yet returned.

Using my right hand, I brushed my fingers against the cool grass, finding the earth between the blades. Closing my eyes, I allowed my mind to connect with the Skills.

I held the meditative state, training my mind to be calm and still.

Searching.

In the distance, I felt a presence approaching.

Opening my eyes, I gently moved the shoulder Akio leaned against.

"Akio," I said softly, "wake up. Rin has returned."

He stirred, raising himself, then yawned and rubbed his eyes with the back of his hand. Grabbing his stave that was leaning against the tree, he used it to stand up. When he peered into the mist, he raised his eyebrows.

"She's not too much farther away," I said, standing.

"You're incredible," Akio said, grinning at me.

I returned his smile. There was still a lot for me to learn about the Skills, but I was happy Finae and Emiko had been able to teach me more. All it had taken were the right teachers and the proper technique to learn how to connect with the Skills.

Rin came from the east, sitting astride a bay horse. She dismounted and let out a long breath. Her hair was disheveled, and there were dark circles under her eyes.

"Sorry it took longer than I said it would," she said, rolling her shoulders back and stretching. "I ran into one of the spies from General Mirai's network, and it delayed me."

"How are things?" Akio asked.

Rin closed her eyes momentarily, inhaling deeply. She looked exhausted. As the Shadows often did, she pushed herself to the limit in times of crisis.

"It's as we expected," she said after a short time. "Multiple towns and villages are fighting over resources in the north and the southern regions of Kiriku. General Mirai's forces are spread thin in an attempt to stop the fighting, and he's not alone." Rin's eyes fell on me. "Phantom Asdar left with a group of Shadows. He's planning on mediating on behalf of the towns. A few of the older Shadows are with him in case things don't go as planned."

Judging by her tone of voice, she seemed to know how significant this was.

The tension had risen so much that even Asdar had been forced to act.

"And Kilo?" I asked.

Rin withdrew some letters from one of the saddle packs, handing them to Akio and me to read. "Kilo sent an urgent message via the spy network. Hitori has sent all of her forces to stir up unrest across the lands. They've been given orders to 'burn everything in their path.' Which is likely the cause of all the fires in the north."

Akio looked up from the letters. "What's their destination?"

"Vaiyene," I said, not needing to read the letter to know.

Rin nodded to confirm.

It was what Phantom Lunia had feared would happen if Kilo's plan didn't work. Hitori had lashed out at Vaiyene to eliminate the cause of the threat.

"I hesitate to leave Konro without any means of protection," Rin said, patting the muzzle of her horse, "but there are others who need us."

"I agree," Akio said, crossing his arms over his chest. "I find it hard to believe the False Shadows and the mercenaries would travel down the cliffs to Konro to attack it again. It would be inefficient for their mission to directly attack Vaiyene."

Something pulled at my mind, and I left Rin and Akio to continue discussing plans, walking to the edge of the lake. After undoing the knot in the decorative string around my waist, I tied up my pants above the knees and waded into the water. Light glowed beneath the water's surface, and I tracked it to one of the massive rock pillars at Konro's border.

Resting my palm and fingertips against the stone surface, I allowed my vision to darken. Awareness, like a gentle *knowing*, came to my mind. The pulse of the Skills filled my mind. When I was quiet enough, I felt the gentle ripple of the barrier we had erected to protect Konro.

Even though she remained deep in sleep, Finae still held the line.

I smiled.

If anything happened in Konro, the Skills would rally to protect the village. Somehow I knew Finae and the Skills wanted us to leave. I withdrew my hand and returned to the shore, untying the length of cloth at my knees.

"We need to leave," I said, drawing Akio's and Rin's attention.

Rin's eyebrows raised.

Akio tilted his head, his lips poised for a question.

"Finae continues to sustain the barrier," I said, waving my hand out toward the lake. "She might not be responsive to us here, but she's ensuring Konro is safe. We'd be of more help if we joined General Mirai and Phantom Asdar."

Akio glanced over at Rin. "To Vaiyene then?"

"To Vaiyene."

————

By midday, we encountered a tragedy caused by the False Shadows.

Rin dismounted from her horse and, eyeing the smoldering piles, walked the perimeter of what used to be a village.

I slid from my horse, waiting as Akio came over.

There was a pained expression on his face. "I've seen many of these villages before. It's…" His voice trailed off, and he shook his head. "The moment you start thinking things are not as bad as they are, it becomes too much to bear. Be careful how much you allow yourself to hope in these situations."

Considering the small number of houses and the rows of plants in the garden, it looked to have been the home of maybe fifty people, if that.

Rin came over and shook her head. "We were too late for this village, but if we hurry, maybe we can save others."

I walked through the ruins, turning away from the promise of the fields, and glanced down at the wreckage of the houses.

"Maybe they got away?" I asked, hopeful.

Rin came to my side and pointed at one of the piles of smoldering wood. The blackened remains of a hand poked up through the rubble.

I shuddered.

"There is nothing we can do for the people here," Rin said, "but we can ensure others do not have to go through the same."

She was quiet for some time before she moved on, heading back to where our horses were. "Kilo struggles with the same reconciliation. He berates himself for not coming sooner—for not anticipating Hitori's moves. My brother and I used to say to one another, 'We do what we must for the good of others.' I believe your Shadows have some similar saying Kilo is fond of."

"'A Shadow does what he can. No more can be asked of him,'" I recited.

"Hopefully, it will alleviate some of your pain. I wish I could say it wasn't this way, but for now, this is what we are fighting against. Ikaru and I went through this more times than I care to admit. It takes its toll on all of us." She looked off into the distance. "I am more than ready for this to be over."

I drew in a deep breath and let it out.

How long would it take for peace to return?

Silently, Akio came toward us, leading the horses. He handed each of us the reins to our horse.

"If we keep riding," he said, mounting, "we should catch up to them by the end of the day."

Rin and I mounted, and together we set off at a steady pace. Smoke in the distance became our guide, and we encountered two more villages, both in the same condition as the first. When we arrived at the third village, we heard shouting in the distance.

Flames raged against a heavy wind.

My hands became clammy, and my throat dry. The heat of the flames blew over us as we approached, and I struggled to keep my breathing normal, remembering the fires of Vaiyene.

"Shenrae, what's wrong?" Akio asked, reaching out a hesitant hand toward me.

I kept my eyes ahead on the fire.

"It hasn't even been a year since the fire in Vaiyene," Rin said, her eyes narrowed.

She kept a tight hold on the reins of her horse. I'd forgotten. She also had been there in Vaiyene.

I tried to swallow against the lump in my throat.

"I'm fine. Just memories," I said, spurring my horse into the town.

A large wooden gate surrounded the castle of the town where residents gathered frantically outside of it. Smoke rose from inside the castle and the inner courtyard. It seemed the False Shadows had thrown their torches over the gate, and for some reason, it was unable to be opened.

"The fire doesn't seem like it's been burning very long," Rin said, turning her horse away from the town. "They can't be much farther away."

Near the gate, a few people lined up on either side of a stone statue, attempting to lift it. It seemed they were trying to gather enough people to break into the castle, but they were too disorganized.

"I'm staying here," I said, knowing Akio and Rin would not approve.

Rin exhaled heavily. "It would be better to leave this town. If we continue to move, we can stop the False Shadows from causing more tragedies."

Akio stared at me, a note of sympathy in his eyes. "I know it's hard to look past these people, but—"

"I'm staying," I repeated.

I understood the logic behind tracking down the leading group and preventing more deaths, but I could help these people now.

Right here. Right now.

Akio and Rin didn't need me as much as these people did.

Akio's brown creased, and Rin's face had become stoic. They were worried about leaving me, but I wouldn't be persuaded.

"I'll catch up with you after I help these people," I said, trying to sound persuasive.

Reluctantly, Akio nodded. "Be careful." He turned his horse and clicked his heels into the mare's side, spurring away at a gallop.

Rin moved her horse close to mine. Reaching out, she placed her hand on my arm, a hardened expression still on her face. "You can't save everyone. Do what you can and catch up to us. We'll keep our direction wherever the trail of smoke is."

I nodded, feeling a bit sad when they both left. Redirecting my own horse, I stopped at the castle gates.

The people scattered at my approach.

"It's a Shadow!" one of them shouted. "Run!"

Leaning closer to my stallion's neck, I ignored the villagers.

They must have encountered the False Shadows at some point.

Surveying the gate, I formulated a plan, chewing on my bottom lip as I narrowed my eyes. Near the entrance, a ledge stuck out from the gate. If I could reach it, I would be able to climb over and help the people inside.

A billow of flames burst into the sky as something inside the castle exploded.

Smoke burned my eyes and lungs as I got closer. Placing my hands on the horse's shoulders, I dropped the reins and crouched in the saddle, holding on to either side of the stallion's neck as I shifted my feet. As I pushed the horse gently with my left hand, he moved parallel to the building. I eyed the metal hook meant for hanging lanterns and jumped at it. My fingers grasped the ledge. Using my momentum, I swung my feet up, finding the edge of the gate with my toes. I heaved myself up, scrambling across the stone tiles and lying flat on my stomach. Down in the courtyard, an older man stood with two young children clinging to his legs. A woman with long hair tied back with a ribbon flung water onto the flames. She moved to a small pond to refill her bucket. I gave a passing glance to the stallion, regretting that he was not Greymoon. Being a horse from Tarahn, there was a chance he would wait around for me, but if he fled I would need to find another means of travel.

Sighing, I jumped into a nearby tree and dropped.

The woman straightened, drawing a dagger from the inside of her robes and holding it across her chest. She eyed the bond on my arm before she moved between me and the others.

I ignored her, focusing my attention on the gate.

A tree had fallen across the gate, preventing it from being opened. Between the tree and the entrance, there seemed to be enough space to stand. I drew the hood of my cloak over my head, keeping my face down as I burst through the flames. Heat wrapped around me, and I coughed against the thin air.

Memories of Vaiyene flashed in my mind, but I pushed them away.

Crouching low, I slipped under the fallen tree and wedged myself against the gate. I put my hands on the slats spanning the entrance and pushed, but it was so heavy it didn't move. With a grunt, I wedged my shoulder against the edge of the beam and heaved.

It moved.

Slightly.

Readjusting myself, I slid the beam across the two supports. Sweat dripped from my brow, and I wiped it away, trying to keep my breathing to a minimum to avoid too much smoke inhalation. Someone shouted from the other side of the tree. The flames and smoke blurred their outline as they approached, a horse blanket wrapped over their body.

When the fabric was dropped, the woman's long black hair cascaded out.

She put her hands on the beam next to me, and I wedged my shoulders under it, sinking my feet into the ground and pushing. The shaft slid the final distance across the posts and dropped from the wooden supports. I pushed open the gate, gasping for air as the woman and I stumbled through.

"Three...inside," I said in between breaths, motioning back inside.

They would have to brave the flames, but I had done what I needed to.

One of the villagers came forward with my horse. After thanking him, I took the reins and led the horse away from the castle.

"Wait!" a woman said from behind me.

I paused to see the woman with black hair emerge from the flames. She bowed to me as the others escorted the old man and two children safely out of the castle grounds.

"Thank you for your help, Shadow. We are in your debt."

I returned the bow, keeping it short. "You should tear down the gate before the fire reaches the other buildings in the area. Isolate the flames and smother them with dirt instead of using water from the ponds. You'll be more successful that way."

It was how we had contained the fires in Vaiyene.

"Sano!" the woman called. A man in red leather armor came over. "Tear down the sections closest to the town. We must prevent the fire from spreading."

"Yes, Lady Igai!" the man said.

I mounted my stallion and spurred him into a gallop. Feeling confident the townspeople would be able to put out the flames without me, I raced to catch up to Akio and Rin.

chapter sixty-two
Lost

Shenrae

Rays of sunlight reflected off the moisture in the air, creating a dense haze in the forest. The area was damp, and a putrid smell hung in the air. Pulling my scarf over my face, I tried without much success to keep the odor at bay. I felt sick as my horse and I continued into the forest. We had gone the same direction as the others, but we had not yet caught up to them.

Or perhaps they had shifted their direction.

The trail we walked led into the forests just outside of the Miyota Mountains—about a day's ride from Vaiyene.

Something about it made me uneasy.

Like something was off.

I dismounted from my horse, placing my hand on his muzzle to stroke his fur. We had traveled a reasonable distance for the day, and he had done well confronting the fires earlier. His ears swiveled, and his tail swished in agitation.

He, too, knew something was wrong here.

As we continued, a sense of dread came over me. The brush and the thick undergrowth became unruly, and I changed our path, finding an area less wild to continue through.

After adjusting our course, I slowed, my throat going dry.

The source of the smell became apparent.

At least half a dozen bodies lay on the ground in a rough semi-circle. My heart quickened. I did my best to maintain my calm, stepping with light feet past the dead. I knew the False Shadows had no reservations when it came to killing.

Were they close?

All at once, I became aware of the absence of noise. The buzzing of insects and the flight of birds couldn't be heard. It was too quiet here, as if the forest itself reeled from what had taken place. Nausea slowed my progression, and I returned my gaze to the dead, trying to be critical so as to gain any information I could. Most seemed to have died from sword wounds, well-placed cuts, though there were a few less skillfully made wounds that would not have been life-threatening.

Nearby, someone moaned.

A chill went up my spine, and I spotted a man leaning against a rock. His torso was bandaged with the same fabric of the fallen men I had seen earlier. Silver threads were wound around his right arm.

One of the False Shadows!

My heart beat faster, but I forced myself to relax. He was too injured to be a threat. In fact, he looked as white and ashen-faced as the dead in the area. Dirt smudged his cheeks, and his clothing was torn and ragged. It looked as if he had sustained an injury to his arm as well. He glanced over to his side, and I followed his line of sight. Another man, with a similar face, slept soundly. Unlike the first man, he didn't seem to have sustained any serious injuries, only a minor wound to his shoulder. They looked young, maybe sixteen or seventeen. Only a few years younger than I was.

I approached slowly, noticing the first man's hand inching toward a sword at his waist. Dropping the horses' reins, I raised my hands to show I meant no harm. His eyes widened at my approach, a note of fear within them.

Even my display of peace made him nervous.

Stopping out of range of his sword, I knelt to the ground. His eyes flickered from me to the horse. I tensed. Was he going to try and steal the stallion? It seemed a rash decision in his condition.

Desperate.

But something I needed to watch out for.

"What's your name?" I asked, keeping my voice quiet.

He held tighter onto his sword. "Daichi."

"I'm not going to hurt you, Daichi," I said, nodding toward the other man. "Is that your brother?"

He hesitated, then nodded. "You're not one of the False Shadows," he said, licking his cracked lips as he eyed the bond on my arm.

"No, I'm not," I said, noticing he grew tenser. "I'm one of the Shadows."

"Are you going to kill me?"

I shook my head. His fear made my heart heavy. "The Shadows don't kill, and besides, I don't think we're enemies. One of our Phantoms has been working to bring peace between the towns and the False Shadows."

"Phantom Kilo."

Trying not to let my excitement show, I nodded. If these False Shadows had been in some sort of a fight and had their wounds tended to, it could only mean someone who cared about the False Shadows had passed by.

"Have you seen him?"

"We fought alongside the Phantom to stop the mercenaries. Hitori sent them here to destroy Vaiyene. They are"—he clutched his torso and grimaced—"the ones who are killing people. We've only been trying to protect ourselves from Hitori by obeying her orders. We never wanted to—"

Someone screamed nearby.

Startled, I jumped, and Daichi tried awkwardly got to his feet.

"You should try and stay still," I said.

"I have to help," he said, taking a step with one foot. "I want to help Phantom Kilo stop the mercenaries. He has been kind to us, helping us train and making sure Hitori doesn't harm us. He's been—" He gasped as he placed his full weight on his leg. His hand flew to his side. The bandages around his torso became red.

"Stop," I said, rushing forward to support him. "Those bandages need to be tighter if you're going to move."

"There's no time."

"Please," I said, keeping my hands on his shoulders as he struggled to get up again. Finally, he sat back against the tree. I backed away, digging out a roll of cloth from inside one of horse's saddle packs.

"Sit up," I said, slipping the cloth behind him and wrapping it tighter around his torso. "There should be a group of Shadows to the east, near the base of the Miyota Mountains. Another one of the Phantoms is there." I finished, tying off the cloth and clicked my tongue for the horse to come. The stallion came over to me, and I pushed my hand on his neck to turn him to the side.

Offering my hand to Daichi, I pulled him up.

"Tell Phantom Asdar you're one of the False Shadows and that Shenrae has sent you. He will give you his protection." I handed him the horse's reins, taking the staff secured to the stallion's side. I wasn't sure why I was so sure of it, but after talking with Asdar and knowing his deep respect of Kilo, I knew it would not be a problem. "He has a group of Shadows with him as well. They'll offer the same protection."

Daichi stared at me a moment before he went to his brother's side. He placed both hands on his brother's shoulders and shook him gently. "Riku! Wake up."

His brother groaned, opening his eyes.

He froze when he saw me.

"She's a friend of Phantom Kilo's," Daichi said, standing next to the horse. "Hurry. We need to leave. You can ride up front so I can hold onto you for support."

Another scream came from nearby.

While Riku situated himself in the saddle, Daichi paused.

"What are you going to do?" he asked.

"I'm going to find Kilo."

Daichi hesitated again, looking at his brother. "I should come with you."

"I'll be fine," I said with a smile. "It's more important you take care of your brother. Besides, you're not in any condition to continue fighting."

Sighing, he nodded grudgingly, then faced the horse, one hand pressed against his torso. I held onto the stallion while he mounted. Daichi sucked in a sharp breath, his hand still covering the wound. I hoped it hadn't begun bleeding again.

"Thank you," he said, looking down at me from on top of the horse.

"Be careful," I said, tightening my grip on my staff.

When Daichi and Riku were out of sight, I drew in a deep breath. I needed to refocus. Whoever was up ahead was a threat, but at least Daichi and Riku were out of harm's way, and once they found Phantom Asdar, they would be safe. I had done what I could for them.

Cautiously, I continued through the forest.

Something clanged ahead, making my breath catch.

It almost sounded like the scrape of metal—of a sword being drawn. A battle? I crept forward, staying hidden behind a large tree as I peered around the trunk. Three people circled a single man. They wore black tunics over fitted pants, and each had a sword in hand. The man in the center kept his sword pointed at the ground. His long black and brown hair was tied up in a ponytail. A single ray of light shone down on him, illuminating the bond on his arm.

The man in the center slid his right leg back, releasing a puff of dirt into the air.

His back was turned to me, and I held my breath.

His presence seemed to command the area.

The circle around the man broke as one of the mercenaries attacked. The man crossed his blade to defend, sliding his back foot across the dirt to brace himself. When his weight had shifted, he kicked out with his front foot, driving the mercenary to his knees and turning as another mercenary raised his sword. Before the sword connected, the man drew a second sword, catching the tip of his opponent's hilt as he slashed the long sword into his side. Swiftly, he sheathed his short sword and ran into the trees. Before he disappeared, I caught sight of his face.

Kilo?

The mercenaries pursued, and Kilo stopped to engage with one of them, sliding his sword back and around the man's blade, slashing into the mercenary's side. The mercenary fell to his knees, pressing his hand to his torso as the wound started to bleed profusely. The other two mercenaries rushed past their companion as Kilo took off into the forest again. Likely assuming Kilo's strategy was to fight them one on one, the men stayed close together. I trailed after them, trying to stay quiet, but they moved with such speed I soon lost sight of them.

Flustered, I disregarded my earlier caution, running faster to catch up to them. I breathed deeply, pushing harder until finally figures came into focus ahead. A branch snagged my foot, and I tripped, landing hard on my hands.

The ground began to shake, and I scrambled back, pressing my back against a tree.

Horse hooves trampled the grass where I'd been, and I looked up as the rider released an arrow at one of the distant figures.

Kilo seemed to have stopped running.

Moving forward, I settled against a large tree, watching as Kilo stood across from a mercenary with a strange weapon. The man held a short metal stick with a scythe in one hand, and in the other hand, he held a weight. Both items were attached together with a silver chain. The mercenary threw the weighted end at Kilo. He dodged, raising his sword as the mercenary lunged at him with the scythe. The chain snaked across the ground, trying to ensnare Kilo's leg, but Kilo stepped over it, sidestepping the chain.

Behind me, someone cried out in pain.

The woman rider had been unseated from her horse. She pulled back a sword from another mercenary's chest, turning her head in Kilo's direction.

A blur whipped past me, and the scythe cut into the woman's neck.

I covered my mouth with my hands, stifling my breath.

Kilo rushed to her side, holding onto her hand briefly before he dodged the weighted end of the mercenary's weapon. Kilo slammed his short sword into one of the chain links and lifted his long sword to attack, but the other end of the chain swept him from his feet. The mercenary slashed the scythe at Kilo, the blade skimming off something I couldn't see. Not wasting any time, Kilo slashed down, cutting into the man's shoulder.

The mercenary fell against a tree, and Kilo's sword slid between the man's ribs.

I looked on in horror.

Silently, Kilo looked up, his eyes locking onto my own.

I froze.

There was something not quite right in his eyes.

He didn't seem to recognize me.

I hesitated to go move, my stomach twisting in knots at the scene before me. Another mercenary moved in the area and drew Kilo's attention from me. He turned on the remaining adversary.

Kilo moved with precision and purpose, his intentions deadly.

Frightening.

Was it really Kilo?

The remaining mercenary stumbled back from him. Something inside me stirred, and my hesitation disappeared as Kilo's sword came up. I ran and threw my staff out to intercept Kilo's swing, spreading my hands across the length of the staff to hold my defense.

"What are you doing!" I yelled, disbelief slowing my movements as I examined his face. It *was* Kilo, but he didn't seem like himself.

Kilo disengaged from me, his feet shuffling back. He seemed not to have heard my words—or he was choosing to ignore them. Unexpectedly, he moved his sword parallel to the ground and lashed out at me. Instincts took over, and I held the staff vertically to block him.

Another mercenary rushed us from the forest, his sword raised. Kilo shifted into a defensive stance, catching the man's attack with his sword.

The attacker hesitated.

And Kilo didn't miss the opportunity.

The sword slashed across the man's chest, and he dropped to the ground. I lowered my staff, trying to process what had happened. Did Kilo just kill a man?

No, he couldn't have, and yet…

I had seen it with my own eyes.

I clutched at my chest as Kilo and another mercenary exchanged blows.

This couldn't be happening.

Something was wrong.

The men earlier in the forest, the ones I had come across before Riku and Daichi, was Kilo also responsible for taking their lives?

Kilo disengaged from his opponent, raising his sword above his head before the man could lift his blade.

"Stop!" I yelled, putting myself between the man and Kilo's sword.

His sword struck my staff, and Kilo shifted back, slicing up. Blocking his sword with one end of my staff, I swung the other end toward Kilo's head. He ducked and pressed forward, drawing the second sword from his side. With speed and accuracy, he slashed at me, and I barely managed to block his attack, the edge of the blade cutting into the staff's exterior.

He seemed dazed somehow.

Unaware of what he was doing.

As if his body moved without awareness and compassion.

"Phantom Kilo!" I shouted again, panic beginning to make my defense slip. His quick moves exposed me for what I was—a novice attempting to defeat a master. I took a step back, and Kilo's eyes narrowed.

He saw my hesitation.

His opportunity to strike.

Rushing toward me, he raised his weapon, angling the curve of his sword at my chest. Forcing my arms to my sides, I squeezed my eyes shut.

Every instinct in me screamed to raise my staff up—to defend—but I remained still, placing my trust in the man I had always admired...

chapter sixty-three
An Act of Love

Kilo

"Turn back!" I called over my shoulder, watching the two brown horses and their riders continue their pursuit. The False Shadow twins had caught up to me.

"We're coming with you!" Daichi shouted. He urged his horse faster, directing him to the other side of my horse. "We want to help stop Gaiden's men."

They were not ready for combat.

Gaiden's men were swords for hire, and unlike General Mirai's mercenaries, they cared nothing for anyone.

"I would prefer you stay where it is safer," I said, trying to keep the extent of my concern masked. I did not doubt their conviction to go into battle, but I did not want to put them in such danger. It would likely take extreme measures to force Gaiden's men to stop their rampage.

Both twins were quiet.

Suspiciously so.

Narrowing my eyes, I looked over at Daichi, who was always the more outspoken one. His eyes were set ahead——on the smoke in the distance. Kameiten, a town that produced and exported much of the rice in the region, was not far from us. Many years ago, I had passed through it on a Shadow mission.

They had the most beautiful Spider Lilies at the edge of town.

"We are grateful you taught us how to use the sword," Daichi said, finally turning his head to acknowledge me. "It was the first time we felt our lives had any meaning. We would be honored to go into battle with you to defend the people of Kiriku."

Sighing, I shook my head.

Once again, I had found companions pure of spirit on my journey. Despite everything that was happening, there were still kind and good people across these lands. It renewed my conviction to do what I needed to ensure our path led to peace.

"Stay close to me," I said, keeping my voice even as I stared pointedly. "If your life is in danger, seek safety. We cannot protect those who depend on us if we lose our own lives. It is always better to live than to give in to fleeting thoughts of glory and self-sacrifice."

"Thank you, Phantom," Daichi said. He bowed his head slightly.

I smiled to myself.

Phantom.

I had stopped correcting them. Occasionally, Hitori mockingly used the title, but most of the False Shadows had started picking it up after Saitou used it. Their use was one of respect and endearment, and it reminded me of what I had left behind.

And the bitterness that lived in my heart because of it.

Would I ever be able to return?

"Are we near Vaiyene?" Riku asked, drawing my thoughts to the present.

Scanning the horizon, I found the distant peaks of the Miyota Mountains. With my forefinger, I pointed northwest. "If you were to ride for another day, you would find Vaiyene."

I had told Daichi, Riku, and the False Shadows about my homeland while we had trained. The stories had captivated them, rekindling their desire to find a place in which they could be at peace. One day, I hoped to unite the Shadows and the False Shadows as one people and provide a place of shelter for all those who had need of it.

"I'll take you there after this is over," I said, watching as Riku's smile widened. Daichi smiled too, though he tried to remain stoic and hide how much it meant to him. Like many of the False Shadows, they had nowhere to go. They'd been drawn to Hitori's group because it was the only option available to them. Training with Riku and Daichi had shown me how lucky I had been to grow up in Vaiyene and how difficult it was for others to have grown up in much harsher circumstances.

If they held onto hope, there was nothing they could not do.

A scream drew my attention.

We were close enough to the town and flames to be able to distinguish individual buildings that had been set on fire. The architecture of the town was quite old, with a gate surrounding a small castle that separated it from the fields and other residents. The lord lived there with his family and a small number of retainers and servants. Outside the gates were areas terraced rice fields flooded with water, which were maintained by lesser families in the area.

It was early summer, but given the weather and the long growing season here, the rice seemed almost ready to harvest. Which meant the stalks could be set on fire despite the water flooding them.

"We'll try and lead Gaiden's men away from town," I said. "If we can stop them from ruining the rice fields and food supplies, we'll be able to save more lives in the coming months."

I had not expected the mercenary leader to be telling the truth when he confronted Hitori, but it seemed he had been. There were at least half a dozen groups mobilizing across Kiriku. The others had made their presence known by the destruction they had left behind, too great for just the group Hitori had sent in her rage. After leaving Leiko, I had sent messages to both General Mirai and Asdar warning them what had happened.

But only time would tell if we were prepared to stop the coming war.

As we drew closer to the main gate, villagers threw water on the thatched roofs of the surrounding houses, making little progress.

"Dirt will help smother the flames quicker," I said, riding past a group of them as I searched for the source of the fire from my mounted position.

The flames had burned through the building in front of me, and it was now smoldering. Judging by the damage, it was one of the first to have been on fire. It seemed to have then spread to the nearby field, where, as I had feared, the rice stalks had lit up like torches.

Spurring Blackstorm forward, I pushed him hard to the other side of the fields. The people on the roads carrying buckets cleared the way as we rode. On the other side of town, the houses and the fields appeared undamaged, which meant our enemies had not come this way.

"Kilo," Daichi said, pointing to the east.

A pillar of fire erupted into the sky, releasing a plume of smoke.

"Good eye," I said, pulling back on Blackstorm's reins and changing our course. A gathering of almost a dozen armed men circled the building, all on horseback. One of them I recognized, Ouiji. He was one of Gaiden's more important subordinates. He had come to Hitori's camp once, and like his commander, he desired power and the Skills. He held a torch; others rallied to him, lighting torches of their own. They surrounded another small building, tossing the torches onto the thatched roof as they whooped and hollered.

Two of their riders spurred their horses toward the rice fields.

I cursed under my breath, reaching for the bow and quiver tied to the withers of my horse. Shifting my weight, I steadied myself, nocking an arrow before taking aim. When I released my hold, the arrow struck one of the horses in the hind end. The horse reared, and the rider fell to the ground.

Readying another arrow, I paused as two arrows connected with the other mercenary heading to the fields. Tracking the direction the arrows had come from, I spotted two riders on a nearby hill. Silver glinted on their arms.

It seemed Daichi and Riku were not the only False Shadows to have followed me. Based on their aim and precision with the bow, it was likely Kaiba and Aida.

"Keep an eye out for them," I said, to the twins.

Clicking my heels into the horse's side, I headed toward the leading group of mercenaries, trusting Kaiba and Aida would cover our approach. I secured the bow and arrow to the horse's saddle.

Noticing us, Ouiji and his men left the house, spurring their horses to meet me.

They had a group of seven, against our five.

"Keep the riders occupied," I called back to the twins. We had not done any drills on horseback for them to engage by attacking. "Distract them and stay out of the reach of their swords. We only need to discourage them enough to move on."

Clicking my tongue to Blackstorm to alert him, I nudged my heels into his sides, and he broke into a full gallop. With a rush of wind, we passed Ouiji and his group. I kept my horse reined in, keeping my focus on driving him toward the house on fire. A loose beam hung from the roof, and I leaned over to grab it, speaking gently to the horse to keep him from spooking.

He shied away from it.

Ouiji's men kept their course, heading toward Riku and Daichi. Kaiba and Aida had left the hill to engage in close combat along with their friends.

"Whoa, easy, trust me," I murmured to the horse, laying my hand against his neck.

The stallion shied, though we were close enough for me to grab the beam. Letting go of the reins, the animal took flight. We barreled back toward the others, the burning beam blazing in my hand. When I was close enough, I swiped the flames close to Ouiji's horse—near his eye.

The horse reared, and Ouiji fell from the saddle.

Handing the torch to Riku, I drew my sword from its sheath. With one hand, I held the sword steady, using the other to guide my horse toward the woman circling Daichi. She was toying with him, darting close with her horse and blade, but not touching him. A spark of anger rose inside me, and I clicked my heels against the stallion's side. The woman tried to reposition herself to defend against my attack, but before she could, I slashed the blade into her shoulder, severing the muscle.

Her sword dropped from her hand.

"Kaiba!" Daichi shouted, his voice pitched higher than usual.

Circling my horse around, I saw Kaiba lying on the ground. Ouiji approached him, sword in hand. I clicked my heels into my horse's sides, and Blackstorm charged while I slashed down at Ouiji from the horse. The mercenary defended against my attack, placing a hand against the dull side of his sword to brace himself. My blade scraped against his, and I dismounted, whistling to Blackstorm to stay close as I ran toward Kaiba.

He seemed unconscious but alive.

Without hesitation, Ouiji rushed me. A gash on his head indicated Kaiba had stood his ground, but other than that wound, Ouiji seemed unharmed, showing no signs of fatigue. When I was within striking distance, he swiped his sword at my neck. Shifting my sword vertically, I bypassed the tip of my attacker's sword, moving with a subtle grace as I slid my sword along his. We struggled against one another, blades screeching, our strength equal.

Ouiji sneered as I feigned weakness, pushing against my blade with renewed strength. Swiftly, I removed one hand from my sword and grabbed his forearm, pulling him forward and using his momentum to pull him close. He stumbled, his sword dipping close to the ground. Crushing the blade with my foot, I pinned the weapon to the dirt.

He tried to reposition himself, but before he could ram into me with his shoulder, I slashed my blade across his arm.

Blood dripped from his forearm.

Abandoning his sword, he threw a punch at my face with his uninjured arm. I dodged, stepping back before swinging the dull side of my sword against the side of his head. He stumbled back, dazed, the wound on his head reopening and covering his face in a streak of red.

After a moment, the sneer on his face returned, and his bloodlust rolled over me.

He was enjoying the fight.

Ouiji threw a sloppy jab at me, and I shifted the sword in my hand, bringing the dull side of my sword into his jaw. Bone cracked as my sword connected. To my irritation, Ouiji remained conscious. He wobbled as he took his next step, and I sheathed the blade, ramming the hilt into his stomach. Doubling over, he spat out blood, his breathing coming in gasps.

The fight was over, yet he refused to yield.

As Ouiji struggled to breathe, I glanced over at the twins, finding them standing around a body.

Ouiji had managed to steady himself on his feet. Warily, I circled him. His bloodied eye tracked my movement. After picking up his sword, I stood opposite him, extending the hilt to him with a calculated look.

"I acknowledge your strength and desire to continue this fight," I said, feeling his resolve harden as he took his sword. "However, the Skills will destroy anyone who uses them out of hatred. You would not be able to withstand them as you are now."

His fingers curled around his sword. "Do you think you're better than me?" he said, his teeth gritted as he adjusted the sword. "That you can deny those you find unworthy of this power?"

His breathing had finally stabilized.

His anger became a foundation he could stand upon.

Even if I spared his life this time, he would find some other time to come after me. In the pit of my stomach and the back of my heart, the Skills stirred—their own will and desire mirroring my own thoughts.

"Why do you want to learn about the Skills?" I asked.

He leaned over, spitting out blood before he sneered. "To become the strongest."

While a person could aim to be the strongest, if they achieved greatness without regard to how they had gotten that strength, they lacked character. Strength was more than being able to best a foe in battle.

His reason was a flimsy one.

One that would be corrupted with the Skills.

"Stand down, Ouiji. If you desire the Skills so much, call off your men from destroying Kiriku. We will talk about what it will take for you to learn them."

He considered for a moment before he lowered the sword.

Exhaling, my attention shifted back to the False Shadows. Riku had begun to wail as he leaned over one of the bodies. I slipped my sword into the sash at my side, dreading what had happened.

"Kilo!" Daichi shouted, gesturing behind me.

I closed my eyes against the impact.

A thin layer of the Skills had woven together in a barrier, keeping the blade from piercing my back. Unsheathing my sword, I thrust it into Ouiji's chest, then yanked the blade free.

A plume of dust wafted as the body hit the ground.

Turning my head slightly, I eyed Ouiji's body and the pool of blood seeping out from him. He would not be getting up again.

I tightened my grip and flicked my blade, ridding it of most of the blood.

I had done what needed to be done.

Ouiji's forces had scattered, abandoning the fight. The rice field on the far end of town had been set on fire, but it seemed to be the only one still burning.

Wiping the blade with a rag from the inside of my robe, I approached the twins with a heavy heart, seeing Kaiba on the ground. His eyes were closed, and his body was still. A sword slash to the stomach told the cause of his death.

I swallowed the lump in my throat.

The twins' eyes were red from crying.

Quickly putting my fingers to my lips, I whistled, and two of our horses returned. One was the black stallion, Blackstorm.

"We take our fallen with us," I said, surveying the area. "Where's Aida?"

"She went off scouting," Daichi said, his voice scratchy.

I nodded, wanting to move on. Untying one of the blankets from the brown mare, I rolled it out across the dirt. I bent down to cradle Kaiba's head, while Daichi and Riku held onto his feet. We moved Kaiba's body onto the blanket and wrapped it, hoisting him up and tying his body to the horse.

My hands fumbled with the last knot.

Grief constricted my heart for Kaiba, but a lingering sense of resignation darkened my mood further. Ouiji's body still lay face down in the dirt.

I let out a deep breath, resting my head on my hands holding onto the horse.

"Phantom?" Daichi asked,

"Head to the main gate," I said, reluctantly standing back. "I'll be along shortly."

Daichi nodded, ushering the others away as I headed in the opposite direction.

I stood for some time, looking down at Ouiji before I knelt and turned him over. His eyes were already closed, his sword still in his hand. After uncurling his fingers, I sheathed the blade, moving his body off to the side of the road against a tree. His sword I returned to him, folding his hands on top of it.

I bowed slightly.

May you find peace.

With a long breath, I left him on the roadside, heading toward the main house. I did not have to walk far to find the others waiting for me. It seemed they had stopped a few paces from where we had parted.

I looked from Daichi to Riku for explanation. Their eyes were still red, and I sensed their guilt at having not obeyed. Riku's hands were trembling as he held Blackstorm's reins.

"I am sorry I left you," I said gently. Riku sniffed loudly, and I buried my own pain, reaching out a hand to each of the twins' shoulders. "We will go together."

Solemnly, we walked through the town, the whispers of the villagers following us as they carried buckets of dirt and water to douse the remaining flames. I headed toward an older woman standing by the main gate. Deep creases were etched across her forehead and around her eyes.

"There were others who came before you," the woman said. She pointed to the forest to the north. "They headed in that direction."

"Thank you," I said, giving her a small bow. Taking the reins from Riku, I held them out to her. "Would you be able to watch over him for us?"

Her eyes widened slightly, but the hardness in her face seemed to ease. She paused for a moment. "I remember you from many years ago. You and another man were covered with blood on that day too. I see the kindness and guilt in your eyes have not changed."

I bowed low.

Vaguely, I remembered her too.

The memory of that night and what had transpired here had stayed with me.

It was the reason I feared the sword.

"Forgive me for not remembering your kindness, Lady Taizen."

She waved off my words. "If you ever get the chance, join me for tea sometime, and we can speak of your travels."

"I would like that," I said. "If it's not too much trouble, I have another request."

She looked kindly on me. "What is it?"

"There's a mercenary down the road whose life I have taken. He's lying against a tree by the road. Would you be able to ensure he is buried with his sword?"

Lady Taizen nodded. "I will make sure of it."

I bowed again. "Thank you."

We left the brown mare and Kaiba's body with her, heading in the direction of the forest. Uneasiness rested on the edge of my mind. I had repressed my memories of this place, desiring to forget the night Asdar and I had been forced to kill. It was one of our first Shadow missions.

One where things had gone terribly wrong.

"Phantom Kilo?" Riku asked beside me.

"Yes?"

When he did not say anything more, I blinked, shaking off the vision and the guilt of that night, my awareness of the present returning.

We were at the edge of the forest.

Grimly, I led us under the shadow of the trees, my hand resting on the hilt of my sword. The atmosphere was tense, the birds and the insects quiet.

An arrow flew past us, striking one of the trees.

Blackstorm reared and jerked free from Riku's grasp. I lunged after the horse's reins, keeping hold near his mouth to keep him under control. "Woo, easy," I said.

Another arrow sailed overhead. This time, Daichi was hit in the shoulder. The arrow grazed his skin, leaving behind a small cut.

"Split up!" I yelled.

Tracing the arrow's path back to what was most likely its origin, I threw my leg over Blackstorm and urged the stallion into a gallop.

Daichi and Riku headed in the opposite direction.

A bowstring creaked ahead.

Urgently, I spurred the horse forward, but even with the horse's speed, I was too far away to stop the arrow. Slashing out with my sword in the air, I recalled the barrier Finae had shown me how to erect back in Konro. As I drew a line in the air with the sword's top, a slight shimmer of the Skills appeared. The arrow shattered against it; pieces of wood splintered and flew off in all directions.

The forest floor became tangled with roots as I continued.

It would be difficult to proceed on horseback, so I slid off Blackstorm, continuing on foot as I listened for the mercenaries. The crunch of a leaf gave me a moment's warning before a group of mercenaries burst through the forest.

I sprinted forward to meet them, slashing at one person and cutting his knee to disable him before heading in the direction I had last seen the twins.

"Riku!" Daichi yelled ahead.

His twin was pinned by two opponents against a tree.

Riku held onto his side, blood oozing from the wound. I swung down at one of the mercenaries, making him retreat. Readjusting the sword in my hands, I lunged at other mercenary. He raised his sword to block me, sliding one of his hands onto the dull side of the blade to block my momentum. Withdrawing, I crouched down, pushing off my back foot to spring forward as I sliced through the man's arm. The first man returned, thrusting forward with his sword. Stepping to the side, I slid my blade along his sword, angling the tip toward his shoulder. He began to retreat, taking a step back. I shifted the line of my attack, and when he swung his sword high, I cut into his foot.

Steel hit bone.

And he screamed, falling to his knees.

I moved to Riku's side, pushing him behind me with my outstretched arm.

Blood still seeped from the wound at his torso.

Without binding it, he would bleed out.

From farther inside the forest, a horse brayed, then leaped over a bush, coming toward us. Aida hugged the horse's neck as she charged the mercenaries, driving them away. She had bought me a moment of time. Ripping the sleeve from one of the fallen men's clothing, I sliced it with my sword before winding the fabric around Riku's chest, pulling it tight.

Daichi dashed over, and I grabbed his hand, putting it to the wound on Riku's side. "Keep pressure on it, and stay with your brother," I said, picking up my sword from the ground and sheathing it before I raced after Aida. It had been a desperate move—a fool's attempt to scatter the enemy.

But it had worked.

I only hoped it would not come at too high a cost.

From somewhere in the forest came a *craaack*, the snap of a branch underfoot. I kept my thumb at the edge of the guard and stepped carefully, rocking my feet from the top of my foot to the bottom with quiet precision. A blur came from my right, and I flicked my thumb against the guard, drawing my blade and lashing out in an arc. The man before me jumped back, but a touch of blood stained his side. I repositioned the sword and lowered my elbow, bringing the blade parallel to the ground.

I waited.

Out of the corner of my eye, I spotted two more figures moving in the forest.

They were trying to surround me.

Behind me, more movement. I drew in a steady breath, visualizing the circle of attack I would execute. First, the man in front of me, then the two behind him, and finally the men on the other side of the forest. Though their positions would likely change, they would come at me from behind.

The mercenary in front moved toward me.

Keeping my sword level, I waited for him. I eyed the line of his sword, removing one of my hands from my sword to draw a second blade. The man rushed me, and I lashing out at his knee with my long sword. He cried out and dropped his guard, and I sank the smaller blade into his chest.

He fell to the ground, and I pinpointed the two other men in the forest.

They hesitated before they ran at me together.

Drawing in a breath, I slashed at the man on the right with my long sword, twisting my arm and stabbing with the shorter blade. I had revealed my second weapon, but it made the combination no less deadly. Slicing into one of my opponent's arms, the man did not drop his sword.

He had seen enough battle to endure the pain.

I would need to be careful of him.

The man on my left drew his sword up from the ground, but the line and position at which he held it was sloppy. Kicking out with my foot, I drove my heel against the man's kneecap. He crumpled to the ground, and I sheathed my second blade, using the less-trained man's hesitation to regain my two-handed grip on my long sword before cutting into his side.

I ran.

The crunch of leaves underfoot gave away my position, but I did not need to travel silently. I only needed to spread the opponents out, to make them easier to eliminate.

Swiftly, I circled around a large tree and ducked low. Hooves pounded through the forest, shaking the ground nearby. Keeping low, and using the horse as a distraction, I sprang from behind the tree, rushing one of the mercenaries.

Aida rode past at the same moment, firing an arrow at my opponent. The arrow hit the man in the chest, and he dropped. Another mercenary stepped from the forest, and I stepped back to analyze him.

In one hand, he held a curved blade attached to a thin chain. In his other hand, he held the weight at the end of the chain.

A sickle and chain.

I had seen it once, briefly, when I was younger and Asdar had brought out the weapon to spar with me. Neither of us had done more than tossing the chain at a fixed target. Its movements were unpredictable.

Deadly.

I ducked as the mercenary threw the chain at me, dodging as the weapon was drawn back. Hastily, I tried to pinpoint where the chain snaked, but the mercenary slashed at me, and the chain wrapped around my leg.

He yanked the chain, and I fell to the ground, rolling to the side as the curved sword dug into my shoulder. Kicking forward, my foot connected with the man's nose.

As he reeled back, I scrambled to my knees.

Aida screamed as the sickle cut into her. The wound was deep at the base of her neck, and I grimaced as blood pooled in her mouth. I dashed over to her, holding her hand as she drew her last breath, before reluctantly moving away from her.

Grief welled up in my heart, my senses becoming numb.

My vision darkened.

I needed to eliminate the threat.

Nothing else mattered.

Sliding my left foot back, I launched forward, stepping on the chain attached to the sickle and slashing down at the man's chest. The tip of my sword broke through the skin, but he let go of the chain and managed to dodge most of the attack. He drew a dagger from within the sleeve of his robe and threw it at me, and I moved my sword to deflect it, the edge of the dagger cutting across my cheek.

Both of us stepped back and began circling one another.

Waiting.

The mercenary leapt for the chain.

Unsurprised, I cut upward, catching the side of the man's leg. Removing my right hand from my long sword, I drew the short sword from my side, thrusting it into one of the loops in the chain to fix it to the ground. The mercenary's arm pulled back, and the chain from the other side caused me to trip and lose my balance.

My opponent slammed his blade into the barrier that had sprung up against my back.

The Skills stirred in the area, coming to my aid.

The fog on my mind grew as my eyes passed over Aida's dead body, and I elbowed the man behind me in the stomach, shifting my hands into their two-handed grip on my long sword before pivoting. The man stumbled back, hitting against a tree.

My sword slid cleanly between his ribs.

Another person moved into the forest. Briefly, my eyes locked with theirs, but I sensed another more pressing threat from behind. Swinging my sword around, I met the new attacker with renewed strength. The Skills invigorated me, warming my muscles and soothing the fatigue. My focus was so narrow, all I saw was the flash of metal and the line of attacks from my opponent, their footwork and the subtle shift of their arm.

Before me, a sword came down in a glinting arc.

I moved to stop it, the silver glow meeting my own curved blade.

"Kilo!" someone shouted.

It was nothing more than a name—one distant to me—but with it came emotions I did not wish to confront. I could not allow myself to think beyond the immediate threat, but something about the voice made me hesitate.

I lowered the sword.

It was not one emotion that dominated the other, but a tirade of emotions that threatened to overwhelm me. Overbearing anger at the death of those I'd thought of as students, followed by denial and a rush of shame for how it had happened.

Each choice, each decision had been mine.

No one had forced my hand.

It had been my decision to get involved with Hitori and her False Shadows, my plan to track down Gaiden's men, and my own hand that had—no! I stopped the thoughts, stopped the spiral that would shake my resolve. I could not afford to let these men go free. No matter the consequences. I pivoted and brought my sword back, swiping down low at the person before me.

She blocked my sword with her staff.

An unusual choice.

I pushed the thought away, not having the luxury of thinking. That led to slow responses, and right now, I had but one duty: kill those in front of me to save the innocents. If it would save those I had sworn to protect, I would give anything.

That desire took hold of me, reflecting in the ancient magic living deep within the land. At the forefront of my mind, an intense pressure weighed on me, pushing me to move on, to eliminate the threat.

It became harder to breathe, and all of my senses faded.

I raised my sword.

To save those I loved…

"Phantom Kilo!" the girl screamed.

This time the voice rattled me and penetrated the silence. I struggled to keep the momentary bliss and peace I had found earlier, the acceptance of knowing my actions would save the people I needed to protect, but the name—the title—dragged its way to the surface as if duty called me.

Kilo.

Phantom.

Once I had been a Phantom. Before that, a Shadow, and now…

My chest constricted, and I sprang forward, silencing the thoughts.

My opponent lowered her staff, her arms falling to her sides.

I blinked, and a moment of clarity came over me. Digging my front foot into the ground, I stopped my attack, my blade sliding against the side of her neck instead of cutting into it. I lowered my sword and backed away, my hands trembling as I maintained my grip on the blade.

The horror of what I had almost done nearly crippled me.

With the crook of my arm, I wiped away the blood from my eyes and let out a long breath. Only then did I lift my gaze to the person I wished had not come.

Shenrae.

I averted my eyes from hers, feeling ill. I had not seen her since I left Vaiyene. Her being here brought memories of friends gone, and with them another layer of shame smothered me.

Zavi and Mia.

What would they think if they could see me now?

"Kilo," Shenrae said as she stepped forward.

Panic gripped me.

A fear she would be harmed further by me. That my own bloodlust would be incited again and I would not be able to stop myself.

"Stay where you are," I said, my voice shaky. The fog, no, the daze on my mind still clouded my judgement. I recognized the Skills' presence in my mind.

Their influence.

Their rage.

In my previous state, I would have attacked friend or foe.

Swallowing, I continued to breathe, trying to regain myself—to separate myself from my resolve to stop those who had been sent to kill without remorse.

The smell of death permeated the air.

I flicked the sword in my hand to rid it of blood, withdrawing a stained rag to wipe the sword edge clean. The exhilaration of battle still pounded in my veins, but the practice of caring for the blade calmed me.

The edge would be dull after today; it would need to be sharpened.

After sheathing my sword, I scanned the forest floor, seeing Aida's body among the mercenaries I had killed. Another loss I had failed to prevent. Her life and Kaiba's life had ended far too soon, and with the end in sight.

Shenrae continued to watch me, but I found myself unwilling to speak.

As if I could deny what had happened.

I kept my eyes low, noticing Shenrae's legs were shaking.

I drew in a breath. There was no avoiding it.

"What are you doing here, Shenrae?"

She clenched her fists at her sides. "This isn't who you are."

His words bounced off the surface of who I had allowed myself to become. The flimsy construct I had created to eliminate the mercenaries and do what needed to be done was shattered.

I inhaled.

My breathing had returned to normal.

"It is who I am now."

I forced myself to meet her amber eyes, which were relentless in their blame. She bent down to pick up her staff, then circled around me.

"What about the Shadows who look up to you?" she said, anger rising with her voice. "We believed in you! Trusted you!"

She thrust her staff at me, and I sidestepped her, startled she would attack.

Building momentum as she brought her staff around again, she aimed a strike at my shoulder, which I blocked with the guard on my right forearm.

I grimaced at the strength behind her attack.

"I gave up the title of Phantom," I said, taking a step back as she continued to come at me. "I'm not bound by the Shadow's Creed any longer."

She thrust low, and I stepped back to dodge it.

I kept my sword sheathed.

I had no desire to raise it against her again.

Shenrae spun the staff, shifting it between both hands. I tracked the movement, watching the end of the pole and her feet to anticipate the attack.

Angrily, she swiped the staff down and to the side, the air rustling around her. "You were never banished!" she yelled. "You left before anything was made official; Phantom Asdar allowed you to leave so that you would be forced into action. Come back to Vaiyene!"

It took a moment before her words sank in.

Then my lips twitched into a smile.

That was just like Asdar. He had purposely said nothing as I was forced into exile for wanting to pursue the dangers of the Skills. I had given up my title, the role of being one of the three leaders of Vaiyene in order to find a way to protect them. Even if it were true, if the Phantoms would allow me to return, there was no going back from what I had done. I had made the decision to end Oujii's life and the lives of the other mercenaries in the forest. I had passed judgement on them, weighing the lives of all of Kiriku above their own and becoming their executioner.

My eyes narrowed at her.

"Do you really believe the Shadows will follow me as I am now?"

Tears brimmed in Shenrae's eyes. Her grip tightened around her staff, and she thrust it at me. I shifted to the side and grabbed her forearm. She pulled back, but I held onto her arm.

"Can you accept I have forsaken the Shadow's Creed and willingly killed others? Is that the kind of Phantom you would want to follow, Shenrae?"

She yanked free of my grasp.

"Can *you* even accept what you've done?" she asked, her voice choked with grief. "You can't even look me in the eye for more than a passing glance! You're too ashamed to admit it's tearing you apart."

She swung the staff at my chest, and I crossed my arms in front of me, her staff hitting the steel-plated bracers on my arms. She used her full strength, and reluctantly, I pushed back against her, shaking her off.

She sniffed loudly, backing away from me as tears fell from her eyes.

Only then did I realize the extent of the pain I had caused her.

The reason she was here.

And the meaning behind her words.

Turning my back on her, I fisted my hands at my side, squeezing my eyes shut as my resolve began to crumble.

"You used to be a man of ideals!" Shenrae cried. "A man people admired! And now, what have you become?"

Her words seemed far away, like I was hearing them through water or thick stone. The Skill poisoning stirred inside me, blurring my vision. The encounter had been too much, too drawn out. I coughed, wiping away the blood with my palm.

I needed to move on.

To stop the mercenaries and to protect the people, I had to continue forward.

Or all of this would have been for nothing.

On unsteady legs, I navigated over the bodies, making my way to the edge of the forest. A breeze brushed against my back, and I held my breath, too disgusted by the tang of iron, of blood, and the decay of flesh, to walk.

Even though I knew I needed to move on, I was too sickened to continue.

In both mind and body.

"I did not mean for this to happen," I said, then stopped, realizing the words were but an excuse. I had intended for it to happen. I had planned it, prepared myself for this very outcome. It was the reality of placing myself in the middle of the conflict and trying to maintain peace without taking a side.

And I had almost found that way of peace.

Hitori's affection had grown for me, as had her desire to uncover more about the Skills. A strained friendship had begun.

If Gaiden had not shown up as a catalyst, plunging Hitori into a rage, would the outcome have been any different?

"I killed them," I said with a shaky voice, staring at the ground as my vision wavered, "to save the people of Kiriku. The villagers—they didn't choose to be involved in this. Nor did Vaiyene or the False Shadows. If I can do nothing else, I will do what needs to be done to keep the people within my sight safe." I clenched my hands into fists and forced myself to meet Shenrae's eyes. "Even if it that means forsaking my beliefs and ideals," I continued, "I can no longer bear the thought of sparing another life if it means others will die because of it."

Some might have called what I had done noble, retribution even. But I did not see it as such. A decision. That's all it had been. Those I had killed had been Gaiden's men, mercenaries with blackened hearts, but it still revolted me. Not all of them had been like Gaiden or Ouiji, but I had chosen to end their lives because I judged them to be worth less than the innocent lives I could save, without acknowledging the possibility that one of them could have been turned from their path.

That they could have been saved.

Could I have done more?

All at once, the world shifted around me, and nausea overwhelmed me.

The Skill poisoning.

Grimly, I smiled to myself. Perhaps I deserved it. The pain and guilt. The sickness that came from reaching for something I could never achieve.

A peace that was doomed to fail.

Leaning back against a tree, I slid to the ground, digging my fingers into the sides of my head.

I had failed.

This had all begun when I encountered my Phantom beheading a man in the forest. He had found no other way than to end the cycle of death by becoming someone who took life.

Was I no different?

No better?

Hot tears spilled from my eyes. My hands slumped at my sides, and I gazed up through the canopy at the darkening sky in search of the fading light—but there was nothing but darkness.

"I'm so tired, Shenrae," I said, feeling her presence close by. Even though she had seen what I had become, she had not left. That small bit of compassion kept me from falling completely into the darkness. "It all seems so pointless. To have such blatant hate and disregard in the world…" I closed my eyes as anguish gripped my chest. "Sometimes, I wonder if we'll ever achieve peace or if the world is too broken to be saved."

Shenrae moved in front of me, and I opened my eyes. She blocked the view of the canopy above. Her lips quivered, and I noticed she, too, was crying.

My heart broke.

"I'm sorry," I said, averting my eyes. "I'm sorry I left Vaiyene and that I have not been able to make this world a better place for you. I'm sorry I left you and Syrane. I'm sorry for—"

"Stop."

My throat tightened, and Shenrae fell to her knees in front of me. She wiped her tears with her sleeve before she held out her right forearm for me to see.

Silver metal encased her arm in an elegant pattern.

She lowered her arm and cradled it with her other hand. "I believe if we stay true to who we are, we can achieve peace. You've never needed to do everything on your own. You only needed to make a path for us to follow."

She sniffed loudly and swiped away her tears.

"The Shadows still believe in you," Shenrae continued, her voice raspy. "And General Mirai has been doing everything he can to support you. Akio and I have also been doing what we can, and Finae and Rin too. They defended Konro in your place. Even Phantom Asdar has taken a group of Shadows outside of Vaiyene to defend our homeland."

Clutching the robes at my chest with my fingers, I squeezed my eyes closed. Those I cared about were placing themselves in danger. As Lunia had feared, my actions had incited Hitori to endanger Vaiyene and those I loved.

Shenrae reached out to touch my hand.

I flinched and met her gaze.

"You're not alone in this," she said.

Her eyes were filled with determination and passion.

"We need you," she continued. "Without you, the Shadows will continue to lose their way. Already they're losing faith in the Shadow's Creed, and Lunia is—"

"Shenrae, I can't," I said quietly.

I wanted to be there for her, to lead the Shadows and to inspire them. It had been my greatest desire since the day the people of Kiriku had found me broken after my father had disowned me. They had taken me in, been kind to me when my parents had rejected who I was, showing me that there my life had meaning. That my strength could be used to defend them.

Shenrae sat back on her heels. "Why can't you? Because you've 'betrayed' what you believe the Shadow's Creed to be? Do you think that because you've made mistakes as a Phantom, you can't continue to be one?"

Her eyes brimmed with tears again.

"Without you, the Shadows are not the same! Phantom Lunia has made it so most are afraid of action. They want to hide away in Vaiyene because they don't understand the Skills and are afraid of getting involved. Phantom Asdar is doing his best to bring the Shadows together, but…" She shook her head as if she couldn't finish the sentence. Her words were strained as she tried to finish. "We need you. I…"

Her voice was so pained and raw, it cut straight to my heart.

The words she could not say hung heavy in the air.

I need you.

Shenrae looked up to me. Even as a child, she had always admired me. I had tried to be the best person I could be, to be worthy of that admiration and love.

Tears returned to my eyes.

Shenrae stood up. "I'm going to get wood for a fire."

I let out a shuddering breath, allowing the tears to roll down my cheeks. A chill went up my spine, and I began shivering, curling my arms around my chest; the blood and sweat had soaked through my robe to my skin.

I closed my eyes, setting my hand on my sword.

An uneasy daze came over me as I listened for traces of Shenrae, flinching at every sound. Feeling restless, I stood up, walking around the clearing in the forest, gazing with unfocused eyes at the dead bodies. Finally, deciding sleep was not the best option, I found a thick branch and began whittling the end down to create a flat shovel-like head. Thrusting the makeshift shovel into the dirt, I began widening a hole to bury the dead.

A twig snapped in the forest, and I paused, tightening my fingers around the branch. I held my breath, ready should I need to act.

But it was only Shenrae.

In her arms, she carried a pile of wood. She set it down and began placing rocks in a circle to keep the fire contained.

Wearily, I continued chiseling at the hard ground, falling into the steady rhythm of digging against the hardened earth. Shenrae continued building the campfire, and after some time, a fire crackled to life, the warmth falling over me.

"You should rest," she said.

I knew she was right, but I was reluctant to do so.

Dreams would come.

Walking over to me, she softly took the stick from my hand. The sharp edge had already blunted; even if I worked all night, I would make little progress.

With a sigh, I relented to Shenrae's insistence and leaned against a tree close to the fire. The warm waves eased my muscles, and slowly, knowing Shenrae was there, I started to relax.

After some time, I fell into an uneasy sleep, the vision and images of the men I had killed returning to me as I relived each encounter. The cold sensation of blood over my hands made me shiver, and I woke with a start, vomiting to the side.

Shenrae glanced up at me from across the fire. "Is that the Skill poisoning?"

"Some of it is," I said, using Shenrae's voice to tie myself to reality. Part of the nausea and the coughing was, but the regret and shame I had carried for many years. Forcing myself to stand, I walked away, trying to clear my head of the visions.

It was not the first time I had thrown up from a dream.

From the guilt that afflicted me.

"Emiko taught Rin and me how to purify the Skills," Shenrae said, coming close and reaching out a hesitant hand toward me. "Maybe it will help with the sickness?"

She glanced up at me, her eyes filled with hope.

I did not know how to tell her I had lived with this shame for most of my life and that her efforts would likely be for naught. Some days were just worse than others.

Still, I tried to smile for her.

Perhaps it would help with the fatigue and the sickness.

"I would appreciate anything you are willing to try," I said.

She blew out a long breath before resting her fingers on my forearm. At her touch, the silver metal of my bond became hot and painful, and the skin showing through the metal threads became darker in color. A crease appeared on her forehead. If not for her determination and desire to help me, I would have told her to give up.

But I knew this was something she wanted to do.

For me.

Shenrae closed her eyes and placed her other hand on my arm. A silver glow outlined the fingers on her hand. It shimmered and grew in intensity, and I felt my chest begin to constrict. I moved my left hand and pressed it against my chest, balling it in my robes. The pain was almost unbearable.

"Are you okay?" Shenrae asked, her eyes watching me closely.

I nodded, not trusting my voice to remain steady enough for her to continue. A wave of nausea came over me, and I drew in a long breath to quell it. Briefly—through the pain—a gentle touch brushed against my mind.

And I realized what she was trying to do.

Shenrae hesitated, as if she was unsure if she should proceed.

"I will be fine," I said to reassure her.

She nodded, and the featherlight touch brushed against my mind again before my vision shifted and everything went black.

chapter sixty-four
A New Task

Shenrae

Intense pain and sadness rushed into me, cutting off my breath and crushing my heart. I squeezed my eyes shut, trying to keep my breathing steady. The Skills I withdrew from Kilo were so intense, so agitated and filled with grief, they nearly overwhelmed me.

How was Kilo able to bear it?

I swallowed the knot in my throat.

The Skills appeared like tendrils of light around him. They were wound tightly around his limbs, his bond, and his heart. Shifting my fingers to Kilo's bond, I gently unhooked one of the threads of the Skills, feeling the flow of the sadness shift to me. Immediately a tendril of light snaked over my finger, building in power and strength. It was filled with life and emotion, as if these Skills held something precious.

A memory of something from the past came before my eyes.

I saw Kilo, my father, and another man in the middle of a field. Rain poured down, soaking the ground and creating large puddles of mud soaked with red. My father stood to the side, his eyes wide as he looked in horror at a man face down on the ground. Kilo pulled the sword from the dead man's back, his hand struggling to hold the sword steady.

Kilo's regret flowed into me, and my chest constricted from the pain.

The memory faded, and in its place a similar regret filled me, the pain and guilt of having killed the mercenaries. With it came the resolve and desire to protect Riku and Daichi, and at the back of Kilo's mind, burning bright against the cloud of darkness, was an image of Vaiyene.

Finae.

My parents.

Syrane and me, along with all of the Shadows.

Somehow, I felt self-conscious at how strong his emotions were and how deeply his love ran. I tried to separate myself, but by drawing the Skills into me, it seemed impossible to create distance between us, but the feeling remained that I had somehow violated his trust by entering his heart in such a way.

The vision in my mind changed, the void of darkness taking its place.

Kilo stood before me, in this place of the Skills.

I sensed amusement from him.

"I have nothing to hide, Shenrae," he said. "That day, I used my sword to end someone's life because your father's life was in danger. However..." He sighed, and the vision came back to me. "It did not end there. The true guilt of the memory lies deeper, known only by the person who was at my side that day."

It was nighttime in the memory, and Kilo stood outside the camp. My father and Phantom Kural were asleep next to the fire. Leaving the safety of the camp, Kilo walked alone, stopping outside the edge of the forest. Two people appeared, carrying swords. Their eyes blazed with anger, and no matter how Kilo spoke to them, the tension only continued to rise. The two men drew their swords and attacked Kilo. It almost seemed as if Kilo were going to lose until a second person came to his aid.

Asdar.

The fight continued, and the vision faded.

I looked at Kilo for an explanation.

"A few days after I saved your father, the man's brother and father came to find me. They wanted revenge for the death of their son. I tried to reason with them, but..." He shook his head. "In the end, Asdar and I had no other choice but to kill them. Even after two decades, the guilt still haunts me. How could we ever justify our actions?"

"Is that why you refused to use a sword for so long?" I asked.

Kilo's eyes shimmered briefly with silver light. "Yes. I saw firsthand the consequence of taking a life. Because I killed that man and saved your father's life, his family demanded vengeance. It is an endless cycle, and it is the reason why the Shadows do not carry out justice in that way. If we accept death for what it is, we stop the cycle. It is the only way."

"This wasn't what I intended to happen," I said, glancing down at my hands. "When Emiko taught me how to draw the Skills into myself to purify him, it wasn't like this then."

Kilo chuckled. "That may be my doing. I became aware of what you were trying to do, so my subconscious may have brought us here to this place. It's become a respite for me lately."

"Where are we?" I asked, looking around at the void.

"This is the veil between the Skills and our world," Kilo said as he began walking into nothingness. "Now that we are here, there is something I want to show you. There may be something you can help me with if you desire to do so."

I felt slightly awkward following after him in a place without direction. No sound echoed from our footsteps, and there was no odor, and except for Kilo ahead of me, I could see nothing.

Kilo paused and drew in a deep breath, letting it out slowly as the darkness changed shaped.

A twisted and gnarled tree sprouted from the ground. Other trees appeared next to it, their limbs reaching toward the sky with finger-like branches. Surrounding the tree, the dirt seemed unstable, as if it had been uprooted or recently dug up.

"There's a tree in the Kinsaan Forest that is sick with the Skills," Kilo said, placing his hand on the bark. "The area has been stained with hatred and memories from the people Hitori has killed. A thick ooze surrounds the area near there. It's in the gulf and in the streams." Kilo lowered his hand from the bark and looked over at me. "What did you mean when you said you know how to purify the Skills?"

He seemed intent on the answer.

"After we defended Konro from mercenaries, Emiko, a former Shadow from Zenkaiko, came to speak with Rin and me because Finae is—" I stopped suddenly, realizing Kilo might not know. "Do you know about Finae?"

To my surprise, Kilo nodded. "In a sense. I have felt her reaching out to me through the Skills. When we were studying the Skills in Konro, Finae and I began to feel one another's presence almost unconsciously. I know something happened to her, but I also know she's okay."

"Rin sent a message that I wasn't sure if you had gotten yet," I said, almost as an apology for not telling him sooner. Kilo gave me an encouraging nod, and I rubbed my hand over the bond on my arm, continuing to answer his question. "Finae created a barrier to protect Konro from the mercenaries. She hasn't woken up yet, although I've felt her within the Skills too."

Kilo was quiet, tilting his head as if listening to some sound I couldn't hear.

"She's here, in this place," he said, giving me a small smile. "Do not worry. I know how to bring her back from the Skills."

His confidence made me feel better.

"What else did Emiko tell you?" Kilo asked.

"He said it was the Shadows' duty to keep the Skills in balance."

Kilo nodded absently. "I have heard the same from the ancient Phantom. It is something I have been thinking about how to approach. If you're willing, I would like you to find other places across Kiriku showing signs of the Skill poisoning. With all that I have to do in Vaiyene, there is little time."

A grin spread across my face.

He was returning to Vaiyene?

"Of course," Kilo said, a wry smile coming over him, "it will depend on if Asdar will allow me to borrow one of his best Shadows for a few missions."

I tried not to look too pleased at his compliment.

Attempting to keep a straight face, I sighed and looked thoughtful. "Well, I'll have to see what Phantom Asdar thinks. He has been keeping me quite busy."

Kilo laughed and waved me off, walking into the darkness again.

This time when the void changed, the peaks of the Miyota Mountains appeared around us. When Kilo stopped walking, we stood on the summit, at the highest point of Vaiyene. The Reikon tree and the village were nestled in the valley below.

It was a place Kilo and I had often gone to talk.

For a long while, we said nothing, looking out across the valley in silence.

"Thank you for reminding me of what I lost sight of," Kilo said finally, turning to face me before he bowed slightly. "If you will still have me as your Phantom, I would be honored to help you and the Shadows find a new path forward."

Placing my right arm over my chest, I bowed in return. When I straightened, Kilo smiled, and then his gaze drifted down to the valley, kindness once again in his eyes.

chapter sixty-five
Parting

Kilo

I awoke with a start, my hand reaching for the dagger hidden in my robe.

"Relax, it's only me," a familiar voice said. The smell of dirt and decaying leaves wafted toward me as she moved across the forest floor. Releasing the blade, I exhaled, finding the dark silhouette against the campfire.

Rin.

"Go back to sleep," she whispered, kneeling beside me.

Across the fire's glow, Shenrae stared out into the forest. Her staff rested across her knees as she kept diligent watch.

"Shenrae told me what happened," Rin said.

I pressed my hand over my face and closed my eyes, exhaustion weighing me down. It was a warm, humid night, and Rin's usual floral scent was masked by the iron tang of blood and the dank forest. The sensation of uncleanliness rose within me, and with it, guilt for what had been done. Earlier, I had found a stream to wash away the blood, but my hands felt clammy.

Stained.

Rin's fingertips brushed against my head, caressing the side of my forehead to check for a fever. The Skill poisoning had lessened after Shenrae purified them. My throat constricted, and I removed my hand from my eyes, resting it on my chest. Rin's touch was gentle, caring, and accepting. I wanted to explain myself to her, but her eyes held nothing but kindness. Of all the people who understood the guilt, the shame... She had lived it.

Rin rested her hands in her lap. "Do you still feel guilty?"

I hesitated, unsure of how to answer. "I had thought holding onto my guilt would make me a better Shadow, but all it did was bring me grief and separate me from those who were trying to help me."

Rin's green eyes watched me closely as I evaded the question.

"Yes, I still do," I said. "It will take time, but after speaking with Shenrae and seeing how you have been able to move past your circumstances, maybe it is time I learned how to forgive myself."

"'A Shadow does what he can; no more can be asked of him.'"

A slight smile spread across my lips.

"When did you learn that?"

Rin shrugged. "I asked Finae to write down the Shadow's Creed for me, and"—she gave me a sly smile—"you may have recited it a time or two. It's impossible not to have memorized that one."

I laughed, watching as Shenrae walked off into the forest.

"She surprised me in Konro," Rin said. "It was clear she was afraid of the Skills and uneasy about fighting the mercenaries, yet she never hesitated to involve herself. I've never seen someone as young as her be so brave."

"Shenrae's parents were the same," I said, remembering Mia and Zavi. "They instilled courage and a strong will into both Shenrae and her brother. When I think of them and Finae, I am reminded of why I want to create a place full of possibilities and understanding—one where they can live their lives without having to endure the pain I have."

But was it possible?

The thought struck me, giving way to self-doubt. It was a thought I would acknowledge, but one I would not let consume me.

Shenrae and the Shadows needed me.

Growing restless, I pushed myself up, and with Rin's help, I stood. The sun had begun to rise, and through the dense forest, a sliver of sunlight peeked through. Moving to one of the trees nearby, I rested my fingertips against the bark and felt the Skills thrumming within.

But more than that...

"I want to be there for them," I said, imagining the Miyota Mountains and the smiles of the villagers. "I want them to be happy, because I never was."

Rin came to my side. "Hopefully, you will allow yourself to be happy as well."

For the first time in a long while, not since I had left her in Konro, I relaxed, breathing deeply. It was easy to get caught up in the flow of life and be thrown from one pressing matter to another, but sometimes it was necessary to slow down and reflect, to enjoy the smaller moments that made the whole worthwhile.

I was happy to be spending a moment with Rin.

We walked away from the camp, finding a clearing in the trees to watch the sunrise. Birdsong trilled in the trees, and the slow clattering of the leaves surrounded us. A stag and his mate ambled into the open field, munching at the grass as they went. Their ears swiveled, and their tails swished. Neither Rin nor I spoke until they had passed, captivated by their presence and the sun's light.

"I want to ask a favor," Rin said, filling the silence.

"What is it?"

"Let me come with you to stop Hitori."

She hesitated as if she were trying to put her thoughts into words. Before, Rin had not cared what happened to Hitori—or had seemed not to. I had not pressed her to come with me. I was aware of the rift between Rin and Hitori and the pain it would cause to both to consider reconciliation.

What had changed?

"It all seems so long ago when Hitori and I were friends. She's always been direct and decisive. Captivated by whatever it is that caught her eye. I always enjoyed her company, and..." Rin shook her head. "I owe it to her to settle things between us."

"She would appreciate it," I said with certainty. Rin glanced over at me, her brows raised in question. "Saitou came to talk to me when I was among her False Shadows—alone. He asked me to save her."

Rin's eyes widened slightly.

"He also told me of Hitori's frustration with not being able to find people who accepted her way of thinking and how devastated she was to lose your friendship. It's strange to think of her in that way, but really, all she ever wanted was to do what excited her and be accepted for it."

"To learn about the Skills," Rin said.

I nodded. "I only hope Hitori is willing to trust me one more time."

Shenrae

Staring down at my fingers, I clenched them together into a fist. My mind churned with the responsibility given to me by Emiko and Kilo. Since learning about the Skills from Finae, my view on them had changed. I'd been ready to give them up, dismiss them, but now, it felt as if I breathed in a new life.

Purifying the Skills.

A Shadow's duty.

Kilo's task.

It was exhilarating.

Leaving behind the now risen sun, I headed back to camp, stepping over the loose roots and rocks of the forest floor. When I returned, Rin was sitting next to the campfire. She held a teacup in her hand and sipped at the contents. A pot had been placed over the flames, and Rin looked contemplative as she watched the fire.

Kilo didn't seem to be around.

Rin lowered her cup and lifted her gaze to me. "Akio went to find General Mirai. He said to let you know."

I nodded, feeling a knot of worry in my chest. Akio had gone to help the general again, which meant he would be on the front lines of the quarrels between the villages. A part of me felt torn. Being with Akio and the general was what I had wanted to return to, but now that Kilo, Emiko, and Phantom Asdar were entrusting me to find out more about the Skills, I felt pulled in a different direction.

Rin reached out to grab the kettle next to the fire. "I think he knew your Shadow duties would take you in a different direction, and so he didn't want to force you to choose. I hope the two of you can meet again." She smiled at me and poured the tea into two cups.

"I hope so too," I said, feeling uneasy.

It was because of Akio I had gained the confidence to become a better warrior. Without him, I wouldn't have had the conviction needed to face the mercenaries in Konro or Phantom Lunia and Syrane in Vaiyene. His belief in my abilities to learn the Skills was one of the reasons why I had never given up.

It would be hard without him being around.

Catching my eye, Rin held out the cups to me. "Kilo went to cleanse himself in the river. Will you take this to him? The rice will be ready whenever you both return."

I nodded and took the cups from her, heading in the direction Rin indicated. I walked slowly, with my hands close to my body so as to not spill the tea. The liquid smelled spicy, with a hint of peppercorns and ginger.

Not far upstream, Kilo sat with his legs crossed and his hands on his knees. His eyes were closed, and he sat on a rock in the middle of the water, wearing only his white inner robe.

He seemed at peace. And I hesitated to disturb him.

Kneeling next to the river, I waited, allowing my senses to feel for the Skills. In the air there was the slightest sense of them gathering around Kilo. Back in the forest, he had been filled with anger and rage. Now, the air around him was inviting and calm.

As it always had been.

"Kilo?" I ventured, keeping my voice quiet.

He exhaled slowly and then drew in a breath, turning his head as his eyes opened. When he noticed me, he stood up and came to the bank of the river, kneeling. I handed him the tea Rin had given me.

He picked it up and sniffed it. "Ah, Rin's famous pain-relieving tea," he said. I kept a close eye on his right arm, the one on which his silver bond rested. The skin seemed less blackened.

"How are you feeling?" I asked, taking a sip of tea from my own cup, the spiciness warming me.

"More like myself, thanks to you." He paused, looking down at the cup and turning it with one hand. "Seeing you has made me realize how I have missed Vaiyene and those I left behind. Even though I have found some level of comfort in how things are now, my heart has always ached to return."

I kept my eyes down so he could not see how relieved I was.

Kilo drained the remainder of his tea and stood, his eyes tracking the height of the sun. He looked down at me expectantly, a question in his eyes. "We have some time if you would like to accompany me for a walk."

I nodded.

Like old times.

We doubled back toward camp, where Kilo set the teacups down next to Rin. Something unspoken seemed to pass between them. It was subtle, but the way he looked at her and she in turn looked at him confirmed my original suspicion.

They had grown close.

When Kilo returned to my side, he led us toward the sun, picking a path through the forest that followed the river. He walked quickly, but not so fast that it was hard for me to keep up.

"Do you remember when I couldn't keep up with you?" I asked, not able to contain my smile.

"You always insisted I should not wait for you," he said, stepping over a large boulder. "I would have to come up with different ways to make it seem like I was not." He laughed. "I never understood why you got so angry. My legs were much longer than yours. It was only natural."

"It was a matter of pride!"

I laughed too. A part of me always knew Kilo had lied, making excuses as to why he would stop and wait for me to catch up.

"If your parents could see you now," Kilo said.

He didn't say anything more, and he didn't need to. I, too, felt the same sadness encroach around my heart. My parents' absence was painful, but I was grateful for what they had been able to teach me in the time we did have together.

"Do you think the people of Vaiyene will accept the Skills?" I asked. Thinking about the animosity between him and Phantom Lunia, I wasn't sure what he had planned.

Kilo considered for a moment. "There will always be resistance to change. It will take time, but I have a feeling the Shadows will come around. Once they let go of their fear and understand how the Skills are connected to our own lives, it will deepen our reason for being Shadows."

"Syrane's not going to be happy about it," I said quietly.

Kilo raised his eyebrows.

"He doesn't like the Skills, and he's angry with me for leaving. Even Phantom Lunia tried to stop me. They don't seem to understand what you're trying to do."

"And how do they feel about me?"

I refused to say it.

Kilo stopped walking, giving me a wry smile as he turned and stepped back, studying something behind me. I frowned, unsure of what he was looking at or why he seemed not to care that people were upset with him. Curious, I came to his side, noticing the peaks of the Miyota Mountains on the horizon.

"It will not be the first time I have upset the Shadows," Kilo said, an amused smile spreading across his face. "Asdar and I caused a good deal of grief when we were your age. We are the reason why the Shadows go to different villages and towns and why we rely on others for our survival." Kilo's smile became even more mischievous. "I'm not sure Lunia has ever forgiven me for that."

"My parents never told me anything about that," I said, trying not to make it sound like I was pouting.

Kilo chuckled. "Were the Shadows able to focus on aspects of training other than defense, I'm sure you would have been told some of it. It was, after all, what led Asdar and me to become Phantoms. Our vision and desire for the Shadows to become more than what they were was something both of us strove for even when we first joined."

I turned a suspicious gaze toward him.

"It will all happen in time," Kilo said, his mood becoming more solemn. "Syrane will come around, and I will deal with Lunia and the others when I return."

"You're not worried?"

"No," Kilo said without hesitating. "Here, hold out your arm, like this." He raised his arm, with his two forefingers outstretched. His other fingers curled into a loose fist. "You begin by drawing a grid in the air with your fingers. Then trace a character over that for whatever it is your spirit requires. It is an ancient tradition I read once in a book about the older Shadows. They would use it to summon courage before battle."

Intrigued, I watched him draw in the air with his fingers. We had all learned how to write with characters at a young age with a brush and rice paper.

"Compassion?" I asked when he stopped drawing.

"And understanding of those I go to face. My eyes have seen the truth behind the actions of the False Shadows' leader, but I am not sure my heart is ready for what I may be forced to do."

I thought for a moment, considering what it was that my own spirit needed.

Raising my arm and forefingers, I sketched a grid in the air, three lines wide and three lines high, drawing the character for "courage."

Kilo wrapped one arm around my shoulder and squeezed me tightly, and for a brief moment, I could have sworn I felt the arms of my parents too.

"Should we head back to camp?" Kilo asked, turning south, away from the mountains. "Rin and I will be leaving soon to head to Magoto. Once I am done there, I will send word. Do you know how to contact the spy network if you need it?"

I nodded. "Phantom Asdar showed me when I left Vaiyene. I've already written a letter to him explaining that I wish to travel in search of disturbances in the Skills, although I'm not sure where to head first."

"Head to Konro," Kilo said, a faraway look in his eyes. He tilted his head as if he were trying to listen to something again. "I have a feeling a certain someone would love to come with you on your journey."

My eyes widened.

"Finae will be waking soon."

chapter sixty-six
Magoto

Kilo

Rin and I stood outside Magoto's gate. The giant wooden door had been charred down the middle, and one half of the gate had been pushed open, allowing us to see inside the town.

We peered inside at the desolate stone walls and buildings.

Rin's posture was unusually stiff, and worry creased her brow. Reaching over, I took the reins of her horse and tied them to the horse's bridle. One of the spies had found us a day after we left Shenrae, urging us to hurry. She had left us two horses to help with our journey, saying to release them when we were done.

Someone from the spy network was likely in the area, keeping watch.

"Let's see if anyone needs our help," I said gently, watching Rin square her shoulders before she walked over the charred remains of the gate.

Releasing the horses, I followed Rin at a respectful distance as I let my gaze wander the area. The once white stones of Magoto were stained red. Some kind of major confrontation had happened here, and judging by the amount of discoloration, quite a few had died. Soot coated the rock walls as well—suggesting the fire had spread from the gate and up the street.

I grimaced.

Hitori would not have bothered to spare those who had turned against her.

Rin headed east, in the opposite direction from where Finae and I had hidden in Magoto's lower quarter last winter. The buildings here were in modest condition, the stone weathered but sturdy.

This was the lower quarter, where Rin had grown up.

I peered inside houses as we passed. The doors were open. Food, furniture, pots, and pans—all had been left unattended and were in disarray, as if the people had fled hastily.

Rin leaned against one of the door frames. "They've all left." Her voice was strained.

Walking past one of the empty buildings, I came into what seemed to be a courtyard. A sculpture of stone lay broken in the center. It appeared to be some sort of fountain, with a large stone basin.

As I drew closer, the Skills prickled against me.

"What is this?" I asked.

The stone resting in the center seemed to have been polished until it was smooth. It must have taken some time to make it that way, which made it seem odd that it had been abandoned. Bending down, I reached out to it.

The Skills surged across my fingers.

"It was one of Hitori's many attempts to win the people's affection," Rin said, coming to my side. "Her idea was to use the Skills to purify the water from the ocean."

"What happened?"

"In the beginning, it seemed to work, but not long after drinking from the fountain, the people began dying. The townspeople destroyed the fountain and blamed Hitori for it, saying it was her plan from the start." Rin picked up the jade sphere and placed it back into the basin. "It's another of the lies the council spread to weaken Hitori's grasp on the town. I have my suspicions that they were the ones who poisoned the people, but I was never able to prove it."

"That's unfortunate," I said, frowning.

There was much more at play than Hitori's own anger and manipulation. The council, the False Shadows, the mercenaries, the group posing as the False Shadows—all of it had been allowed to spiral because of Hitori's reputation. The hatred they showed her only bred more anger.

"Hitori was devastated," Rin continued, holding up one of the broken pieces of the fountain. "She had asked her father for the materials, begging for his permission to build it. It was one of the only things she had ever had the motivation to do to help the people."

"The council didn't approve?"

Rin shrugged. "They didn't care. Making the townspeople hate Hitori allowed them to tighten their grasp on Magoto. Everyone's been so focused on Hitori that it hasn't been hard for them to manipulate the people."

"And what did happen to the lord? To Hitori's father?"

"The council made it look like Hitori had killed him. They hoped the unrest would be enough for people to rise up."

A miscalculation on their part.

Had the fountain worked, and had the people appreciated Hitori's research into the Skills, she might not have resorted to attacking other villages for necessary supplies. With everyone believing she had killed her father, no town would trust her. She had been forced to use any means required to take care of Magoto.

It all made sense, but there was one thing I still did not understand.

"Why is the council doing this to their own town?"

"If the Lord Shingen, Hitori's adoptive father, had not appeared and been favored by the people, the council would have taken charge of the town."

I sighed.

It was a power struggle.

"Pathetic, isn't it?" Rin said. She spread her arms out at the deserted town. "All this happened because someone was upset they didn't get the title they wanted." Rin dropped her arms and looked back at the empty houses, her voice becoming pained. "I hope they find someplace to call home."

"The people will return when Magoto begins to flourish."

Rin looked sharply over at me. "Do you really believe that?"

"I do."

With my newfound understanding, I began walking around the courtyard, imagining what it would look like when Magoto was rebuilt. "We'll restore the buildings and keep the gates open to those who will travel between towns." I lifted my hand, pointing behind Rin. "Over there, we'll plant a tree. It will be a big one that will grow as tall as the mountains. We'll salvage the fountain and create a garden surrounding it to lift the people's spirits."

Rin raised one eyebrow suspiciously. "A garden?"

I shrugged, trying to contain my amusement. "For color."

She rolled her eyes.

"In time, the Skills will return and the gloom that hangs over Magoto will pass like the wind. When the people return, it will not be the same. The town will become bigger and better than it was, and others will be envious of its greatness."

"That seems a bit ambitious."

I laughed. "Every good story begins with a fool's dream."

Behind Rin, a man and a woman appeared inside the doorframe of one of the houses. They approached with caution, but when Rin turned around, their faces lit up.

Rin ran toward them. "Shoya, Ianai! I'm so happy you're safe!" She threw her arms around both of them, holding on tighter when they tried to push her away.

More people began to gather, their courage seeming to grow as their number increased. Quietly, I slipped into the background, against the buildings, allowing myself to become an observer.

The people needed her.

Loved her.

And she had finally risen to meet that challenge.

Rin exchanged words with many of the people, giving many hugs and talking animatedly to each and every person. There was a lightness to her steps I had never seen before, likely stemming from a place of affection.

It was the same fondness I held for Vaiyene and the Shadows.

At the people's insistence, Rin stood on one of the rocks from the fountain. Then they waited with bated breath for what she was about to say.

She looked abashed at their attention, her words spoken softly.

"We've been through a lot these past few months, and I know it has been hard for all of us. After researching and considering how best to confront the situation and the power that Hitori wields, I believe it is finally time to confront Hitori." She paused for a moment, contemplating her words. There was a subtle shift to her posture, and her shoulders drew back and her voice rose. "After tonight, Magoto will know peace!"

The people cheered, and Rin savored the reaction before she searched for me in the crowd. When her eyes fell on me, I bowed slightly to her.

Her smile grew.

I waited for Rin to make her way over, and when she was ready, we left the lower quarter to a small fanfare of well-wishes. Rin's spirit had been lifted, and I felt more resolved to see this through to the end.

It was time.

Magoto's castle rested on top of a hill, near cliffs that dropped down to the Ame Ocean. The white stone tiles and the arched pagoda were a contrast to the rich blue sky.

As we drew closer to the castle, Rin became anxious. She clenched her fingers in her robes, occasionally fiddling with the charm hanging from her sword.

Unease had retaken hold of her.

I recalled what it had been like the day I became a Shadow, when the weight of being a leader for the people made me doubt my capabilities. The Shadow's Oath had empowered me that day, and there were many days when my mind drifted back to the vows I had sworn for strength.

"'I will stand strong in the face of adversity, though I do not know the way. I will nurture hope, being a light to the darkness around me. I will search for the truth, with eyes of kindness.'"

Rin glanced over at me. "Is that another part from the Shadow's Creed?"

"Part of the oath we take."

"Is everything about being a Shadow just as idealistic as your creed?"

"Foolishly so," I said, grinning from ear to ear. "I prefer it that way. Even if my ideals fall short, I would rather have hope in this world than believe what I do will never save it." I closed one eye and winked at her. "Isn't that why you sought me out?"

Rin laughed. "Maybe."

We continued along to the castle, our footsteps echoing off the hollow walls of the town.

"Thank you," Rin said after some time.

I nodded. It was a small gesture to help her feel better. If I could have done more for her, I would have.

From up ahead, we heard voices.

Breaking away from the main path leading to the castle, we slipped between two stone buildings. A small gathering of people—guards and False Shadows—waited outside the main gate. A few of the False Shadows I recognized from Leiko, though most I did not. I had hoped to settle things without a fight. It was possible they would be sympathetic to our cause, but they could also be loyal to Hitori.

"There's a pathway along the cliffside," Rin said, turning to retrace our steps. "It's dangerous, and it will take a bit of time to navigate, but if we can scale it, we should be able to drop down inside the castle gates without anyone noticing us."

"I always did like your sense of danger," I said, catching a sly grin from Rin.

We followed the white brick wall surrounding the castle to the side of the cliffs. Rin leaned down near the edge of the cliff and peered under a pile of rocks, then reached her hand into a small crevasse, drawing out a coil of rope.

A metal barb had been tied to the end.

When I eyed it curiously, she shrugged. "I did say no one would see us."

She walked along the cliffside, gazing down at the water before wrapping the rope and pronged end around a tree. I leaned over the edge. The roots of the tree had wound themselves into the cracks of the rockface, creating an almost spiderweb-like pattern.

Rin held the rope out to me and pointed down at the cliffside. "The roots act as footholds. If you climb down to that stone platform there, you'll find a small cave that spans the cliffside. It was Ikaru who found it. He used to be quite different than he is now. Full of energy and ambition."

"Once this is over, Ikaru will be able to smile again."

She nodded absently.

Taking the rope in my hand, I pulled on it, testing the strength of the tree's trunk. I placed my feet on the pile of rocks and jumped, rappelling down the cliffside. When my feet touched the rock platform, I released my hold on the rope, kneeling before I crawled through the cave's opening. The light canteen at my side glowed. In a short distance, the cave opened up, and I stood, waiting. Rin crawled through and coiled the rope, carrying it with her as she led the way. The cave we followed was not fully enclosed, as the outside edge had been eroded away. Wind buffeted us, and we hugged the narrow pathway, keeping close to the rocks of the cliff as the tide crashed below, breaking against jagged rocks and spraying mist into the air. I paused for a moment, looking out over the darkening sky to where clouds billowed on the horizon. Bolts of lightning crawled from one cloud to the other.

A storm was coming.

And soon it would be upon us.

Rin swung the rope at her side, and when it began to hum, she released the pronged end, hooking a tree at the top of the cliff. Pulling on it to check it was secure, she began climbing. I kept an eye on her footing, watching her grace and agility with quiet admiration. When she reached the top, I began my own climb.

Pulling myself up, I stared in quiet awe of Magoto's castle. While I had been here before, this angle made it seem immense, more daunting. Perhaps it was the light of the oncoming storm that gave it that impression.

A group of shadows moved within the courtyard. At least two people—guards, most likely—were on patrol. Rin and I sneaked across the area and pressed ourselves flat against the castle wall. When the guards were almost upon us, Rin darted from our hiding place, her arm grasping the wrist of one guard before she pinned her to the ground. The remaining guard threw a punch at me, but I dodged and grabbed her hand, jerking it behind her in a hold.

She struggled against me.

"Be still," I said, keeping my voice quiet. There was a brown birthmark on her neck. She was one of the False Shadows I had trained.

Relaxing my grip, I stepped back. "We're not here to fight, Ai."

When I released her, she spun around and drew her sword, pointing the blade at me. Her eyes were sharp, her black hair framing her angular face. She drew in a deep breath, preparing for her next attack.

"Your reflexes have improved," I said mildly. Ai had promising talent with the sword. Rin frowned at me from her position on the ground. Her knee was still pressed into the other guard's back. I gestured for Rin to let her up.

I kept my voice even as I addressed them. "We came to settle things with Hitori."

Ai's gaze rested on the swords at my side.

She tensed as if she were going to attack, but instead of raising her weapon, she met my eye. "You abandoned us," she said, gesturing back toward the town. "They all died! The council members, the guards, the people you trained—all of them are dead! This is the first day in a week the air hasn't stunk of corpses.

You—" She choked on her emotions and fought through them, her sword shaking in her hands. "Where were you?"

Her words were a desperate plea.

I swallowed the knot forming in my throat. "I am sorry I could not come sooner."

Her eyes began to well up with tears, and I felt my chest tighten with regret. I bowed to her, then waited for Rin to stand beside me before we continued to the castle.

The False Shadows did not follow.

And Rin said nothing about the exchange.

There was nothing to say.

I had known when I left Hitori to pursue Gaiden's men that a battle would break out in Magoto. And as much as it pained me to admit it, I could no longer focus on individual people to save. Even with the help of General Mirai, Kefnir, Shenrae, and now Asdar, the extent to which people were dying had eclipsed our capabilities. The only way to stop it, to reduce the numbers and make the most difference, was to put an end to Hitori's influence and power.

I knew it in my heart.

"You did what you could," Rin said at my side.

Her eyes reflected my own pain. Neither of us wanted to confront Hitori knowing if she did not yield, one of us would have to kill her. But it had to be done. She needed to answer for what she had done to the people of Kiriku.

The castle's inner courtyard was little more than white stone surrounded by a gate to keep others out. A few dead trees were planted in the area, their limbs and branches twisted in an eerie display. Traces of vines, flowers, and misplaced rocks gave the indication a garden had existed in this area too, though it had long been neglected. I rested my hand on one of the trees, not surprised to find the Skills absent from them. A piece of bark stuck out, and I picked at it, revealing an ash-like interior.

Rin was crouched next to the cliffside.

She plucked bits of dried grass and arranged them in a pile.

When I drew near she looked up briefly. "Can I borrow your light?"

She began adding rocks around her pile to contain the grass.

Untying my light canteen, I handed it to her, and she removed the top, feeding a thin piece of dried grass into it. When it caught fire, she laid it on her pile. Patiently, she guarded the fire with her hands, placing larger sticks onto it until it could withstand the wind.

Rin sat back on her heels and focused on the castle. "This was my signal to Hitori to let her know I was off guard duty. Despite how late it usually was, she would always come."

I knelt beside the fire, adjusting the two swords at my hip.

Time passed, and all seemed calm until the air shifted and pressed in against us. The Skills howled with anger, rising like a storm as Hitori walked toward us.

chapter sixty-seven
Confrontation

Kilo

Hitori's presence had become immeasurable.

Even without knowledge of the Skills or her title, anyone would have found her intimidating in her present state. She held her head high as she walked over the stones leading to the cliffside, her demeanor commanding obedience. A long robe flowed behind her, tied at the waist by a magenta ribbon. Her blonde hair was tied up with a silver dagger thrust through it. Following behind her, Saitou wore his usual leather armor. His face seemed more hollow than usual, as if he were fatigued or sick.

Hitori's attention immediately snapped to Rin. "I see you brought the Phantom. How nice of you to continue working together against me."

"I don't regret what I've done," Rin said, meeting Hitori's gaze. "I would do the same again. You've grown too reckless, too unyielding in your pursuit of knowledge. The Skills are too powerful—"

"Too powerful?" Hitori laughed. "Only the weak of mind would use such words. The Skills are limited by the user and their strength. There is no one more capable than I to control them. I told you that the first time you defied me."

"Hitori, please," Rin said, taking a step forward. "You can't continue like this."

"This has all been a temporary setback," Hitori continued, pacing about the cliffside, her fingers clenching and unclenching as she walked. "I will take back what is ours. I've already begun teaching the guards and the mercenaries how to use the Skills." Her smile deepened, and a touch of madness rose in her eyes.

"Take back what?" Rin asked, throwing her hands behind her. "Magoto? There's nothing left of Magoto! You're the lady of nothing. You saw to that yourself."

Hitori smirked. "I never considered myself the 'lady' of this pathetic town. The people have hated me since I came. Do you really think I mourn what has happened? No, what I will take control of is the Skills. I will build an army who can wield them so none will dare stand against me again."

A subtle shift in the air brushed against my awareness. Though they were few, the Skills in Magoto had begun awakening at Hitori's unrest.

She was losing control again.

Walking to Rin's side, I caught Saitou's gaze from behind Hitori, and the conversation we had came back to mind. This would be my last attempt.

"And then what?" I asked Hitori. "Will you be satisfied when your father's legacy is no more? When Magoto ceases to exist? I do not believe you are as heartless as you pretend to be. You can lie to yourself, but your actions betray you. The fountain you created, the villages you've attacked for supplies, all of it has been to provide for the people of Magoto and protect the legacy your father entrusted to you. The power you desire, the knowledge of the Skills, it has been to earn the people's respect—their love.

Even your hesitation with the council betrays how you hoped things could be settled without killing them."

A vein at Hitori's temple twitched.

I had hit a nerve.

"You have not given up hope for Magoto," I continued, feeling Hitori's anger begin to take control of the Skills. "Your purpose for the Skills has and always will be to acquire the affection of others. You were disappointed, hurt, that the people could not see the Skills' worth. The fountain was the one thing you created for them. How it must have hurt to watch them destroy it."

As the pressure in the air increased with Hitori's own rage, I resisted the urge to pull at the collar of my robe. Swallowing, I reminded myself there was enough air to breathe, and should I need to, I could calm the Skills in an instant.

"You think you're clever, do you?" Hitori mocked. Her glare deepened as the Skills crackled in the air. "Just because you were able to create meaning from what I've done doesn't mean it's the truth. I did what I did because I felt like it. Not because I desire someone's approval."

Her words were accented by the Skills. It was almost like fire in my lungs. *Relax*, I whispered to the Skills. I was the one in control here—not Hitori. Saitou's fingers were wrapped around his sword, his knuckles white and his eyes closed tight as he fought to remain silent and diligent against the Skills in the air.

Beside me, Rin coughed.

Hitori seemed unaware of what she was doing—or she didn't care. I reached out to the Skills, drawing them to me, reassuring them as Shenrae had done with me.

I was strong enough to withstand this.

There was nothing to fear.

Trust me.

The tension lessened.

"The people have not abandoned you," Rin said, picking up the conversation as my focus shifted to calm the Skills. Her voice grew louder and more adamant. "There are people who stayed in the lower quarter. They still believe in you, Hitori."

"Don't make me laugh!" Hitori shouted. Her hands were rigid at her sides as she began pacing more rapidly, her eyes darting back and forth, unfocused as if she were seeing something we could not. "They are there because they have nowhere else to go. They have no desire to move forward, to search for something better, because their vision is shortsighted. All they think of are their own needs, disregarding the path of progress I've laid at their feet. Even the False Shadows left here are too hesitant. And the guards—"

"There's still time to start over, Hitori," I said, sensing that we were beginning to lose her to her own thoughts and madness.

Hitori stopped pacing. "Are you still talking like that? I've hated your ideals since the day I met you." She spread her arms out around her. "You could have ended this, saved countless lives, if you'd only had the will to kill me. I shudder to think what your Shadows must think of such a spineless leader. You've done nothing but delay the inevitable." Smiling, she lowered her hands to her sides. "Your mercy and compassion are lost on me. If you want to save the people you love so much, harden your resolve, Phantom. I am done talking."

Rin stiffened beside me. "Hitori, please—"

"Enough!" Hitori yelled, unleashing a wave of the Skills toward us.

Planting my feet, I held my right arm before me, calling to the Skills. Rainbow light sparked in the air as Hitori's wave and my own wall of Skills collided.

As they dissipated, the Skills sizzled in the air, crawling like branches of lightning. In their wake, a charge remained in the air, full of possibilities. Swiftly, I closed the distance between Hitori and me, intent on stopping her, but Saitou drew his sword and blocked my path.

I caught Rin's eye, and she gave a small nod. She would have to face Hitori alone while I dealt with Saitou.

Saitou's eyes were thin as slits as he fixed me in his amber gaze.

Ever since I had joined the False Shadows, I had known it would come to this—Saitou and I would have to face one another. Though we both wanted Hitori to stop, duty had bound Saitou's actions. Even if it came at the cost of the late lord's town, a man he had admired, he would not falter. His love and devotion for Hitori were unbreakable. His duty was to protect her, to stifle any personal desires of persuading her onto a different path because he wanted her to live. Being Hitori's retainer, his only job was to obey her, to be an obstacle for me to pass through to get to his master.

Saitou spread out his feet, sinking into an offensive stance.

"I will be your opponent, Kilo, servant of Kiriku."

My hand went to the sword Orin had given me, my fingers curling over the silk wrapping. Within seconds, I had pinpointed the weaknesses in Saitou's armor: at the armpits, the groin where the legs connected to the torso, behind the knees, the space between the neck, and his unprotected head. He held his sword with his left hand, and I reminded myself it was his dominant hand, but I had seen him lead with his right hand before. I would need to watch for attacks from the left but be cautious if he switched his grip.

Allowing the battle with Rin and Hitori to fade from my mind, I let out a long breath. This duel would require all of my focus, and I knew Rin could hold her own against Hitori.

Shifting my own stance, I curled my fingers around my sword.

Analyzing.

Anticipating.

Saitou's command of his sword was absolute.

While I had always desired to test my skill against him, this was not the circumstance I would have chosen. Strong swordsmen exuded an aura around them, subconsciously dissuading people of power from challenging them. Until now, I had never felt much of Saitou's, as it had been masked by Hitori's own commanding presence.

Saitou's aura was fierce, pointed, and immense.

A bead of sweat ran down my brow as my thoughts stilled and my breathing steadied. Each of us waited for the other to make the first move.

The wind howled as the moments dragged on.

Then, suddenly, Saitou's right foot shifted, and he sprang forward, drawing his sword. With my thumb, I flicked my sword loose from its sheath and swiped his attack to the side, turning my blade over my head and slashing down. Saitou blocked me and slid his sword along mine, cutting horizontally against my neck.

The sword skimmed my neck, drawing a thin line of blood.

"That was your only warning," Saitou said, his voice cold as he held the sword at the side of my neck. He stepped closer. "The next time I catch you off guard, I will cut off your head."

Instincts took over, and I elbowed Saitou in the chest.

He stepped back, his sword pointed at the ground.

He was fast.

Swifter than Asdar and more agile with his long limbs. His technique was flawless, and he possessed a speed that came from instinct instead of experience.

I wiped the blood from my neck with the back of my hand.

In the forest against the mercenaries, I had shaken off the restraint of not killing, moving instinctively and without hesitation. It had unlocked the deadly training of my craft, allowing me to release my full potential with the sword.

But it had come at too high of a cost.

As the person I was now, could I defeat Saitou?

My breathing escalated, and I forced myself to inhale and exhale more slowly in a steady rhythm. The Skills lay at the edge of my mind, but honor kept me from reaching for them. When the time came, I would draw my second sword. I would need the same ruthless instincts and conviction I'd had back in the forest, but with the compassion and kindness of my heart.

This was a death match.

I needed to acknowledge what it was.

Taking a defensive stance, I watched as Saitou angled his sword parallel to the ground. When he swung the blade at my side, I slashed down with my long blade, drawing the shorter sword at my hip to slash between the leather plates at Saitou's knee. He pivoted, bringing his sword high up over his head, not even flinching as the wound near his knee bled.

Shuffling back, I crossed my blades in front of my chest, catching the sword. I pressed forward, holding Saitou's sword.

In matters of strength, he also had the advantage.

Saitou's foot shifted, and I jumped back, dodging his kick before it could connect with my kneecap. He swung at me, and I raised my short sword to block him. The blades screeched against one another, and I maneuvered the short sword free. I slashed at Saitou's chest, but he blocked it with uncanny precision, using the armor on his right forearm to stop the strike from my long sword. In a flash of movement, he withdrew. A blade in his right hand glinted. Hastily, I raised my arm to block his blow, but the knife sliced across my face. The curve of the blade skimmed across my left eye and forehead, releasing a stream of warm blood.

Stumbling back, I swiped at the blood with the inside of my arm, trying to clear my eyes. But the world had been plunged into darkness.

I heard a scuffle behind me.

An approach.

I slashed out with my long sword, feeling it cut into flesh. There was a sharp intake of breath, and panic gripped me.

Without my sight, I did not know what had happened to Saitou.

Calming my breathing, I listened, picking up on quiet footsteps to my right. The rustle of clothing caused me to raise my sword, and my blade met resistance with a clang. Saitou's swing seemed at half strength—as if my last blow had injured him. I held my sword steady against his, sliding against his weapon briefly to gain a reference to what his stance was.

Crosswise against his body.

Pressing down, I pinned Saitou's sword to the rocks with my long sword and flipped the short sword in my left hand before ramming the hilt into Saitou.

Something cracked.

Bone shattered.

And Saitou fell to the ground.

I stepped back, all too aware of the damage I had caused.

Sheathing my long sword, I used the short blade in my hand to cut the sleeve from my left arm. I slashed the fabric into long strips and wrapped it over the wound on my forehead, binding my left eye to stop the flow of blood. Dragging the back of my hand across my right eye, I cleared the blood. It watered, but I could make out some semblance of shape and form.

Saitou lay nearby.

There was blood at his temple where the hilt of my sword must have connected. I pressed my fingers gingerly against his head, holding my breath as I tried to assess the damage. His hair was damp at the side, and even though I had heard a crack, his injury seemed minor in comparison to what it could have been.

I breathed a sigh of relief.

He would live.

Using the remainder of the cloth from my sleeve, I bound the wound on Saitou's head and eased the armor from his chest to elevate his head with it. As I shifted him, he groaned, but he seemed only semi-conscious of what I was doing.

I laid my hand on his shoulder. "I will keep my promise."

Standing, I took a moment to orient myself. Without the use of my left eye, I would need to rely on my other senses to judge distance and space. The pain in my eye was not unbearable, but my breathing remained labored, and the lack of blood weakened me.

Voices ahead were muffled by the wailing of the wind.

A fog had rolled in.

It seemed the storm I had seen earlier was now upon us.

With shaking fingers, I gripped the handle of my sword, moving into the mist. Silhouettes appeared ahead, and with the Skills, I was able to confirm one was Rin.

"Rin!" I called.

One of the figures shifted in response, but before I could move to her side, a thicker white mist enveloped me. Thin strands, as precise and elegant as a spinner's thread, held onto my ankles. I tried to move, but the strands tightened to keep me in place. The Skills illuminated within my bond, and I guided them with my fingers, swiping at the threads until the Skills from Hitori released their hold on my legs.

Rin yelled something.

But her words were lost in the encroaching storm.

Despite the pain and my lack of clear sight, I braced myself against a gust of wind and fought my way forward, taking slow steps as the wind whipped against me.

Rain pelted my face.

"Rin," I said, extending my hand toward her.

Her breathing was ragged, and she held onto her side. I saw no outward wound, but her fingers clutched at her torso. Was it something to do with the Skills? When I wrapped my hand around her wrist to draw her closer to me, the Skills burned my hand. The Skill poisoning in Rin's body had spread across her neck and over her face.

Her resolve to see this to the end humbled me.

She was willing to give everything to save her friend's life.

"Can you continue?" I asked.

Rin tightened her grip on her thin dagger, which was charged with the Skills.

"I have to."

"I'll follow your lead."

She nodded and ran forward, the dagger held in her hand. She slashed at Hitori in quick, successive strikes, her blade skidding around a barrier Hitori had erected. Her movements were swift and fluid, hitting a range of areas.

But Hitori did not even flinch.

Rin's attacks did nothing to her or the barrier.

I came at Hitori from a slightly different angle, drawing my long sword and sliding my hand over the blade to illuminate the Skills around the edge. Hitori caught sight of it and drew the blade from her back. Metal screeched together as Hitori's sword hissed, evaporating the raindrops. I pushed against her, disengaging as Rin slashed at Hitori with her dagger. The glow of Hitori's sword burned brighter. It sputtered against droplets of rain, releasing steam into the sky.

A bolt of lightning struck the castle's spire.

Within seconds the top of the pagoda caught fire. My ears rang from the impact of the bolt. The ground lifted, and another bolt of lightning struck the castle, splitting rocks as the energy headed for Hitori.

Rin sheathed her dagger and leaped at me.

A blast hit us as the Skills connected with Hitori, sending both Rin and me flying backward. Rin cradled the back of my head with her hand, protecting me as we crashed into the rocks of the cliff.

I gritted my teeth at the impact; the air was forced from my lungs.

Rin pushed herself off of me. "Are you okay?"

I nodded, stunned momentarily.

The place where I had been standing moments ago was now cracked open, the edges of the rocks blackened from lightning.

"Was that Hitori?" I asked, disbelief hanging on the words.

Could she now direct the lightning's energy?

"It seems that way."

Her command of the Skills was incredible.

She far surpassed Rin and even me with the energy she could draw.

With a hand from Rin, I stood and retrieved my sword from the rocks. Hitori stood with her head tipped back toward the sky. Her arms were raised, her sword held high as she drew the Skills—the lightning—to her. The wind whipped against the folds of her robes, and when she turned toward us, her eyes momentarily glowed white.

Rin drew a handful of daggers out from the pouch at her side. "I think we'll have to use the Skills to even get close to her."

We both hesitated because of the strain the Skills placed on our bodies.

"Let me see your hand," I said, holding out my own to her. Rin raised her eyebrows in question but placed her hand in mine. I recalled the sensation of the Skills being drawn from me by Shenrae.

Rin pulled her hand back. "Don't."

I tightened my grip on her.

"I'll be fine," I said. She was angry with me, but we both knew she could not summon the Skills any more without endangering her life.

"What's Hitori doing?" I asked, to turn her mind back to what mattered.

Rin sighed. "She still seems to be absorbing the Skills. I don't understand how she's not suffering from the Skill poisoning with that much power."

"I think she has more of a tolerance for it than we do," I said, running my fingers along Rin's bond. "A lot of her experiments were on how to increase a person's limits with the Skills."

I glanced up briefly, to find Rin's attention fully on Hitori. When I returned my focus to where our hands were joined, my bond awakened. The silver tendrils grew hot against my skin, winding and swelling around the bond on Rin's arm.

By the time she realized what was happening, it was too late.

"Kilo!" she said, yanking her arm back.

I held up my hands as she took a step back from me. The pattern of my bond wrapped around her hand and upper arm, creating a casing that covered her entire right arm.

"Now we're even," I said with a sly smile.

Rin glared at me. "It was different with Finae. And now you have nothing to protect yourself from the Skill poisoning."

I lowered my arms to my sides, becoming serious. "I will be able to dispel the Skills from my body without it. Besides, I would never be able to forgive myself if there was something I could do to prevent you from dying. It's selfish of me, but I can no longer imagine a future without you by my side."

The clouds continued to swirl above Hitori, and the unsettling realization came to me. She was drawing too much power. Even with her tolerance, dispelling that much of the Skills would be difficult.

I let out a deep breath and returned my attention to Rin.

There was a slight smile on her face from my words, but she was still mad.

"I know what I'm doing," I said. "Trust me."

"You have a plan then?"

"I'm going to take Hitori into the Skill world."

The details would take too long to explain now, and beyond the basic idea, I did not know *exactly* how it would work, but I had an idea.

Rin nodded. "What do you need me to do?"

"Place the daggers around Hitori so I can create a barrier to contain the area," I said, unsheathing my long sword. "I'll keep her attention on me. When you sense a shift in the Skills, come close to me."

Rin pulled a blade from the pouch at her side.

"And just so you know," she said, her eyes crinkling at the corners as a smile spread across her face, " it's not selfish, because I feel the same way."

I smiled back at her, and she lingered for a brief moment before disappearing into the mist. Warmth blossomed in my heart and spread throughout my body.

With renewed strength, I rushed Hitori.

The Skills crackled at my approach, and I sensed a force gathering. When Hitori released them, I drew my sword, slashing out in an arc to create a line of the Skills. Planting my feet, I stood my ground as rocks and water broke against my barrier.

Rin's silhouette darted behind Hitori.

Reaching out with the Skills, I confirmed Rin had completed the circle. A glint of metal flew through the air toward Hitori, coming from the place where Rin had been. Hitori, distracted by the projectile, did not notice Rin's approach from the other side. Rin lashed out with her blade, and Hitori cursed as she grabbed onto Rin's arm. The edge of Rin's blade inched closer to Hitori's neck as Rin began to overpower her.

Dark, thin whisps of the Skills dropped from Hitori's bond, coming off in thick chunks. The rocks under her hissed and began to corrode.

The hair on the back of my neck rose as the air became charged.

Lightning.

Dropping to the ground, I slammed my palm against the rocks, closing my eyes and letting my thoughts reach out to the dagger Rin had placed. *Awaken.* I felt the presence of Rin and Hitori nearby—and at the very edge, Saitou. When the lightning bolt struck, my vision shifted, and I drew all of us within the barrier into the darkness and to safety.

The wind and the rain disappeared.

And all sound fell away.

I pushed a long strand of wet hair off my face, slicking it back against my head. My clothing hung close to my body, drenched from the rain.

"Is this the Skill world?" Rin asked, her voice strained as she walked over to me. Her reflection rippled against the glass-like surface that was the ground. She held her bond with her left hand. The arm was blackened, but the Skill poisoning across her face had begun to fade.

The bond I had given her seemed to be helping.

I nodded. "This is the place where the Skills reside. Where their energy and presence are purest."

In contrast to the pressure and pain Hitori projected from the Skills, this place was one of peace and healing.

Extending my hands, I held my palms up. Tiny balls of light floated from them into the air like fireflies. Colorless at first, they began to shimmer with various hues. Blues. Reds. Purples. Greens. Yellows.

Hitori was on her knees not far from us, her hand pressed against her neck. When she saw me, she removed her hand and glared. The small wound on her throat continued to bleed.

I walked to her, sending ripples of water across the ground.

Hitori stood, staring at the water that was not water.

"Where are we?" she demanded.

"It's not a place," I said, stepping back to show her the silver light and the void behind me. "This is the Skills."

A momentary flashed of excitement passed across Hitori's eyes.

Rin let go of her arm and came to stand next to me. "There's still a lot we don't know about the Skills," she said, "but Kilo and I have been learning how to use them."

Hitori scoffed. "You always hated the Skills."

"I never hated them. I hated what you became because of them." Rin's voice was pained. "Please, Hitori. I miss talking with you and being friends. I might not have always understood your desire or your obsession with the Skills, but I think I'm beginning to."

"It's too late," Hitori said. "You're just as much a fool as your precious Phantom." She raised her hand, the blade catching the light as she thrust it into Rin's chest.

"Rin!" I shouted.

My grasp on the Skill world broke.

Lightning struck behind us, backlighting Hitori's figure as she withdrew her dagger from Rin's chest.

Rin slumped to the ground, and I dashed forward, drawing my sword and slashing at Hitori's torso. She side-stepped the edge of the blade, throwing the dagger at my head. I dodged to the side, but the blade's handle struck the side of my head in just the right way to reopen the wound above my eye.

Blood oozed down my face, and I pressed my hand to the wound.

My vision became blurry.

Dots merged together and created shapes, melding and dancing before my eyes. There was a gentle pressure around my bond, and I looked down at it, surprised to see a vibrant blue color emerge from the Skills. It swirled around my arm and shimmered. A smile crept onto my lips, and I shifted my sword, angling it as I painted a blue line in the air with the blade.

I did not need to see the blade with anything other than the Skills.

As I retreated deeper inside myself, reaching a meditative state, the outline of things in the area became silver.

Time seemed to stand still as the Skills revealed themselves to me, and I drew in a deep breath, allowing the Skills in my right arm to grow, giving permission for them to flourish and be as they were. Stepping forward, I felt the Skills seep into the rocks beneath me. There, they illuminated everything in a silver light: the dirt, the pebbles, the shoes beneath my feet, even dead leaves trapped in the cracks of the cliffside. I took another step, the Skills spreading out from my feet and outlining the scene before me. The cliffside lay to my left, with piles of rocks and boulders weathered by the wind's hand. Under my feet, the illumination extended. A small line of dots floated beneath the stones to the cliffs and into the ocean.

I could sense the Skills, the energy, the life force within each thing.

A smile spread across my face.

I had never seen so clearly.

With my newfound sight, I scanned the area, sifting through the illuminated outlines and meandering light. Hitori's outline glowed. Tiny pulsing dots hung in the air, creating multiple streams of light. They converged toward Hitori, making a current in the area.

Like a gust of wind, Hitori drew in the Skills and expelled them. A shockwave of Skills came toward me, and orbs of light kicked up dirt and gravel from the ground, pushing the air outward. The force pelted me, cutting and bruising my skin. But there was nothing to fear. The wind tousled my hair and my robes, and once the initial shockwave passed, the Skills began to draw back to Hitori the same way they had before. She was not exhausting them like I thought but gathering them to her in a constant cycle. Instead of becoming too inundated with the Skills, she made sure she lessened the damage done to herself by becoming only a temporary vessel for them.

Holding my sword parallel to the ground, I diverted the flow of the Skills from Hitori and drew them to me, using the metal of my sword as an anchor point for the Skills. They churned through the sword and gathered inside me, pooling up until they became too great of a force to contain.

Extending my hand, I released my hold, unleashing the Skills toward Hitori. They broke the ground, sending rocks and pebbles flying as an equal forced barreled toward me.

A blur rushed from the side, and Saitou threw himself directly into the path of both attacks. I dashed in front of him, thrusting my sword into the ground and bracing myself to absorb the Skills from Hitori's attack.

I shuddered against the collision, grimacing.

"Next time, warn me of your intentions," I said to Saitou beside me.

He gave me a slight smile.

Closing my one good eye, I endured the onslaught.

Saitou shouted, "Hear him out, Hitori—please! You can't go on like this." His voice was pained, yet it held the same resolve he carried in battle.

Another burst of Skills rammed against my barrier. I steadied myself, leaning into the wave and letting it wash over me. Compared to her first attack, the intent behind it seemed weaker.

Hesitant.

Saitou's plea had shaken her.

Pulling my sword from the rocks, I sheathed it and crossed the distance between Hitori and me. Slowly, I took my second sword from the sash around my waist. I laid both swords on the ground and knelt, bowing low to her.

"I do not wish to fight any longer, Hitori," I said, raising my face to her. Her eyebrows were turned down, a deep crease running between her brows. She dismissed me, her attention fixed solely on Saitou.

She was furious at his interference.

Hitori drew back her arm, drawing the Skills to her with a wind that rustled my clothing. I remained as I was, placing my trust in Saitou, watching as a jolt of energy split, unearthing the rocks in a swift line toward me.

Before it hit its mark, Saitou stepped into its path.

The force of the Skills diverted around us.

Rain began to fall from the sky again, washing the caked-on blood from my face. The acrid tang of blood sickened me, but I remained still.

Hitori strode over to Saitou, her lips pressed thin.

"Why would you betray me like that?"

"I will not stand by and watch you destroy your last chance for redemption." Saitou's voice was unwavering. "The day my lord found you on the battlefield I swore to him I would protect you. Dying at the hands of the Phantom you have befriended seems a terrible end." He pressed a hand to his side where he was bleeding profusely, his expression never once faltering. "Do not throw your life away out of spite."

Saitou thrust his sword into the rock and leaned heavily against the hilt. He sank down to the ground, using the sword as a crutch. He bowed his head and knelt before his master.

A pool of blood expanded underneath him.

"Allow me to continue serving you," he pleaded. Coughing, he spit out blood to the side. "I want to see what you and Phantom Kilo can accomplish with the Skills. Together. It is my only desire."

From across the cliffside, Rin stirred.

Relief washed over me.

Hitori looked down at Saitou with a mixture of horror and rage. He had acted against her wishes, and it seemed she could not understand his reasoning. Her hands were clenched at her sides, and her eyes shifted from Saitou to me.

My swords remained on the ground.

If she made an attempt to strike Saitou again, would I be able to intervene?

Would her rage go beyond her affection for him?

Saitou's breathing became more ragged.

But Hitori remained indecisive.

To protect me instead of obeying his master… It was a deep wound Hitori would have to process another time.

"He will soon lose too much blood to survive," I said, not breaking eye contact with Hitori. "I would decide quickly what you wish to do. He has been loyal to you to the end. Do not question him."

"What do you know of—"

"He is dying for you, Hitori!" I said, my anger growing. "Despite everything you have done, he has never faltered. What loyalty have you shown him?"

To put someone else's life above one's own was the greatest act of love. Whether or not Hitori could see the action for what it was, it was Saitou's devotion that made me question Hitori. A person's character could be judged by those they kept in their company. It was because of Saitou, Rin, and Haru that I had come to learn Hitori's true nature. Their devotion made me search for the meaning behind their loyalty.

Huffing, Hitori started to turn away, but Rin dragged herself up, staying Hitori's departure. Rin's hands were wrapped and bleeding, and a small bloodied gash was on her chest. Like Saitou, Rin's conviction to see this to the end—to save Hitori—had given her the strength she needed to stand.

"Please, Hitori," Rin said, her voice choked.

Saitou set his sword on the ground next to mine and pressed his head to the rocks. "I beg you, Lady Hitori. Let someone who knows how to unite the people bring peace back to Magoto. Let Phantom Kilo calm the people's bloodlust for what you've done so that you may finally live without that burden."

I held my breath.

Everything had led to this single moment.

One final chance.

Hitori was silent for some time, her nose crinkling in disgust before she turned her anger on me. "And what would you have me do, Phantom? Surrender Magoto?"

"I have no desire to take Magoto. Besides"—I nodded toward Saitou—"there is one who has already earned that honor."

Saitou raised his head slightly at my words. It was the most logical solution, and given Hitori's affection for him, it was one she would consider.

"Why can't you just kill me?" Hitori asked bitterly. She gestured toward the castle and then at the fires still smoldering in Magoto. "After all this, you're telling me you can forgive what I've done?"

"What good would your death bring?" I said evenly. "Vengeance serves no purpose but to create more hatred in a world dying because of it. The peace we wish to create cannot be accomplished with ideals of personal justice. Do I despise you for killing your own people? Did you deserve what came to you? None of those actions are mine to judge. I serve the people of Kiriku. To spread more hate would be a betrayal of their trust."

I swallowed, thinking of Zavi and Mia.

Kaiba and Aiden.

The Shadows and False Shadows.

Even Gaiden's men.

I had given up on my own judgements long ago.

Placing one foot on the ground, I stood and walked to Hitori. She raised her head, staring up at me as I stopped a few feet away from her. In her eyes, a fire still burned. Her desire and will had not been broken, but it was possible the words of Saitou and Rin had humbled her enough to listen.

Or perhaps she was finally tired of the cycle she was trapped within.

I stood before her not as a Phantom or a Shadow, or even one of her False Shadows, but as an equal trying to bring peace back to the world. Only with courage could we lead the people of Kiriku through the ruin around us.

The Skills had reemerged into the world, and the ancient Phantom had given us another chance to find a path that would not lead to destruction.

With Hitori's help, it might be possible.

From a small pocket inside my robes, I retrieved a silver coin that had been given to me by Phantom Kural the day I had asked for sponsorship as a Shadow. As a Phantom, I could defend the people, spark hope in the hearts of others. But the ones who made the battle worth the sacrifice were the ones who would rebuild the world in their own vision. The ones who dreamed of a better tomorrow. Those who were unafraid to do what needed to be done to create a new path.

People like Finae, whose wonder remained untouched.

People like Shenrae, who searched for their own sense of purpose.

And people like Hitori, who saw no limitations.

I rubbed my thumb over the silver coin and held it out to Hitori. "Surrender the False Shadows to me, and become one of my Shadows. You and Saitou will have my protection, and I will ensure you can explore the extent of the Skills. Your discoveries will help shape a new world for all those in Kiriku."

Hitori's eyes widened.

"There is a place for you in this world, Hitori," I said, watching as her breath caught in her chest, "even if others do not believe it to be so."

Hitori shook off her initial shock, her expression changing into a sneer. "Did you forget you are no longer a Phantom? Do not think you can fool me by withholding information and making such claims!"

She was desperately trying to grasp onto something— anything—to refuse my offer, but I saw her words and outward appearance for what they were. She was afraid. Everything she had tried to do with the Skills had only ever created distance between her and others. She had tried to create something beautiful, useful, and others had sabotaged her. All her life, she had been fascinated by the world, but none had ever seen her as something more than a threat.

Tightening my grip on the coin, I looked over at Rin and Saitou.

Even they had hesitated with the Skills—as had I. While the Skills were dangerous, I believed aligning ourselves with them and their desires would lead to a better tomorrow.

For all us.

"I am sorry that others cannot see the Skills in the same way as you or I do. You did not deserve to be treated as you were." I held out the coin to Hitori again. "This is a symbol of the promise between a Phantom and a Shadow. I can only offer my protection and guidance. The rest will be up to you."

Hitori gave me a calculating look, her eyes searching for any deception in my actions. Her eyes were locked on mine for some time before I gave her a small nod, reassuring her.

Finally, she took the coin from my hand. "I'll hold you to your word."

Smiling, I placed my right arm over my chest and bowed to her.

"I expect nothing less."

Behind us, Saitou remained kneeling, his hands still gripping his sword. He seemed to have passed out from the pain. He needed immediate attention.

"Where's Seiji?" I asked.

Hitori shook her head. "Gone."

"He sometimes frequents the lower quarter," Rin said, coming toward us. "I'll see if I can find him." Her hand was still wrapped tightly. Blood had soaked the cloth she had used to bind it. As she came closer, it became clear that her wounds were not as severe as they had seemed.

Relief rushed through me.

"Hurry," I said, giving her a pointed stare.

There was something else she needed to tend to as well.

And the sooner we told the others, the better it would be.

Nodding, she ran through the courtyard, and I turned my full attention to Saitou.

"Before I struck her, she infused her hands with the Skills to catch my blade," Hitori said, taking off the outer layer of her robes. "Her temporary collapse was due to the tremendous concentration of Skills in my dagger. She blacked out because of them."

That was…incredible.

Hitori knelt next to Saitou and draped her white robe over his body, the silk immediately absorbing the blood. The rain had stopped, and the clouds had broken, lighting the two of them in a warm ray of light. Hitori seemed unsure of what else to do, or perhaps because of my presence she felt uncomfortable trying anything.

"Saitou?" I called, kneeling next to him and placing my hand on his shoulder. His body twitched at the contact, but he still seemed unconscious.

Moving in front of him, I reached my arms behind my back.

"Help me get him onto my back."

Hitori adjusted his arms around my neck, and I shifted him, looping my arms underneath his legs before pushing off from the ground. He groaned but didn't wake up as I moved with him. Hitori retrieved his sword and began walking with me, staying close to my side. My knees felt weak, but we were not far from the castle. Saitou needed to be somewhere out of the cold and the damp. Though it had stopped raining, there was a breeze that made me shiver.

I breathed heavily, taking one step at a time.

The False Shadows Rin and I had encountered earlier, the ones guarding the castle, Ai and Shizuka, rushed toward us, opening the doors to the castle.

"Bring medicine and bandages," I said to Shizuka. "Warm water, too, and thread and needle."

Hitori led me up the stairs and down the main corridor into a room where blankets were already laid on the floor next to a bed. With Hitori and Ai's help, we put Saitou down and leaned him up against a stack of pillows.

Shizuka came in with the supplies I had requested.

While Ai and Hitori worked on removing Saitou's armor, I pressed a damp cloth to his head, cleaning the wound there. Once it was clean, I applied a thin line of the ointment Shizuka had brought before sewing the wound together and wrapping a fresh bandage around his head. He had a second injury on the underside of his arm. A thin piece of fabric had been tied around it. Judging by the amount of blood that had soaked through, this must have been the wound that had weakened him. Carefully, I untied the soaked cloth, stitching the wound and applying ointment before rewrapping his arm with a fresh bandage. Another wound was at his side, though it had only broken the skin. This I cleaned, applying one of the thin pastes Shizuka had brought.

Sitting back on my heels, I pressed the back of my hand to my temple. While I was not as talented as Seiji was, I felt confident in my administrations.

Exhaustion had finally caught up to me.

Hitori looked over at me expectantly, her back stiff.

"It looks worse than it actually is," I said, realizing she probably could not tell his condition. "He will be dazed for a couple weeks from the impact to his head, but as long as infection doesn't develop in any of the other injuries, he'll be fine. Saitou's love for you is strong. He'll pull through."

Hitori let out a long breath.

I stood and walked to the window to gaze up at the cliffside, relief flooding through me. The glow of three fires lit the blackened sky—a message to General Mirai's spy network.

We had succeeded.

chapter sixty-eight
The Road Ahead

Kilo

At last, it was over. After everything we had done, finally, the False Shadows were no longer a threat. Other complications had arisen across Kiriku, but like a ripple across a lake, the waves would soon calm, and peace would return.

I pressed my hand gingerly against my eyes, trying without much effect to soothe the pain. The bandages wrapped around my head itched—annoyingly so—and I had little tolerance for it.

A gentle breeze blew over me, rustling my hair and the loose bandages around my eyes. I could taste the salt in the air—a reminder of the ocean on the other side of the cliffs. It was hard to imagine such a vast ocean full of possibilities outside the walls of Magoto.

I released a breath.

Magoto's people were now free, and with it Rin's duty to them.

Sensing someone approaching, I turned my head.

"I've made something for the pain," a man said. I recognized the voice as Seiji's. He had returned during the night the battle took place, nearly a week ago.

Stepping close to me, he reached toward my head to unwrap the bandages. I kept my eyes closed, feeling the cool paste as he smeared it over the wounds. He paused for a moment before he began rebandaging my eyes. "They're healing well. In a few more weeks, you should be able to remove the dressings. I don't think you'll lose much of your eyesight."

"Thank you," I said, gratefully as I bowed slightly. "Without your care, things may have turned out differently. What will you do now? Will you stay in Magoto?"

"No, I want to travel and learn more about different medicines across these lands. Now that you've released the False Shadows to do as they please, I find myself drawn elsewhere."

His voice had a touch of wanderlust to it. I knew it well.

"It will be good for you," I said, thinking fondly of my time during Shadow missions. Seiji would learn much from researching various methods, and he would become an even better doctor because of it. "If you ever wish to study in Vaiyene, let me know. My offer to sponsor you as a Shadow still remains."

Seiji laughed, knowing how much I wanted him to say yes.

"It's a very tempting offer."

"It is important to follow one's own path," I said, recalling the pain he had suffered from Hitori's manipulations. "I know there are amends you wish to make in regards to your father's work and how it was used by Hitori to learn about the Skill poisoning."

"Yes," Seiji said, his voice quiet. "I'm not sure how much of a difference I can make, or what good it will do, but I want to at least try."

I nodded. "I think you'll find solace in your work."

Seiji's studies would help restore his father's honor, and undoubtedly, the methods he would learn to counteract them would be necessary in time. Parting ways did not make me sad, for I knew our paths were likely to cross again in the future.

I turned my head, catching the chatter of voices below the gates.

Not long from now, Saitou was to address the people and the guards as the new lord of Magoto. It was something I did not want to miss.

"People are gathering down in the lower quarter," Seiji said, letting me know what I could not see. "Would you like me to guide you there?"

"I would appreciate it. Haru was supposed to come before it began, but I feel he might have gotten distracted with everything going on. I hear there's going to be a celebration."

"The first of its kind!" Rin said from somewhere behind me. "The guards were up early this morning helping with the daily catch. You should see the baskets of fish and oysters they brought back." Her enthusiasm and excitement pitched her voice higher. "We even found a store of sugar inside the castle, so the people from the lower quarter have been baking sweets for tonight's celebration as well. It won't be extravagant, but this will be a night the people will remember."

"I'm happy to hear the people's spirits have lifted," I said. What pleased me more was hearing Rin's happiness. Though I could not see him, I could almost sense Seiji's hesitation and unease. "You should stay and join the celebration, Seiji. What's one more night with the False Shadows?"

He chuckled. "I suppose one more night wouldn't matter."

"Oh, I heard from Phantom Asdar," Rin said, her tone becoming serious. "The group of Shadows he took to defend the perimeter of Vaiyene and the towns nearby was successful. He indicated there were no casualties, only a few minor injuries among the Shadows and the two twins in the False Shadows, Daichi and Riku are safely with him. He made a specific note that one of the mercenaries who attacked previously knew of the Silver Foxes."

Good. We could begin tracking down this group creating chaos across the lands. It was a relief to hear Asdar was doing well, as were Daichi and Riku. I had worried about the previous attack on Vaiyene and was thankful to hear it was not Hitori's doing. Tensions between Lunia and the Shadows were already high, and further involvement on Hitori's part would aggravate them.

"We've also recovered the bodies of the False Shadows you asked about from Kameiten, Kaiba and Aida. The guards have already prepared for their bodies to be burned this evening."

"And their swords?" I asked, the sadness of their deaths returning.

"I asked Haru to keep them separate. They're in possession of the guards for now. Whenever you're ready to tend to them."

"Thank you," I said, feeling an immense gratitude for everyone's help in taking care of the matters after the battle.

A cheer came from the crowd below.

"Hurry or we'll miss it," Rin said, grabbing my forearm and guiding me along the wall. Her enthusiasm returned in full force. As we descended the steps, she held onto both my arms to steady me. The gossip and chatter from the people grew louder.

"Many of the people from the lower quarter have even begun to return, too," Rin said, pulling me through the crowd.

"I met a few people in the neighboring towns asking for news of Magoto," Seiji said. He trailed after Rin and me, but his voice grew louder as the crowd pressed in; he had to move closer to be heard. "They seemed pleased to hear Saitou is now the lord and told me they would return. He carries the hope of Magoto."

I wished I could see Rin's expression, but I did not miss the gentle squeeze of her hand against my forearm. It would not take long before word of Saitou's reign spread across the lands of Kiriku. Already, Rin had sent letters to General Mirai and Asdar, in addition to using the spy network to spread the word of the resolution.

This was a turning point for Magoto.

And I could not be happier for the people here.

"Phantom Kilo! It's good to see you again," someone said.

"Haru and his father are heading over," Rin said, alerting me before they reached us.

"Gai, captain of the guard," Haru's father said, introducing himself. "It's an honor to see you again, Phantom. We are in your debt for everything you have done for Magoto."

With a smile, I bowed to him. "While I am humbled by your kind words, I played but a small part. It is because of your hard work and your guards' loyalty that this day has come. Your son's guidance helped a great deal with Hitori. I wish you nothing but the best in the coming years."

"We are needed at Lord Saitou's side," the commander said, "but I hope we can talk more before you depart."

"I'm happy you are well, Phantom," Haru said, hanging back for a moment. "While most of the False Shadows have decided to stay in Magoto, I am pleased to hear the twins are in Vaiyene. Once things settle here, I hope I can come visit you and meet your Shadows."

"You are always welcome," I said.

Haru placed his hand on my shoulder before departing.

The crowd had become quiet.

Rin grabbed my hand and pulled me through the crowd. "Saitou is standing next to the fountain. He's wearing the old lord's armor and sword," she said, giving me a running commentary. "I know he is uneasy with his new position, but he looks the part. I think Lord Shingen would have approved, even if it is different from what he originally had planned."

Rin released my arm as the crowd drew a collective breath. I used the opportunity to reach out with the Skills and get a sense of what was going on for myself. As I extended my awareness with the Skills, silver outlines drew themselves around the buildings and the people. Saitou stood in the center, with Gai and Haru next to him. The other guards were lined up on one side, the townspeople on the other side. Counting all of them, there were maybe two hundred people.

Fewer than the people in Vaiyene.

Saitou began to speak, his voice echoing across the stone buildings. "It is with mixed emotions I stand before you today. It grieves me Lady Hitori has bequeathed the title of lord to me, but I know to most of you that comes as a relief. I ask you to not judge Lady Hitori too harshly, as there was more to Magoto's corruption than most were aware of. Behind the scenes, the council members tightened the strings, controlling Hitori's actions and forcing her hand. They killed Lord Shingen and are to blame for the aftermath that followed."

I smiled to myself.

Despite Hitori no longer being his master, he remained loyal to her. He would likely always keep his actions reflecting his devotion to her.

Through the Skills, I became aware of another presence at the edge of the crowd. I sensed no ill will from Hitori, but I was mindful of the conflict this would cause her.

Rin pulled on my arm, and my meanderings were cut short.

"Phantom Kilo," Saitou said, raising his voice.

Rin pushed me forward, and the crowd parted around me. I stood next to Saitou, unexpectedly put into the spotlight. Using the Skills, I could see the outlines of the people gathered.

"It is due to Phantom Kilo's assistance and goodwill we were able to come to an amicable end. Together with the strength of the Shadows and Vaiyene, we will rebuild our once great town. I am honored to be able to serve you, and I will do my best to make Magoto a place we are all proud to call home. Let us remember tonight as the beginning of new friendships and of hope."

Something within my Skill sight streaked across the sky—an arrow shot from the gate by one of the guards. The people pointed and cheered as a gong rang out. Music began to play, and the crowd whooped and hollered before they began to disperse. The guards started setting fires to begin cooking their feast.

Saitou remained where he was.

When Saitou, Rin and I were alone, the gravity of the situation settled among us, creating an atmosphere somber in comparison to the people's celebration.

"It will not be easy," I said, sensing the misgivings in both Saitou and Rin, "but this is the best option for Magoto—and for

Hitori." I could still feel Hitori's presence, and I continued for her sake also, as she was close enough to hear. "I have found the hardest part of moving on is not knowing if the decisions we made were the correct ones. But whether they were or not, all of us will have to come to terms with the things we have done. Do not let misgivings of the heart dissuade you." I glanced from Saitou to Rin, letting my gaze drift over to Hitori as she began to slip away. "All of us will become stronger because of this."

I allowed my words to rest in the air before turning the conversation to a lighter note and addressing Saitou.

"Rin tells me you are wearing your lord's armor and sword."

"Yes," Saitou said, "Hitori came to me earlier and showed me where she kept them. At first, I refused her, but she wanted me to have them. She said it would be fitting."

"While I didn't know the lord as well as you and Hitori," Rin said, "I know he always held you in high respect, as do the guards. It should have always been you. Even Hitori wished for it. This will finally set her free of that burden."

"I only hope she can find peace," Saitou said softly.

A mischievous grin came over me. "Hitori will be too busy with my sister to even worry about anything other than the Skills. Her questions will be endless."

Rin laughed at my side. "They will become quick friends."

With Finae's free spirit and curiosity, it certainly seemed likely. Finae would have little hesitation allowing Hitori to live as one of the Shadows. In due time I would answer to the Shadows and reclaim my title as Phantom from Lunia, but for now...

The people began singing, and a small number began to dance. The scent of fish and smoke wafted over us. The drums had become quicker and more intense. I no longer felt Hitori in the area, but there was one person I had yet to see tonight, someone I knew was in the area.

Knowing Rin, she had invited Ikaru to the celebrations and he had refused. Rin pulled on my arm, trying to drag me into the crowd, but I found myself missing the Miyota Mountains and Vaiyene, and my heart was not entirely in the celebration.

"There is someone else I should go talk with," I said.

Rin hesitated. "He took the first watch tonight, although his shift has been over for quite some time ago."

I did not miss the sadness in her voice.

"Do you need me to guide you there?" Rin asked.

"I'll find my way."

"You shouldn't be using the Skills without a bond."

I waved her off. "I will not overdo it. Allow me some form of independence."

"You're so stubborn."

I laughed, and using the Skills' sight, I navigated around the lively group of people and along Magoto's walls. It had been some time since I had last spoken with Ikaru. After Hitori had released him, I had tried to speak with him, but for the most part, he had kept to himself, refusing to talk with anyone.

When I neared Magoto's gate, I saw a figure sitting on top of the walls, gazing out across the Plains of ReRiel.

"Ikaru?"

He moved in my Skill sight but said nothing.

I sighed.

Without him speaking, I could not confirm it was him. He had little reason to be mad with me and refuse to talk, but perhaps something weighed on his mind.

"If you're there, Ikaru, I would appreciate you letting me know," I said as I continued along the wall. "In case you have not noticed, my eyes are bound. But, if you would rather, I can talk to this wall instead."

Turning my back to the stone wall, I leaned against it, allowing the Skill sight to fade from my mind. The music from the lower quarter reached even here. The scent of fish cooking carried as well.

"Rin misses you," I said, feeling perhaps he needed the reminder. "I am happy the two of you will no longer need to be apart."

I paused, trying to figure out if Ikaru was listening.

I carried on as if he was.

At least the wall seemed to be listening.

"You are free, Ikaru. You can do whatever it is that you want to."

"Why didn't you kill her?" Ikaru asked. His voice betrayed his bitterness.

So it was anger that had kept him from speaking.

I could deal with anger.

"Hitori has caused a lot of pain for a lot of people, but her knowledge of the Skills can be used for good. " I paused for a moment before continuing. "Besides, you know the Shadows do not take life."

Ikaru was silent.

"Would her death make you feel better?" I asked, pausing to consider it from someone else's perspective. "Her death would be a temporary catharsis, soothing the initial anger at what she has done. In the end though, it would do nothing to change what has been done. Hitori has divided the people, creating hatred and fear. What we need is not vengeance, but something to bring us together as one people. Something we can rally to."

"And you think Hitori can do that?"

"Hitori will play some part," I said, trying to gather my thoughts. "But even I do not have all the answers as to how. Something tells me we will need her in the end."

Ikaru scoffed. "Do you often rely on such nonsense?"

I smiled, trying not to laugh.

It was true I did rely heavily on my instincts, and I was aware my quick judgements annoyed more than a handful of people.

"Rin will be busy with General Mirai's spy network," I said. "She'll be going between Vaiyene, Magoto, and many of the other towns. Would you like to come with me? To Vaiyene?"

"I have no interest in becoming a Shadow."

The venom in his voice was palpable.

"Leaving Magoto may give you some peace," I said with an even voice. After being in the False Shadows, he would never consider becoming a Shadow; that I was certain of. "Rin seems to have fond memories here, but that is not the case for everyone. A few of the False Shadows will come with me and join the Shadows, but not all of them will."

Standing, I placed my hand on the wall. I used the Skills to redraw the image of the area in my mind, seeking some hint of Ikaru's body language—but I could see nothing.

His demeanor was hard to read.

Something about his hesitation made me wonder if there was more to his anger and resentment. An underlying emotion was darkening his thoughts, but without knowing him better, I could not figure out what it was. I feared the more I forced myself on him and asked him what bothered him, the more he would distance himself from me, as he had with Rin.

In time, I hoped he would come to trust me.

"If you ever want to talk," I said, casting a sightless glance over to Ikaru, "I am always here to listen."

A sharp pain near my temple cut off my use of the Skills.

Thoughtlessly, I took a step forward and tripped over a rock, hitting my head against something wooden. Throwing my arm out, I managed to catch myself against the wall.

I pressed my other hand to my head and gritted my teeth against the pain.

Ikaru sighed overhead. He scuffled against the stone of the wall, dropping down next to me. "Let me help you get to wherever you're heading. Here, put your hand on my shoulder."

Breathing through the pain, I did as he said, feeling the extent of his anger and unease through the Skills.

"Sorry for the trouble," I said against the dizziness coming over me.

"It's fine."

"If you wouldn't mind, I would prefer to sit outside Magoto's walls, in the forest. Being surrounded by all this stone has never been my favorite feeling."

Ikaru turned, and I followed after him, keeping my hand on his shoulder. A breeze blew over us once we passed under the gate. I exhaled, already feeling better. Before long, the sounds of birds chirping reached my ears, and the music and commotion of the town faded away.

Ikaru stopped, and I removed my hand from his shoulder.

"Thank you," I said, holding out my hand as I continued into the forest. My fingertips brushed against a tree, and I knelt in the tall grass.

"Do you want me to wait, or…"

"I am not sure how long I will be," I said, resituating myself, crossing my legs in front of me. "Rin should be in the lower quarter if you would like company, or if you would prefer, you are more than welcome to stay here with me."

Ikaru moved a short distance away, twigs cracking under him, before he settled against a nearby tree. I drew in a cleansing breath, allowing my thoughts to quiet and my mind to reach out to the Skills.

Was Finae still within the Skill world?

It had been some time since I had felt her try and reach me.

Guilt immediately rose within me.

What if she was in trouble?

I let the feeling pass, reminding myself Finae understood my duties and my obligations. I drew in another deep breath, holding it in before letting it out. The Skills began to move at the edge of my awareness. Remaining silent, I allowed time to elongate and my mind to think of nothing, to expect nothing.

However long it took to reach the Skill world, I was prepared to wait. My impatience only prolonged the time it took. That much I had learned when trying to speak with the ancient Phantom.

At some point, I became aware of the absence of birdsong and any odors in the air. The void had dampened my senses. Standing up in the Skill world, I opened my eyes and left behind my physical form. As I wandered listlessly, the water under my feet spread out, reflecting my own appearance across the small waves. I paused for a moment, seeing the Reikon Tree in the water. Vaiyene. It seemed so long ago since I had been there, though it had not even been a year. My heart ached when I thought about the people I had left behind. Not just Syrane and Shenrae, but the villagers and the Shadows I had sworn to protect. Serving them had always been my purpose, and now that they were no longer in danger from the False Shadows, I could return.

As I walked across the water that made no sound, small orbs of light rose around me. A multitude of colors came before my eyes, brilliant hues of purple, red, yellow, and blue. They remind me of someone as vibrant and as colorful.

Someone I missed dearly.

I held out my hand, watching as silver light outlined my fingers. Beneath my feet, a steady silver trail flowed like a river, reminding me there was a purpose to my journey even if I did not know the destination.

Being here in this moment had a purpose.

It brought me peace, knowing I was but a single part of something much bigger. I was insignificant. Small. Impermanent. All things changed, and the Skills, the cycle of life and death, all of it would happen in its own time.

Off in the distance, a bridge came into focus.

The silhouette of it reminded me of a memory—a time when Finae and I had left Vaiyene's borders. The weathered boards of the bridge groaned under my weight, and I rested my hands on the railing. Moss had grown over the damp wood. As I recalled the memory, details began to take shape.

I closed my eyes and breathed in the earthy scent deeply, recalling Finae's wonder...

"It's so high up!" Finae said, hoisting herself up onto the railing. One knee was bent under her as she gazed longingly into a cavern so deep one could not see the bottom.

She leaned closer to the edge of the sheer cliffside, peering below.

She was fearless.

Beside her, I rested my back against the railing, looking up to the darkening sky. Stars shimmered across a deep-blue-and-purple backdrop. A passing whisper of clouds formed a shadow across the moon, creating a delicate scene.

I blinked as one of the stars fell, leaving a trail of light in its wake.

"Finae, look," I said, pointing up to the stars. She turned around, sitting on the railing, her eyes wide as another star streaked across the sky.

"Why are they falling?"

"Because it is their time," I said, finding the North Star that would lead us back to Vaiyene. "They've fulfilled their purpose, and now they are free."

Fine reclined back, holding onto the railing with her hands and rocking back and forth.

The wooden bridge dissipated under my feet, and with it, the memory faded. But the feeling of Finae's fearlessness stayed with me.

Another memory rose…

Finae and I stood on top of the waterfall in Vaiyene, looking down into the valley. People ran to take shelter, but neither Finae nor I moved.

Our father had returned from a Shadow mission, though not in the same manner he had left. The Shadows carried his wrapped body into the Phantoms' house. Our mother stumbled after him.

Numbness kept the tears from my eyes, but I wrapped my arm around Finae. We shared no great love for our father, but he remained our father nevertheless. Our mother had told us to leave her, saying she wished to be alone. It was her reaction that had shaken me more than what had happened.

To calm down, I had taken Finae to the top of the waterfall where we could listen to the roar of water.

"Are you okay, Finae?"

She nodded.

I pulled her close, and she began sobbing quietly against my chest. Perhaps what hurt the most was not that our father had died or that our mother had not wished for us to be around her, but the loss of what could have been. Some part of me had always hoped for reconciliation, a time when both our parents would realize Finae and I were just as precious as their eldest son. That we, too, were worthy of their love.

But with our father now dead—

"We should probably get out of the rain," I said, pushing Finae gently away. Raindrops fell on her cheeks, mixing with the tears. "We should probably be there. Grief makes people lash out. I am sure our mother will appreciate us being there."

Even as I said the words, I did not quite believe them, so I amended the statement.

"It is our duty to be at her side."

The vision wavered, and I held onto Finae's grief.
Another memory rose in the void…

Rain pattered against my straw hat, and a stream of water fell onto the woven straw cape hanging on my shoulders, running off at the sides. Beside me, Finae walked and hummed in the rain, swaying as she splashed into a giant puddle.

In her hands, she twirled an umbrella she had painted with koi and green lily pads.

We walked through the forest of Vaiyene, having come down from the Reikon Tree. One of the village girls, not much older than five years, ran past us. She tripped and fell into the mud, bursting into tears.

Finae rushed forward, bending down next to the girl and helping her up. "You're okay. Here, take this." Finae offered the girl her umbrella.

The little girl's eyes lit up, and she took it, skipping back to her mother, who stood nearby under a pagoda. A baby was strapped to the woman's back.

I untied my straw hat and pressed it down over Finae's head.

Finae tilted the brim up and was about to protest when I nodded toward the woman. Her name was Yuya. Her husband had recently passed away from an illness, and I had been stopping by every couple of days to make sure she was doing well.

"Her husband had a fondness for koi," I said, smiling as the woman took the umbrella from her daughter. She focused quietly on the designs Finae had painted on it, tears brimming in her eyes.

Yuya scooped her young daughter up and came toward us, extending the umbrella out to Finae.

"Keep it," Finae said.

The woman bowed, tears falling from her eyes. "Thank you."

I bowed in return and placed a hand on Finae's shoulder.

Her kindness had always touched people…

I stood quietly in the Skill world, letting the memory fade.

Briefly, from out of the darkness, a figure appeared, taking the shape and form of the ancient Phantom.

A sense of what I needed to do settled over me like a guiding hand.

The Skills illuminated the void with memories, spreading their glow into the dissonance that was Finae's consciousness. I knelt, keeping my breathing calm as Finae's memories came in greater force. These thoughts, these emotions and fragments of Finae rushed into me. I tried to fill myself with as many memories and facets of Finae's character and personality as I could, gathering the times when she had been hopeful and happy, as well as the times when she had been sad, lonely, and angry.

When at last the memories quieted, I waited in silence, holding the pieces of her together in my heart. With no thoughts or feelings of my own, I waited for Finae's self to become whole again.

Silence permeated the air.

Then came a subtle shift in the Skills, so delicate I dared not breathe. A hand touched my shoulder, and a familiar presence brushed against my mind. I turned my head to see the Skills gathered together in a brilliantly colored form.

"I knew I would find you here," I said.

Finae grinned at me, her presence separating from the Skills. Her eyes were alight with a subtle glow. She was taller and looked older than she should have been, as if, somehow, more time had passed while she was in this Skill world.

Her grin, however, remained the same.

"Kilo, I was having the most incredible dream! I don't know how long ago it was, but there was a time when this"—she spread her hands out across the area—"was almost the same as the world we live in."

I tilted my head, a smile appearing on my face.

How I had missed her.

"But there's something wrong here," Finae said, her initial happiness wearing off. She spun in place, her eyes searching for something in the darkness. "Something's *off*."

She looked back at me, her brow knit in concern.

I shifted my attention to the Skills in the air, focusing on the feeling of the Skills. Finae's presence created a bright area, a ray of light in the darkness, but somewhere deeper…

It weighed on my mind and seemed to mar the landscape.

Unrest and worry came over me.

Reaching out to the Skills, I let them show me what they would. The silver ripples beneath my feet stilled, becoming like glass. My own thoughts and emotions dimmed, allowing whatever it was to show itself without my own judgement. A black liquid began to burble across the water. It throbbed as I drew closer, pulsating as if it breathed. It pushed against me, creating a force as I reached out a hand. Tendrils burst forth, wrapping around my hand and winding around my arm.

The skin of my forearm blackened.

Skill poisoning, but why was it here?

A pull at the edge of my mind strained my concentration. My vision became blurry, and I held onto the impure skin with my other hand to dull the pain.

I had stayed too long in the Skill world.

"Finae, do you know how to return to Konro?" I asked.

She considered the question.

Across the glass surface, flowers blossomed, and the white petals floated around Finae, enveloping her in beauty. A chasm opened in the ground between us, and the ground she was on remained illuminated while the ground near me withered and died.

"I know the way," Finae answered.

Her attention seemed to be focused on something else in the distance.

"Finae," I said, waiting until I had her full attention before continuing. "Don't stay too long. Next time I might not be able to separate you from the Skills. You could lose yourself."

She grinned, a touch of mischief in her eyes.

"Be careful," I said, letting go of the Skill world as awareness came back to me.

The pain in my eyes.

The scent of damp earth.

The numbness in my legs.

Removing my hands from my knees, I dragged myself across the dew-laden grass.

Something moved near me, and then there was an inhale of breath near me. I reached out with the Skills, recognizing the person's presence beside me.

Hitori.

"It's been five days since you were last conscious," she said. "Ikaru brought me here after the first night. You've been using the Skills in some sort of meditative state since then. Give me your arm," she said, grabbing hold of it. She turned it over in her hands, her fingers warm against my skin.

There came a familiar pull, a drawing of the Skills from my arm. The sensation was the same as when Shenrae had purified the Skills in me. A realization came to mind. Hitori had been absorbing the Skills while I was in the other world.

"Thank you," I said, feeling grateful.

As she regarded me, Hitori's expression was full of curiosity. "What made you lose sight of your usual restraint?"

I considered withholding the information, to tease her, but if she had helped me out of her own inclination to do so, I wanted to show my gratitude in a way she would understand. Clearing my throat, I felt the last bits of the Skill world fade away from my mind.

"I've been using the Skills to talk to someone who lives in a different time and place."

Hitori inhaled sharply, and I smiled.

It was the beginning of a beautiful friendship.

Gratitude & Acknowledgements

First and foremost, thank you to you, dear reader, especially as you find your way to the end of my second book. It's said a reader will forgive the author of their flaws if the story is good enough, which I'm grateful for, as there have been many!

A span of three years has passed since my first book debuted, and I am happy with my progress as both a storyteller and student of this craft. I spent over two years finding the heart of this story, and I can't wait to see where these characters and this journey will take me in the coming years.

Thank you for continuing to follow Kilo's, Shenrae's, and Hitori's journey and for sticking with a humble author as they question the world around them through fiction.

This book would not have been made possible without the help of these wonderful patrons whose generous donations have helped to keep my publishing funds going:

Frank Nichols
Joe Gillespie
Margaret Dunkhorst
The Pol Family

Thank you for supporting my writing and believing in me! It means the world to me. And thank you to everyone who has purchased a book, left me a review, or has ever engaged me in conversation about my characters. I will, and have, spent many hours talking to each of you. It makes the years of work worth it and quite possibly is one of my favorite things of being an author.

Special thank you to my editor Emily Cargile for her dedication and time with this book. She helped me smooth out my writing and has taught me more than ways to hone my craft. There's still a lot I have to learn, but I am grateful for her keen eyes and wit with this book.

To my very early beta readers (Jason Dias, Amy Lemke, Malcolm Barber) and developmental editor (H.A. Lynn) who read this book in its first incarnation: what a mess this story was! I hope you are as pleased and as proud as to where this has gone. I would not have been able to find my way without your comments and questions, and I am eternally grateful for the time and energy you spent.

To my friend, Laura Pol, whose enthusiasm and love for this story has quite possibly surpassed my own: I never thought it would be possible, but your passion has made me realize more than ever how special an author's world can be and how a creation can live on in the hearts of others.

To all you who have tagged me on social media sharing my book: thank you! It lights up my day seeing people enjoy my stories.

If you've made it to the end of this long and rambling letter, thank you again for being here and supporting me.

Want to follow my writing journey?

Sign up for my newsletter on my website, or find me on social media (noellenichols). I actively share what I'm reading on #bookstagram, give out ARCs opportunities, and a lot of other fun authorly and reader things.

www.noellenichols.com

And if you enjoyed this book, please consider leaving a review to help others know if they want to read my books.

Noelle lives in the mountains of Colorado with her husband and their three border collies. When she's not dreaming of fantasy worlds and contemplating life, she's creating art and doing as many things as she can.